HOWLING ACROSS BRIDGES

a novel

Dorothy & Clyde —
Blessings to you —
J.M. Miller
10/2015

JAMES RANDALL MILLER

Copyright © 2013 by James Randall Miller

Cover Design by Damonza
Interior formatting by Benjamin Carrancho

Inquiries should be addressed to the author by email at:
jamesmillerbooks@gmail.com

Printed in the United States of America

ISBN 978-0-9834150-1-5 (paperback)
ISBN 978-0-9834150-2-2 (eBook)

DEDICATION

To those
in uniform
promoting a higher good
and to my friend
Sergeant First Class Mario Frisby,
Purple Heart recipient,
U.S. Army Ranger, retired,
and his faithful dog, Jekyll

...and when you turn to the right hand, and when you turn to the left, your ears will hear a voice behind you, saying, "This is the way. Walk in it."

– Isaiah 30:21

"What you seek is seeking you."

– Rumi

FOREWORD

"Until one has loved an animal, a part of
one's soul remains unawakened."
— Anatole France

Animals enrich our lives in so many ways; they love us unconditionally, they bring us joy and they even help improve our emotional
and physical health. For those returning from Iraq and Afghanistan,
dogs can be the life-saving therapy they need to fight the battle of combat stress. More veterans are dying by their own hand after returning
home than have from conflict. As the founder of Pets for Vets, Inc., I
have seen first-hand the benefits that a rescue dog can bring. At Pets
for Vets, Inc. our goal is to help heal the emotional wounds of military
veterans by pairing them with a shelter dog that is specially selected to
match his or her personality. Professional animal trainers rehabilitate
the dogs and teach them good manners to fit into the veteran's lifestyle.
Each of our veteran-pet matches receives a Welcome Package of equipment to start their life together; in addition, each dog is healthy and up
to date on vaccinations. We also provide a life line of support for our
veterans. Our program is provided at no cost to the veteran.

Pets for Vets is unique in that we strive to find the right pet for each
veteran. We match the temperament of the dog to the personality and
lifestyle of the veteran. It is because of this and the positive reinforce-
ment training we use that we are able to facilitate long lasting bonds
between each dog and veteran. This bond can lead the dogs to anticipate what their veteran needs, in certain situations, from waking them
up from a nightmare to alerting to noises such as ambulances when
driving. I hear stories daily about how having their Pets for Vets dog

has allowed our veterans to have a second chance at health and happiness. This can include finally turning the lights off at night, taking less medication for depression and anxiety, feeling comfortable going out in public and stating that without their dog they would have become another statistic.

As a Vietnam Era veteran, Jim Miller knows how war can affect someone for a life time. However, one does not need to be a veteran to identify with *Howling Across Bridges'* hero, Ranger Colt Mercer. Jim's story mirrors the stories of our Pets for Vets veterans. One veteran told me that his heart and soul were killed in Iraq. For the eight years since returning home he did not care about anyone or anything. He was constantly looking for fights. When he found Pets for Vets, he said he was either going to get a dog or a gun. Fortunately he received a dog, Rakassan, who opened the door to his heart and the window to his soul. Rakassan gave him the gift of love which in turn he is now able to share with other people.

In 2008, the Rand Institute estimated that 20% of the 1.6 million U.S. soldiers who served in Iraq or Afghanistan suffered symptoms of PTSD. This affects not only the veterans but also their families, communities and our country as a whole. It is crucial that we all understand what our servicemen and women are experiencing as they transition back to civilian life. *Howling Across Bridges* helps to provide that insight.

In closing, we are not rescuing our dogs, they are rescuing us. Said an anonymous Pets for Vets, Inc. veteran, *"If they can heal, we can heal…"*

Clarissa Black

Clarissa Black
Founder of Pets for Vets, Inc.
www.pets-for-vets.com
Long Beach, California 2013

PROLOGUE

JUST BEFORE PULLING the trigger, I focused on my breathing. The perfect time to shoot is between breaths, when your breathing muscles and diaphragm are relaxed. *Boom!* I unleashed a fifty-caliber bullet, sending it sizzling through the thin mountain air at supersonic speed. I watched its swirling vapor trail as it headed to my foe, who was 1400 meters away. Crimson-colored spray and flying body parts marked the end of the man's existence. It wasn't even noon and I had my third kill. This was turning into a productive day.

I am a United States Army sniper. I prowl the mountains of the Hindu Kush in search of prey, but I don't limit myself to the Kush. I pursue my quarry throughout the rugged landscape of Afghanistan, stalking its expansive deserts, valleys and plains, and even city streets. I'm quite good at my craft, a master hunter who kills unseen by transforming into a ghost with stealth and camouflage.

"One shot, one kill" is the sniper motto, and I take this motto seriously. My ability to deliver a bullet with stunning accuracy up to 1800 meters away requires me to be a wizard at factoring in variables such as range, gravity, wind speed and direction, temperature, barometric pressure, and even the spin of the Earth. My bullets cost four bucks apiece. In comparison, taking someone out with a Hellfire missile fired from a Predator unmanned aerial vehicle costs around seventy thousand dollars, and often results in "collateral damage," a euphemism for a bunch of innocents being killed. Simply put, I am a highly-valued military asset who provides a cost-effective way to send insurgents on express flights to Allah.

My effectiveness transcends my kills. I am a fear merchant, a dispenser of doom. I toy with psyches. If you are my enemy, you must ponder the possibility of me whenever you venture out. You know I'm everywhere and nowhere. I am invisible, I strike from great distances, and I might have you in my crosshairs. Have a nice day.

My name is Colt. This would've been my story. But, the brutality of war intervened with an unceasing attack on my psyche. I'm not sure when or where my soul was stripped from me. Perhaps it was a gradual erosion of my humanity rather than a singular event. Finding my soul is now my story.

1

"EVERYTHING IS IN order." The Sergeant Major frowned as he closed the folder containing my discharge paperwork. "I still don't understand why you're doing it, but you're free to go."

"Thank you, Sergeant Major." I did an about-face and left the building.

My career as a United States Army Ranger was over. I was "free to go." Those are potent words when Uncle Sam has owned your freedom for the last nine years. As heady as emancipation sounds, Uncle Sugar faithfully gave me the basics of living—food, shelter, clothing, health care and a monthly stipend. Now, I'd have to hustle for the basics and all I had was a vague plan for doing this. I'm not sure if renting a crystal ball or perhaps seeing a fortune teller would qualify as having a plan. Any thought of retirement now required lotto assistance.

I got on my bike, which I rode to the post every day, and cruised through the Fort Benning gate for the last time. I caught the Chattahoochee River bike trail and headed to my apartment, which is located near the RiverWalk in the Georgia town of Columbus. Some angry-looking thunderheads were fast approaching from the west, so I shifted the drive train on my Cannondale to its highest gear. My leg muscles burned as I blazed down the trail. The flower-scented wind felt good in my face. My vision was filled with a passing assortment of pink dogwoods, azaleas, antebellum plantation homes and high-rise office buildings. This would be my last bike ride in Georgia; tomorrow I'd be boarding a plane for Alaska.

I made it to the apartment as the heavens unleashed a torrential rain. My lungs were pumping hard. Lightning flashed, followed by an immediate clap of thunder. I was glad to get home safely.

"Is that you, Colt?" my roommate Kenny yelled from his room.

"Yeah, I just beat the rain. I had to speed down the trail."

"You want to go out for dinner?"

"Not in this mess. Let's order pizza. We still have plenty of beer."

He came out of his room. "I could go for that. You want Marco's?"

"Yeah. I'm hungry. How about a large Deluxe Uno and a White Cheezy?"

"I'd like a Meat Supremo over a Deluxe Uno. The White Cheezy is cool."

"The Supremo's fine, but tell them to double the pepperoni. I'll take a shower while we wait."

I went to my room and took off my ACU (Army Combat Uniform). That's when it hit me: this would be my last time wearing an Army uniform. I looked at the Velcro-backed Sergeant First Class insignia and ran my fingers over the raised thread stitching on my Combat Infantryman's Badge, Senior Parachutist Badge, and Ranger Tab. Each of these made me flash to the intense training or active ground combat required to get them. The vivid images of war ended my reminiscing. I tossed the uniform on a pile of clothes I was giving to Kenny, who was also a Ranger.

I turned the temp toward cold in the shower to cool down. After toweling off, I put on jeans and a T-shirt. Kenny was looking out the window as I walked into the living room. "Check out this freakin' monsoon. The pizza guy's gonna get soaked to the bone."

The rain was near biblical. I reached into my pocket and pulled out a twenty. "Let's give him a decent tip. Here's my share."

"Put your money away. With all the stuff you're leaving me, this meal's on me. By the way, I found the perfect movie for your farewell dinner. *Jurassic Park.*"

"Thanks, Ken. I'm sure there's some ironic reason for your choice." He smiled. I went to the fridge, pulled out a couple of beers, and brought one over to him. "Oh, I added my uniform to the clothes heap. A few of them are clean," I said with a smirk.

"Pizza's here!"

We watched the poor guy sprint through the downpour to our door. He wasn't wearing a raincoat and looked none too happy as he handed over the goods. Fortunately, the pizzas were high and dry, being in a waterproof case. Kenny thanked him with a ten dollar tip.

I put in the movie while Kenny opened the pizza boxes on the coffee table. We consumed them before the velociraptors ran amok.

After the movie, I got up and gazed out the window. The rain had stopped. Kenny cleared his throat. "Colt, don't get pissed, but I have to say this. You can still change your mind. Hell, you know they'd take you back in a heartbeat."

"Kenny, I just can't do it anymore. I can give you a hundred reasons for staying in, but every fiber of my being is screaming for me to get out."

"Well, I guess you gotta do what you gotta do." Knowing it was pointless to keep pressing, he mercifully let it go. "So, Mr. Civilian, are you all ready to go?"

"Yeah. Everything's packed. I'm traveling light. It was nice of Colonel Henderson to let you run my ass to the airport."

"He's a good guy. By the way, he pulled me in today, demanding I talk some sense into you. That's how much he respects you."

I smiled. "Before the farewell barbeque yesterday, he pushed hard to get me to reconsider. Hey Ken, switching gears, do you mind if I take one last walk along the RiverWalk?"

"No problem. Take your time. I'll probably turn in before you get back."

"I might be back soon if the monsoon returns."

I put on my raincoat and headed out. Once on the trail, I went north, away from Fort Benning, and toward Lake Oliver. At the 14th Street Bridge, I came to the Battle of Columbus historic site. Here, the last major land battle of the Civil War began at 1400 hours on Easter Sunday in April of 1865. Union Brevet Major General James Wilson's raiders were charging across Alabama, hell-bent on taking Columbus, which was then the second largest manufacturing center in the Confederacy. Right here, where I was walking, Confederate Major General Howell Cobb's war-weary troops made their last stand. Hours of intense hand-to-hand fighting ensued and, by 2000 hours that evening, the battle was over. Wilson's troops then danced pretty hard on the city, destroying anything having military value. Back then, they didn't split hairs on what qualified as military value. So, what wasn't plundered and pillaged was burned by the Yankees. In so many ways, the Civil War was brutally savage. I winced at the thought of how devastating those cylindrical-shaped, soft lead Minié balls were when they tore through a human body.

Enough about war. I pressed on to Heritage Park, a wonderful oasis offering sculptures, water features, and exhibits focusing on the city's history and its relationship to the adjacent Chattahoochee River.

I came to a bronze statue of John Pemberton, who was posed sitting on a bench with a mortar and pestle next to him. Dr. Pemberton, a Confederate, was a chemist and druggist by profession. He was wounded in the Battle of Columbus and, following the war, invented what he called *"a pure, delightful, diffusible stimulant"* we know today as Coca-Cola. I took a seat on the bench with John. I was the only person in the park, given the late hour and the possibility of more thunderstorms. "How are you doing, John? My name is Colt. If you don't mind, I'll share a seat with you for a while. This is my last night in Georgia. I'm heading to Alaska tomorrow."

As I sat reflecting with John, we were graced with a soft gentle breeze that carried the smell of rain and the scent of seasonal flowers. The sweet sounds of the Georgia night added to the reverie. When I first came to Georgia, the distinctive and loud noises of katydids and crickets nearly drove me to distraction, but now I found their singing to be comforting. There would be many things to miss about Georgia, from sitting on the deck with a big glass of sweet tea to rafting down the Chattahoochee on a warm summer day.

I looked at John and wondered about his life. He too knew about war and had suffered from its consequences. "Hey, buddy, I read how you were addicted to morphine after getting your ass shot and you eventually concocted Coca-Cola in an effort to find a cure for your addiction. Not bad, dude." He just sat there with a stoic smile on his face. "I don't think I'll hit one out of the park and get wealthy like you did. Right now, I have to tell you, I don't have a clue about anything. Tell me, did you feel the same way as I do after you got out of the army?"

More silence.

I tilted my head upward and saw a few stars through a break in the clouds. I turned my attention back to my bronze friend. "John, you wouldn't know it to look at me, but I'm a bad-ass killer. Yes, it's true, trust me. The Army taught me how to kill someone twenty different ways without a weapon. Give me a rifle with a good scope and I can shoot the ass end off a cicada from a mile away. If General Cobb had me and a few of my boys equipped with some of our weapons, well, we would've kicked ass at the Battle of Columbus. Of course, I guess you wouldn't have invented Coca-Cola because you wouldn't have been wounded, but you get my drift.

"Now, let me tell you something that'll have you howling with laughter. Get this. I can no longer stomach what I've been trained to do. Isn't that a hoot? A trained killer who can no longer kill. What irony, huh? How's that for being pathetic." I looked to see if his slight smile had increased to an ear-to-ear grin. He looked the same. John was good at keeping his thoughts close to the vest. "So, what the hell am I supposed to do now? I'm a washed up soldier with no skills, who's never spent one day in my entire adult life as a civilian. Geez, I feel like I'm hosed, John."

We sat in reflective quiet. I broke the silence. "John, I'm lost. My path used to be so clear and I felt invincible. Now it's like a great fog has descended, and I'm blindly trying to find my way. I guess you must know the feeling, yet you eventually took root and thrived. I admire you, John. You give me hope." A pigeon suddenly took flight and flew by just inches from my face. It scared the crap out of me. I almost dove to the ground, a now instinctive reflex acquired from a few too many tours in hostile country. I sheepishly looked at my bronze friend to see if the bird fazed him as well. But old John just sat there nonchalantly like he'd seen it a hundred times before.

A flash of lightning appeared to the west. Another flash. I counted aloud and got to fifteen before the boom sounded. Since sound travels about a mile in five seconds, the lightning was about three miles away. It was time for me to head back to the apartment before the next monsoon hit. "John, it's been a pleasure meeting you and talking to you tonight. Tomorrow, I'm off to Alaska where I'll be living on God's good humor. I hope I'll find some success as a civilian. Wish me well, buddy, because I'm going to need it." I stood up, put my hand on his shoulder, and said goodbye.

I made it a hundred yards down the path when the downpour hit, but I didn't mind. In fact, there had to be something metaphorical about being alone in a deluge. As if to embellish the notion, I took my time walking home.

Kenny was snoring away when I walked by his room. I hung my jacket in the shower and tossed my dripping pants and socks into the dryer. The walk had done me good. I fell asleep quickly and didn't wake until the alarm clock sounded the next morning.

After an instant waffle breakfast, we loaded my stuff into Kenny's car and headed to Atlanta. We chatted sporadically along the way, mostly about the scenery. Kenny knew I didn't have a clue regarding the future, so he saw no need to press me on it. Like most guys, silence is the best course of action when things become awkward. I was grateful for it.

When we arrived at the airport, I had him drop me off instead of going through the hassle of parking. After a round of goodbyes, I made my way in with all my possessions fitting comfortably into a carry-on bag and a suitcase. In fourteen hours I'd begin life as a newly minted civilian in Alaska.

2

Five months later...

"SORRY, COLT, TODAY will be your last day. I'm letting you go."

"Come on, Marty, let's talk about this some more."

"Colt, face it, you suck at selling cars. One lousy sale in the last three weeks and you practically gave that ride away because he was a soldier. You're wasting your time being here."

I sighed. He was right; I had no talent for smooth talking someone into believing a tired old heap was akin to a late-model Ferrari. I guess this deficiency ruled out me being a politician too. "Look on the bright side, Colt. Me firing you in early November puts you one up on all those who'll be looking for holiday jobs."

"Thanks, Marty. You're a prince among men." He smiled at the comment, which I think he perceived as genuine.

"I'll give you a recommendation if you want on your next job."

"Thanks, but I don't think I'll need a character reference to sell my blood."

He laughed but I wasn't joking. He reached into his pocket. "Here's ten bucks. Call it your severance pay. Have dinner on me."

"Thanks, Marty. I love eating at McDonalds." I took the bill and left. So much for my car-selling career.

It was cold outside; we'd been having a run of sub-zero nights and days in the single digits. I reached into my coat pocket and pulled out my gloves. I'd need them to hold the ice-cold steering wheel. I decided to take Marty's generous severance pay and get a bite to eat at my main sustenance center, the place with the familiar golden arches. I walked in and looked at the value menu. If I did this right, I could stretch my severance pay into two meals. I ordered a double cheeseburger, fries, and a drink. Excellent. Plenty left for a meal tomorrow. I waited patiently for my food, filled my cup with Coke, and smothered my burger in catsup because it's important to have a vegetable with your meal. I took a seat and watched a bunch of high-energy kids burn off some of their high-calorie happy meals. Some parents smiled and waved at their playing kids while others seemed to revel in their temporary solitude.

I ate slowly to make it feel like I was eating a bigger meal. Not that it helped a couple of hours later when my stomach would start growling, but at least I could pretend to be having a feast. I opened four more packets of catsup and dunked my fries in the red ambrosia. Yeah, I was living large.

I finished my meal, refilled my soda, and contemplated the magnitude of being unemployed again. Unless I found something quickly I'd have to dip once more into my savings. A quick mental calculation of my financial burn rate put me at a few months of solvency; after that, well, let's not go to that dark space. I decided to spend the next day searching Craigslist for a job. Who knows, maybe I'd land one of those brain surgeon positions that doesn't require previous experience or a lot of education. Yes, life was shaping up. I went home, watched something stupid on TV, and decided to turn in early. I made a mental note to cancel my cable subscription tomorrow because eating matters more than watching inane drivel.

The next day I woke early, got on the computer, and searched for jobs on Craigslist. After a half-hour of fruitless searching, I needed to get out and clear my head. The sun was coming up. With no clouds to trap the heat, this would be a frigid day. Still, it would be fun to spend a few hours cross-country skiing. I had gotten a deal on used waxless Alpina Red Tail skis and wanted to test them in the back country. My plan was to ski up Powerline Pass in the Chugach State Park, a half-million acre wilderness bordering Anchorage. No matter how bad I was feeling, my soul always found solace in the Chugach.

I put on my ski clothes, filled a backpack, and went out to warm up my car. After ten minutes of chiseling ice off the windows, I headed out. At the Upper Hoffman parking lot, I put on my skis, gloves, and hood, and made my way to the trailhead. The vapor from my breathing hung for a while in the air before disappearing. It was probably between zero and five below.

I suddenly heard strange noises behind me. With my full-face hood my vision was restricted and I couldn't easily pivot around with my skis on. An alarm sounded in my head because humans aren't the apex hunters in the Chugach. By the time I turned around, the animal, a dog, was nearly upon me, growling, barking, whining, yelping, crying, and baring its teeth, almost all at the same time. It stopped about four feet away and kept up its almost eerie repertoire of noises. I kicked off one of my skis, figuring to either kick the animal or use the ski to ward it off. It kept vocalizing—words couldn't describe the odd sounds—but it didn't come any closer. I got a chance to look it over. Geez. It looked like it'd been through a war. One of its upper incisors was broken off, its left ear was practically gone, and the other looked like a cauliflower ear you'd see on a tired old boxer. Its scarred face looked like it had been on the losing side of many catfights. Crisscrossing the older scars was a newer round of putrid-looking, pus-filled gashes that were oozing blood all over its face. Its right eye was draining fluid and there was a big knot under its upper left lip, like someone had put a golf ball inside its mouth between its lip and teeth. Probably some sort of abscess. Its tail was bent at a peculiar angle about half way up, and its fur was missing in several places. As if all this wasn't bad enough, the mutt was emaciated.

As the verbal tirade and teeth-baring aggression continued, I noticed something odd. The poor thing was wagging its broken tail. Well, it appeared as if it was trying to wag the appendage. This was a sign. Dogs don't wag their tail when they attack. My fear began to subside.

"You know, if you mean to intimidate me, you might want to stop wagging your tail."

At the sound of my voice, the dog stopped its tirade. It stared at me, still baring its teeth. Geez, this dog was a mess.

"Look, I see you have a Jekyll/Hyde thing going on here. Your teeth say one thing but your tail says something else."

We stood looking at each other some more, each sizing up the other. I broke the silence again. "I don't think you're crazed; you're just a dog needing help. I'm going to make a call for someone to come and help you." I got out my cell phone and dialed 911.

"What is the nature of your emergency?"

"I'm at the Upper Hoffman trailhead and found a dog in bad shape."

"Sir, we only respond to human emergencies."

"Well, what the hell am I supposed to do with this dog? It's in bad shape."

"Sir, there's the pet emergency center on Lake Otis Parkway near Tudor. You can take the animal there."

"I can take the animal?" I emphasized the 'I' in my response.

"I'm sorry sir, that's the best we can do for you."

"Great," I replied sarcastically. "Thanks for all your help." The mutt's pathetic eyes bore into me, pleading for help. Damn. "Well, hell, I guess I'm the one who'll rescue your sorry ass today. I'm going to pick you up and take you to a doggy doctor. Bite me, and I just might bite your scrawny ass back."

I warily put my hand out. The dog appeared to have spent the last of its energy reserves with the barking tirade and made no threatening moves. I scooped it up. "Don't worry. I'll get you some help. Let's get in my car and go to the doc."

I sat the dog on my lap because I didn't want the dirty thing sitting on my car seat. It didn't so much as whimper as I drove. About halfway there, the car's heater started to unthaw some of its scruffy fur, releasing a wicked brew of noxious odors.

When I got to the pet center, a lady at the front desk winced upon seeing the poor dog.

"I found him at the Upper Hoffman trailhead."

"Oh my. Please follow me back to the exam room. Does he have an ID tag?"

"No. This dog is traveling incognito." I then recalled something funny. "Remember that old joke, *Reward for missing dog: three legs, blind in left eye, missing right ear, tail broken, recently castrated, answers to the name of 'Lucky'?* Well, I think that might be this dog." The lady halfheartedly smiled at my devastating wit.

I put 'Lucky' on the exam table. The vet came in and frowned when she saw the pathetic creature. "Hello, my name is Rosanna Dickens. Let's see what we have here." She put on a pair of latex gloves, performed a quick assessment, and looked at me with a grave expression. "Sir, I don't even know where to begin with what's wrong with this little dog. He's frostbitten, emaciated, and has two abscessed teeth. Did you notice how he winced as I brought my hand near his face? That's a good indicator that he's been abused. I could feel where several of his ribs appear to have been broken. More signs of abuse. He's about a year old, but trust me, that year must've been hell for him. I'm sorry to say this, but I recommend putting him down."

I gazed at the dog lying motionless on the table. Tough break, I thought. Life sucks. "Okay, Doc, you know what's best. Kind of a shame, huh?"

"There are lots of abandoned animals like this one. Alaska in the winter is terrible on them. Most just lie down and never get back up. The cold gets them." She tenderly touched the dog. "One of my techs will prep him to be put to sleep. It's humane and he won't feel a thing."

"Okay. Do you mind if I say a quick goodbye to him?"

"Go right ahead. I'll tell the tech to give you some time. She smiled, touched my shoulder in silent sympathy, and then left me to say my goodbye.

I turned my attention back to the dog and frowned at the sight of his distorted face. All I wanted was a nice ski outing and here I was at a vet center saying goodbye to some wretched mutt. Lucky looked at me and tried to wag his tail. Damn, I thought while looking at him, life didn't deal you a good hand. I guess we had one thing in common—we both knew the feeling that comes from being dealt a bad hand or two. "Well, little fella, this is goodbye. Life sucks, as we both know. I bet there'll be nothing but sunny days and lots of bones in doggy heaven. I wish you well on your journey. When you get to heaven, look up my friend, Johnny Matthews. He's a good guy, and I'm sure he'll show you around. I bet he knows where all the good bones are buried."

I flashed on Johnny and the awful day when an Afghan's bullet found its way to his head. I started to choke up. Damn, I needed to beat a hasty retreat from this scene. "Goodbye. Fair winds to you on your new journey."

The tech entered the room with some syringes in his hand. I nodded and left the room. At the sight of me departing, Lucky struggled to get up and go with me. The tech grabbed the flailing animal. He began yelping, a terrified kind of yelping—I think he knew what was coming. I quickly headed to the front door. The yelping seemed to increase in volume, if that was possible. I stopped. Damn it. I looked at the exit, only a few feet away. *Keep walking,* I told myself as the yelping echoed in my head. "Crap!" I turned around and walked back. Seeing me, Lucky tried even harder to escape the tech's grasp, frantically yelping. The vet walked back in with a *"what the hell"* expression. I put my hand on the dog's head. His yelping stopped and he collapsed back on the table.

"Well," said the vet, "this little dog seems to have bonded with you."

"Oh joy," I cynically replied.

The dog was staring at me with a *help me, help me* look on his face.

I looked at the vet. "Maybe I could take him home for a while."

She looked at me with a puzzled expression. "What's your name?"

"Colt."

"Colt, I appreciate your gesture, but this little guy has major health issues. He's probably in staggering pain and he's damaged psychologically from the obvious abuse. If you want a pet, I have several more suitable candidates for you to consider."

"Ma'am, I don't want a pet. Believe me, that's the last thing I need in my life right now. But I just can't turn my back on this dog."

She frowned and looked back at the dog. "If you decide to do this, I have to tell you, there'll be a considerable expense to get him back to any semblance of health. He'll need dental work, all his shots, de-worming, and who knows what else from there. My professional opinion is to end his suffering."

Now I frowned. "How much to get him back into shape?"

"It'll be pricy, especially if there are internal injuries needing attention. Plus, he'll never look a lot better than he does now. We can't replace ears, remove scars, or fix a tail, and I don't know of any dog psychologists to help mend his mental traumas. Colt, truly, putting him down would be the best thing to do."

I knew she was right. Damn. I thought about it for a few moments. "Can you give me a break on the bill?"

She sighed. "Well, I suppose. If you want to tackle this, I won't bill you for my time. But, you'll still have to pay for facility and medicine costs."

I cringed. More money taking wing. "Let's do it." Geez, what a sap I was.

She smiled at the tech. "Let's start the paperwork. This little dog now has an owner." He left to get the paperwork, probably thinking I was an idiot.

I put my hand on the emaciated dog and frowned. "Well, this'll be interesting." Lucky tried to wag his broken tail. I think he sensed his rescuer had truly arrived.

The tech came back holding a clipboard. "If you fill this out, we can get started."

I took the clipboard, dreading how expensive this was going to be. I got to the box wanting the dog's name and stopped to give it some thought. 'Lucky' sounded a bit cynical, and God knows I didn't need any more cynicism in my life. What to call him...? I flashed on when he first approached me, all the odd barking, snarling and then the tail wagging, that Jekyll and Hyde thing. I smiled. There was his name, right in front of me. Jekyll. It sounded nice, but a bit unpretentious. It needed to be dressed up a bit. I thought some more and smiled again. I had the perfect name for this homely creature. Jekyll von Bickerstaff. I penciled it in. I read it aloud and couldn't help but laugh. Yes, it was indeed a grand name.

The vet came back and read the chart. "Jekyll von Bickerstaff?" She smiled at the majesty of the name for such a wreck of a dog. "I like it." I didn't respond. My thoughts were on my wallet getting skinnier. She turned her attention to the dog. "Well, Jekyll, or should I say, Mr. von Bickerstaff, we're going to help you get better." She stroked his head and then gave him a shot to knock him out. Her game plan was to x-ray him to look for internal injuries and pull the teeth causing those painful abscesses.

I spent a couple of hours in the waiting area. She called me to her office and showed me his x-rays. "This confirms what I suspected," she said, pointing to his ribs on the x-ray. "You can see here, here and here where his ribs were broken and subsequently healed. Here's where his tail was broken. We could amputate it at the break, but I'd let it go since I don't think it's causing him any pain. I don't see any other internal injuries needing attention. His real issues are with his fur and skin. He's frostbitten in several places. I think those areas will heal with the help of antibiotics. His teeth are in bad shape. I pulled two abscessed molars, the broken incisor and another decayed tooth, and had to insert something called a Penrose drain to drain fluid from one of the wound areas. The antibiotics should help those heal too."

She let out a sigh and went on. "I put some antibiotic drops in his eye, which should cure the infection. Plus, I gave him all the normal shots, so he's now up-to-date for those, and I gave him de-worming meds. I'm having my tech shave off his fur because it's matted so badly. We'll have to keep him warm until his fur grows back."

I squirmed. "Wow, he sure has some major malfunctions."

"He does. Jekyll has no body fat, so his body is cannibalizing muscle tissue for calories. I'm not sure how this will affect him long-term. The big thing is to get calories into him. Massive amounts of calories. We'll need to start slowly and then increase the amount of food. Too much food all at once will kill him. He should stay here at least a week. I recommend you come by daily to bond with him." She looked at me with sympathy. "You know, you'll have your hands full for a while to get him back on his feet. I'm not sure he's even housebroken."

"Guess I picked a winner, eh, Doc?"

She smiled at my weak sarcasm. "I think that little dog picked you."

The following week passed quickly. Being unemployed gave me plenty of time to visit Jekyll. Each day I could see him gaining weight and strength. He loved seeing me and got upset when I left. I guess you could say the damn thing had indeed bonded to me.

I took Jek home on Saturday. Before picking him up, I stopped by a pet store and bought everything the kind saleslady said a dog would need. Ka-ching, ka-ching, ka-ching, more money moving out. I nearly fainted when the vet clinic receptionist handed me a bill for $873 to "spring" him from the clinic. She had to practically pry the MasterCard from my hand. I made a mental calculation of how many value meals I could buy at the arches for 873 bucks…gasp.

When we got home, I showed Jekyll the big cedar-filled pad I bought for him to lounge on. I put an old blanket on it. He still looked pathetic, what with being bald, bent-tailed, scarred, and those absurd-looking ears. But, he seemed happy to be hanging with me. I let him sleep with me at night to keep him warm. The damn dog had a nasty snoring habit, and, from his many motions, he sure dreamed a lot. Some nights he'd wake up whimpering. That was something we had in common. We both had more than our share of bad dreams.

I spent a lot of time hustling him outside to use the outdoor facilities and got a kick out of seeing the shocked expressions on the faces of my neighbors when they saw good ol' Jek, out doing his business. They all acted like they'd never seen an alien dog from another planet before. To my delight, in no time, Jekyll was housebroken. Like the vet noticed earlier, he winced every time my hand moved toward him. His previous owner obviously smacked him a lot. I'd love to put a few "love taps" on that jerk's head.

A week after Jekyll came home, we were running out of the complimentary dog food provided by the clinic. My vet recommended Blue Buffalo because it was made with a lot of good crap. Since Jek needed something packed with nutrition, I splurged. Another hit to my wallet. I needed to hunker down even more to cut costs, but after dropping my cable service and cell phone, there wasn't much left to chop. Life was back to basics.

My austerity measures were becoming creative, or I should say, desperate. For internet access, I pirated a neighbor's unsecured Wi-Fi signal, and used Google Voice for free telephone service. I prowled Costco to stretch my dollars. Staples for my subsistence included bulk packs of macaroni and cheese, refried beans, and mega-bags of rice, apples, potatoes, carrots, and onions. I took advantage of their free samples. Because I was polite to the people who dispensed the samples, they didn't say anything when I came back for seconds. They knew I wasn't there to taste. I was there to put food in my belly. On Fridays, I'd buy a five-buck rotisserie chicken and dissect it. Mixing the pieces into rice, refried beans or mac and cheese would give me meals for four or five days. I'd freeze the carcass, and later put it into a big pot with potatoes, carrots, and onions to make chicken soup. To my surprise, when I dropped a piece of carrot on the floor, Jekyll was on it in a flash. It seemed he loved carrots, so I began feeding him as many as he wanted.

Although I'm not proud to say this, I also got my toilet paper from Costco. I'd go into restroom stalls and stuff my pockets with it, but I always left enough for someone not to get caught short. After Costco, I made the rounds at fast-food joints for condiments and napkins. I hit a new low at the arches, swiping some fries and chicken nuggets from a kid who'd left his table to play. I gave up shaving cream and settled for lathering my face with soap in the shower. I could make a six-pack of disposable razors last half a year, and a mega-container of Johnson's baby shampoo was good for an entire year. My one stick of deodorant is used only for special occasions, like a job interview. Fortunately, I don't have body odor, or maybe I do, but I can't tell anymore.

I also cut my use of laundry detergent by half, and when that didn't seem to affect the cleanliness of my wash, I cut it by half again. I bought a used hair clipper and gave myself haircuts. Keeping my hair short meant less shampoo being needed. My weekly showers were done in the dark to save electricity and it was kind of fun; I pretended to be standing under a waterfall in Hawaii. I was getting so frugal that I could probably figure out a way to breathe less if they ever started charging for air.

I contemplated surrendering my single biggest expense, my apartment, and living out in the woods. Doing it wouldn't be that hard since I once lived close to the earth as a sniper. I could eat for free at Bean's Café, which feeds the homeless. I gnawed on a carrot to quiet my growling belly and decided to table this notion until the weather got warmer. Jekyll wanted a carrot too. That he loved carrots amazed me, but at least they were cheap.

3

IN THE COMING days, I camped on the Craigslist site, trying to find a job. Jekyll seemed to like being wrapped in a blanket and sitting on my lap as I pounded away on the keyboard. After a while, he started getting used to hearing 'damn' or some other colorful expression that always came with each fruitless round of job searching.

After a couple of weeks, I found a lead. Rico's Bar and Grille had an opening for a food server. After scanning the net for "lessons" in food serving, I called Rico's, telling the manager that I was his man. My bunk was good enough to land an interview on Wednesday. That gave me time to write a résumé and check out more table-waiting tips on the net. I looked at Jekyll. "Fake it till you make it, right boy?" He gave me a few tail wags as if to say *You got that right, bwana.*

I woke up early on Wednesday to give me time to mentally prepare for the interview. I mulled over what to wear and went to the bedroom closet. I had two ties to my name, one teal-green and the other metallic red. I put them on the bed next to my distinguished fashion critic, who was observing my every move. "So Jek, which tie should I wear?"

"Woof!" He put his paw on the green tie. "Woof!"

"The green one? Are you sure? I was leaning toward wearing the red one."

"Woof!" He put his paw again on the green tie and wagged his tail to emphasize the point.

"Jek, red ties convey confidence and power. Believe me, I need something to convey confidence since I haven't a clue about serving food."

"Woof!"

"Okay, okay, I'll wear the green one, but if the interview doesn't go well, it'll be on you." After putting on black slacks, a freshly washed white shirt, and the tie demanded by El Fashionista, I looked in the mirror and was pleased with the reflection. If nothing else, I'd show them I knew how to dress. I had a flash of insight and ran to the bathroom to get the deodorant. I was going all-out for this interview. With one last look in the mirror, I was satisfied, and turned to Jekyll for a final appraisal. "Well?"

"Woof! Woof!" I interpreted the woofs as *way cool, dude, way cool!*

"Thanks for your help on this, Jekyll. Wish me well. Let's get you out to do your business and then I need to split."

While Jekyll did his sniffing and squatting, I thought about what to say at the interview. I was nervous because I needed to land this job to stop, or at least slow down, my financial hemorrhaging. I was proud of my new résumé, which reflected my vast food-serving experience. 'Vast' was a bit of a stretch. In the Army, I had brought a tray of food to my friend Johnny when he was laid up with the flu. That was the total of my food serving experience. My résumé was all bull crap, but it looked good on paper. Besides, nobody would ever go to the Army and ask for verification.

I arrived at ten and knocked on the front door, as requested. An overweight guy came to the door smiling and waving. He looked to be really old, somewhere in his forties. "How ya doing; my name is Eddie Rico and I own and operate this place. You're Colt, right?"

"Yes, sir," I said with enthusiasm in my voice while holding out my hand for him to shake. *Remember to grip his hand tightly,* I told myself. *That conveys confidence.* He shook my hand with equal confidence.

He locked the door and motioned for me to have a seat at a table next to the bar. "Hey, I like your tie. Is it an Armani?"

I smiled and gave silent thanks to my dog for his impeccable fashion sense. "Thanks, sir. No, it's a Wal-Mart special. I don't orbit in the same sphere as Armani."

He laughed at my reply. "Can I get you a Coke or some other soda?"

Crap. What's the protocol when someone offers you something during an interview? If I said no, I might offend him. Saying yes might imply I was being too casual, especially in an interview. *Damn.*

"Um, if you're having one, then that would be great."

"I'll get us a couple of Cokes," he said, pleased that I took him up on his offer. He came back and handed me a mug of soda. "Do you ever notice when you go to most eating places how seventy percent of your mug is filled with ice? You can have people thinking they got three or four free soda refills, when in fact, they really got only one glass of actual product." He seemed proud of that tidbit of knowledge, which indicated the man knew his craft. *Crap.*

"Yes, sir. Ice is a lot cheaper."

"Exactly. You know, I'm a local business having to compete against the big boys. Every little bit of savings helps."

"It must be a constant challenge," I said in empathy of his plight.

He rolled his eyes and nodded affirmatively. "So, if you worked for me, what could you think of to help reduce my costs?"

Damn. My goose was cooked. I took a sip of my soda to stall for some time to think. "Well," I said with a little hesitation, "I guess I wouldn't offer a free soda to anyone I was interviewing until after I decided to hire him." He laughed heartily at my remark. I went on, not wanting to appear like a smart ass. "I'd also take a hard look at everything on the menu and see where my true profit was. I'd question whether to continue offering the marginal-profit dishes and I'd have my staff push the meals that were making me money."

"Interesting," he said, apparently pleased that I had some semblance of a brain. "Did you bring a résumé?"

"Yes, sir." I reached into my coat, pulled out my two-page masterpiece, and offered it to him.

He took it with a smile, put on his bifocals, and started reading. After about a minute he put the résumé down. "U.S. Army. Ranger School. Sniper. A bunch of medals. E-7. Impressive. Why did you get out after nine years?"

My stomach tightened. *Should I buffalo him or level with him? Damn.* I looked him in the eye to decide if my reply should be trash or truth. He noticed my hesitation in replying but seemed truly interested in what I had to say. I couldn't stop myself. The reply was going to be the truth. "Mr. Rico, I could no longer take watching someone be blown into pieces when I nailed them with a fifty-caliber bullet, nor could I endure having any more of my friends die in my arms." *Well, so much for this interview.* My afternoon was now shaping up nicely. After explaining to Jekyll how I had blown it, I'd be back on Craigslist looking for another job.

He winced at the verbal mortar shell I tossed his way. But, I think there was empathy in his eyes. "Colt, I too was in the Army. Infantry, 82nd Airborne Division, Desert Storm. It got nasty there more than a few times."

That got my attention. "Sir, I apologize for the candidness of my remark, but there's no way to sugarcoat what I've been through. Maybe you can understand having been over there yourself."

"I do. You said what you needed to say perfectly." He mercifully ended the exchange by putting on his bifocals and returning to my résumé. After a couple of minutes he took off the glasses and tossed them on the table.

"You don't know squat about the food service business, do you?"

I looked him straight in the eye. "No sir, not a damn thing. But, I'm a fast learner and I know I can do this job and do it well."

I think he appreciated my honesty, well, my in-person honesty, and not the résumé crap. Finally, his stony expression turned into a smile. "I'll start you at five an hour for the first two weeks while my staff trains you, then I'll bump you to ten if you work out. Plus you can keep all your tips after your training. I expect hard work from my employees and I have zero tolerance for tardiness or dishonesty. How does that sound to you?"

"It sounds great and more than fair."

He smacked the table with his hand. "Done! Can you start next Monday?"

"I sure can. Thank you for giving me this chance, sir."

"Colt, I was enlisted just like you, so drop the "sir" crap. Call me Eddie." He reached across the table and shook my hand. "Tell you what. Follow me back to the grill and I'll give you a lesson on how to make a killer burger. You can even eat your lesson after we're done. It's on me."

"Thanks, Eddie, I could use a good burger. I'd be happy to get a lesson on how to cook a steak too."

"Wise ass," he said with a smile. "We could probably rustle up one of those. My T-bones are impeccable."

I had a delightful meal with Eddie. He introduced me to the staff and they all seemed friendly. I couldn't help but smile as I drove home. My belly was full. Things were looking up.

Jekyll was at the door to greet me. His ridiculous tail was wagging at staggering speed and he had an expression on his face that demanded to know how things had gone. "Well, Jek, we did it. I got the job!" I scooped him up and danced a jig. He was as excited as me, licking my face and woofing up a storm. "You were right about the tie choice. Just to show my appreciation, I brought you a little something." I reached into my coat pocket and pulled out the T-bone remains from Eddie's. Jekyll's eyes lit up like Christmas arrived early. I found the perfect way to say thanks to my wunderhund. He pounced on the bone with a gobbling frenzy that would impress a hungry school of piranhas. In no time, the bone was history. Jekyll then waddled into the kitchen.

"Woof!"

I walked in to see what he wanted. His paw was on his food bowl. His look said one thing—he'd completed the appetizer and was now ready for the entrée.

"Are you serious? You want more to eat?"

"Woof!"

"Jek, I left a lot of meat on that bone. Maybe you might just want to let it settle for a while."

"Woof!"

"Okay, I'll give you a half ration of Blue Buffalo, but that's all. Deal?"

"Woof!"

I rolled my eyes and got out the bag.

"Woof! Woof!"

"Geez, Jek, hold on for a second."

"Woof!" He tore into the food and practically inhaled it. I shook my head. To say that Jekyll had an appetite would be a titanic under-statement. He'd already gained a good four pounds since the day I found him, or should I say, the day he found me.

Since the weather had warmed to the high teens, I began going on walks with Jekyll stuffed into my parka with only his head hanging out. He enjoyed getting outside as much as I did. It made me smile when I walked past people on the trail and saw how they looked after catching sight of my seriously non-GQ mongrel. Jekyll, to his credit, didn't seem to be aware of his shortcomings. He appreciated people and wanted to meet everyone he saw. Even my neighbors, after they got used to the sight of him, appeared to succumb to his charms. The kids loved Jek, and would run yelling, "Jekyll von Bickerstaff, Jekyll von Bicker-staff," whenever he was out. One girl, a five-year-old named Lilly, was especially enamored with Jekyll. She'd wait by her window and scream with delight when I brought him outside. I think her parents gave up saying "no" to her running out to see him. Some days she never got around to putting on her shoes, even though it was winter. Lilly would always come out with a carrot for Jekyll. I never heard of a dog liking carrots, but this dog ate them like they were candy. It seemed like every kid in the neighborhood had a carrot stuffed in their pocket in case of a chance encounter with Jekyll von B. Yep, my dog was a charmer. I think he had an "Abe Lincoln" thing going on. He was just so homely and friendly that nobody could resist him.

I brought Jekyll back to Rosanna for a follow up appointment. Everyone on the staff was amazed at his progress. Just like the neighborhood kids, they'd say 'Hello, Jekyll von Bickerstaff' as he walked by. He marched into the exam room like he didn't have a care in the world. It made me smile.

"Hello, Colt," Rosanna said cheerfully as she walked into the room. I'd already put Jekyll on the exam table so she went right to him. She patted his head and he licked her hand in response. "Wow, what a change!" She moved her hands over his body and then lifted up his lips to look at his teeth. She then put him on a scale. "Goodness. Five pounds up! Did I say wow already? Jekyll is making a remarkable recovery. Whatever you're doing, keep doing it. I can't believe I'm saying this after his first visit here, but if you keep feeding him at this rate, you'll be having an overweight dog before long. He should weigh no more than twenty to twenty-two pounds, so we'll see where he is next month. Truly, you've done an exceptional job with this little fella." Jekyll was wagging his tail briskly, apparently agreeing with what she said.

"Thanks, Doc. Now, if only I could get him to work, life would be sweet. I was thinking about having him be a dog model. What do you think?"

She chuckled at the thought of Jekyll posing for some big magazine spread. "I think you better have him earn a living using his wits."

"So, can you hazard a guess regarding his lineage?"

"Hmmm…my best guess is Jekyll is a mix of Pembroke Welsh corgi and, oh, maybe a Jack Russell terrier. But that's a guess. From his appetite, there might be a little wolf in there too." I laughed at her remark. I liked this woman. She had a kind heart.

For the first time in a long while, I felt happy. I wasn't sure if it was me landing the job or maybe Jekyll taking my mind off things. I decided not to analyze it and simply enjoy the feeling.

Monday came and I showed up at Rico's early. Eddie had me shadow Tommy, a balding twenty-something guy with an easy smile. After watching him work the lunch-hour crowd, I concluded that this man was a genius. He could take ten orders at once, remember everything without writing it down and, with his great attentive service, would have the patrons feeling like they were royalty. I was astonished at how people responded with generous tips, but he deserved it. Geez, this guy was making enough to buy a yacht.

As the days went by, Tommy navigated me through the tricks of the trade. He taught me about serving techniques, establishing a rapport, not only with the customers, but with the staff, and how to handle heavy trays of food, dishes, and glassware. He even gave me tips on tips. Report less than ten percent to the IRS and they will get nasty. Not declaring anything after ten percent was up to you. I learned that the big money comes from those undeclared tips. Sorry, Uncle Sugar, but servers need to make a living too.

Soon, I was hustling tables on my own, charming the patrons, and making good money. After coming home at night, Jekyll and I would sit on the couch and count our tips for the day. I even worked a ten-bucks-a-week deal with Lilly to watch Jekyll during the day. After a month, she thought she was becoming a tycoon. There was generosity with her new-found wealth. She always used some of her earnings to keep Jek in carrots.

The months were clicking by. It was mid-April and financially I was in the black. I even paid off my vet bill. Eddie was generous in terms of food. He gave us a free meal if we worked both lunch and dinner.

Jekyll's stamina had markedly improved. At first, he couldn't go far without getting winded. Now he was able to keep up with me for miles. I never put him on a leash because the blasted dog glued himself to me whenever we went out. To celebrate Jek's progress, I got Eddie's okay to take the weekend off. I planned an overnight trip to Eklutna Lake, with a twelve-mile hike to a glacier. The hike would be mostly level, so Jek could manage it. If not, I'd just carry him. I had a nice backpacking tent and the gear we would need, so I was looking forward to the outing.

On Saturday, I got up early and headed out with Jekyll in tow. He seemed excited. I had my rain jacket in case of any showers and could stuff His Jekyllness in it if necessary. He still needed to be kept warm since his fur was still growing out.

I parked at the trailhead and we headed out. By noon, we were six miles in and Jekyll was keeping up with no problem. Even the weather was cooperating. We were having a blast; he'd run from one thing to another, smelling everything along his path, and then would race back to me.

Eklutna Lake is an eight-mile-long, glacier-fed body of water bordered on all sides by mountains, and beyond the lake, the trail continues to Eklutna Glacier. There were a few people on the trail including an occasional all-terrain vehicle, or ATV. About nine miles in, we came to a slight elevation rise. I got ahead of Jekyll after he became preoccupied with a frog. After cresting the rise, I caught sight of movement. Something rocketed out of the brush and hit me—I went flying through the air and landed hard on my side. In a second, whatever hit me was on me. Damn, it was a bear! It swiped me hard a couple of times with its paws, causing my backpack to fly off. I curled into a fetal position thinking, *kiss your ass goodbye, Colt. This is it, you're dead.* Geez, I'd made it through Iraq and Afghanistan and here I am on a trail in Alaska being an hors d'oeuvre for some damn bear. The bear, a grizzly, and probably a female with cubs, bit into my calf and shook her head. I screamed out in pain. She was really pissed, roaring and snarling and chomping her teeth. Another bite. Another scream.

Suddenly, I heard a familiar growling, barking, whining, yelping, crying noise above the din of the bear. Jekyll came roaring in and jumped on that she-bear with all the force his nineteen pounds could muster. Startled, the bear turned around to face what had just entered the scene. Upon seeing Jekyll, I bet the bear had to fight the urge to double over in laughter. She smacked him away and turned back to have another chomp on me. Jekyll would have none of it. He jumped back up like his legs were made of coiled steel springs and was on the bear in an instant. He latched onto her face with his mightiest chomp. The bear had him flying again with a simple flick of her head. Once more, I became the chief target. Just then an ATV came roaring over the rise, practically running into the bear and me. Between that, Jekyll now back and bellowing, and me kicking as hard as I could, the bear decided enough was enough. She disengaged and went running back into the brush. I caught a glimpse of two other fur bundles running after her.

The guy on the ATV gasped when he saw the blood pouring from my leg. He tore off his T-shirt and wrapped it around my calf saying, *"Jesus, Jesus."* He was shaking from the adrenaline surge. "Are-are you okay?" he said, his voice trembling.

"Yeah, but how's my dog?" I couldn't see Jekyll.

The guy stood up and looked around. "Oh God, your dog is hurt bad! The bear bit off one of his ears and broke his tail!"

Jekyll pounced on me, licking my face with more concern than a mother tending to a kid after a bike wreck. "I'm okay, Jek, I'm okay." I sat up and looked him over. He had a nasty gash on his side that was bleeding, but the calamities scaring the crap out of the ATV driver were just his normal everyday ugliness. Despite the pain, I couldn't help but laugh. I stood up and felt my world go black. I collapsed, nearly hitting Jekyll.

As I came to, the guy's face was about an inch from mine. "Mister, hey, mister!" I think he thought I'd died.

"I'm okay, just a little light-headed. I'd appreciate it if you could help me back on my feet and give me a ride to my car."

"Sure, no problem. Wouldn't it be better if I go and get some help?"

"No, let's put some distance between us and that bear."

"You're right. Let me help you up." I felt better this time. I pulled off my bandana and handed it to him.

"My name is Colt. Would you mind putting this on my dog's wound?" He nodded and did as asked. Jekyll didn't make a fuss when he wrapped him with the makeshift bandage.

"Colt, my name is Ben. Let's try to get you on my ATV."

"Good idea. If you could get my backpack, I'll put on my raincoat and my dog can fit in under it."

He went over and got my shredded pack. I pulled out the raincoat and put it on. He handed Jekyll to me and I put him inside my coat. I was able to sit on the rear rack with my feet dangling off the end. Ben slowly began heading back to the trailhead. He warned all the other hikers we passed about the bear. With all the blood on me it was obvious he wasn't issuing a false alarm. Jekyll was on full bear alert the whole way back.

It took an hour to make it back. I was grateful Ben was there. Not only did he stop the bear attack but he was kind enough to give me a ride. The pain was now cutting through the fading adrenaline surge. Now, each beat of my heart produced lightning bolts of pain. I looked pretty rough hobbling over to my car.

"Colt, why don't you wait here and let me get you some help."

"Thanks, Ben, but I just want to get back to town. I need to get my dog patched up and then me."

"I think you have the order mixed up. You need to get patched up first." I smiled weakly, unzipped my raincoat, and gently put Jekyll into the car. He moved gingerly to the passenger seat and curled up. He was feeling pain too.

"Thanks for everything, Ben. God knows how much more that bear would've danced on me if you hadn't appeared."

"Are you sure you don't want me to get some help? Can you drive okay?"

"Yeah, I'll be fine. Thanks again for all you've done." He nodded but still looked concerned. I smiled to show him I was okay, started the engine, and headed down the road. After getting out of his sight, I let out a large moan. It hurt badly when I breathed. Jekyll took note of my pain and started to get up. "It's okay Jek. Stay put. We'll be all right soon."

By the time I arrived at the pet clinic, my pain was intense. I turned off the engine and got out. When I stood up, nausea swept through me. I forced myself to walk to the passenger door to open it for Jekyll. Fortunately, he was able to walk on his own. At the entrance, it took all my strength to pull the door open. "A bear got us," I said to the receptionist. "I'm going to leave Jekyll here and go to the VA hospital." That's all I remembered. I woke up later at the VA hospital. The doc was polite and told me I'd be okay. I had a couple of broken ribs, and of course, a bunch of puncture wounds. He sewed up the worst of them, and said I'd need antibiotics for a while because bear bites can easily become infected. The ribs would take some time to heal, but it wasn't serious. Overall, for a bear attack, I got off pretty easy.

I called Rosanna. She assured me Jekyll was okay and he could come home anytime. He had needed stitches, but that was the extent of his injuries. He'd need antibiotics too. She said it took her whole staff to pry him away from me when I collapsed. I told her how Jekyll went after that bear with fearless abandon, and how Ben thought he'd been savagely attacked by the bear after seeing his normal looks. We both laughed.

I called Eddie, who told me to take off as much time as I needed. He even offered to run a burger out to me. Eddie was a good guy.

The next day I decided to pick up Jekyll. Rosanna sent one of her staff over to pick me up. My ribs hurt like hell when we hit the slightest bump. Everyone greeted me heartily at the vet clinic. Jekyll leaped with joy when he saw me. It was kind of embarrassing to see his shameless display of delight. I couldn't help but smile at my bliss puppy. After a few pats, I got down to business. "How much do I owe you, Rosanna?"

She smiled. "This one's on us, Colt."

I couldn't resist the urge to give her a hug. I thanked her and the staff, and Jekyll made the rounds too, giving them tail wags and licks.

When we got home, Lilly was waiting. Her whoop of joy ended when she saw us hobbling down the sidewalk. Her mom, Jamie, came over. "What on earth happened to you two?"

"A bear attacked me and Jekyll saved me. He's a true hero."

Lilly's eyes went wide, "A bear, a real bear?"

"Yes, Lillybean. She was a momma bear protecting her babies. We're okay. The momma bear was just telling us to stay away."

"Can I get you anything?" Jamie asked.

"Nah, Jek and I will be fine. Thanks though."

"Can I still watch Jekyll tomorrow?" Lilly asked.

"We'll see, sweetheart. He had some stitches so he might not feel like playing. You're welcome to come over with a carrot. I'm sure he'd love that."

She beamed with delight. "I'll see you tomorrow, Jekyll von Bicker-staff." She kneeled down and gave him a tender hug. He wagged his tail and licked her a few times. This satisfied her concern that her beloved dog was all right.

Inside our home, I looked at Jek. "I don't know about you, but I'm wasted. Let's grab a quick bite and then crash." I poured him a bowl of Blue Buffalo and made myself a PBJ sandwich. Neither of us finished our meal, which, for Jekyll, was saying something. He followed me into the bedroom. I picked him up, which caused my tender ribs to sing, and put him on the bed. He burrowed under the blankets. I joined him and brought him close. "You know you saved me on that trail. You're my hero dog. I'll pin my Silver Star on you when you get enough fur." He licked my face. In no time, we were snoring.

I learned a lot about people when we were recovering. I also learned a lot about myself. My neighbors made sure I had a hot meal with abundant leftovers every single day. Lilly practically demanded to be Jekyll's personal nurse. Her parents said she wouldn't sleep at night unless she came over before bedtime for one last check of his health. The neighborhood kids provided a steady stream of carrots, which Jek downed with delight. I began entertaining the notion of his father be-ing a rabbit. Eddie came every other day with a bag stuffed with enough food to last me a good week. Jekyll ate Eddie's fries like they were a new form of carrot. One day, Lilly put catsup on some, and from that point on, he insisted that his fries come with catsup. Even Rosanna dropped by for a house visit, giving Lilly some pointers on caring for JvB.

After a week, I felt a lot better. My calf was still tender and my ribs hurt like hell, but I didn't need pain pills. I was getting bored sitting at home. Jekyll, however, was in hog heaven. He appreciated not only my full attention, but that of the neighborhood. It seemed like every five minutes someone knocked on my door inquiring about the health of you-know-who. Questions regarding my health seemed an afterthought. I began feeling like I was sharing a home with a rock star. No one would consider knocking on my door to pay homage to El Perro de Gran, the grand dog, without having a carrot to offer. Though I didn't think it possible, judging from a carpet strewn with half-eaten carrots, even Jekyll's bottomless pit of a stomach was discovering the concept of limits.

I was touched by so many acts of kindness. I thought "real" people existed only in uniform. It pains me to say this, but I never trusted anyone not in uniform. That's a stereotypical statement, but when you're steeped in a culture demanding service, honor, and integrity, well, most civilians don't rise to the level of those in uniform. But events occurring lately couldn't be ignored. My shallow view of the world was being reformulated.

Before Jekyll, I just existed. I could no longer endure the rigors demanded by the uniform, yet I was lost in the world of the civilians. Between these diametrical opposites is the infernal region, the place where I dwelled. I could no longer talk to those in uniform. Their words would ignite the chatter of war that was always in my head. The civilian language was mostly words I didn't understand or even care to fathom. That was me, adrift in the infernal regions. Then Jekyll came into my life and that began my renaissance. A vet tending to my dog became a friend. Neighborhood kids I'd never spoken to before began knocking on my door to play with my friendly beast. That was the catalyst for their parents to strike up conversations with me. When we hiked, passersby couldn't help but ask about my odd little dog, sparking still more interactions with the mysterious people known as civilians. Through my dog, I began to learn their language. I found there were many kindnesses offered by the people in this alien world. Lilly alone showed me how to love.

Things began to look up. I was feeling alive again.

4

I HAD JUST finished breakfast when the doorbell rang. It was Scotty, in his ACU. I'd known Sergeant First Class Scott Morey since Ranger School. He halfheartedly smiled. The expression on his face meant something wasn't good. *Crap.* The faces of soldier-friends started racing through my head. One of them was dead.

"Who?" I said to Scotty in lieu of shaking his hand.

He walked in and sat on the couch. "Sit down, Colt. The news isn't good."

Damn. I sat on the other end of the couch, with eyes already brimming with tears. Jekyll jumped into my lap, concerned, and threatened Scotty with a menacing stare.

"Who, Scotty, damn it."

He grimaced at being the grim reaper's emissary. "Manny. A bad firefight in Paktika Province."

"Manny? Oh God, no!" I gasped in disbelief.

Scotty fought to keep in control. "Manny. God, how we loved him."

Jekyll licked my face, comforting me as best he could.

Emanuel "Manny" Otero, Scotty, and I had endured Ranger School together, emerging as the three amigos. I was an only child, but after Ranger School, I had two brothers—Manny and Scotty. I had just lost a brother. I fought to breathe.

"He loved Alaska. He wanted to be buried in the Fort Rich cemetery."

"When?"

"Next week. Colt, it'll be closed casket ceremony." I gasped again. Closed casket for KIAs—Killed in Action—means a mangled corpse or only parts left of a body. My friend, Johnny, had such a ceremony. The thought of him dying in my arms with a bullet drilled into his head flashed before me. I got nauseous.

Jekyll had enough. He started growling at Scotty, as if to say, *you can leave now and take the anguish you brought in with you.*

Scotty turned his attention to the snarling monstrosity of a dog. "Damn Colt. That dog looks like a mortar went off in his face."

I put my hand on Jekyll's muzzle, silently telling him to knock it off. He stopped but kept up his menacing stare at Scotty. "He may be ragged, but he's a good dog," I said in defense of my beast. "He took on a she-bear that attacked me."

Scotty gave me a *'really?'* expression and then nodded at Jekyll in a sign of respect.

"This is ripping me apart, Scott. Our friends are dying in droves. My dear God."

"It's eating me up too. I go back for another tour in six weeks. You can run through the shooting gallery only so many times before a bullet finds you."

"Get out. Now. I'm pleading for you to get out."

"I've got a wife and three kids. Short of soldiering, I don't have a lot of skills that'll pay the bills. Another four years and I can retire. I have responsibilities I have to meet."

"You're no good to them dead!" I was pissed, not at Scotty, but at war. Jekyll started barking after my outburst. "Shut the hell up, Jekyll!" I shoved him off me. He landed hard on the floor.

"At ease, Colt!" Scotty ordered in his terse sergeant voice.

I tightened my jaw and glared at him. Rage rose from deep within me. In the last few months, I'd thought this rage had withered away, but the news of Manny brought it roaring back. The rage didn't die, it never would die—it simply had been on a hiatus. "Fine, Scotty, stay in. Keep soldiering. Get killed. I'll show up to your damn funeral and say pleasant crap about you. I'll tell your kids you were, like Manny, a hell of a guy. Scotty, I'm running out of Army friends. Damn, I'd love to move to another planet that outlaws war."

Scotty didn't respond. We both knew he had to do what he had to do.

"I have to get back, Colt. The service is next Tuesday at 1000 at the Soldier's Chapel." He stood up and put on his tan beret. He let out a sigh. "I loved him. Truly, I did. He was one of the good ones."

I nodded my head in agreement. Tears started flowing again.

"I have to go." He opened the door and stepped out.

"Scotty..."

He stopped and looked back at me.

"Thanks for dropping by in person to tell me."

He nodded and walked away.

I closed the door and stared blankly into space. *Manny was gone. Manny. My incredible brother Manny.* I went to the kitchen and grabbed a bottle of Canadian Club. Jekyll walked in and stood next to me. Even a dog can figure out when something dreadful has happened. When I brought my gaze to him, he responded with a few tentative shakes of his bent tail. I ignored his gesture and walked past him to the bedroom. He followed me. I got to the door, turned around, and gave him an icy stare. "Leave me alone." I closed the door.

I sat in my room and drank, trying to numb it all away. I stared at the ceiling, remembering the times spent with Manny.

The doorbell rang repeatedly after Scotty left. The damn neighbors could get their entertainment elsewhere. At eight, the persistent ringing meant only one thing—Lilly. She was coming over for her nightly Jekyll fix. Reluctantly, I got up. There she was, on cue, with a look of concern on her face.

"Hello Mr. Colt," she said in her bubbly, adorable way. "Is Jekyll okay?"

"Yes, sweetheart, I'm sure he's fine."

"Jekyll, Lilly is here." No response. "Jekyll!"

"Where is he, Mr. Colt?"

"He's in here somewhere. Let's find him."

"Jekyll, Jekyll von Bickerstaff, where are you?"

I saw his scrawny tail sticking out from behind the couch. "There he is, Lilly, behind the couch."

"What are you doing behind the couch, Jekyll? Come on out." He wouldn't budge. Lilly's continued pleas had no effect. I pulled the couch out. Lilly got on the floor and hugged him, but Jekyll didn't respond. Her face filled with anguish. "What's wrong with him, Mr. Colt?"

"I don't think anything is wrong with him, sweetheart. Let's take him out to do his business. Maybe then he'll be better." This satisfied her. She put a carrot treat back in her pocket. "Come on, Jekyll, let's go outside." Reluctantly, he got up and slinked out. He took care of business and finally gave Lilly a few licks, which assured her that he was okay. I walked Lilly to her door because I needed to talk to Jamie and Brian Gilgren, her parents. I'd met them several weeks ago when Lilly was playing with Jekyll.

They greeted me with smiles, but when they smelled alcohol on me, their mood soured.

"Jamie and Brian, if you have a second, I need to talk to you. I...I got some bad news today. A dear friend of mine was killed in Afghanistan."

My alcohol consumption appeared less egregious with this disclosure. "Oh Colt, I'm so sorry," said Jamie.

"Me too," added Brian. "Did you know him long?"

"I did. I considered him to be my brother." A tear rolled down my cheek. Jamie gave me a hug.

Brian put his hand on my shoulder. "Is there anything we can do, Colt?"

"His funeral is this Tuesday. I'd appreciate you watching Jekyll."

"Sure. Lilly will love to spend the day with him. Tell us if you need anything else."

"Thanks, Jamie. Thank you too, Brian."

I said goodbye and walked home with Jekyll. I went to the kitchen and popped my pain and antibiotic pills. "I'm going to bed. Are you coming?" He didn't respond. I slept without him.

5

FUNERAL TUESDAY CAME. I got up early and took a long, hot shower. I dreaded today. I dreaded sitting in the chapel again. I dreaded seeing Manny's family—his parents, brothers, and sisters; I dreaded hearing what the chaplain would say; I dreaded hearing what his commander would say; and I dreaded the high possibility of me falling apart during the service.

I'd spent the last few days in a fog. My recent optimism had been stripped away, leaving me raw and exposed. I didn't give Jekyll much attention and he did his best to avoid me.

I went to my closet and got out my one and only suit. I call it the death suit because the only time I wear it is when I go to a funeral. I hate the death suit. It was eight-thirty; I needed to leave early to get a Fort Richardson visitor pass. With all that I've given to my damn country while wearing a uniform, I should be given a lifetime pass to access a post. "To hell with it," I said aloud while putting on my tie.

I dropped Jekyll off with the Gilgrens, headed to the post, and got through the post's security forces without any hassles. The guard at the gate wanted to give me directions to the chapel, but I tersely told him I knew the damn way to that building by heart.

Scotty was pacing outside when I arrived. When he saw me, he hustled over. "Colt, Manny's family wants to meet you." I looked at him and nodded. He put an arm around my shoulder and pointed the way with the other. "Christ," he whispered, "dear Christ."

I almost started to hyperventilate as we got closer to the reception room.

The room was full of men and women in uniform. Manny's parents were surrounded by their remaining children and Manny's commander. "Come on, Colt," Scotty said. "Let's get it done." He had to push me to get me moving to them.

When they saw me they walked my way. They knew me from the many "Three Amigos" photos Manny had sent to them. His mother hugged me. I lost it. I began weeping, sobbing without shame, in her arms. Scotty lost it too. He could act like the tough Sergeant First Class for only so long. He wrapped an arm around me and the other on Manny's father. After a while, one of their children came up and offered Scotty and me several tissues. I took them and thanked her. Manny's mom and dad barely understood English, so I asked their daughter to interpret for me.

"Mr. and Mrs. Otero, I loved your son. He was the brother I never had. I…" I wanted to speak forever about my friend, to tell them what a wonderful human being he was and how big of a hole his passing had left in my heart. But no matter how much I wanted to be eloquent, I was too choked up to say another word. In the end, what I said, or didn't say, didn't matter. His parents already knew how special their oldest son was.

Mr. Otero gave me a tender, fatherly look and took my hands in his. He spoke to his daughter. His wife nodded, saying "Sí, sí, sí" as he talked. "My father says he's never seen such an outpouring of love as he has today. God should bless all of us with friends like Manny had."

I smiled weakly at this humble, yet proud man as she translated his words. Manny's mom hugged me again. The commander, a lieutenant colonel, looked at his watch and motioned for us to head into the chapel. Manny's mother insisted that I come and sit with her family. Never in my life have I been so honored.

In the chapel they had a large picture of Manny on a poster board near his closed casket, which was draped with the American flag. Next to that was a Battle Cross, consisting of a helmet balanced on a rifle balanced on combat boots. To the military, the helmet signifies the fallen soldier; the inverted rifle with bayonet signals a time for prayer, a break in the action to honor their comrade in arms; and the combat boots represent the soldier's final march of his last battle.

The service began with a prelude of soft music, then the posting of the colors. The National Anthem was played and the chaplain gave his invocation. The commander stood up for the memorial tribute. He choked back the tears as he spoke. "Sergeant First Class Emanuel 'Manny' Otero was killed in action during an intense firefight in Afghanistan while leading his Rangers against enemies of the United States. He has been posthumously awarded the Bronze Star Medal, the Purple Heart and the Meritorious Service Medal. He is by any measure a hero to his family, the 75th Ranger Regiment and the nation."

The chaplain read something from the *Bible*. Then came a hymn and a few moments of silence for everyone to reflect. The chaplain gave the benediction, which was mercifully brief, ending with "and so we will remember Manny Otero, a brave Ranger who will now dwell in the house of the Lord."

Then it was time for the last roll call, the part of the ceremony that's difficult for me and most soldiers to bear. The commander stood up and began calling the names of the Rangers in Manny's platoon who were able to attend. They stood at attention when their name was called and responded "Here, sir." The commander then called "Otero." No response. He shouted the name again. "Sergeant First Class Manny Otero." Still no reply. More silence.

Then Scotty stood up. He spoke in a voice loud enough for all to hear. "Sergeant First Class Otero is no longer with us, sir. Killed in action. But he will never be forgotten."

There were more words in the ceremony, but I didn't listen much after the roll call. I just sat and hung my head. I rode the short distance to the Fort Richardson National Cemetery with Scotty and his family. Not a thing was said inside the car. A large group was making their way to the gravesite when we pulled in. I followed Scotty and other Rangers. We all filed by Manny's casket. Many of them left Ranger tabs or coins on his casket. I put a picture of me, Scotty and Manny on the casket. We were having a grand day on a Georgia beach. None of us had to shave more than once a week when the picture was taken. Now the three of us were down to two, and the two living ones were old before their time. I kissed his casket. *God, how I was going to miss Manny.*

The platoon was called to attention. "Present arms" was ordered for all in uniform to render a final salute. I could give a crap about being in uniform or not. I stood at attention and saluted my friend. The bugler started playing "Taps." We all held our salute throughout the song. A river of tears was pouring from my eyes. Another order was given and rifles were fired.

"Goodbye, Manny," I said softly. "Goodbye, my dear friend."

I went over and hugged all of Manny's family. I had to get out of there, and started running down the road. I ran as fast as I could back to my car, my chest heaving when I finally got there. No matter how fast I ran, I couldn't outrun my grief.

6

AFTER THE FUNERAL, I drove up the six-mile-long Arctic Valley Road on Fort Richardson. The road goes back to a small ski resort in the mountains and the views along this drive are breathtaking. I pulled off the road about five miles in, got out of my car, and walked to a stand of stunted spruce trees. I sat down, leaned against one of the trees, and eyed Ship Creek Valley, a broad glacier-carved landscape looking as pristine as it did a thousand years ago. I thought about Manny and wondered if he and Johnny had already met in heaven. Surely heaven must have a special place for Rangers. I felt an urge to join them.

I thought about my parents who were also in heaven. A speeding drunk driver had plowed head-on into them on White Spar Road just four miles from our home in Prescott, Arizona. I was seventeen when it happened. I joined the Army one day after graduating high school. All the physical and mental demands of being a soldier kept my grieving at bay. Some days though, I'd sit quietly and remember them. They were wonderful people. My dad had taught math and science in high school. Mom was a healer, a nurse practitioner. Together, they were quite a team.

I wonder what they'd think if they saw me now. Surely they'd be disappointed that I didn't turn out to be someone of status like a doctor or engineer. Instead, I made a living killing people until I couldn't do that anymore. I sold cars poorly, and now, here I was being a food server. I never developed any serious relationships with women since I was always deployed. I had no assets to speak of, but I did have a dog that's world-class ugly. Yeah, hell, I'm sure I'd be the apple of their eye. They were gone for nearly a decade now and my heart had yet to mend. My friends were dying in droves and every time one succumbed, my heart took a new pummeling. I began to think I was a Jonah, a bringer of bad luck, dooming everyone loving me to a premature and often tragic death. I looked with envy at an eagle soaring over the valley; it could take wing and fly away from everything.

I sighed.

Well, enough damn reflection. Time to get my sorry ass up and back to…to…what? It was just time to get the hell up. Anything beyond that was long-range planning. I headed to the car and dusted off the death suit as I went.

After getting home, I didn't feel like getting Jekyll or talking to Lilly and her parents. But, after a half-hour of moping on the couch, a wave of guilt swept through me for taking advantage of my kind neighbors. I went over to pick him up.

"Hi Mr. Colt!" Lilly said in full cheer. I marveled at how she could brighten even the darkest of days.

"Hello, sweetheart. How's Jekyll?"

"He seems sad, Mr. Colt. He only ate one carrot."

Jamie came up and smiled. She knew I must've been through hell today. "Hey. Was it a nice ceremony?"

"It was. Thank you for asking." I bit my lip to ward off the tears.

"We'd be happy to keep Jekyll longer if you need some space. He's welcome to stay the night."

"Jamie, I'd love to take you up on the offer. You really don't mind?"

"Of course we don't mind, do we, Lilly?"

She started jumping up and down doing a victory dance. "Do you mean it, Mr. Colt? Can Jekyll von Bickerstaff really stay with us tonight?"

"He sure can. Why don't you come over to my place and I'll give you some dog food to feed him this evening." I mouthed a silent *"thank you"* to Jamie. She smiled understandingly in reply.

After equipping Lilly with Blue Buffalo, I decided to head over to Scotty's. I didn't want to be alone. I stayed the night with them.

The next morning I went to see Eddie about going back to work. My way of dealing with grief is to ignore it by staying busy. I suppose it's analogous to sweeping the proverbial dirt under the rug. You can't see the dirt, but it's there. Anyway, I thought I could try a few shifts and see how it went. Eddie was both surprised and happy to see me. With Eddie being Eddie, a hello had to come with food. He told Tommy to bring me a T-bone, medium rare.

"So, are the bites and ribs healing well?"

"They are. Still some pain, but nothing I can't handle. I'm losing my mind sitting in the apartment, Eddie. I'd like to come back to work."

"I got no problem with that. When do you want to start?"

"Tomorrow would be fine."

"Okay, but don't push it. I miss having you around. If Tommy makes any more money, he might buy me out." I laughed at the comment. Tommy had been working extra shifts to cover for me. Knowing the way he charmed people, he was making some tall green.

I got home and a while later the doorbell rang. It was the Gilgrens, who were coming back from a picnic. Lilly gave me a summary about everything she and Jekyll had done along with an accounting of what he had eaten. Apparently, her two toy dolls qualified as edible goods. Jekyll looked tired. He headed over to his pad, plopped down, and was asleep within thirty seconds. I told them about me going back to work tomorrow and asked if Lilly could resume watching Jekyll. Predictably, Lilly lit up at the news. Jamie said it'd be fine, but they were going on a camping trip for the weekend. I said that Jekyll would just have to entertain himself for a few days. After a bit more small talk, they were ready to head home. Lilly gave me a big hug and thanked me for letting Jekyll stay with her. "Lillybean, I hope someday to have a little girl just like you. You're a gem."

Jamie laughed. "One week with her constantly at your side might make you want to be a monk." I smiled at her remark. After saying goodbye to them, I walked into the bedroom and saw my photo scrapbook still lying on the bed. I had gotten it out earlier to find a picture to put on the casket. I sat down and opened it. As I turned the pages, tears began flowing. The tears quickly turned to anger, and I slammed the book shut. I needed a change of venue, so I tiptoed past a sleeping Jekyll and went for a walk. The scrapbook pictures danced in my head as one mile turned into two. Maybe I should get some help to get through this, I thought. Manny was going to be a huge hurdle to get over. After a few more miles, I decided to hell with going to shrinks. The only therapy I needed was work. When I got home, Jekyll was still asleep on his pad, so I went to bed without him. The walk had done me good. I fell asleep in no time.

7

I GOT UP early the next day, excited about going back to work. I tried serving customers in my head—what to say, taking orders, bringing out trays of food, and all the nuances Tommy had taught me. I hoped for a slow day to re-hone my skills. After showering, I roused Jekyll from his slumber, and took him out to drain the dragon and lay a few land-mines. I headed to Eddie's at ten. Everyone greeted me heartily, offering help if things got sporty. I felt welcome.

Customers started streaming in and soon I was hustling. The mechanics of serving came back quickly, but my ability to act cheerful and make small talk had withered. I just didn't have it in me. My robotic people interactions were reflected in anemic tips. I wanted to greet someone saying I could give a crap about taking your order or acting pleasant because I buried my brother this week—just give me your damn order and be quick about it, and leave a nice tip when you move your sorry ass out of here.

After the lunch crowd came and went, Eddie called me over. "Colt, you've been terse with customers, and sometimes downright nasty. What's up?"

"May I talk to you in private, Eddie?"

"Sure, let's go to the office. You want a Coke?" I shook my head no. With an apprehensive expression, he motioned for me to sit. Eddie always conducted employee business in one of the restaurant booths with the office being reserved for firing someone or dispensing a serious ass chewing.

"Eddie, I have something I need to tell you." I bit my lip to ward off the tears.

"Damn, Colt, what the hell's wrong?"

I said the words fast to get them out. "We buried my friend Manny this week at the Fort Rich cemetery. He was KIA in Afghanistan."

Eddie sighed. "Did you know him long?"

"I called him brother. We went through Ranger School and did a tour together in bad country. He helped fill the holes in my heart from losing my parents and another Ranger friend who died in my arms with a bullet in his head."

"Crap. Life dealt you a few tough hands."

"I'm having a hard time being pleasant. I wanted to come back because staying busy helps take my mind off the hurting."

"Colt, I'm sympathetic to your situation, but customers don't want to be served from someone who doesn't give a crap about them. You have no business being here if you can't meet professional standards. I can give you another two weeks off, but after that I'm going to have to hire someone to take your place."

I nodded. Business is business and he wasn't running a recovery clinic. "I'll get it together, Eddie. I like working here and need this job. Keep an eye on me on the dinner shift. You'll see I can do it."

"Okay, Colt. Truly, news of any KIA saddens me. You deserve some good luck to come your way. You want me to make you a burger?" Eddie's solution to resolving any challenge or hardship always came with calories.

"No thanks. I'm not hungry."

I served the dinner crowd with my pearly whites sparkling and my tête-à-têtes dazzling. The tips grew respectable as a result and Eddie rendered several *you're doing good* smiles throughout the evening. My shift ended an eternity later. I walked to my car and slumped on the seat, mentally and physically spent. I sat for a while before driving home.

Jekyll made a beeline to the yard and whizzed like a racehorse. He hustled to the kitchen and whacked his food bowl. Another customer wanting service. He practically inhaled his chow. "Geez, Jekyll, you might want to eat a little slower and savor your meal." He ignored my comment and gave me a *"what's for dessert?"* gesture. I went to the fridge, pulled out some carrots, and watched him annihilate them. Then he wanted to play. "Jek, I've had a hard day and I'm exhausted. I'm heading to bed." He was disappointed, but too bad.

I found a bedroom strewn with chewed up pieces of my scrapbook. Every picture was shredded to bits. He must've spent all day chewing through my memories. "Jekyll, damn your ass. Get in here. I'm going to tie a knot in your tail!" He wisely elected not to come. I slammed the door shut. *Damn him.*

I brushed my teeth hard, threw the toothbrush in the sink, and went to bed muttering *"idiot dog"* several times. I decided to ask the Gilgrens if they wanted my mutt permanently. Lilly would want him for sure, but Brian and Jamie might be a tough sell. I could play dirty by making the offer to Lilly, knowing they would be faced with breaking her heart by saying no.

It's hard to fall asleep when you're pissed. I tossed and turned for over an hour before drifting off.

I woke up the next morning still in a foul mood. Jekyll hung his head when I walked into the living room. He didn't wag his tail and when I reluctantly moved my hand to pet him, he cringed like I was going to smack him. I guess we all have a past to deal with. It was time for his nature call. "Get your sorry ass outside and do your business." He slinked past me. He paced and circled, paced and circled until he found the ideal spot to squat. *Damn, I thought, one part of the yard is as good as any other part of the yard—just squat the hell down and go.*

I threw a few dog treats on the kitchen floor. "Your ass doesn't deserve these, so consider it an unwarranted kindness." He slinked by me and began eating them. I went to the bedroom to clean up the mess. Seeing the carnage got me pissed again and I lost all desire to clean. Maybe I didn't want to face the symbolism of tossing away the remains of images that once reflected my life. I showered and dressed for work, and then took Jekyll out for one last chance to relieve himself. On the drive to work, I gave more thought to giving him away. He needed more than what I had to give. Lilly would love him eternally and he'd be happy with her. Besides, I thought cynically and darkly, anyone I care about seems destined for tragedy. I clenched my jaw and stepped on the gas, hoping to put some distance between that thought and me. "Remember," I said aloud as I pulled into Eddie's, "smile your damn smile and say your damn pleasantries. Make the schmucks think they're damn royalty."

8

IT WAS A busy day at the Grille. The lunch crowd packed the place and we scrambled to keep up. At least the tips were good. The pace eased after the lunch rush, but remained brisk. I dreaded the thought of a tsunami of dinner patrons. Eddie said the big Dimond Mall sale brought the hordes our way. He likened us to scavengers feeding on the carcass after the lions had their fill. A good analogy, I thought.

The dinner crowd was huge, with every table filled and people outside waiting for a seat. Eddie was in hog heaven and even hustled a few tables on his own to get the mob in and out faster. Finally, around eight-thirty, the crowd began to thin. That's when trouble arrived. Two scruffy looking guys in their late teens, each with a bedraggled female in tow, came in with attitude. It was my misfortune to be their server. Eddie looked at me with empathy. He knew I wouldn't be having a pleasant experience.

"Good evening. My name is Colt and I'll be serving you tonight. If you follow me, I'll take you to your table."

"Yeah, whatever," the alpha punk said.

I brought them to the table farthest away from the other guests and forced myself to have a pleasant voice. "How's this?"

"This sucks. We want to sit by that window."

"Um…sure." My hesitation was due to a family with young children sitting next to the table the punk wanted. Thankfully, they had nearly finished their meal. The four ne'er do wells plopped on the seats. I gave each of them a menu. "May I get you something to drink while you decide what you want?"

"Get us all a beer. A draft beer."

"No problem, but I'll need your IDs first."

The alpha punk pulled out an ID and tossed it my way.

A cursory inspection revealed an obvious fake. "I'm sorry, but I'll need something more definitive, such as a driver's license."

"Screw you. This ID is fine. Now, get me and my friends a damn beer now."

I fought the urge to smack his pimpled face. The mother at the adjacent table responded to the nastiness by bringing her youngest to her lap.

I stood silently, waiting for him to produce a real ID. "Just get us some Cokes and be quick about it," he said tersely.

"Good choice. I'll be right back."

"Lousy retard waiter." Alpha made sure his voice could be heard by me. That was enough for the family sitting next to them. They gathered their brood and quickly left.

I came back with the sodas. Alpha took a sip and acted like I'd handed him a cyanide cocktail.

"I told you I wanted a root beer."

"You said Cokes, but no worries. I'll change your order. Do any of you want something other than Cokes?"

One of the chicks with a ring in her nose smirked. "Bring me lemonade instead."

I went back and changed the order. Eddie came over from the grill and witnessed my tightly clenched jaw.

"Colt, don't let them get to you." I glared at him and filled the damn glasses again.

I returned to the table with the drinks. Alpha had dumped out the contents of several sugar packs and drawn a heart in the mess, presumably to impress his girlfriend. A man of true class and proper upbringing.

"Took you long enough."

I gave him and ring-nose their drinks. "May I take your order now?"

"We all want burgers and fries."

"What would you like on your burgers?"

He acted like I was an insect annoying him. "Just put the normal stuff on the damn burgers and bring them out. Can't you do something as simple as that?"

"I'll have your order out ASAP."

Eddie promptly prepared their meals. His 'Order up!' came in less than five minutes. I brought the burgers and fries to their table. Alpha looked at the food with disdain. "Why isn't there cheese on my damn burger?"

"Because you didn't order a cheeseburger."

"Who the hell would serve a burger without cheese? Take the damn burgers back and bring us cheeseburgers." His pals enjoyed the show, happy to have me as their amusement for the night.

I put the dishes back on the tray, went back to the grill, and slammed it down in front of Eddie. "The little darlings want cheese on their burgers."

"Colt, you need to calm down. They'll be gone in no time."

I glared at Eddie. "I think you better put Tommy on this table."

"No can do. He's swamped right now and I can't pull him off his tables." He put the cheese on the burgers and I headed back to my scruffy buddies.

Alpha looked at the burgers with disdain. "The damn cheese should be melted on the burgers, not placed on cold. Take them back and do it right. The fries better be hot when you get back."

I left without saying a word, telling Eddie to fix the order. I stood in the bar area waiting for Eddie. The alpha punk headed for the restroom, making a joke about the "retard waiter" as he left. They all laughed as if it was the funniest thing they ever heard.

I waited a minute and decided it was time for me to use the restroom too. Alpha was finishing up at the urinal. He smiled contemptuously when seeing me. I pounced on the little bastard, throwing him into the wall with a body check so powerful that it busted the wallboard. Alpha gasped—the blow had knocked the wind out of him. I grabbed his neck and lifted the scrawny kid off the floor and up against the broken wall. His eyes were bulging, partly because of me having him in a choke hold and partly out of sheer terror.

I stared straight into his bugged-out eyes. "Well, punk, it's just you and me now. You picked a former Army Ranger to dick with, so let's see how tough you are, tough guy. Your first lesson in good manners will begin with me rearranging your smart-ass face." I cocked my arm back to rocket my fist into his nose.

"Don't do it, Colt!" Eddie screamed in a voice an octave higher than normal. He grabbed me just as my fist started forward. Though I couldn't coldcock Alpha with Eddie on me, I still had the bug-eyed punk in a firm chokehold. If he could say anything right now, he'd be crying out for his mommy. Eddie swiftly placed himself between me and my foe. I released my grip on Alpha's neck. He dropped as if he'd melted and gasped for air on the way down. From the floor, he looked at me in panic knowing I might pounce on him again. I had the urge to leave an imprint of my boot's tread on his pimpled face.

Eddie pushed me back, swiveled around, and yanked Alpha up by his vest. He went nose-to-nose with the prick and shook him to get his full attention. "Listen to me, you little twit. This can go one of two ways. You pretend nothing happened, go back to your seat, and have dinner on me. Or, you can file charges and I'll claim I saw you attacking one of my employees when I came in here. Two against one. Care to guess who the judge will believe? Come to think of it, I can walk out and leave you with Colt. What'll it be?"

"Ev-everything's c-cool," Alpha gasped in a raspy voice. "Dinner is fine."

"Good. Now go back to your friends and behave yourself. I'll have your meals out in a minute." Alpha nodded and shakily headed to the door. He flinched as our eyes met. I wanted more of him and he knew it. I was tempted to tell the tough guy to wash his punk-ass hands.

"Colt, for God's sake!" Eddie bellowed after the door closed. "I thought you were going to kill that kid."

"I'd be doing humanity a service if I did."

"Damn it, you assaulted him. You could go to jail right now if he wants to make something of this. And me, it's a slam-dunk lawsuit that would kill my business."

"I don't give a damn."

"I know, and that's why I'm firing you right now. Go to your car and I'll bring your things out to you. Colt, you leave here without a fuss and maybe we can get through this."

"Fine. Whatever you say, Eddie."

"I say leave now." He headed to the door and opened it. "I mean it, leave and don't come back."

I walked by him and left without saying another word. I sat in my car for a few minutes after Eddie brought out my things, contemplating on the notion of waiting for Alpha and his friends to come out. The adrenaline dancing through my veins demanded I hit someone. "Damn!" I smacked the steering wheel after deciding to leave Alpha and his cesspool pals behind. I started the car and pealed out of the parking lot. Another job just went poof. What now? Nearly a year out of the Army and what did I have to show for it? Nothing. Absolutely nothing. I was a dismal failure as a civilian. I drove past a bar and was tempted to go in, but I knew I'd either get into a fight or get busted later for DUI. Heading home was the only viable option.

I pulled in to my apartment's parking lot. It had been a long day that ended poorly. Well, I thought, at least my mangy mutt will be greeting me with a hearty tail wag, not that his broken tail could muster much of a wag. The home reception didn't meet even those meager hopes. Instead, the smell of feces assaulted my nose. A large pile of dog crap decorated the living room carpet along with a couple of nice-sized wet splotches. Trash from a garbage bag being ripped to shreds was scattered throughout the kitchen. Jekyll cowered in the kitchen, trying to hide amid the debris. I exploded. "What the hell have you done?" He winced at my screaming, looking even more pathetic than normal, as if that was possible. He was trembling, utterly terrified. I liked seeing the fear. It ignited the rage in me. "You miserable no good mutt! You worthless piece of crap! You ruined my place!"

He lost control of his bladder, which enraged me further. "Why don't you just die? You're no good to anyone!" I lunged at him, trying to slap his head. He ducked and I missed, striking my knuckles against the counter's edge. "Damn!" I yelled in pain. I raised my hand again. Jekyll braced himself for what was coming. From his many past abuses, he knew hell was about to visit him. His eyes met mine. The anguish in those eyes stopped me in mid-swing. I gasped. *I was a monster—I was a monster going after a defenseless animal.*

The enormity of it hit me like a lightning bolt. I staggered out of the kitchen and collapsed on the living room floor. *My God,* I thought, *what have I become?* The floodgates opened. I cried uncontrollably, sobbing from this and all the other hurts in my life. Waves of despair rolled over me. I knew the dog wasn't the worthless piece of crap in the apartment. That distinction belonged solely to me. I had the longest cry of my life. When no more tears were left, I curled up in a fetal position, in a stupor. The word "worthless" echoed inside my head.

Something touched my shoulder. I opened my reddened eyes. It was Jekyll. In a supreme act of courage, this dreadfully abused dog came over to me, the man who was going to beat him, and put his paw on me. I stared at the pathetic-looking creature. He stood his ground, bravely looking at me with eyes ablaze in empathy. He wagged his bent tail. This poor dog, with an existence of unyielding mistreatment, was tendering one the most poignant acts of love I'd ever experienced. I reached out and gently pulled him close. He licked my chin.

"Jekyll, I'm so sorry. You picked a real loser to be with, you know that, don't you?" He sat up and eyed me in a playful way. His scruffy fur, tattered ears, and scarred face made him look like a caricature of a dog. I smiled at his silly-strange expression. "Aren't we grand? You and me, here we are, broken and battered, both of us not much good to anyone. I guess all we have is each other." He gave two shakes of his tail and a soft woof in response. He nudged his muzzle under my hand. I responded by patting him softly. What a pitiable sight we'd be to anyone seeing us—each down on our luck, haunted by our pasts, with nothing but a bleak future. But, I realized I had at least one thing in my miserable life. I had my dog.

9

I SLEPT WELL into the next morning, after being so emotionally spent from the day before. I could've slept for two days straight had it not been for my furry friend fetching me back from dreamland. "What's up, Jekyll?" I said in a half stupor. "Remind me to buy you some breath mints."

"Woof! Woof!"

I forced my eyes open and was rewarded with a full-screen view of Jekyll in my face. He looked like I had him in my riflescope with a million-power magnification. His scarred mug had the effect of a defibrillator, slamming into full awareness. "Geez, Jek, you scared the crap out of me."

"Woof!"

"Do you need to go out?"

"Woof! Woof!"

"Okay, give me a second to find my pants."

He was jumping at the front door as I walked up. I let him out and he laid a huge landmine in the yard. Thank goodness for his heads-up.

After Jekyll made an unsuccessful scan of the area for Lilly or anyone else sporting a pulse to play with, he roared back into the apartment and straight to his dog bowl. He woofed again, which probably meant *would you mind rustling me up some Belgian waffles, a few eggs over easy and some thick slices of applewood-smoked bacon?*

"All I have is Blue Buffalo or cereal, what's your pleasure?"

"Woof!"

"Blue Buffalo it is."

I poured his favorite dog food into the bowl. He switched on his inhaling mechanism and vacuumed up the morsels in a heartbeat. He gave me his custom *you shortchanged me again* look, but I didn't buy his baloney. "Forget it, Jekyll. You had your vittles."

"Woof!"

"Okay, I'll give you a few carrots but that's all. I mean it." He tore into his dessert oblivious to my advisement.

I started to clean up the apartment and left the front door open to let the place air out. Between the scrapbook litter, trash in the kitchen, and Jekyll's indiscretions, it took a while to get everything squared away. I took a shower and thought about the day before and how poorly I had treated not only Jekyll, but Eddie. They deserved much better from me. I decided to apologize to Eddie, although not right away. I think he'd throw me out if I put so much as a toenail inside his place. I'd give it a couple of weeks before offering my apologies.

I also would give Jekyll another chance to change his mind regarding me. I planned on telling him all about me. If he wanted to opt out, I'd try to give him to Lilly. I know it sounds odd, but I swear he understands me. Any conversation involving food proves my point. Anyway, today I was going to sit down and tell him, but I wanted the place to be somewhere other than the apartment. Heaviness permeated the air here from all the drama last night. I thought we could go to Kincaid Park. I loved going there to sit and think and I'm sure Jek would like it too. I packed a few snacks. Jekyll was excited to get out after being cooped up while I worked.

At Kincaid, a short walk brought us to my favorite place, a mound of dirt that used to be a World War Two artillery battery. Built for coastal defense, it afforded a spectacular view of Cook Inlet, Mount Susitna and Denali—what Alaskans call Mount McKinley. After admiring the scenery and playing a little with Jek, I sat down and got serious. Jekyll plopped down in front of me, his tail wagging. He could tell my mood had changed and was attentive to that.

I cleared my throat and hesitantly began. "Jekyll, I need to tell you some things about me and after you hear what I have to say, I won't blame you for wanting to leave. If you do, I can try to get you a new home with Lilly and her parents." He listened attentively, cocking his head to the side as if to hear me better. He looked peculiar when he did the head-tilting thing. I fought the urge to laugh at his antics because this was supposed to be a serious conversation.

I cleared my throat again. "You know, I was happy all through childhood and into my teens. I liked school, was good in sports and had lots of friends, including a few girlfriends. I planned to go to Arizona State University and be a Sun Devil, playing baseball. I didn't know what I'd major in, probably whatever my dad recommended. You would've loved my parents, Jekyll, and they would've loved you. My dad was such a good man and parent. If I ever have kids and was only half as good as he, that would be more than enough.

"I could talk to him about anything. He always treated me with love and respect, but he wasn't a pushover. I had limits, and he wasn't the kind of guy who took well to having those limits be tested. But, he was always fair and quickly forgave my indiscretions. I loved to go floating down the Colorado River with him. We did float trips every year since I was seven. He was the best storyteller in the whole world. There's nothing grander than hearing your father telling a good story around a campfire at night.

"My mom, oh how I loved her. She had such a warm and tender heart and her easy smile just lit up the world. No one could be sad for long around her. She moved with such grace, like a leaf on a soft summer breeze. I loved to watch how fluidly she danced with my dad. She loved life and her compassion always provided a safe harbor for those in peril. This made her a wonderful nurse practitioner. All my friends wanted to play at our house just to be around my mom.

"All this came to an end when I was seventeen and just a couple of months away from graduation. My wonderful safe and secure world ended when that damn drunk slammed into my parents. I was supposed to go with them to the Gateway Mall, but a friend called at the last minute wanting to do some dirt biking at Alto Pit. I had just gotten a used Kawasaki KX 250. So I lied to my parents, saying I felt sick and wanted to stay home and sleep. I was sailing over the trails while they were on their way to heaven. I remember the police car waiting in front of our house when I got home.

"Jek, when your parents are instantly stripped from you as a child, especially if you're an only child, there are no words to describe the tsunami of grief slamming through your heart and soul. At seventeen, I learned that hell on Earth is being alone. Their passing created an emptiness within me that I've never been able to fill."

I gave Jek a hug before going on. "My grandparents offered to take me in, but they were ancient, in poor health, and lived out of state. The judge was going to ship my ass to them, but after some quick searching, I found an alternative that he agreed to let me do, which was to join the Army. So, I stayed with a foster family until the day after my high school graduation and then I was off to basic training.

"My age of innocence ended on the day my parents were killed. It was also the exact date when the rage within me was born. You felt that rage last night. Anyway, in the Army, I learned to fight and became skilled in the art of self-defense. I became quite proficient with guns, knives, my hands, elbows, feet, head, and a ton of improvised weapons. I was an eager student because my rage fed on it. I'd lie in bed thinking about using my skills to inflict pain on the drunk who killed my parents.

"I signed up for Ranger School to enhance my killing skills. That's where I met Scotty and Manny. We became inseparable. I got real depressed after my grandpa died. He lasted only four months after my grandma passed from a stroke. Without her, he saw no need to go on living. My other grandparents passed long before and I had no aunts and uncles. I was alone. Manny and Scotty knew how much I was hurting. They told me I'd never be alone because, in them, I had two brothers. I went from having no one to having a family. Manny and Scotty, how I loved them. They pulled my ass out of the fire and their friendship kept my rage at bay.

"I met a lot of other good people in the Army and experienced many kindnesses. I was reasonably happy. Manny and Scotty then got transferred to other posts, leaving me adrift. I tried to replace their love with the love of women, but none of them could measure up to my mom. Invariably, they'd say something that would ignite the rage in me and I'd dump them. Being deployed a lot didn't help relationships either.

"The war in Iraq began heating up. That's when some of my friends got the dreaded 'KIA' attached to their name. Each KIA was like a dart to my heart. I already had enough holes there from losing my parents. Afghanistan kicked in and more names rolled in. More gasps and more grieving.

"I decided to apply for the Army's five-week-long sniper school and was accepted into the program. I knew this demanding course would keep my anger down. I thrived there. I loved crawling through thick underbrush loaded with thorns, vines and nasty slithering things, matching my wits against experienced snipers with high-powered binoculars, who were hell-bent on finding my ass. Although it may have seemed macabre, I found it exhilarating knowing that as a sniper the slightest mistake or movement could be my last.

"I met Johnny Matthews at sniper school. He was a tall, slow-talking hombre from Dallas. We hit it off immediately and were lucky enough to get teamed up after graduation. As a sniper team, Johnny was the spotter and I was the shooter. We got so close that we would often know what the other was thinking.

"Let me tell you about Johnny's last day in Afghanistan. We were called in to help out the soldiers operating from Forward Operating Base Joyce in the Kunar Province. They needed a sniper team to raise a little hell with the insurgents who were getting rowdy. Johnny and I quickly owned the territory. He was a wizard at using his spotter scope to locate the enemy and talk me to the target. In the blink of an eye, he'd calculate a dozen variables and give me recommendations for scope adjustments. We had seven kills in just a couple of days. I would always try for a head shot, Jek. You hit someone between the eyes or in the back of the head at the brain stem and that is that. A shot to the chest works just fine too, but a head shot delivers a horrific psychological calling card that's guaranteed to scare the crap out of the dead guy's Talli-pals. I packed a .50 caliber M107 rifle with a sweet scope. When I hit someone, Jekyll, their head would explode, and I mean explode. If I hit them in the chest with that big-ass bullet, their body would fly apart in chunks and pieces.

"It's hard to describe the feeling when you're looking at someone through a telescope and you know, when you squeeze that trigger, whoever's in your crosshairs will cease to exist. You'll witness the carnage of blood, brains, and guts in hideous magnified detail through the lenses of the telescope, and the butchery you just created will forever be etched in your memory.

"After our tenth kill, we left our hide and moved back to FOB Joyce to resupply. It was quiet at the FOB, if you don't count the occasional rocket or mortar the Taliban would lob into the camp, as their fun little way of saying 'buenos dias.'

"Late in the afternoon, we heard a distant boom and then came an urgent call for assistance. The Chinook helicopter, carrying replacement troops, had been shot down on a ridge on the other side of the valley. The captain organizing a rescue team asked Johnny and me to come along and provide them with firepower. He didn't have to ask twice. We grabbed our gear and hopped into one of the MRAP all-terrain vehicles. We pushed as far as we could to the crash site in the MRAPs, but we had to go the last 1200 meters on foot.

"The Taliban were there in force. They launched a barrage of mortars and machine-gun fire our way, using the terrain to their advantage for concealment. Johnny and I scanned the area and decided to take a position on a knoll about 300 meters from the downed helicopter. We had to haul some serious ass through gunfire to get there, but it was worth the risk because it was the perfect place for providing suppressive fire to cover the others.

"I ran about fifty meters when I got nailed in my upper arm by an AK round. It stung like hell, but it didn't slow us down. We got to the knoll and Johnny patched me up. In seconds, he was scanning the field with his scope. He found a nest of them and guided me in. I got one and then another. Johnny had me swing sixty meters to the left and I got three more as fast as I could target them and shoot my weapon. It didn't take long for them to see us picking them off, so they charged our location. Johnny whipped out his M4 carbine and dropped a bunch of them with several three-round bursts from the semi-automatic weapon. One insurgent got so close that Johnny nailed him at point-blank range. I couldn't help with my long rifle, so I grabbed my Beretta and nailed another one that got close. We were able to hold off the rest of the fighters until an Apache swooped in and did some serious carnage with its thirty-millimeter chain gun.

"We rescued the helicopter crew and the four replacements. It was a miracle that none of them died. Three of us were wounded, but we were okay. Johnny and I headed to the tail-end MRAP where they were loading the last of the crash survivors. Johnny let out a sigh of relief that we made it through this firefight intact. He put his hand up to high-five me when a shot sounded. I could feel and hear the bullet whiz by my ear. Johnny fell to the ground. An insurgent had popped up from behind a rock nine meters away and drilled him. Two troops immediately shot him dead in his tracks.

"I dropped down to see where Johnny was hit and gasped. He had a hole in his forehead that was oozing blood. The back of his head, where the bullet exited, was nothing but bloody goo. There's no other way to describe it. His eyes were fixed. I felt his neck for a pulse. He had one. But a minute later he died in my arms. Now I knew how it felt to be on the other end of the barrel, how all those people felt when I dropped the guy next to them. I ran over and jumped on his killer, flailing away on his dead body. My rage was on fire. It took four troops to pry me off him. I was covered in blood, my blood, the insurgent's blood, and Johnny's blood. They had to tie me up; I was thrashing and screaming, completely out of control. They got me out on a medevac, along with Johnny in a body bag and the other wounded.

"The Army awarded Johnny and me Silver Stars and Purple Hearts for that awful day, but no medal could compensate for the horror I experienced. Nightmares began plaguing me, laced with graphic scenes of the people I'd killed. Something inside me, for lack of a better word, broke. I told the Army I'd never fire a gun again. They said I had post-traumatic stress disorder and sent my ass back to Fort Benning. I got an Honorable Discharge three months later. I needed to find a place to live, but Prescott had too many memories of my parents. I always liked Alaska, so I came up here. Scotty and his family were also here. I thought it'd be nice to have some family nearby.

"I took Johnny's death really hard. He joined the list of other good soldier-friends of mine that were KIA, either in Iraq or Afghanistan. Between Johnny, my other friends and my parents, I thought the holes in my heart were beyond repair, but then I met you and things seemed to get better. Then Manny got killed and we buried him just like John-ny. Now, I don't know if I can ever recover. Maybe I'm jinxed. Maybe I should put a sign on me saying, 'Hey, if you get to know me, you're going to die before your time, and most likely in a very bad way.' Scotty is next, I fear.

"And just to bring you up to date, my prospects for employment are in the toilet, and I'm not that far from being homeless. My past sucks, the present is crap, and the future looks dreary. My life is a disas-ter and is starting to sound like a sad country song."

I looked into Jekyll's eyes half expecting him to run for the hills. "Well, Jekyll, that's my story. What do you think of my sorry-ass ex-istence?" He didn't run off. Instead, he hopped into my lap, put both paws on my shoulders, and began licking my face. He woofed a few times and wagged his tail as if to say, *'None of your stuff scares me a bit, I'm happy to be with you. Oh, and one more thing. I could curl your toes with my stories.'* He settled himself into my lap and kept wagging his tail. I gently stroked his fuzz fur. A feeling swept over me that I haven't felt since I was a teenager. It was unconditional love. I realized how much I missed it. What irony, that a dog with a garbage-heap existence was gifted beyond measure with a heart of purest love.

10

A WEEK PASSED with me spending most of my time with Jekyll. I was still feeling raw from the emotional trauma and was glad to have mended fences with my furry friend.

The doorbell rang. I was surprised to see it was Eddie. He was carrying a bulging plastic bag. "May I come in?" he said hesitatingly.

"Sure, come on in, Eddie."

He handed me the bag. "Just a few things in case you get hungry." For Eddie, food was the universal peace offering.

"Knowing you, there's enough for an army. You want to share some of this treasure?"

"Nah, nah, it's for you and Jekyll."

"Can I get you a beer or anything?"

"Nah. Well, why not?"

"I have your favorite. Alaskan Pale Ale." His face lit up. His fondness for this brew was legendary. I went to the fridge to get a couple. "Take a seat, Eddie."

He went over to the couch. Jekyll got the scent of French fries and went over to Eddie to offer profuse thanks in the form of some rapid-fire licks. Eddie patted his head in response. I handed Eddie the beer, and could tell he was bothered by something. He was fidgeting with the bottle and coughed nervously before getting down to business.

"Colt, I have something to say man-to-man."

I looked at him puzzled. "Sure, Eddie. No matter what you say, you'll always be a person who is welcome in my home."

His eyes brimmed with tears. Something was obviously troubling him. I gave him time to find his words.

"Colt, I'm a soldier of the 82nd Airborne. I don't care if I've been out for a dozen years or a hundred years, I'm a soldier. I treated you like crap the night I fired you. Like crap. I let those punks come into my restaurant, when I should've tossed them out. I was afraid of losing business, and chose those creeps over you, a fellow soldier. You begged me to put Tommy on the table and I said 'no.' You told me how you were hurting from losing a dear friend in the war. But hey, I had a business to run, so I said 'tough.' I lost friends in Desert Storm and the hurt has never left me. Yet there I was, playing the insensitive bastard. I'm here to tell you I'm ashamed of myself, completely and utterly ashamed. You deserved a whole lot better than what I gave you. I am so, so sorry." He looked relieved that he was able to get it out before choking up again. Jekyll looked at him, then me, then him again. He started licking Eddie on his cheek. Eddie brought him in close.

"Eddie, I have no hard feelings for you or anything that happened while working at your place. You gave me a job when you knew I had zero skills, took care of me after I danced with that bear, and have been nothing but a friend to me, and a lot of other people who pass through your eatery each day. Every place has to be run with rules or there'll be anarchy. My actions put your business in jeopardy and you had every right to fire me. And if you hadn't stopped me from clocking that kid, he'd be in the hospital now, and I'd be in jail. Thank God you came in when you did. You have nothing to apologize for. In fact, I planned to apologize after giving you some time to cool down."

My response seemed to brighten him up. "Thanks, Colt, but I mean it, you deserved better. Your old job is yours if you care to have it back."

"Eddie, I appreciate your offer, but can I say no, at least for a while? I have to make some changes in my life. What those changes are, who knows? But lately, and don't laugh, damn it, I've warmed up to the notion of there being a God. I think we've been put here for a reason, whatever the hell that might be, and need to start looking for my noble purpose in life. I've already squandered too much of my life doing deeds that won't get me to heaven."

"Well, you do know how to write good crap on a résumé. I'm sure you could write something to bamboozle Saint Peter."

"Shoot, Eddie, you saw through the bull on my résumé in a nanosecond. I think they're pretty damn good at spotting crap up there."

He lifted his bottle to salute me. "Right you are, Colt, right you are." He consumed the rest of his beer in a few gulps. "I can't stay long. I've got a business to run, don't you know? By the way, word has gotten out in 'Punkville' that no one had better go to Rico's and act up. They have some maniacal server who eats punks like they were sardines. I've had nothing but happy patrons since you went nonlinear."

"Give me a call any time you need a 'punk exterminator.' I can also rent out Jekyll if you need entertainment."

"It's a deal." He turned serious. "Colt, I mean it. I'm sorry for treating you poorly, and a job will always be there if that 'noble thing' doesn't work out for you."

"Thanks, Eddie. Now damn it, quit getting stressed about anything you did to me. We're cool and always have been cool."

"Sure. Drop by anytime and bring the furry fry-eater with you. I'll make you two a mean burger."

"Maybe I will if you 'up the ante' with a T-bone."

"Wise ass." He gave me a hug which I returned with enthusiasm.

"Eddie, you're one of the good guys."

"Yeah, yeah…bye, Colt."

"Bye, Eddie, and thanks for dropping by." I closed the door with a smile. Jekyll gave me a *'Let's eat!'* woof.

11

THE NEXT MORNING Scotty called. "Hey, Colt, we're having a barbeque today over by my place and you're going to come. That's an order from Maggie. She says to hand the phone over to her if you say no."

"When your request comes with such a potent threat, how can I decline?" I long ago learned the wisdom of yielding to the woman with a Southern-accented silver tongue that could turn sharp on a dime if you crossed her. I'd rather go single-handedly against a rogue band of Taliban than face Maggie if she was on a tear.

He laughed. "Be at our house at ten-thirty. We'll go over to a little park across from the school."

"Sounds like a plan. Can I bring anything?"

"Bring a smile. We've got things covered."

"Thanks for the invite, Scott."

I took a shower and puttered around the house. By nine-forty Jekyll and I were heading to Southport, a subdivision where Scotty and his family rented a nice two-story home. When we arrived, his three kids came running. Julianna, the oldest, hugged me. "Hello, Colt! Where's your dog?"

"He's right here, sweetheart." Jekyll jumped out in full tail-wagging mode. He ran up to the kids, who all dropped to the grass to be on his level. In a microsecond, my snake charmer of a dog had made three new friends.

Maggie came out after hearing the commotion and gave me a hug. "Hey, sailor, you come here often?"

"That's *soldier* to you, ma'am. And no, I rarely frequent these parts. Pickings for single women are slim."

"I suppose you're right. This is a subdivision for families."

Sophie, the middle child, piped up. "Hey, Colt, what's his name?"

"Jekyll von Bickerstaff." I had to shout to be heard above the ruckus.

Scotty came out with a big tray covered in foil. "Jekyll von what?"

"Jekyll von Bickerstaff, an elegant name for my prince of a dog."

Maggie laughed and said it in her luscious Southern way.

"Hey Mag, did you get a good look at that ugly dog?"

"You be nice to my pooch, Scott. He's got feelings too."

Maggie turned her attention to Jekyll, who was jumping and cavorting with the kids. "Oh my, he does look a bit rough around the edges. How did you come by him?"

"He found me. Last winter at the Upper Hoffman trailhead. He was in bad shape."

"Hell, Colt, he's still in bad shape."

I smiled at his remark. "Scotty, he's one amazing dog. Just you wait. In a while, even you will be singing his praises."

He laughed, like that'd be a cold day in hell. "Hey, would you mind hauling this tray and the beer out to the park?"

"No problem."

Amy came up, doing her best to carry my dog. "Colt, can Jekyll von Bickerstaff come with us?"

Maggie gave me a silent yes. "Sure honey, he'd love to go with you." Jekyll didn't need an invite. He soon was in their car, helping Maggie as best he could to get the kids in their seats. I had to smile when I saw Maggie holding his head in both her hands loving on him. God, that dog had all the right moves with women.

I followed Scotty about a half-mile to the park. In no time, we had the grill going and the burgers sizzling. Scotty handed me a beer and took a long swig from his. "Ah, that hits the spot."

"Eddie was planning on giving me beer tasting lessons. I stress the word 'was' because he fired me the other day."

Maggie frowned, looking none too happy. "Colt, what happened?"

"Some punks came in with attitude. So, I decided to administer a few lessons in good manners using physical persuasion rather than verbal eloquence."

Scotty laughed. "I wish I could've seen Professor Colt teaching Good Manners 101."

Maggie didn't take the news as humorously as Scott. "So, what are you going to do now?"

"I don't know Maggie. I just don't know."

"Hey you two, today isn't about sitting around feeling sorry for ourselves. From now on, I decree that only positive things will be discussed." He held his bottle up.

"Your motion has been seconded." I clinked my bottle against his. Reluctantly, Maggie touched hers with ours, sealing the pact.

The day went on and we sat around eating our burgers, laughing and telling jokes. Jekyll roosted in Scotty's lap acting like they were buds from way back. In seeing how delighted Scotty was interacting with JvB, Maggie floated the idea of getting their own dog. He didn't object.

Jekyll later excused himself and headed over to the girls. After an hour of Jek romping with the kids on the playground and eating his fill of carrots and leftover burgers, he took roost on Maggie's lap and was out before you could say dessert.

I had a piece of her homemade Southern apple pie and couldn't resist a second helping. By three, we were all tuckered out and ready to go home.

"I can't thank you both enough for this day. How I envy you, Scotty, for having a wife and kids. You picked a good lady."

Maggie smiled and hugged her man. "We're blessed, for sure. When are you going to jump back into the dating game?"

"I need to get my act together before doing that. Right now, I'm not even close."

"You will be some day, Colt, and you'll make someone a wonderful husband. It's easy to imagine you with a bunch of kids."

"For now, my dog will do. We get along fine together."

Scotty laughed. "Jekyll von Bickerstaff. He's a hell of an interesting little dog."

"See, I told you. Already you're singing his praises."

Maggie picked him up and kissed his muzzle. "Bring him by anytime you want. The girls will fight over who gets to entertain him."

I hugged Scotty, Maggie, and the girls. All of them hugged my furry four-legged friend goodbye. He made sure every one of them had several licks of love before we left.

I decided to take 100th Avenue to get home. When I got to the intersection, there was a makeshift sign with balloons saying *"Huge*

Garage Sale—Voyager Circle!" On a whim, I turned left instead of right and drove into a posh subdivision called Resolution Pointe. To me, the homes looked like mansions.

I turned on Voyager Circle, got out of the car with Jek, and started walking down the street. Who knows, I might hit the jackpot and find some treasure for pennies on the dollar. Jekyll was eager to meet the hordes of people who were bargain hunting. We came to a house where they were clearing out a lot of good stuff, including a mountain of books. From the driveway, I watched the man of the house. He was trim with fair skin and red hair. I could tell he was pissed when his face turned red as he argued with some idiot who probably wanted a ninety percent discount. Finally, he pointed his finger to the street and told the guy to get the hell off his property. The scorned bargain-hunter stormed off in a huff. I admired the homeowner's directness, a trait I always appreciated.

I worked my way into his garage and nodded a hello to him. He acknowledged me with a slight smile. In the single-car portion of the three-car garage sat an impressive three-wheeled motorcycle—a Harley Davidson Trike with a 'For Sale' sign on it. The gloss-black dream bike was like a magnet, pulling me over. I touched the leather seat and ran my hand along the gas tank and up to the handlebars. One hundred percent sweet. As I ogled, the owner walked up. "Isn't she nice? She's a Tri Glide Ultra Classic with a ride smooth as silk."

I nodded and patted the beast a few times, as if it was alive. "What a beautiful ride. There's something about a Harley that can't be duplicated. I've always dreamed of owning a Trike one day. I envy you."

"Well, I can make you a good deal on it right here and now."

I laughed. "Tempting. Very tempting. Why are you selling it?"

His wife walked up with an exasperated look on her face before he could reply. "The guy over there wants your air compressor for ten bucks. You put eighty dollars on the tag. Do we have a sale?"

He gasped. From across the room he shouted "no" to the bargain hunter who frowned at the response. "Geez, Annie, why don't we load all the stuff up and head to the Salvation Army. I'd rather get a tax deduction than deal with these people."

"Pat, you agreed to participate in the street sale. Now you need to buck up and tough it out." He rolled his eyes in reply. Just then, Jekyll came with a book in his mouth. He dropped it at my feet and let out a woof, followed by some serious tail shakes.

"Annie, check out this dog." He turned to me with a quizzical expression. "Is this your dog?"

"Yes sir. His name is Jekyll von Bickerstaff, a noble dog that saved me from a she-bear while we were hiking at Eklutna."

"Jekyll what?"

"Jekyll von Bickerstaff. I kind of figured he needed a good name given his, well, his obvious challenges."

His wife kneeled down and patted Jekyll on the head. "Well, hello, Jekyll von Bickerstaff. My name is Annie. I see you're interested in purchasing a book."

"Woof!" He wagged his tail and licked her hand.

"Annie, what did he pick?"

She looked at the title and laughed. "He picked our Zen book."

"Wow, a dog with sagacious inclinations."

I smiled at his remark. "Jekyll, why don't you take the book back and find one on dog obedience." He pawed at the book and woofed again. His bent tail wagged fiercely.

"I think he really wants this book. My name is Pat Brennan and this is my wife Annie."

I shook his hand. "Pleased to meet you, sir, and you, ma'am. My name is Colt Mercer. How much is the book? And before you reply, I assure you I won't haggle about the price."

He laughed. "Well, there's a first. For you, good manners and no haggling have just earned you a hundred-percent discount."

"That's the only time today my husband has smiled. You're welcome to go pick some more on us if you like. Oh! Pat, did you make him an offer he can't refuse on the MLC?" He frowned in an animated way when she said MLC.

"What's an MLC?"

She pointed to the Harley. "This monstrosity. Pat's Midlife Crisis." He rolled his eyes.

A teenaged girl bolted into the garage. She was pretty with a face full of freckles and long flaming-red hair. "Daddy, can I take the Subaru out for a while? I'll go to the commissary for you before we see the movie."

"Who wants to go with you?"

"Jen."

"Oh no, not her." He turned to Annie, wanting concurrence.

"Pat, she's not a bad girl. Let them go."

Outnumbered, he reluctantly conceded. "Katie, raise your right hand and repeat after me." She did as requested, raising her hand. "I promise I will act responsibly, obey the speed limits, and not talk on the cell phone when driving." She quickly repeated the words.

"Get the list off the fridge."

"I love you. Momma." She pulled out her phone while bolting back into the house.

"Pray you never become the father of two girls" His expression demanded empathy.

"My only encumbrance is my Zen-loving dog. I noticed from the word 'commissary' that you must be military."

"Retired. My last duty assignment was the commander of the 3rd Mission Support Group on Elmendorf."

"An officer in the Air Force."

"Yep, a has-been colonel. From the way you act, I'd say you're in the military too."

"Yes sir, I was. An Army Ranger, Sergeant First Class. I got out last year."

"Tired of the Army life, eh?"

I looked at him and decided not to say something glib. I leaned in close to his ear for others not to hear. "Sir, I was a sniper. You can only take so much of seeing heads exploding in your scope view and having too many friends get killed. I buried my dearest friend last week after he was KIA in Afghanistan."

He silently nodded, and, to my surprise, gave me a hug, the kind of hug that said "say no more, I understand." Annie, who was tending to someone on the other side of the garage, gave us a quizzical look. I guess her husband wasn't prone to hugging strangers.

"Thank you, sir, for the book. I'm not sure I'll ever read it; but you never know, maybe my dog will insist that I do."

"Hey, I'll make you a deal. If you help me haul all the crap we have sitting outside back into the garage, you can take the Harley out for an hour. What do you think?"

"Are you serious?"

"I am. Come on, help me wheel her out. Maybe we could run over one of these civilians if we try."

I smiled and eagerly took him up on the offer. He shifted the transmission into neutral and we pushed it through the pack of people milling about.

"I assume you've ridden motorcycles before."

"Yes sir, I owned a few as a teenager."

"Where are you from, Colt?"

"Prescott, Arizona."

"Nice town."

"Yep, it was a great place to grow up. Plenty of space for motocross."

Pat gave me the low-down on how a Trike differed from a regular motorcycle. He started the beast and gave me the helmet. Jekyll interrupted his book perusing and thundered over. He leaped up on my lap and wouldn't entertain the thought of not going with me. Pat smiled an okay for Jekyll to take the ride with me. I wedged him between my legs, put on the helmet, and gingerly put the trike in gear. The big machine felt good under me. When I got to the end of the street I instinctively wanted to lean into the turn. That's where a trike and a two-wheeled motorcycle differ. You don't need to lean on a Trike, you just turn the handlebars. Plus, when you stop, you don't put your feet on the ground as you do with a two-wheel motorcycle. Other than that, riding this beast was heaven.

Jekyll and I went down Minnesota Drive and then headed east up O'malley to the mountains. The Harley's big motor purred, oblivious to the elevation gain. Jekyll acted like he was having the time of his life. He sat perfectly still except for his head, which was swiveling to and fro. He was a natural born motorcycle rider. At the top of O'malley, I headed over and took DeArmon all the way down to the Old Seward Highway. My watch showed twenty minutes remaining. Since Scotty was close and on the way back, Jek and I motored over to his place. You should've seen his eyes pop out when we rolled into his driveway. "Where the hell did you get that?" He acted like I stole it.

"I was at a garage sale and the guy let me ride it for an hour in exchange for helping him put his crap back in the garage after the sale."

"Tell him I can be by tomorrow to help him if he gives me the same offer. I can't believe you took the damn dog with you."

"I think he could drive it himself if I let him."

"That's an interesting dog you have there, Colt."

I smiled and nodded. I looked at my watch. It was time to go. "I need to get rolling, Scotty. Just wanted you to see this incredible machine."

"Wow. Thanks, Colt. Now I can tell everyone you have an ugly dog that fights bears and rides motorcycles with fearless abandon." I laughed, shook Scotty's hand, and put the Trike into gear.

In no time, I was back at Pat and Annie's house. There weren't any people around, so I carefully pulled into the garage. Pat heard the Trike and came out. He smiled at my ear-to-ear grin. "Pretty sweet, isn't she?"

"Pat, you made my day. Hell, you made my whole year and possibly the decade. I can't thank you enough." I shook his hand. "I mean it, Pat. You've been incredibly kind."

"No problem. Now, do you want to start negotiating a price?"

"Your reaction to the joker wanting the air compressor proves you're not a man who likes to haggle."

He laughed. "You got that right, but with you, I'll make an exception."

"How much are you asking for it?"

"Just make me an offer I can't refuse."

"Pat, I barely have a pot to piss in. If I had the money, I'd write you a check right here and now."

"Tell me, if you had this cycle, what would you do with it?"

I mulled the question over and a response came to me like an epiphany. "I'd head down the road and visit the families of my friends who died serving their country. I'd hope, while on the journey, to rediscover my soul, because right now, I've lost it, and fear I'll never find it again."

He looked at me with compassion. "I'm still waiting for your offer."

"Sir, I got fired the other day for physically teaching a punk some lessons in good manners. Before that, I got fired because I couldn't sell a car to someone in uniform without giving away all the profit. I'm not kidding about barely having two nickels to rub together. Riding this magnificent machine is a poor man's dream come true. For the first time in a long time, I was totally in the moment, without a single bad thought the whole trip. For me, that's saying something. I'm grateful to you."

"Okay Colt. I had to try to negotiate. We're planning to buy Katie a car for school this fall. If this bike doesn't sell, my car will be the one sitting out all winter. If that happens, I'll be farting snowflakes well into next summer."

I smiled at his remark. "I'm kind of curious, sir. Why are you selling this magnificent ride?"

He laughed heartily. "Between you and me, Annie is right. It was a midlife crisis. I looked at all those guys cruising the roads on their hogs and thought I wanted the wind in my hair too. But after getting my ride, I quickly learned there are bugs in that wind and idiots in three-ton pickups who relish toying with you. Sitting in my car's comfort co-coon listening to Bach on the JBL surround-sound system trumps bugs in my teeth any day. I bought the Trike from a guy my age, lowballing him with a ridiculous cash offer, which, to my surprise, he accepted. In retrospect, I should've seen it as a sign."

"Well, Annie should be glad you chose something with wheels rather than a nice pair of legs."

"Hey, do you mind if I use that the next time Annie gives me grief for buying the MLC?"

"Not at all, sir. Good luck selling the ride. Hell, you'll probably sell it in a heartbeat."

"You would think, but all I've been getting are half-price or less offers. I shouldn't complain, because I did the same thing with the previous owner."

I switched gears and moved on to business. "Sir, I'm ready to complete my part of the deal. Let me help you bring your stuff back into the garage."

"Thanks. By the way, Annie set a place for you at the table. She'll be serving her secret family recipe, cannelloni and garlic bread. In my opinion, it's the Eighth Wonder of the World."

"Sir, you've been over-the-top kind. We're more than square."

"Alright, I didn't want to do this, but now I'm going to have to appeal to your sense of brotherhood. I'm outnumbered in this house two-to-one and three-to-one when Rachel, our oldest, is with us from college. Just once I'd like to bring the number of men up a little. Consider it your duty, young man. I'm appealing to you in the name of all that's holy."

"You sound rather pathetic, sir," I said laughing. "Well, since you've elevated it to a humanitarian issue, how can I say no?"

"Good man. Now lend me your humanitarian hand and help me move this crap back in."

"Yes, sir. Happy to oblige."

We were bringing in the last few things when Annie yelled, "Dinner!"

"You'll remember this feast for a long while, Colt. I guarantee it."

"I'm looking forward to the meal, sir. What did you call it?"

"Cannelloni."

"Is it similar to a certain chef's canned pasta with mini meatballs that I used to eat as a child?"

"The two are often mentioned in the same sentence, son."

We went in, washed up, and headed to the dining room. Three place settings at the table verified that men would be outnumbering the women. Pat winked at me. I smiled in reply. Colt, the Great Humanitarian, I thought. Jekyll was lying on the floor snoring. For him, the day had been long. Annie brought the plates out, which were filled with the pasta and bread. It smelled heavenly. She sat down and reached for my hand and Pat's hand. "Time for grace." We all bowed our heads. "Dear God, we thank you for this food and we thank you for each other." She squeezed my hand when the simple prayer was over. I smiled and said a quiet amen. "Well Colt, dig in."

"Can you give me a tour of the plate before I begin?"

"I sure can. The cannelloni is filled with ricotta cheese, spinach, and several meats and spices. The béchamel sauce is made with butter, flour, sea salt, nutmeg and a few other ingredients. The wine is a lovely Ladoucette Pouilly-Fume Sauvignon Blanc from Loire, France."

I took a bite of the pasta and nearly swooned. Pat smiled at my reaction. "Didn't I tell you it was every bit as good as the canned pasta of your youth? We keep Annie's recipe in the Brennan family vault."

"How about a tour of the vault after dinner?" They laughed. I sipped the delicious wine and tried the garlic bread. Both were perfect accompaniments to the cannelloni. In no time, I was powering through the meal, futilely trying to pace myself in an effort to show some semblance of table manners. Annie was pleased to see my unabashed wolfing.

"Annie, this is the finest meal I've ever had. Thank you for having me."

"You're more than welcome. So, tell us about yourself."

"Not much to tell, ma'am. I grew up in Prescott and joined the Army at seventeen. I saw a bit of the world and ended up here."

"Are you still in the Army?"

"No, ma'am, I got out last year."

I prayed she wouldn't ask me why. If she did, there'd be a bogus response. "Do your parents still live in Prescott?"

I stopped chewing and swallowed hard before replying. "No,

ma'am. They were killed by a drunk driver when I was seventeen."

"Oh, Colt, I'm so sorry."

"It's okay, Annie. It was a long time ago. They were wonderful people."

"I see the connection between the Army and you going in at seventeen."

"Yes, sir. It was a memorable year in many ways." I needed to change the subject or there'd be tears. "What about the two of you?"

"Well," said Annie, "Pat and I have known each other since seventh grade. We're from Spokane, Washington. We dated in high school and then I went to college at the University of Washington in Seattle while Pat attended the Air Force Academy. We were married a month after he graduated. We travelled all over with the Air Force, Langley, Misawa, Eglin, Hickam, Lakenheath, and finally Elmendorf. Did I leave out any, Pat?"

"Yeah, you left out my tours in Prince Sultan, Balad, and Bagram."

"We may have passed each other in Balad and Bagram."

"None are places I'd want to live." I nodded my head in agreement.

"So, Colt, what are you doing now?"

"Well, Annie, in the immortal words of Mark Twain, the secret of success is making your vocation your vacation. So, right now, I'm trying to find such a vocation."

"Seriously, what are you doing with your life?

I hesitated before replying. It's never any fun to tell someone you're a complete failure. "Right now I'm unemployed and living on hope and a prayer. To be honest, I was a good soldier, but as a civilian, I'm an utter disaster. I just don't have a clue regarding what to do. That's a pathetic thing to say at twenty-seven years old."

"Colt, I work as a counselor at Dimond high school. Why don't you drop by and I'll have you take one of our career placement tests? They're great at showing possible vocations compatible with your interests."

"I'm open to anything, Annie."

"Great. I have some openings next week. Give me your number before you leave, and we can work something out."

"I will. You two are very kind. Your children are lucky to have parents like you."

"Thanks. Perhaps you can share that tidbit with Katie."

"I'd be happy to, sir. So, are you fully retired?"

"No, I'm only fifty-one and our daughter, Rachel, is in graduate school at Yale. Her tuition alone will keep me working for years to come. I work as the chief of military construction for the Corps of Engineers."

"Do you like the Corps?"

"Well, it's not as stressful as running an Air Force Support Group, so, yes, I suppose I don't mind it. Don't take this personally, but my only knock against the Corps is that it's Army run."

"No offense taken, sir. I'd make a million changes if I ran the Army. So, what's Rachel majoring in?"

Annie lit up with my question. "She recently got her Master's degree in astrophysics and is now pursuing her doctorate. She loves the academic world and hopes to be a professor one day."

"Like I told you," Pat said, "I plan on working for a long time. Who would've thought buying a telescope for her tenth birthday would cause me to work until I'm eighty." I caught on to his dry sense of humor. He was every bit as proud of his daughter as Annie.

"Maybe for a graduation gift you could buy her an Alaska mountaintop to put her telescope on."

"Don't get Annie thinking." She smirked and winked at his response.

"My dad would've liked Rachel. He was a high school science teacher and his three passions were astronomy, geology, and wilderness hiking. His impromptu stargazing sessions at Pronghorn Park, in Prescott, were like a magnet for the whole community. Some of my earliest memories were of him lifting me up to look at the heavens through a telescope and rock hounding in the Grand Canyon. He and my mom were inseparable, so wherever Dad was, there was Mom. She became an accomplished amateur astronomer and geologist in her own right."

"Was your mom a teacher too?"

"No, ma'am, she was a nurse practitioner, an exceptional one at that. But, her true calling was being a mother. My father was an incredible parent too. They were my best friends as well as my parents."

Annie saw the tears welling up in my eyes and wisely changed the subject. "So, Colt, do you think we'll win in Afghanistan?"

I was grateful for the conversation shift. I thought about her question for a while. "Pat, I believe you'll agree with this. Afghanistan is a cauldron filled with toxic, centuries-old, and unfathomably deep hatreds and rivalries that we, as outsiders, will never be able to understand. But we as a country disregard these facts in the calculus of our decision making, and arrogantly wave our standards and philosophies in front of them, telling these proud people to drop thousands of years of tradition and adopt our ways. We tossed in a boatload of dollars as a catalyst to accelerate our will. Well, though they may live in meager surroundings, they aren't going to bow to the whims of an outside "infidel" power. They're smart and tenacious, with levels of patience I marvel at. They spanked the Russians and believe we can be defeated too. But, there's one wild card that could save the day."

"What's that?" Pat asked inquisitively.

"Mineral deposits."

"Mineral deposits?"

"Yes, sir. Since the US has been in Afghanistan, we've discovered what could be huge deposits of copper, iron, gold and even lithium. If we switch to cars powered by lithium batteries, imagine the fortune that commodity alone could generate. The key is to extract these minerals and distribute the wealth to the people, like Alaska does with the Permanent Dividend Fund. Do that and you'll fundamentally alter the Afghan economy for centuries to come. But, getting that done will be an enormous task."

"I've never heard of huge mineral deposits."

"Look it up on the net, sir. There's stunning potential."

"So, what's your assessment of the immediate future?"

"I think we'll stay a little while longer, lose a lot more good men, and then leave, just like the Russians. If I was a woman, I'd be doing everything I could to leave the country, because it'll revert to the burqa once we're gone."

"Did you see much action over there? You don't have to go into details."

"Yes ma'am, I did. But it's not over for me. Last week, I lost—"

It was like the tears just opened up and I couldn't stop them. My parents, and then talk of Afghanistan. *Damn.* My sobbing brought Jekyll to life. He jumped into my lap, frantically licking my face. Annie slid her chair over and hugged me. Pat put his hand on my shoulder. "It's okay, Colt, we understand."

"Please forgive me for ruining this fine dinner. Last week we buried Manny Otero, my friend since Ranger School. He and my other friend Scotty pulled me out of the enormous pit of grief I'd fallen into after my parents died. I didn't have blood-related siblings, but I considered Manny and Scotty to be my brothers. Manny was killed in action, over there, and Scotty will be back for another deployment in less than six weeks. Right now, there's a huge hole in my heart. If something happens to Scotty, you might as well call me a dead man with a pulse."

"Oh Colt, I am so, so sorry. I can't even begin to imagine all you must have been through." She was in tears too.

Pat brought tissues from the kitchen. I wiped my tears, which helped restore some of my dignity. "Thank you, sir. I used to never cry, but lately it seems like my tears are on a hair-trigger."

"Colt, we've only met, but you'll always be welcome here if you need someone to talk to."

"Thank you, sir, but something happened recently that I need to work through on my own."

"What's that, Colt?" asked Annie.

"I can't yet articulate what I want to convey. It's still a bit murky."

"Tell us anyway. It's okay if you don't have it all laid out. What's on your mind?"

"Annie, after my parents were killed, I took a long hiatus from the concept of God. Only lately have I drifted back to believing in God, and more importantly, that I've been put here for some purpose, a noble purpose. What the noble purpose is, I haven't a clue. But, I feel compelled to find it. Does this make any sense?"

"It sure does. As a counselor, my focus is helping students find thier calling."

Pat pulled his chair over. "It makes sense to me too. You're on the right path with those thoughts. Colt, I'd like you to read the Zen book Jekyll picked out today. It's packed with wisdom, and may help you through tough times and to find your noble purpose. Promise me you'll read it, okay?"

"Yes sir, I will."

"I know one of its passages by heart. It's from Buddha: '*On life's journey faith is nourishment, virtuous deeds are a shelter, wisdom is the light by day and right mindfulness is the protection by night. If a man lives a pure life, nothing can destroy him.*'"

"That's nice, sir."

Annie jumped in. "I'll offer another passage for you to consider. It's about God, from Psalm 32, and has always brought peace to me. '*You are my hiding place. You will preserve me from trouble. You will surround me with songs of deliverance.'"*

Jekyll snatched a piece of pasta from my plate. It disappeared in one gulp. He then looked at us sheepishly, with a *'what?'* expression. After the heaviness, I couldn't help but laugh.

Annie rode on the levity. "I have something that'll take your mind off any trouble. Häagen-Daz mango sorbet."

"That sounds good."

"I'll get us some."

Pat looked at me. "So, what's been swaying you back to God?"

"There are dog-centric events causing me to reflect." I felt like an idiot for saying that.

"Dog-centric events?"

"Forgive my odd response, sir. What I'm trying to say is my thoughts of God have been aroused by my semi-furry beast. Last winter, I was cross-country skiing and found him at the Upper Hoffman trailhead. If you think he looks rough now, you should've seen him then. He had a bunch of abscesses and was frostbitten and emaciated. The vet practically demanded to put him down. For some reason, I said no. Maybe he reminded me of me. Maybe my internal hurts and anguish felt a kinship with his suffering. So, I adopted him and gave him his name. Slowly, he got better. In seeing him get better, I felt better too. Not long ago, on a hike at Eklutna, I was attacked by a she-bear and he fought her fearlessly, saving my life. He's the bravest dog I've ever seen…then, after the news of Manny, I was on the verge of losing it, but he was right there by my side, offering comfort. I'm also amazed at how many people I've met because of him, which has helped me understand civilians. I'm convinced God brought this homely little dog into my life."

Pat patted Jek on the head. "I bet he did too."

Annie yelled out from the kitchen. "I think he deserves a scoop of sorbet. He's a God dog."

I laughed. "I have, on more than one occasion, used an extra word after God to describe him."

She put a dish on the floor for Jekyll. He made short work of the treat and acted like he just tasted heaven. Tonight, Jekyll and I discovered two new loves—cannelloni and Häagen-Dazs mango sorbet.

Following dessert, the evening passed with easy, enjoyable conversation. Jekyll sat on Annie's lap and then shifted over to Pat. Katie drifted in around nine and, after putting a bag of groceries on the kitchen counter, came in and sat next to her mom on the couch. She gave me a casual look and winced when her eyes met Jekyll.

"So, my dear, did you and Jen have fun?"

"We did Momma, and, Papa, there are no new dents or dings on the car."

"Thank God for that," he said with an exaggerated voice expressing relief. He was stroking Jekyll as he spoke to his daughter. If Jek had been a cat, he'd been purring.

Katie looked at me. "What happened to your dog?"

"He took on a she-bear who was attempting to have me for dinner. You're looking at a hero dog."

"What's his name?"

"Jekyll von Bickerstaff."

"Jekyll von Bickerstaff?" He took her saying his name as an invite and rocketed off Pat's lap and into hers, giving her some impressive licks.

"Whoa! Hey boy, I'm Katie." She wrapped her arms around him and gave him a hug. Soon, she was cooing at him and he was wagging his tail like they were long-lost friends. Once more, my furry friend's charm overcame his homeliness. I felt like bowing to his greatness. "Colt, do you mind if I take Jekyll von Bickerstaff over to my friend Jen's house for a little while?"

I looked at Annie and nodded an okay.

"Sure, Katie, but be back in thirty minutes," said Annie. "We've kept Colt here far too long already."

She headed out the door with Jekyll in her arms.

"Don't be surprised if she comes back asking if she can adopt Sir Bickerstaff," Pat said.

"Hey, if you apply Rachel's telescope analogy to Katie, maybe you'll be working to put an aspiring veterinarian through school."

Pat laughed. "I guess I'll be the first centenarian ever to work at the Corps."

"Sir, your daughter is a beautiful young lady. I can see where the red hair comes from."

"She inherited all her daddy's Irish-ness," said Annie, "right down to the freckles."

"Well, thank God she got your even temper, dearest."

After a while, Katie came back with Jekyll looking like he'd enjoyed his sabbatical with her.

"Colt, I was wondering. Can Jekyll von Bickerstaff stay the night with me?"

Before I responded, Annie jumped in. "Let's give them a break and maybe ask him and Jekyll to visit us some other day."

Katie frowned but didn't protest. She had request number two locked and loaded in the firing chamber. "Well, I guess you're right. Do you mind me spending the night at Jen's? Her parents say it'll be okay."

"Alright," said Annie, "but be back home by ten tomorrow."

"Thanks, Mom!" With that, she ran to her room, did some quick packing, and was gone in a flash.

I used Katie's leaving as my cue to head out as well. "Pat and Annie, I think it's time for Jek and me to say goodbye too. Thanks for having us over tonight. I had a great time."

"We loved having you."

"I second that," Annie said with a smile. "Hey, before you go, give me your phone number."

"Pat and Annie, I have a favor to ask."

"Sure. What can we do for you?"

"Let's say goodbye and leave it at that."

Pat looked perplexed as did Annie. "Why would you say something like that?"

"Because, sir, it's easy. The last thing you two need is an anchor like me. I've got issues to work out and I won't burden you or others with my problems. Nothing is more pathetic than someone trying to solicit friendship through pity. I thank you for this wonderful day and evening. I'll never forget the fabulous meal and trike ride. So, let's leave it at that and move on with our lives."

Annie turned to Pat, no doubt wanting her man to respond in a military way. His response lacked terseness.

"Colt, I learned this while at the Academy. '*No man is an island entire of itself; every man is a piece of the continent, a part of the main; if a clod be washed away by the sea, Europe is the less, as well as if a promontory were, as well as a manor of thy friends or of thine own were; any man's death diminishes me, because I am involved in mankind. And therefore never send to know for whom the bell tolls; it tolls for thee.*'"

"Yes sir, I know the poem. It's by John Donne, and it doesn't end with the words you recited. A few lines later are these words: '*No man hath affliction enough that is not matured and ripened by it, and made fit for God by that affliction.'"*

"You, sir, are a philosopher."

"No, sir, I'm more of a pragmatist adrift in a sea of jaded negativity."

Annie looked at me with a combination of empathy and sternness. "Pardon me if I interrupt you two philosophers, but let me add my two cent's worth. Colt, you're being a bit arrogant saying who can be your friend and who cannot. If my husband and I want to be your friend, then it's our responsibility to tell you if you're dragging us down. So, you have a couple of friends here, Bucko. Suck it up and get over it."

Pat laughed. "You've just witnessed my woman putting her foot down. I agree with her."

I smiled weakly. I was outnumbered. "Does your friendship include my dog?"

"You bet," said Annie. "Should I get him a doggie bag of pasta to seal the deal?"

"If you do that, he might decide to change owners."

I thanked them again for the lovely evening. They walked us to my car and gave me a hug. "See, Pat," said Annie, "this is why we need to have more garage sales. You can meet some nice people this way."

"You're right, dear. We should have one every weekend." They looked at each other and shook their heads "no" in unison. I laughed and said a final goodbye. Jekyll gave them one of his best yodel-bark farewells.

12

IN THE FOLLOWING days I gave a lot of thought to the "noble purpose" notion while searching for jobs on the net. My thoughts kept drifting to the Harley. I remembered how powerful the feeling was when Pat asked me what I'd do if I had the Trike: *"I'd head down the road and visit the families of my friends who died serving their country. I'd hope, while on the journey, to rediscover my soul, because right now, I've lost it, and fear I'll never find it again."*

I imagined Jek and me going on a quest to discover my noble purpose, and mentally ran through the hometowns my KIA friends— Wenatchee, Washington; Tioga, North Dakota; Eureka and San Luis Obispo, California; Santa Fe, Dallas, Roanoke, and Orlando. They sounded like interesting places to see, but I'd dread saying hello to the families of my friends. Maybe that wouldn't be such a good thing in terms of my emotional health.

On the net, I viewed my bank account: $4,257.56. That was my entire net worth. Well, maybe a bit more if you counted my ancient Honda. A new set of studded snow tires now cost more than what the car was worth. Fortunately, it still ran okay after 161,000 miles. Thank God for duct tape.

I wondered what my parents would think of the paltry assets I'd amassed in my twenty-seven years. Their modest inheritance went to my grandparents; they thought they'd need the money to care for me. Grams and Gramps wanted to give me some of the money, but I insisted they buy a grand headstone for my mom and dad instead. After that, the Army gave me all I needed to get by.

I didn't mind living a life of simplicity. Possessions, in my humble opinion, require care and, if you're not careful, they'll start possessing you. I was always happier being out in the country, hiking or exploring the Chugach Mountains. Being outdoors costs nothing and is infinitely more satisfying than staying home tending to possessions. Jekyll prefers being out in the country too. I think we both love the peace and solace offered by nature.

My reverie ended with the phone ringing. "Hello, this is Colt."

"This is Annie Brennan. Remember me?"

"Of course I remember you, Annie. We met at a bar last week, right?"

"Har, har. Hey, I have an open slot today at three. Can you come to the school and take the assessment?"

"Um…sure. How long will it take to complete?"

"Not more than an hour or so at most. Do you know how to get here?"

"I think so. Just take Dimond Boulevard to Arlene, right?"

"Right. Come into the main entrance and ask for me. See you at three, okay?"

"I'll be there."

Jekyll and I spent the time before I had to go by taking a walk. When we got back, Lilly and Jamie offered to watch him while I was gone. He and Lilly were in full play when I headed to my car.

I pulled into the Dimond parking lot. At the front desk, a student-receptionist greeted me with a smile and seemed to know I'd be showing up. Behind her were three attractive young ladies who definitely weren't students—they looked to be in their early twenties. If they were teachers, they sure didn't look like any teacher I'd ever had. Annie walked in sporting a big smile. She gave me a warm hug.

"Wow, this is one nice high school. I don't mean to be a know-it-all, but I think you spelled Dimond wrong. Aren't you missing an 'a'?"

"Our school was named for Anthony Joseph Dimond, an Alaskan pioneer legislator and federal judge who promoted statehood for the young territory."

"Well, maybe somewhere in his family lineage there was a poor speller."

She smiled. "Let's get on to business." I nodded at the three ladies, thanked the receptionist, and followed Annie to a nicely appointed room equipped with a round table with six chairs. She handed me a packet. "Colt, this assessment focuses on left brain/right brain theory, and tries to identify your unique skills, traits and preferences. The left brain predominately controls linear reasoning, mathematical concepts and language functions, while the right brain processes audio/visual stimuli, spatial manipulations, and the like. So, engineers are typically left-brain oriented, while writers and artists are mostly right-brainers."

"From what you've seen of me, where would you put me?"

"That's a good question. You puzzle me. Some people are equally adept at left and right brain functions. I think you might be one of those."

"That's the ideal thing to have, right?"

"Yes and no. These people can be good at anything they do, but because so many things interest them, they can bounce from one thing to another. Those who focus are often brilliant and successful, and those who don't can be forever dissatisfied and eternally poor. Their gift of having an incredibly agile mind becomes their weakness."

"Uh, oh. That sounds like me alright."

She laughed. "Just take the assessment and we'll see. It'll be fun to see how you do." She left the room and I got down to business. I finished quickly and waited for her to come back. Memories of my days in high school came flooding back. That time seemed an eternity ago.

Annie popped her head in to see how I was doing. "I'm all done. It wasn't difficult to get through."

"Great!" She came in and took a seat next to me. "I'll have the results by Saturday and I'll give them to you when you come over for dinner."

"Dinner?"

"What do you want me to make for you?"

"If you're really asking, I do have a request. Be it ever so humble, I loved my mom's meatloaf and mashed potatoes. What do you think?"

"Well, my boy, are you ever in luck. My meatloaf recipe will bring tears of joy to you at first bite. And, Pat, with his Irish roots, can do wonders with a humble potato. Hey, bring Jekyll von Bickerstaff too. You two are a dynamic duo. He's the yin to your yang."

"You don't mind if I bring him?"

"Of course not. Pat and I like your dog with a face only a mother could love. Katie will be thrilled to know Jekyll is coming over too. Be at our place around five, okay?"

"Sure. Thanks, Annie, for everything."

"Yeah, yeah. Now, on to more business. Remember those three young ladies you saw at the front desk. Well, they practically accosted me wanting to know everything about you."

"Who are those ladies?" I said with a smile. "They look like they're barely out of high school."

"Well sir, they're in college and are student teaching here, which is a requirement for getting a teaching certificate. They're most eager to meet you."

"Annie, as tempting as your offer is, I'll respectfully pass."

"Colt, I'm not trying to be a matchmaker here, but I've worked with these ladies for the last semester and I can tell you that they're all very nice. You couldn't do better than dating one of them."

"I'm not sure how to say this in a way that won't sound crude or cynical…"

"Talk to me, Colt. What's on your mind?"

I hedged some more. "Annie, I want to make a general statement that's independent of those ladies."

"Okay," she said, looking at me earnestly.

I paused again to compose my thoughts. "If all I wanted was sex, well, it's easy to get laid. But, that's not what I want. I want the total package, the kind of relationship my parents had, which was based on mutual respect and genuine love. But, I'm not a whole person. I've seen too much. You can't do the things I've done, and lose as many friends as I have and still be whole. It's like the light within me has died and I fear it'll never shine again. I have nothing left to give. Those young ladies are untainted and tender. They deserve much better than someone like me."

She put her hand on mine. "I want you to listen to me, really listen to me. I, too, lost my mother when I was young. I was only twelve when she died of ovarian cancer. She went quickly after being diagnosed. We were extremely close and I took her passing really, really hard. I know about the light you talk about. I lost that light when Mom died."

Her words brought back with alarming suddenness the awful feeling of losing my parents. I fought back tears. "Annie, I'm so sorry. How did you get through the ordeal?"

"I nearly didn't. I rebelled. I tried drugs. But something remarkable happened. I met Pat. Then I met his family. His mother became my new mother. My dad remarried but I'd already bonded with Pat's mom. To this day, I love her immensely. With her love and gentle guidance, I became whole again. I found a new light within me. It's a different kind of light, but it shines just as brightly as the one before. You too will find a new light. You will see."

I was overwhelmed by what she'd shared. "Annie, I've never heard more eloquent words than what you just said to me. Thank you so much for sharing your life with me. We both know dark nights of the soul…" My words trailed off. She knew what I was trying to say.

"Never lose hope, Colt. Never, never, never lose hope. I'm living proof that people can survive and thrive despite having to endure an enormous loss." She stood up. "Alright, enough of this. When you're ready to date one of those young ladies, let me know."

I nodded and gave her a hug. "Thanks for everything. I mean it."

"I know you do. You're one special guy, Colt Mercer. You need to find that light in you. I guarantee it will be there when you're ready to find it."

"Charge!" I said lightheartedly.

She laughed. "Okay, Bucko, let me get on with my day. I'll walk you out to your car."

The rest of the week went by quickly. Saturday came, and when we pulled up to the Brennan's home, Jekyll was beside himself. He leaped out of the car and made a beeline to the front door. I was beginning to think his bent tail might undergo complete structural failure given the way he was red-lining it back and forth.

Annie beamed at seeing my dog's shameless display of enthusiasm. "Welcome to our home again, Jekyll von Bickerstaff. I'm so pleased to have you as our guest." She reached down and scooped him up. He showered her with his best glad-to-see-you licks.

When Pat came out to say hello, Jekyll leaped from Annie over to him. "Whoa!" He grabbed Jekyll in mid-air. "I guess you missed me too."

"Please forgive my overzealous dog. I'm sure he remembers your cannelloni and béchamel sauce and is here for more. Heck, when I think of that meal, I have to fight the temptation to jump into your arms."

"Thank you for the compliment on my cooking. I hope your expectations will be met with this evening's meal."

Pat gave me a hug like I was a long-lost friend. "You want an Alaskan Pale ale?"

"Yes, sir. That'd be nice."

Annie took my hand after Pat handed me a beer. "Colt, c'mon, I have your assessment laid out over here."

We sat at the table and Jekyll jumped on my lap. He was acting like a hopeful parent at a parent-teacher conference. "So, do my natural proclivities dictate a career in rocket science?"

"Interesting you might ask that," Annie began. "You are a fascinating subject. Before I answer, let me ask you a question. Did you ever get an IQ test in school? If you did, I bet it was high, something over 130, right?"

"Yes, ma'am, it was 170-something, as I recall. I remember my dad being impressed since he was a teacher."

"Well, your high score doesn't surprise me. It shows up throughout your assessment."

She thoroughly went over the findings. Pat came over and listened as his wife talked to me in her professional mode. He'd been outside for a while. I heard the garage door open and close when he was away.

"So, can you bottom-line-it for me, Annie? In other words, what do you think I'd be good at?"

"Colt, do you remember when we talked about some people having equal left/right brain dominance? Well, you're one of those people. You can do well at just about anything you set your mind to, and you certainly have the intellectual horsepower to take you anywhere."

"Uh, oh. That's not good, as I recall you saying."

"It's not good or bad. Your challenge will be having the discipline it will take to focus on one thing and not act like a butterfly flitting from one thing to another."

I nodded and sighed. "I was hoping you'd give me a clearer direction for my noble purpose."

Pat came in from the family room and tossed a big paperback book on the table. "This will help you on your noble quest." It was a road atlas of America.

"Sorry, I don't get it."

He was beaming. "Since you were last here, I wanted to see if you were the real deal and not some slick con man trying to play us."

"Play you? I wanted to say goodbye after we met." Now I was really puzzled.

"Hang on a minute and this will all become clear. I called my friend who is the Security Forces commander at Elmendorf, and asked him to run a background check on you. Turns out you're the real deal. Silver Star, Purple Heart, and a bunch of other medals."

"Security Forces background check? Talking to Security Forces about me isn't making anything clear," I said in a voice conveying my lack of amusement. I got up from the chair. What the hell was going on? I needed to leave before saying something ugly.

Annie stood up sporting a huge ear-to-ear grin. She could see the steam rising in me and gave me a reassuring hug. Pat was looking at me with the same goofy grin. Even Jekyll looked perplexed. "Come outside for a minute. We have something to show you." She took my hand and gently urged me toward the front door.

"Come on, Colt, humor us," Pat said in a playful tone.

I decided not to protest since I was going to leave anyway. Outside in the driveway sat the Harley. It had a big red bow on it. I looked at them. "Did you sell it?"

"In a manner of speaking we did," Pat said. He reached into his pocket, pulled out a set of keys, and tossed them to me. "These will go nicely with the road atlas."

"What do you mean, Pat?"

"He means the Harley is yours," said Annie. "We're giving it to you."

I looked at them, stunned. "You're giving me the Harley? Did I hear you right?"

"You heard her loud and clear, son. You and von Bickerstaff have worked your way into our hearts. You deserve this more than anyone. Annie and I have been blessed financially and we want to share some of our blessings with you. Please accept this with our profound thanks for all you've done for our country. It's time for you to go on your quest. Go find your noble purpose."

I was overwhelmed and couldn't utter a single word. But they could read my tears just fine. Annie wrapped her arms around me and hugged me tenderly. It was the kind of hug that only a mother knows how to give. "We love you. If we had a son, we'd want one exactly like you. If I could speak for your mother, I'm sure she'd say it's time to leave the sadness behind and open yourself to happiness. Each night, our prayers now include you."

I nodded my head at what she said and hugged them both for a long time. *What incredibly wonderful people you are,* I said to myself over and over. I loved both of them, but not because of the gift. I loved them because they were honest, genuine people. I saw in them a re-flection of my parents. It felt like I was hugging my own parents. The feeling was sublime.

After we got back home, I was giddy with excitement and stayed up late with a thousand ideas dancing in my head. Jekyll and I were going on a quest, a quest to find our noble purpose.

The next day I went to the Brennans, got on my new ride, and rolled in to Scotty's place. His eyes about popped out when I told him it was mine. "Tell me this again. They *gave* it to you?"

"They did, along with an atlas of road maps for America."

He couldn't fathom how someone would give away the finest Harley he'd ever laid eyes on. "You need to take me, Maggie and the kids over to meet them. We could use a nice big house."

"Scotty, I'm sure they're way past their limit for generosity."

"You know, Colt, if you're going to take that dog with you everywhere you go, you need to get some sort of harness made so he won't take a dive."

"Oh, so now you're concerned about my dog?"

He patted Jekyll on his head and accepted a few Jek-licks in response. "I know a parachute rigger who lives right around the block. He might be able to rig something up for Jekyll to ride more safely." He pulled out his phone, made the call, and ended the conversation with "cool." He smiled at me. "He'll be right over."

"Thanks, Scotty."

A muscular black man pulled into the driveway. Scotty went over and gave him a hug. "Colt, this is my good friend, Jamal. He's a Ranger and a damn fine parachute rigger."

I shook his hand. "Rangers lead the way."

"Pleased to meet you. So, what can I do for you?"

Scotty jumped in. "Colt, get on the Harley with Jekyll so he can see."

"Man, this is one sweet ride you have here," said Jamal. "Looks like your little friend already fell off a few times."

"Thanks, Jamal. This is Jekyll von Bickerstaff. He got this way from saving me from a big-ass grizzly."

"Cool," said Jamal. He patted Jekyll on the head. "Can you get me a measuring tape?" he asked Scotty.

"Sure, I'll be back in a sec."

"So tell me, how does she ride?"

"Like a dream, Jamal. She's ultimate cool."

"How long have you had her?"

"I got her yesterday. Still learning her idiosyncrasies."

He laughed. "Yeah, man, I'm still trying to figure those out with my wife."

Scotty handed the measuring tape to Jamal and he took enough measurements to impress a fine tailor. Jekyll give him a lick every time he came near with the tape. "Tell you what, man, give me a couple of days to rig something up that'll do the trick."

"Thanks, Jamal. I appreciate you taking time for the fur ball and me."

"No problem. We Rangers stick together."

"We sure as hell do," said Scotty as he returned with some beers. The three of us talked for a while. Jamal and Scotty took turns sitting on the Trike, but they couldn't do it without you-know-who having to sit on their lap. I think Jekyll was protecting our newly acquired interests.

The following day the Brennans and I went to the Alaska Department of Motor Vehicles to register the Trike in my name. While there, I applied for a special license plate Alaska offers for veterans with Purple Hearts. I figured if I had one and got pulled over, maybe the cop would cut me a little slack and not write me a ticket.

A couple days later I went to Scotty's for dinner. Afterward, Jamal came by with an impressive army-green harness made of ballistic nylon and parachute straps. "Come on man, let's try it out," he said, beaming with pride at what he'd constructed. I put it on and then Jamal put Jekyll inside of it. He adjusted the straps that went through some nice metal buckles that looked like they were salvaged from an armored personnel carrier. He padded the straps where they fit on my shoulders for comfort. Jekyll was tentative at first in the strange contraption that looked like a kangaroo's pouch. But after a minute, he lit up with satisfaction. Jamal had made the pouch with netting in order to let air circulate; otherwise Jekyll would roast in it.

"Thanks, Jamal, this is perfect." Jekyll looked comfortable and pleased, and seconded my thanks with a few big woofs.

"It's my pleasure. Put some miles on it and let me know if we need to fine-tune the mother."

Maggie came out holding a bag and laughed at the sight of me wearing the harness stuffed with my happy dog. "Now you know how a pregnant woman feels. Colt, I have something else for you," she said with a huge smile, scarcely able to contain her excitement. She reached into the bag and handed me a box. "This is for Jekyll von Bickerstaff."

I opened the box and started laughing. "What the hell is this?"

"It's a helmet for Jekyll. I also got him some eyewear protection called *Doggles*. Try them on him."

I pulled out the orange-colored helmet. We put the helmet on Jekyll, took it off, made some adjustments, and tried it on again. It fit perfectly. Jekyll didn't seem to mind and loved the attention. I then put the Doggles on him and had them fitting nicely in a couple of minutes. The well-designed doggie-goggles had orange-colored lenses and racing flames on the sides. I stood back, looked Jekyll over, and reached my limit for holding it in. I collapsed to the ground in laughter, as did my friends. We were howling—it was just so ridiculous. Jekyll loved his new look. He came to each of us as we were laughing hysterically and gave us all a bunch of licks. He looked like a poor imitation of Snoopy going after the Red Baron. I never laughed so hard or so long in my life. After regaining my composure, I thanked everyone and decided to take a quick drive down to Beluga Point to try out all the new equipment. There was a must-stop to make before taking the ride to Beluga. I borrowed Scotty's cell and called the Brennans. "There's something you have to see. I'll be over in two minutes."

As I rounded the corner on their street, they were outside waiting for me. When they saw Jekyll in the harness with his helmet and Doggles they were rolling. Pat was laughing so hard that tears streamed down his face. After regaining use of her motor functions, Annie ran into the house for her camera. She began taking pictures of me and my Hells Angels wannabe, but was laughing so hard that the pictures would probably be blurred. Jekyll loved the attention and yodeled away while Annie took pictures. I was thinking about getting him a tattoo saying *Born to raise hell with carrots*.

We left Pat and Annie and headed down the Seward Highway to Beluga Point. I could tell Jekyll liked his Doggles, which kept the wind out of his eyes, allowing him to get a clear view of the surroundings. He was swiveling his head back and forth taking in all the sights, letting out a few choice hello yodels to kids in cars we were passing. You should've seen the expression on their faces. I'm sure they'll never forget the day they saw ol' Roadin' Hood and me on our Trike cruising down the highway.

13

A COUPLE OF days had passed since we had cruised to Beluga Point and I was itching to head out again. We needed to go on an extended local trip on the Harley to work out any kinks before we embarked on the Grand Adventure. I was thinking the Kenai Peninsula south of Anchorage would be a great place for camping and fishing, and the mountain passes and many curving roads would test the viability of our ambitions. I spent the morning with Jekyll perched on my lap, gazing at the computer screen, trying to figure out where on the Kenai we'd go.

"How about this, Jek? We head to the Russian River, catch a salmon for dinner, and spend the night. Then motor over to the town of Kenai and go up the coast to the Captain Cook campground. Hang there for a day, then head south and knock around in Homer. What do you think?"

"Woof!"

"Glad you agree. Okay, let's eat, pack a few things, and then drive over to get the Trike." He ran to the kitchen, whacked his food bowl, and bellowed a high-spirited yodel. "Yeah, I kind of figured your food bowl would be the first thing you'd want me to pack." His tail was wagging fiercely. "Just remember, we need to pack lightly, so I'm taking a collapsible food bowl instead. Don't worry, it holds your normal ration of food."

"Woof!"

While I loaded our gear, Jek played with Lillybean. It was almost two before we were ready to go. As I was saying goodbye to Brian and Jamie, Lilly ran to me. "Goodbye, Mr. Colt. I hope you and Jekyll von Bickerstaff have a good time." She always found a way to melt my heart. I gave her a hug.

Jamie smiled at how tenderly I treated their little girl. "You'll make a wonderful father one day." I smiled. It felt good to hear a mother say those words to me. A part of me would love to have kids. I think I'd be a good father.

The three of them walked Jek and me to my car. Jekyll was torn between wanting to go and staying with Lilly. He reluctantly jumped into the car and poked his head out after I rolled down the window. Lilly reached into her pocket and pulled out a carrot. "Goodbye Jekyll von Bickerstaff. Have fun with Mr. Colt." He accepted her offering and yodeled a goodbye as I pulled out of the driveway. Pieces of carrot flew out of his mouth when he tried to hit a high note. It was hilarious.

Although sad to say goodbye to the Gilgrens, we looked forward to our first long trip together. When I took the 100th Avenue exit off Minnesota Drive, Jekyll lit up. He knew the way to Pat and Annie's house and stood up, putting his paws on the dashboard. He didn't want to miss a thing. His tail wagged a mile-a-minute. I smiled at how much he loved life. His attitude was infectious.

After a mile or so we reached the Resolution Pointe entrance. There, the road forks around an elongated island loaded with flowers. As we were coming in, a dilapidated truck shot out from the lane leaving the subdivision. I could have sworn I saw a shock of red hair peaking above the dashboard on the passenger side and the driver appeared to be shouting and pushing the passenger down. Our passing the truck happened so swiftly that I couldn't discern what was going on, but Jekyll unleashed an enormous bark that caused me to jump. It sounded eerie and wasn't his typical bark. He jumped around to face backward and continued barking at the truck. He was seriously agitated.

"What is it, Jek?" As I said the words, it hit me—that shock of red hair—I'd seen it before. Coming out of this subdivision, it had to be Katie! I jammed on my breaks, did an abrupt U-turn, and stomped on the gas. Jekyll fell into the seat, but quickly stood up with his front paws on the dashboard, howling like a banshee. The truck was speeding down the road about a half mile ahead. I had to catch them before he got on the four-lane Minnesota Avenue. There was no way my four-banger would be able to keep up on a big open road, and I didn't have a cell phone to call the cops.

Through the truck's rear window, I saw him struggling to hold down the passenger, causing him to drive erratically. My mind raced. How to stop him? I decided to attempt a Tactical Vehicle Intervention, which I had learned in the Army. I was now twenty feet behind him and closing. Since his focus was on the captive passenger, he hadn't noticed me. The front of my vehicle became even with his rear tire. *Perfect!* I swung my car's steering wheel to the right and rammed him. I nailed him good—his rear tires lost traction and spun out as hoped. *Bang!* The rear tire on his passenger's side snapped off from the force of hitting the curb. The impact had sent me reeling into the other lane. I jammed on the brakes, jumped out, and began sprinting to the truck. Jekyll barreled past me, shrieking an eerie-sounding attack yodel, the same yodel he had used going after the she-bear at Eklutna.

The guy jumped out of his truck, looking dazed. He quickly recovered when he saw me sprinting his way, and pulled a pistol from his windbreaker. His passenger was screaming—it *was* Katie! He leveled the gun at me at near point-blank range. I knew I was dead, but maybe my momentum would bowl him over, giving Katie a few precious seconds to run away. He grinned wickedly at me before pulling the trigger. Jekyll leaped on him with all his might. The gun discharged and the bullet whizzed by my head, coming so close that it set my ear ringing. I was on him before he fired again. I grabbed the barrel of the pistol with my right hand, and the butt of the gun with the other. Then, with both hands acting in unison, I flipped the pistol around to where it was facing him. I pulled his trigger finger twice. *Boom! Boom!* He gasped. I swung my forearm up and nailed him in the throat with my elbow. It was classic Krav Maga self-defense fighting, developed by the Israelis as an efficient way to brutally end your opponent's life.

The guy dropped to the ground like a rock. Frothing blood poured out of his mouth, a sure sign his larynx was fractured, causing him to asphyxiate. Jekyll was baring his teeth, ready to pounce if he stirred. I tore the pistol from his hand and threw it away. Katie was screaming and frantically banging on the passenger door, trying to escape. Her abductor must've rigged the door not to open. "Jek, let's help Katie." He ran to the truck and jumped in to comfort her. She was hysterical and mistook him for another attacker and began kicking at him. Her foot connected with his muzzle, sending him reeling to the truck's floor. He yelped in pain from a bloody upper lip.

"Katie, it's me, Colt! You're okay now. Give me your hand." She frantically began kicking at me, like she did Jekyll. I grabbed a leg, pulled her toward me, and pinned her down on the bench seat. She was screaming and thrashing about. "Katie, look at me! It's Colt. You're safe!" Her eyes fixed on mine. They conveyed but one thing—pure terror. Then, suddenly, she recognized me. My words had cut through her panic. She stopped screaming. "Sweetheart, you're okay, you're okay.

It's me, Colt. You're okay." I brought her close and hugged her hard. She melted into me and started weeping with relief. Her heart was pounding from the adrenaline and fear coursing through her body. "It's okay, sweetheart, you're safe now. We'll sit here until someone comes to help." Jekyll wiggled his way between us and began licking her face, doing his best to comfort her. I stroked her hair and comforted her in my softest, most soothing voice. "You're okay, sweetheart, you're okay. Just breathe…you're okay…"

A few minutes passed. I heard a car stop in the other lane. A guy walked up asking what the hell happened. "Are you okay in there?"

"Yeah, we're okay. If you have a cell phone would you please call 911."

"I already did." At that moment he saw the bloody body of the other man and gasped. He started to back away.

"Mister, that man abducted this girl. I need your help for one more thing. Can I use your phone to call her mother?"

"S-sure." He handed me his phone.

"Katie, what's your mom's number?" She was in shock and couldn't remember the number.

I called 911, told them to call Dimond High School and tell Annie that Katie was in a car accident on 100th Avenue near Minnesota, but she was okay. I handed the phone back. "Thanks, sir. We appreciate your help." He nodded and went back to where other people had gathered.

As I was comforting Katie, the gut-wrenching image of Johnny lying dead in my arms flashed before me. Katie would have a similar image forever etched into her memory if I didn't get her away. I had to act quickly. "Katie, we need to leave. It's important you don't see the bad man because he's dead, so close your eyes and I'll carry you away from him, okay? Do not open your eyes until I say so, is that clear?"

She meekly nodded yes and closed her eyes. I carried her to the other side of the road where the truck shielded any view of her assailant. We sat on the curb waiting for the police to arrive. Jekyll looked at me as if to say *Are you okay?*

"I'm fine boy, I'm fine, but let's check you out." He had a battered lip, but it was nothing serious. "You'll be okay, boy. Your tooth punctured your lip a little."

Katie wrapped her arms around him. "I'm sorry for kicking you, Jekyll von Bickerstaff." She tenderly stroked his head, oblivious to all the people staring at us.

Suddenly the frantic screams of "Katie! Katie!" pierced the air. It was Annie. She must've driven to the scene at the speed of light. Katie started to bolt upright, shouting "Momma!"

I grabbed her and pulled her back down. "Katie, I don't want you to see the man." She immediately understood and nodded. Jekyll was still firmly in her grasp. "Annie, we're over here!"

She sprinted around the truck, and upon seeing her little girl, let out a wail of relief. Annie assumed, from seeing the accident that Katie was in the car with me. She started checking her over for injuries. I grabbed her arm and pulled her toward me, which startled her. "Annie, the police will be here soon, so I need you to listen to me."

She was shocked that I had grabbed her so forcefully. "What's wrong?"

"Katie was abducted, and I crashed into the truck to save her. Now listen to me. Take Katie and walk that way, away from the truck. I don't want Katie to see her abductor. Do it now and don't come back to this area." The police showed up as I said the words. Annie started to say something. I reached behind her neck and pulled her face close to mine. "Annie, I had to kill the guy. Do not let Katie see the body or it'll haunt her for the rest of her life. Get away from here quickly. Go!"

Annie gasped at the enormity of what I'd said. "Katie, Colt is right; you don't need to see anything. Let's take Jekyll and get out of here." They ran fifty yards down the road, stopped, and looked back at me. I waved to show them I was okay. Annie was holding her daughter tightly and Jekyll was in Katie's arms. He was looking at me with obvious concern.

A tough-looking cop surveyed the scene. When he saw the man had been shot, he talked into his portable radio, probably calling in the cavalry. The man who loaned me his cell phone pointed to me and the cop came my way, his pistol drawn. I raised my hands up to show him I meant no harm.

"Lie on your belly and put your hands behind you. Do it now!" I did as he requested. He kicked my feet apart, dropped his knee into the small of my back, and handcuffed me. I could hear multiple sirens. Yep, he had called the cavalry.

"Sit up." He grabbed my arm and pulled me upright.

Before he could say anything more, I jumped in. "Officer, the dead man abducted the young lady over there and I chased him down."

"You did a lot more than chase him down. He's dead. Did you shoot him?"

"No, sir. He shot himself. I just pulled his trigger finger twice and gave him a love tap to the throat."

"Hey smart ass, don't get coy with me. That man is dead over there and you just said you're the one who did it."

"I'm not being coy. You might want to read me my Miranda rights before you start interrogating me."

"Alright, smart ass. *You have the right to remain silent. Anything you say or do can and will be held against you in a court of law. You have the right to speak to an attorney. If you cannot afford an attorney, one will be appointed for you. Do you understand these rights as they have been read to you?*"

"I do, and thank you for being so attentive to my rights. Now, how about you stuff me into your ride and take me away." He grabbed me up and forcefully began moving me to his police car. I abruptly stopped and he almost ran into me. "I have one request. Do not bring the young lady back to see the dead guy. Do not bring her back, okay?"

"Shut the hell up and start moving to the car." That was enough for me. I whirled my leg around and caught him in the back of his knees. He dropped on his back in an instant, and I drove my knee into his chest, pinning him to the ground.

"Listen asshole, my Army friend died in my arms with a bullet between his eyes and that image haunts me to this day. Do not bring the young lady back to see the dead guy. *Do you hear me?*"

He was wide-eyed at how quickly I had him on the ground. A second later, four policemen gang-tackled me and rammed me to the ground. I was screaming like a lunatic now. *"Don't let her near here, damn it! Keep her away from the body!"*

One of the cops zapped me in the face with pepper spray. I gasped. It felt like a thousand bees and a flamethrower were assaulting my face and eyes. They lifted me up and threw me into a police car. "I'm taking you to the station to book you," said the cop who handcuffed me. "Any more nastiness and I'll spray you again. Got it?" I didn't reply. I couldn't. I was gasping for air. He began to drive away.

Katie must've told Annie what happened because Annie leaped in front of his car causing him to jam on his brakes and swerve to avoid her. He jumped out of the car. "What in the hell do you think you're doing, lady? I nearly ran into you."

"That man saved my little girl. She was abducted and he chased them down. He saved her. Now you let him go, now!"

"Lady, he's going to the station and we'll sort it out there." He said something into his radio and several uniforms came running toward his car. While Annie was engaging the cop, Katie snuck around and opened the rear door. When she saw me gasping, she screamed and jumped in after me. She frantically began trying to get me out of the car. I couldn't see a thing. My eyes were swollen shut and I could hardly breathe.

Katie's screaming really fired Annie up. She ran to Katie and they both tried to pull me out of the car. Jekyll joined them, grabbed my pants leg, and pulled with all his might to extract me. The other cops arrived and had to pry Annie and Katie off me. I had no idea what the hell was going on, but I sure heard Jekyll bellowing and the ladies screaming.

Thank God Pat arrived at the scene. Annie must've called him when she got the news. I could only imagine the look on his face at the sight of me in a police car and his two ladies and Jekyll doing their best to pull me out. Annie frantically told him what happened. After some swift negotiating, he was allowed to see me. He gasped when he saw my condition. "Colt, it's me, Pat. You'll be okay. I'm coming to the station to be with you. Thank you for saving Katie. Thank you, thank you."

"T-take c-care of J-Jekyll. C-call Scotty to get m-my c-car."

"We will, I promise. I'll be there for you."

I weakly nodded. The cop tapped Pat on the shoulder.

"I have to go," Pat said to me. "Don't worry about Jekyll."

The cop got back in the car. "Mister, I might owe you an apology when the dust settles." I couldn't respond. My lungs were burning and I was frothing at the mouth. "Let's get to the station and I'll get you cleaned up. Blinking rapidly will help flush the pepper spray out of your eyes."

True to his word, when we got to the station, the officer took me to a restroom where he practically drowned me with soap and water. After ten minutes, I felt like I might live. I now had a profound new respect for pepper spray.

The detective made me go through the story of what happened from the time I left my house until when the police arrived. Another detective had me tell her my story again. They wanted to see if my story was consistent. After that, a guy came in holding a clipboard loaded with paper. "Hello, Colt. My name is Detective Mark Cameron. You took on one bad-ass dude today, did you know that?"

"No, sir, I never met the guy. What's his story?"

"He's got a rap sheet a mile long, a former gang-banger who has served hard time for manslaughter, and has multiple violent assaults, a history of grand theft auto, including the truck you took out today, drug trafficking, robberies, several vicious rapes, etcetera, etcetera. A lot of his finest work was done before he turned eighteen. He just finished a twelve-year stretch in Pelican Bay, where California incarcerates their most serious criminal offenders, the baddest of the bad. I'm not sure how he ended up here in Alaska, but I'd be willing to bet it has something to do with drugs. Anyway, the outcome for that young lady wouldn't have been good. How you disarmed the guy and took him out was nothing short of phenomenal. Your military training no doubt saved your life today." I nodded a silent yes. They must've done their homework regarding who I was.

"You're free to go, Colt. The DA will have to look into this, but it's a slam-dunk case of self-defense, if ever there was one. Before you go, though, I want to thank you for what you've done. I have two young daughters, which makes me cringe when I think about what this man was capable of doing. It was a brave thing you did and you, sir, are a true hero. Let me be the first to shake your hand and say thank you for saving that young lady's life. Some of my colleagues want to say thank you, too, before you leave."

I shook his hand and he patted me on the shoulder. Several other police officers, including the one who cuffed me, entered the room and they each shook my hand and offered me their thanks.

Katie was taken to the police station with Annie to take her statement. They let her and Annie go home long before they said I could go. Poor Katie, she had been walking home from school and noticed she was being followed by the guy in the truck. She nearly made it home before he jumped out and forced her into his truck at gunpoint.

Pat came into the room and hugged me about as hard as I've ever been hugged in my life, saying thank you over and over. He knew I saved his baby girl from unfathomable cruelty. I hugged him back and told him I was fine and everything would be okay. The cops were touched by Pat's emotions and offered him their empathy. They were good people. It reminded me of the closeness I felt with my fellow soldiers.

We left the station and headed down the road. "Colt, let's go to my home," Pat said.

"Sir, just drop me off at my place. You need to be with your family. I'm fine, truly, I'm okay."

"Colt, Annie wasn't going to leave the police station without you, but I insisted she get Katie home as soon as possible. I promised to bring you home the minute you got released. The mother in her needs to make sure you're okay. She also needs to thank you for saving her daughter's life."

"Okay, sir, we'll do it that way. Do you mind me using your cell to call Scotty to let him know I'm okay?"

"Sure."

I made the call and handed the phone back. "He says my poor car is at his place and is drivable, but it's going to need a whole lot more duct tape on the right front fender." Pat smiled weakly. After that, we didn't say much; we were both exhausted. When we pulled into the garage, Annie came out and wrapped her arms around me without saying a word. Pat came over and the three of us hugged each other. After a while she turned to her husband. "She's asleep now. Our doctor has her on sleeping pills. He wants her to sleep for a good twelve hours and then we need to get her into therapy tomorrow."

Pat nodded and excused himself to go look in on his daughter.

Annie kissed me on the cheek. "I can never, ever find an adequate way to thank you for what you did today."

"Annie, there's no need to thank me. I did what needed to be done. Besides, Jekyll is the real hero. He knew something was wrong when we passed that truck, and he was on that guy like white-on-rice after we rammed him. When he jumped on the guy, it caused his pistol to deflect slightly as he fired, and that saved my life. By the way, where is Jekyll?"

"He's with Katie. Your little dog refused to leave her when the police said we had to go to the station. They finally agreed to let him come with us, and he sat on her lap while they took her statement. When we got home, he crawled into bed with her and really helped calm her down. She fell asleep holding him. He's one amazing dog. From now on, Jekyll von Bickerstaff gets as much mango sorbet as he wants when he comes here."

"Whoa, you better be careful making such a statement. He'll have you buying it by the gallon."

"It'll be a small price to pay for saving Katie." She hugged me again. "Thank you Colt, thank you. You're a true hero, the bravest man I've ever met."

"You're welcome. Does that mean there might be more cannelloni in my future?"

"You can have it morning, noon and night for life if you want."

I smiled. I knew how mentally exhausted she was. "Annie, let me call Scotty to drive my car over. You need to be with your family now. Really, I'm okay."

Pat came back into the garage. "Katie and Jekyll are sleeping peacefully."

"Can I use your cell phone again to call Scotty?"

Annie jumped in. "Colt, how can you be okay? You killed another human being today and nearly got killed yourself."

"It's no big deal, Annie. I'm fine."

"How can you be 'fine'?" she said with an edge to her voice.

"Annie, I was a sniper. It's not just a title. You kill people when you're a sniper, and you get shot at. This is nothing new for me. That guy crossed the line when he abducted your daughter and tried to shoot me, so I cashed in his ticket. Do I feel remorse for killing him? No. Not a bit. Believe me when I say I'm fine, because it's the truth."

The magnitude of what I did while in the Army dawned on her. She didn't know what to say. The events of the day had drained her.

"Annie," said Pat, "please go in and be with Katie and let me stay here with Colt."

She sighed, gave me another hug, and headed back into the house without saying a word.

"Let's go sit on the porch." He headed out of the garage and I followed. There were two Adirondack chairs on the porch. It felt good to just sit for a while. "Colt, are you really okay?"

"Yes, Pat. But, I need to get something off my chest and it needs to stay between us. I deliberately took the guy out. I could've disarmed him, but the image of him stalking Katie, after he got out of jail, flashed in my head just as I grabbed him. I pulled the trigger twice and then fractured his larynx just to make sure he'd never harm her again."

Pat's eyes went wide. He just looked at me, speechless.

"You did the right thing, Colt," he finally said. "You saved my little girl from that animal and your actions will help other girls in the future. You did the right thing. Do you need anything? I mean *anything*?"

"No, I'm fine. I really would like to go home and get some sleep."

"Okay, son. Let's go get your car."

"Thanks, Pat." I got up and headed back to the garage.

"Do you want me to get Jekyll?"

"No, sir. It sounds like Katie wants him to be with her, so I'll leave him here if you don't mind."

"That would be great."

I called Scotty to let him know we were coming. They were waiting outside when we got there. I jumped out before Pat could say anything and waved goodbye. He looked relieved, not having to converse with my friends.

Even though Pat had told Scotty what happened, he and Maggie took an hour to debrief me. She hugged me as hard as Annie did, saying the guy could've just as easily taken one of their kids. Though she didn't say it, I knew she was glad he would no longer be on the streets stalking children.

I said goodbye to them. Scotty had done a good job making my car drivable. A few good hits with a sledgehammer got the fender away from the tire. It now had only one functioning headlight, but that wasn't a problem in the land of the midnight sun. After getting home, I went straight to bed. I missed Jekyll, but didn't dwell on it. In a few minutes I was asleep.

I didn't sleep well, though, tossing and turning most of the night, and woke up several times wondering where Jekyll was. I had gotten used to his snoring and leg twitchings, and it felt peculiar without those background distractions. The image of that idiot's pistol pointed at me and the sound of the bullet whizzing by kept flashing in my head. The bullet sounded like the one that whizzed by me and got Johnny. Then there were the thoughts of what he would've done to poor Katie. The lingering effects from the pepper spray caused me to cough throughout the night. I made a mental note to buy a can for the Grand Adventure. Heaven help the guy, or animal, on the receiving end of that stuff. I looked at the clock. It was five-thirty. Any further attempt to sleep was pointless. I got up and made a pot of coffee. While it brewed, I jumped into the shower. It felt so good letting the hot water cascade over my body. I closed my eyes and enjoyed the moment. "Thank you, God," I abruptly said. It was like the words came from my mouth without me thinking to say them. I began crying.

14

AFTER EATING, I needed to run. Nothing clears your head better than a six-mile jog. The sky was crisp and clear, so I put on my running suit and did a few stretches in the yard to warm up. I decided to run to Taku Lake on a trail having a generous assortment of hills and flats. After a while, I got into a rhythm and it felt good to put my body on autopilot. A gentle peace came over me. I had a thought that was powerful. Since it was me who had saved Katie, maybe, just maybe, I wasn't a Jonah after all...

I took another shower after returning and thought it would be good to spend some time with Scotty and Maggie before picking up Jekyll. Katie needed to sleep, so I didn't want to get there too early.

It was noon when I left the Moreys and headed over to the Brennans. Jekyll would be starved, so I planned to treat him by going to Eddie's for fries and maybe a burger for myself. As I turned on their street, I had to jam on the brakes. Several news cars were in the street and Pat and Annie were in their front yard with Jekyll talking to what looked like a bunch of reporters. Pat saw me and motioned for me to come. I parked my car and the horde drifted my way. Pat hugged me and Annie kissed my cheek, and Jek acted mighty pleased to see me again. "Everyone," Pat said, beaming, "this is Colt Mercer, a true American hero."

The media circus ended a half-hour later when Annie mercifully said we had to go inside and be with Katie. Jekyll loved the attention and would've spent the entire afternoon giving interviews. I let out an audible sigh after Pat closed the door. "Dear God, let's hope all this is over now."

"Colt, why not enjoy your fifteen minutes of fame?"

"I don't know, sir, I have an uneasy feeling about all this. Anyway, hopefully it's over. How's Katie doing?"

"She's still sleeping. The pill really knocked her out," said Annie.

"How are you doing and don't say 'I'm fine'."

"I didn't sleep well last night. It doesn't take much to stir my pot of unpleasant memories, and I kept flashing on what could've happened to Katie. But, after a long run this morning and seeing my fur ball here, I feel a lot better. I want to head down to the Kenai tomorrow and have some fun. After that, there'll be no worries."

"Colt, how can you act so unbothered after taking a man's life and nearly being killed yourself?"

I looked her straight in the eye. "Annie, forgive me, but you just don't get it. I had 38 confirmed kills as a sniper in the Army, and a whole lot more if you count those killed from the airstrikes I called in. I've seen heads and bodies literally exploding as a result of me pulling a trigger. When I told you that day at the school how the light in me had died, maybe now you can better understand what I was trying to say. As cold as it sounds, killing one more person doesn't make any difference to me. It's like if you're drowning, it doesn't matter if there's ten feet under you or ten thousand. My soul started drowning with the first person I took out. No, that's not true; I really took the deep plunge the day that drunk crashed into my parents. I cling to the words you said about finding a new light within me. Maybe I'll find that light on the Grand Adventure. So, to answer your question about me being okay, what can I say?"

"You answered just fine." She came over and hugged me gently. "I more than ever understand what you're saying."

"Colt, I'm convinced God brought you into our lives," said Pat. "Not just because of Katie but for what we can do for *you*. The Brennan family, and von Bickerstaff over there, will find a way to pull your ass out of the water. You can count on it."

"You two have already done so much for me. I'll never be able to say 'thank you' enough times."

"You saved our little girl," said Annie. "We're the ones who can never say thank you enough."

"My dear wife is so right. What you did yesterday won't be forgotten by this family. If I live to be ninety, I'll still be saying thank you for what you did."

"You two have already been so kind to me. I still can't fathom the depth of your generosity when you gave me the Trike, and how you've welcomed me into your lives while asking for nothing in return. It's an honor for me to call you friends. Now, if you don't mind, I'd like to take my dog out for one of his favorite treats, French fries at Eddie's."

"Why don't you stay for dinner?"

"Annie, thanks for the invite, but Katie will need your full attention when she wakes up. Have you got a plan on dealing with the mental trauma of her experience?"

"We do," said Pat. "She'll be starting therapy tomorrow morning, and we'll keep her in it for as long as it takes."

"Sounds like a good plan. If you don't mind, I'd like to drop by tomorrow and pick up the Trike. I'll leave my wreck-of-a-car inside."

"Sure. We likely will be gone with Katie when you get here."

"You take care of yourself on the trip," said Pat. "Don't cross paths with another she-bear."

"I'll do my best, sir." I turned and faced my half-asleep wonder dog that was sprawled out on the floor by the couch. "Hey, Jek, you want to go to Eddie's for some fries and catsup?"

"YYYY-o-oo-oooo-oww-ee-ooh." He bolted upright and scrambled over to the front door. I couldn't help but laugh.

"Drive safely," Annie said while smiling at the antics of my dog.

"Yes ma'am, I will."

"Goodbye, von Bickerstaff. You're welcome to come over any time." He ignored Pat and raced to the car without as much as a goodbye lick. His stomach was now in control.

After a delightful meal at Eddie's, Jek and I went home. Lilly howled with delight upon seeing her best friend. I spent a few minutes with Brian and Jamie, telling them about the news interviews and my plan to leave for the Kenai in the morning. Jamie laughed, saying she wondered what trouble I'd get into this time. I cringed at the thought, and hoped Jek and I would have an uneventful trip.

Jamie turned on the TV. "Hey, Colt, the news is on in a minute. Let's see if you're on."

"Are you going to be on the news tonight, Mr. Colt?" Lilly asked.

"I might be, sweetheart. I helped another girl yesterday."

"Did she fall off her tricycle?"

"No, Lilly, um, someone wasn't having good manners, so I helped her get away from the mean man."

"Oh. Can I give Jekyll a few carrots?"

"He ate a lot of fries, so you better wait on the carrots, but I think he'd love to sit on your lap for a while."

"Okay!" She jumped on the couch and clapped her hands. "Come on up, Jekyll von Bickerstaff, let's sit together."

Jekyll waddled over, but was so stuffed that I had to pick him up and put him on her lap. He snuggled in after giving her a few choice licks. Brian put on Channel 2, and to my surprise, I was their lead story. They showed the Brennans and then me and Jek. We all laughed when we saw Jekyll. I have to be honest and say the camera didn't enhance his looks, but he exuded his usual charm. Brian turned off the TV after the story ran. "That was some kind of thing you did yesterday. The father in me thanks you."

"So does the mother in me," Jamie added.

"Well, I was fortunate to recognize her. If I'd waited just a few minutes longer before leaving here, it wouldn't have turned out good. That rattles me a bit, I have to tell you."

"Thank God you showed up when you did," said Jamie.

"I know. Well, if you two don't mind, we need to turn in early so we can hit the road by seven."

"No problem, Colt," said Brian. "Lilly, Jekyll and Mr. Colt are going to bed. You need to say goodbye because they'll be out camping for a while."

"Can I walk with you and Jekyll to your place?"

"You sure can, Lillybean."

We walked across the courtyard and I gave Lilly a hug after she said her goodbyes to Jek. He headed straight to the bed. I could tell he was bushed. He probably didn't sleep that well with Katie last night.

"Hey, boy, you can go to sleep but I'm going to stay up for a while to repack a few things for our trip. Thanks for saving me yesterday. You really came through, my friend. We did good saving Katie." I gave him a hug and he licked my cheek a few times. I lifted the covers and he crawled in. I closed the door and headed into the kitchen. After a couple of minutes, he was snoring away.

15

WE HAD A grand time on the Kenai. Jamal's harness worked well as did Jek's goggles and helmet. We caught a red salmon on the Russian River and grilled the magnificent fish at the campground. The Harley performed flawlessly and we even went through a good downpour without a hitch. Jekyll had a ball the whole trip—his nose was always exploring something new, and he made many new friends. Several people said they saw us on the news. We got invited to a few lunches and dinners as a result of our newfound celebrity; I was overwhelmed at how appreciative people were for what we'd done. We were ready for the Grand Adventure.

I felt great, but tired when we rolled into Pat's driveway at about two in the afternoon. I thought Pat and Annie would be at work and Katie at school, so I was surprised when Annie came out looking haggard. Her eyes were bloodshot like she'd been crying. "Annie, what's wrong?"

"We haven't had a good week, Colt. Katie is refusing to go to the counselor anymore and she's beyond belligerent. We're at our wits end regarding how to deal with her."

"I'm sorry, Annie. What can I do?"

"Nothing, Colt. We need to be patient and loving with her. There's another problem and it's not good. Come in so we can talk." The anguish in her eyes made my stomach cringe. I nodded and followed her in. Jekyll sensed something was wrong too, and shadowed me with his head hung low.

Katie and Pat were sitting on the couch and, from their body language, you could tell both were fuming. He stood up when I came in and wearily greeted me. "Hello, Colt. I have some bad news involving Jekyll."

"Jekyll? He's fine. Nothing's wrong with him."

"Colt," said Annie, "after you were on the news with Jekyll, a guy called saying Jekyll is his and he wants him back."

"What?"

"He said Jekyll ran away and he tried desperately to find him." Tears were rolling down her face.

"Who the hell is this guy? Jekyll was horribly abused when I found him. I'd love to dance on him like he did with my dog."

"Colt, that's not the way to handle this and you know it. Let me work it out for you. I'll hire a lawyer if necessary."

"You listen to me, Pat. I'm not giving Jekyll up to anyone, period. No damn way."

"I know. I'm asking you to stand down and let me handle it."

I raised my hands in total disgust. "Fine, you handle it."

No one said anything for a while. It finally hit me that the anguish on their faces involved more than Jekyll. Katie was sitting on the couch, scowling. I must've arrived when they were having an argument. Jekyll slinked over to her and she picked him up. He licked her face but she didn't seem to notice.

"Okay, forgive me, but obviously I walked into an edgy situation here. What's going on?" Nobody said a word. "Look, I'm tired after being on the road for seven days, so let's not play games. What's going on? Katie?"

She lit up defiantly. "I'm not going back to that damn therapist!"

"Watch your language, young lady," Pat boomed. "You *will* go back and that's the end of it."

"No, I won't and you can't make me!"

"The hell I can't!"

"Pat, stop!" Annie wailed. "Katie, you're having trouble sleeping and you're not getting through this. Your dad and I believe you may need more intensive therapy. There's an in-patient program for teens going through some rough times where you stay for a month or so."

"No! No way am I going to the funny farm. I'm not going!"

"All right everyone, knock it off. Pat and Annie, sit on the couch and we're going to settle this now." They did as I asked without saying a word. Katie looked more defiant than ever. "First of all, Katie, please forgive me for being so selfish. I should've stayed here with you instead of taking off for a week. I'm truly sorry."

"Why did you leave me? Some of his friends might come after me."

"Katie, your dad and I will protect you"

"No Momma, you and Daddy can't. These men are really bad."

"Katie," said Pat quietly, "is this why you keep looking out your window at night? Do you think they're coming for you?" She nodded yes as tears rolled down her cheeks.

I started to choke up. God, the thoughts she must've been having while I was having fun. I felt incredibly guilty. My mind raced about what to say. She didn't need a tender "there, there, it will be okay" speech and other platitudes. She needed a crash course on the real world, and I knew I was the one who had to deliver it.

"Sweetheart, you've had nothing but a life of milk and cookies and now you've been rudely introduced to the real world, and parts of that world, as you now know, aren't so pleasant. I was introduced to that world when I lost my parents to a drunk driver at seventeen. I joined the Army and have been in two wars. I've killed people and there've been many who tried to kill me. I've learned a few things and want to share them with you. What I have to say isn't pleasant, but you need to hear me. Okay?"

She nervously nodded yes.

"Okay then. Let's begin. Katie, tell me if I am wrong. You've already replayed what happened over and over in your head about a million times, correct?"

"Yes."

"Here's a newsflash. It'll never get better no matter how many shrinks you see. You'll continue to replay that day, and you'll let the reprehensible behavior of that twisted, disgusting individual haunt you for years, or maybe for the rest of your life."

Annie was stunned. "Colt, how dare you say something so utterly callous."

Pat stood up. His face was bright red. This was his way of saying the conversation was over.

"Colt," Annie said tersely, "I want you to leave…"

I leaped up and grabbed Pat's throat with my right hand and rammed him into the wall. His eyes bulged just like the punk I nailed at Eddie's place. Annie and Katie both screamed at my sudden violent act. With his throat in my tight grasp, I turned around to see the horrified looks on their faces. I let him go, and he half-dropped to the floor gasping for air. Annie was beside herself, looking at me with a combination of disbelief and outright fear.

I returned my attention to Pat. "Sit back down on the couch, sir, and that's an order." Annie started to say something, but I cut her off with a stop motion of my hand. "Sit down, sir. Now!"

Pat didn't have any fight left in him. He sat down and didn't say a word. Katie was bawling, and Annie embraced her while glaring at me. "Leave this house, Colt, and I mean now!"

"I will, Annie, but I want two minutes to say something to all of you. Two minutes is all I ask."

Pat glared at me, but I think he felt he owed me at least this for saving his little girl. "Go ahead. You have two minutes starting now."

"Thank you, sir. I grabbed you to show you a bit of what Katie went through. It was pure fear."

"We know what fear is. You didn't have to frighten us so. We've already been through enough."

"Two minutes, Annie. I still have the floor." She tightened her jaw and nodded a terse okay.

"When our ancient ancestors experienced the fear you just experienced, it triggered one of two actions, fight or flight. We've lost these two basic elements since we became 'civilized.' Now, when we're confronted with fear, we tend to be paralyzed like the three of you, and what you did the other day, Katie. We've lost our basic survival skills." I looked at each one of them. Pat was pissed and Annie stared menacingly at me while embracing her daughter. "Katie, whenever you replay in your head what happened, you feel powerless and with this powerlessness comes a wave of fear. Am I correct?" She nodded yes. "Sweetheart, you'll always feel this way because you don't know how to fight, and you don't know how to flee. Until you do, you'll forever be trapped in fear. I—"

"Colt," said Annie tersely, "we're going to get Katie help. We don't need your help."

"Annie, I have a minute left. Let me speak."

"Let him finish, Annie, and then he can be on his way." She unhappily yielded to her husband's dictate.

I turned my attention to Katie. "Katie, look at me." A tear ran down her cheek. "Sweetheart, there's a way out of this mess and it's called empowerment. I want to tell you a quick story about a guy named Imrich Lichtenfeld, who went through what you experienced, and much worse. This won't take long, okay?" She nodded hesitantly.

"Imi was a Jew living in Czechoslovakia when Hitler took over the country. Things soon turned horrible. Nazi thugs rampaged through his Jewish community, brutalizing residents, raping women and burning down homes and shops. After a while, Imi formed a group to confront the Nazis; and whenever these thugs came into his community, he'd fight them with all his might. From his many confrontations, Imi developed a way to fight and defend himself. His fighting method would later come to be known as Krav Maga, which means 'contact combat' in ancient Hebrew. Imi was able to flee to Palestine, and began teaching Krav Maga to members of the Jewish underground. When Israel became a country, it adopted his Krav Maga method for personal protection, and has taught it to its soldiers ever since."

I took Katie's hand in mine and looked into her eyes. "Katie, I used Krav Maga against the guy who attacked you. I want to teach you this self-defense method and I guarantee that, once you learn it, you'll know how to act in scary situations. When you replay what happened, you won't respond with fear, because you'll know how to defeat him just like I did. You'll never be afraid of him or anyone else again, because you'll have the skills to either remove yourself from the situation, or defend yourself if you have to."

I turned to Annie and then Pat. "I offer this training to all of you."

"Colt," said Annie, "I don't think this is what Katie—"

"No, Mom, everything Colt said is true. I can't stop thinking about what happened, and don't want to fear him anymore. I don't want to live in fear."

"Katie, your mom and I think the best thing is for you to see a counselor to help you get through this."

"Daddy, I don't want to go to a counselor. I want to meet that man in my dreams and defeat him. I want to stand up for myself. Teach me, please, will you Colt?" Her voice sounded clear and decisive.

"Sweetheart, with your parents' permission, we'll begin tomorrow. But, I have two conditions: one, your mom and dad will learn Krav Maga with you; and two, you *will* go to that counselor and you *will* participate fully, and I mean fully."

"I will, Colt. I promise. I'll do anything you say."

I shifted my attention to Annie and Pat for an answer. Annie eyed her husband and slowly nodded her head yes.

"Okay, Colt, I guess we'll try it." He looked like he'd gone through a war.

"Alright then, Pat and Annie, you'll need to take a week off from work beginning tomorrow. We'll muster in your backyard each day at 0800, and I promise you this is going to be one intense week. Deal?"

"Deal!" said Katie before her parents could say a thing. She had perked up noticeably and seemed eager to start the training. Pat and Annie didn't share her enthusiasm. That their baby girl's innocence had been forever lost was almost too much for them to bear.

"Well, my two minutes are up, and I'm out of here." Pat nodded, but Annie didn't respond.

Katie stood up and came over to me. She wrapped her arms around me. "Thank you for saving me, and for offering to teach me how to defend myself."

I hugged her back. "You're welcome, sweetheart. You'll get past this and I promise, you'll be fine."

"Thank you, Colt."

I cupped her face in my hands. "When he pops into your thoughts again, you tell him that you aren't afraid of him anymore and he'd better run, because you're going to learn how to kick his butt."

She laughed meekly. "Okay, Colt. And, I'll tell him he'll have to deal with you and Jekyll von Bickerstaff too."

"There you go. Jekyll von Superdog will defend all of us. I love you, Katie. You'll be fine. Trust me. And if you need help dealing with your fear, you call me anytime, day or night, okay?"

"I will. Thank you for protecting me."

I hugged her again, and then looked at Jekyll. "Jek, are you ready to head out?"

"Woof!" He ran to the door and we left without saying goodbye.

16

LILLY WAS BESIDE herself when we got home. Jekyll was just as excited to see her, and they were soon on the ground rolling and cavorting. I brought out a lawn chair and watched them play. I needed time to think. It saddened me to find the Brennans so distraught, and I felt badly for not being with them the past week. I needed to rise to the occasion and teach them how to deal with fear. Dealing with fear was one thing I was good at, but I wasn't born that way. Rather, I had to learn how to control my fear and so did the Brennans. Krav Maga is a brutal, no-kidding defense whose basic tenet is to destroy its enemy swiftly and without mercy. I knew I couldn't start at that level—Annie would end the training on the spot if I did. Rather, I had to ramp up, starting with basic moves and methods.

I was running through the basic Krav Maga moves in my head when Lilly threw a ball for Jekyll to fetch, and it bounced off the ground and into my lap. Jekyll leaped up on me to get it. I was so lost in thinking that he scared the crap out of me.

"Sorry Mr. Colt. Did you see how Jekyll von Bickerstaff jumped up on you to get the ball?"

"I did, Lillybean. He scared me for a second."

She giggled and ran to me, joining Jekyll on my lap. He treated her to some choice licks, and then licked me. I hugged them both. "You two are very special to me. I love you both. Do you know that?"

"We sure do, don't we, Jekyll von Bickerstaff?"

"Woof!"

I hugged them again. Jamie came out and smiled at the sight of the two of them on my lap. "Hey, Colt, do you want to come over for dinner? I've got a big pot of spaghetti on the stove."

"You don't mind?"

"We'd love to have you. Dinner will be served in about twenty minutes."

"Thanks for the invite. That'll give me time to shower and feed Jek."

"Sounds good. Lilly, you need to come in and wash up."

"Okay, Momma. See you in a few minutes, Jekyllbean."

Her new nickname for Jekyll cracked me up. "C'mon boy, let's get you some chow."

"Woof!"

I had a wonderful meal with Jamie and Brian. She made some killer garlic bread. We talked about the mini-Grand Adventure on the Kenai, and how much we liked being on the road. They were as steamed as I was regarding the idiot wanting Jekyll back. We agreed to keep Lilly out of the loop regarding this mess. I told them about Katie and my plan to teach her self-defense. Brian liked the idea, but Jamie was doubtful of the approach.

Jek and I said goodbye around eight and we went for a walk. It felt good to stretch my legs. I thought more about tomorrow and practiced some basic Krav Maga moves as I walked, which seemed to amuse Jekyll. I'm not sure, but I think he tried to emulate some of my moves. We went straight to bed after our walk.

The phone ringing jarred me awake. I looked groggily at my clock. It was two in the morning. "This is Colt."

"C-Colt, this is Katie."

"Are you okay, sweetheart?"

"No."

She was crying.

"Talk to me, Katie." I sat up, now fully awake.

"I-I can't sleep, Colt. Are you sure no one will come after me?"

"Oh, Katie. You're really hurting, aren't you?"

"Yes."

"Do you want me to come over and be with you? I can be there in ten minutes."

There was a pause. "Y-yes."

"Okay, sweetheart. I'll bring Jekyll too. Will you watch for me? I don't want to wake your parents by knocking on the door."

"Yes."

"I'm on my way. We'll get through this. Hang tough."

"Okay. Bye Colt."

"Bye sweetheart. See you in a few." I got up and quickly dressed. Jekyll was now awake, wondering what happened. "Katie needs us. Let's go over and be with her."

He jumped off the bed and went right to the front door. I grabbed the keys and drove quickly, arriving in less than eight minutes. Katie had the door open as we walked up. She looked ragged. I closed the door, whispered for her to sit on the couch, and tiptoed into her room for a blanket and pillow. I sat at the end of the couch, put the pillow on my lap, and had her lay her head on it. Then, I put the blanket on her. I didn't say a word and neither did she. Jekyll jumped up and she drew him to her. I stroked her hair gently and felt the wetness of her tears. Her breathing began to slow, becoming more rhythmic. In a while, she was asleep. The night faded away.

In the morning, something roused me from my tenuous sleep. I forced my eyes to open to see what it was. Annie was standing in front of me in her bathrobe with a *what the hell?* look on her face.

I whispered. "She called at two in the morning and pleaded for me to come over."

Her lips quivered and her eyes teared up. She kissed me on my forehead. "Thank you," she mouthed. I smiled and nodded.

Jekyll was awake and gazing at Annie, but he kept perfectly still. Annie touched his head and mouthed a "thank you" to him as well. He didn't make a sound.

She went back to their bedroom. In a couple of minutes, Pat came out with tears rolling down his cheeks. Annie must've told him what happened. He put his hand on my shoulder and smiled weakly. He gently stroked Katie's hair. "Can I get you anything?" he whispered.

"No, sir. I'm fine. She's sleeping peacefully. We shouldn't wake her for a while. She's had a rough night."

He nodded okay and went back to their bedroom.

After another hour or so, Katie began to rouse. She opened her eyes and looked at me. "What time is it?"

"Oh, around seven or so. How are you doing?"

"I'm fine with you and Jekyll here."

I smiled and stroked her hair. "If you work hard, you'll get through this and will be fine. It'll be tough and unpleasant, but you can do it. I promise you'll have a good life. Have faith, okay?"

"Okay, I believe you."

"Good. Now get up and get ready for the day."

"Yes, sir," she said with a half-smile.

"That's the spirit. And hey, would you mind pulling me up, because my legs have fallen asleep."

She laughed. "Thank you so much for everything, Colt. I love you."

"I love you too. Go on now," I said with mock exasperation.

Pat and Annie heard us and came out. "How is she?" Pat asked.

"She's fine now, sir. She just needed some comforting and sleep."

"That should be my job," he said dejectedly.

"Pat, that will come. Right now she thinks I'm the only one who can fight off her demons. That's why you two need to participate in learning Krav Maga. She needs to know she can be safe here with you."

"You're right and we will fully participate," he said.

"I still don't agree with your approach," said Annie, "but, right now, you're the only one who seems to be able to give her a sense of comfort. So, I'll do my best to participate. And, thank you so much for coming over." She wrapped her arms around me and held me tight. I could tell she was in agony as a mother.

"Annie and Pat, I know you view her as your baby girl, but she isn't a baby anymore. She needs for you to treat her as a capable young woman. You need to cut the apron strings a little and let her grow. She'll rise to the occasion and have a good life. If you try to shelter her now, she may never want to leave that shelter. You two need to have faith. Now is the time to empower her."

"She's just a little girl, Colt. I don't think she's ready for all of this."

"No, Annie, she isn't the one not ready for it. You are."

"Annie, Colt is right. We need to let Katie grow in order for her to get through this. I see it clearly now." Annie smiled weakly and nodded her head in agreement. Her maternal instinct was demanding walls be built around her daughter to shelter her forever.

"Okay then. When she comes out, I want you to greet your daughter with some enthusiasm and an eagerness to get on with our day. Empowerment 101 begins in forty-five minutes. Act like this is exactly what she needs. Oh, and you both might want to switch to jogging suits or shorts, because I'm going to work your butts off."

"Yes, sir," Pat said with a smile.

"That's the spirit. Let's make this happen. By the way, what's for breakfast?"

Annie smiled. "I'll check for a special breakfast recipe in the Brennan family vault."

It hit me that I needed a couple of props for the class, and Scotty would have them. I gave him a quick call and told him how to get to the house. He said I just caught him going out the door heading for Fort Richardson and he'd be right over.

The doorbell rang and Scotty came in and handed me a bag. He was dressed in his ACU and looked sharp for so early in the morning. Pat and Annie were surprised to see a soldier in their living room.

"Pat and Annie, this is Scott Morey, my best friend from my Army days. I asked him to come over with some props. Scotty, Pat's a retired Air Force colonel."

"Pleased to meet you, sir and ma'am."

"It's good to meet you too, Sergeant," said Pat. "Would you like to stay for breakfast?"

"No thank you, sir. I need to get to the post. We've got a heavy duty fitness inspection going on this week."

"Colt has told us a lot about you, and we appreciate you being such a good friend to him," said Annie.

"It works both ways, ma'am. Colt has been a true friend to me and my family over the years. He's family as far as we're concerned."

I put my arm around Scotty's shoulder and smiled. "By the way, there's something I need to ask you two on behalf of Scotty. Since you so graciously gave me the Trike, he was wondering if maybe you would be willing to give this house to him and his family."

Scotty gasped.

Annie laughed.

"That will be all, Sergeant," Pat said in his colonel's voice. "You're dismissed."

Scotty stood at attention. His face turned red. "Yes sir!" He popped me on the chest and shook his head.

"C'mon Scott, let me walk you to your car."

"It was a pleasure meeting you, sir and ma'am."

"Hey, Scotty, we'd love to have your family over sometime. How about a barbeque when everything settles down?"

"Sounds nice, ma'am. By the way, I'm sorry for all you've been through. As a father of three daughters, I know how hard this has been for you."

"Thanks," Pat said. "We're coping as best as we can. Your friend, here, has made things a whole lot better than they could've been."

"C'mon, you're going to be late." He nodded a final goodbye to the Brennans and we walked to his car. "Thanks again for bringing the things over. The pistol's unloaded, right?"

"It's just a piece of iron, Colt. No bullets and no magazine. The combat knife, though, is fully sharpened, so be careful with it. Are you really going to teach them Krav Maga?"

"I am. Heaven help the next idiot who messes with this family."

"You know, I've been thinking about giving Maggie a few lessons. Hell, can you imagine if she's pissed and knows Krav Maga? The thought scares me."

I laughed. "She's already a force to be reckoned with, that's for sure."

I gave him a hug and went back in the house. Annie was making breakfast and Jekyll was ready in case any food scraps filtered down.

"You have a real nice friend," Pat said.

"Yes sir, he's a good guy. So is his family."

Katie came out of the bathroom looking fresh. The sleep had done her good. She came over and hugged Pat, which surprised him, especially after all the tenseness of the past few days. He hugged her back and kissed her on the forehead. "Momma, can you make some scrambled eggs and bacon?"

"I sure can, Sweetie. They'll go well with the cantaloupe I'm slicing."

We had an enjoyable breakfast. Annie did wonders with the scrambled eggs, which were topped with smoked salmon and brie cheese. After a last sip of coffee, it was time to get down to business. "Annie, I'll help you with the dishes and then we can start our first lesson."

"Okay. Let's just put the dishes in the sink and I'll do them later. Don't forget, we have a counselor appointment at one this afternoon, so we'll need time to get ready for it." Katie frowned at her comment.

I jumped in. "Great! Katie can tell the counselor all she learned today, and give him some pointers on self-defense." My comment brought a smile to her face and seemed to lighten the thought of having to go.

I asked everyone to take a seat on the couch. Katie sat between her parents. "Let's begin with some basic insights about self-defense, which we can do indoors." I moved the coffee table out of the way. "Okay, here we go. The first rule in Krav Maga self-defense is simple. Do anything it takes to survive. Anything. The second rule in Krav Maga is 'there are no rules.' We'll concentrate on your reflexes and how you can use them to your advantage. Don't worry about what I mean by this because I'll discuss it later. We'll focus on basic stances from which to fight or defend. We'll work on them over and over until you get them right.

"Krav Maga isn't about defensive fighting. You'll never win if you're always on the defensive. We'll focus on moving from defense to offense so you can end things quickly. All the defenses we incorporate will come with built-in counter-attacks. I'll drill into you the words block and attack, block and attack. After that, we'll focus on delivering strikes, including palm strikes, hammer fists, uppercuts, throat strikes, hook punches, and fun things to do with your elbows. You'll learn how to defend against someone coming at you with his fists or what to do if you're in a body hold. I'll teach you how to use your attacker's momentum against him. We'll cover attacks with guns, clubs, and knives. You'll learn to use those weapons against your opponent."

I took a deep breath, and had a sip of coffee before continuing. Annie was squirming, and Pat sat stoically, but I knew there must be a million thoughts racing through his head. I'm sure it dawned on him that being in the Army is a hell of a lot different than the country-club atmosphere of the Air Force. Katie was hyper-focused on everything I said.

"Okay, here's what I plan to do today: teach you the moves and techniques to quickly shift from defense to offense; show you how to counter and quickly end a threat; teach you about reflexes and how to use them to your advantage; focus on taking out your opponent by striking vulnerable parts of his body; and lastly, talk about never putting yourself in a position where you have to defend yourself. Is everything clear?" They all nodded yes.

"Let's go outside for our first lesson." While they went to the back yard, I pulled the pistol from the bag Scotty brought over, checked to make sure it was empty, and placed it under my waistband. Jekyll was frolicking with Katie when I came out. "Jekyll, come here boy, we've got some serious work to do." He sensed from my tone that this wasn't playtime, and obediently came over and stood next to me. "Okay, Katie, the first thing we're going to do is re-create how the guy came after you."

Annie gasped. "Oh no! No, no, no!" We're not going there."

"Yes, Annie, we are. That's square one in getting through all this."

"Katie, this is a mistake. You don't have to do this. Let's go in and, Colt, we thank you for wanting to help."

"No Momma, I want to do this. You go in if you want, but I'm staying out here." A tear rolled down her cheek, and I could tell she was summoning all her strength to rise to this challenge.

Annie was surprised at her resolve. She started to say something else but decided to go a little while longer before pulling the plug.

"Okay," I said before Annie could change her mind, "I'm going to be the bad guy. Scotty brought over this pistol for us to use. It's unloaded and doesn't have a magazine in it." I pulled the pistol out and gave it to Pat. He examined the piece and agreed with a nod it was empty. I could tell he had doubts about my approach, but he didn't say anything. "Alright, Katie, I just got out of my truck. Let's run through what happened from there."

"W-well, h-he pulled the gun out of his c-coat and pointed it at me. He s-said g-get in the truck or I'll k-k-kill you."

"How far away was he when he spoke to you?"

"H-he was real close. The gun was right here." She put her hand about a foot in front of her body.

"Okay, good, that's good. Now, we're going to reverse roles, and I'll be you and Pat, you'll be the attacker. Annie, you stand here and Katie, over here so you can see."

I gave Pat the pistol, and he halfheartedly pulled it out and pointed it at me. "No. C'mon Pat, put some enthusiasm in this. Do it like you mean it. Let's do it again."

This time Pat rose to the occasion. He charged up to me and pulled out the pistol. "Get in my truck or I'll kill you!"

I grabbed the pistol and swiveled it around and out of his hands, and then rammed my elbow into his throat. I didn't put much force behind it, but it was enough to send him reeling backward. I picked up the pistol and had it pointing at him in a flash. The speed at which all this happened caused everyone to gasp.

"That's how fast you can go from defense to offense. You'll learn to do it just as quickly."

"Wow," Pat said. "I couldn't believe how fast you turned things around."

"Alright, Katie, now we'll do it again, but this time you mimic my actions." I had Pat hold the pistol again, and went through the motions of disarming him and striking him with my elbow with Katie mimicking the moves. I then had Annie and Pat do it with Katie being the attacker.

After being satisfied that they all had the moves down, I assumed the role of the attacker. Katie skillfully whipped the pistol from my hands and delivered an elbow to my throat that connected a little too effectively. She actually knocked me back, and I added a little drama by falling to the ground gasping for breath.

"That was good, Katie, very good. Let's run through it again." She was beaming at how well she had done, and I think she surprised herself at what she was able to do. She did it the second time just as deftly as the first. We did the moves at least thirty times. She began to lose her fear, and was shifting to bold reacting. I could see the light coming on in her. She wasn't feeling like a helpless little girl anymore; she was learning that she had power, real physical power. This girl had talent for martial arts.

Next, I had Pat and Annie go through the same drill over and over until they, too, had it down. I loved it when Katie offered pointers to them. Both parents looked proud after performing the moves. The family had noticeably gained some confidence, which was good to see.

It was almost time to leave for Katie's appointment, so Annie made lunch. We ate PBJs on their picnic table. Katie fed Jekyll some sandwich crust and laughed when he wolfed it down.

"Pat, do you mind staying while Katie goes to counseling? I'd like to chat with you regarding Jekyll."

"Sure, but like I told you, I'll handle it. In fact, I'm going to meet with Detective Cameron later today."

"We have to leave now," said Annie. "Colt, do you want to stay for dinner?"

"No, ma'am. I plan on hiking up Flattop to work off all the splendid food you've served me."

"Okay. I guess we'll see you tomorrow at 0800, correct?"

"Correct. Eight sharp. Be ready to go when I get here, okay?"

"Yes, sir," she said with a smile.

Katie came over and hugged me. "Thanks for everything. I love you."

"I love you too, sweetheart. Now, you will fully participate today with the counselor, right?"

"Yes, sir," she replied just like her mother.

"Hey, I'd like to hear some of those 'yes sirs' directed to me when I ask you guys to do something," said Pat with a mock pained expression on his face.

"Yeah, right, Daddy." She hugged him. "I love you, Daddy."

"I love you too, Sweetie. Now go on and get out of here."

Pat gave Annie a quick kiss and they left. I sat down with Pat, and Jekyll jumped on my lap.

"Hey, do you want a beer?"

"I'd love one."

He got up and came back with a couple of brews. He handed me a bottle and clinked his against mine. "Here's to us. I had my doubts on your approach to handling this, but Katie was beaming after she disarmed you and knocked you on your ass. Even Annie seemed to perk up."

"Thanks. Remember, you have to empower your little girl, not shelter her. She'll grow from all of this, and it will be for the better. You'll see."

"I sure hope you're right."

"There's one more thing for you to consider. Remember how you said you had to sell the MLC to make room for a car for Katie. Well, the time to get her a car is now and not later. Also, after giving her the basics in self-defense, I recommend she continue to learn by attending regular self-defense classes. They'll do wonders for improving her confidence, and it's a great way for her to get physical fitness. Remember, now is the time to put her out in the world and not shelter her from it."

"You have some good points. Can you recommend any school for her to attend?

"No, sir, but if you want, I'll check some out."

"I'd appreciate it. Would you be interested in going with me to look at some cars?"

"I'd love to. I used to sell them, so my vast experience in negotiating a deal is at your disposal."

"As I recall, didn't you get fired as a car salesman?"

"Let's not get into the weeds on this," I said with a smile, rolling my eyes.

He laughed. "Well, I was thinking about an econo-box that gets about a million miles per gallon. Do you have anything in mind?"

"I could make you a good deal on my Honda."

"Um, tempting as it is, I'll pass on that. I was thinking about some kind of import."

"You can't go wrong with a Honda. As you can see with mine, they run forever. A new Honda would get her all the way through college and still be running just fine."

"If you have time, why don't we look at a few dealers this weekend? I'll even talk to the head cook about throwing a meal in for your troubles."

"That sounds good. I need to take the MLC to the Harley dealer and have them go over it stem-to-stern to make sure it's ready for the trip. Maybe we could drop it off first and then look at cars."

"Looks like we have a plan. Going back to Katie, I want to thank you for the kind act of coming over last night. She's bonded to you and believes you're her lifeline to get through all of this and, as her father, I can't thank you enough."

"Sir, plenty of people have done many kind things for me. So, I'm doing nothing more than repaying the universe for the kindnesses done for me. Speaking of kindnesses, what are you up to regarding Jekyll?"

"Well, I called Detective Cameron and told him about you finding Jekyll and how the vet said he'd been abused. He said he wants to talk to the vet, and then he'll chat with this guy. So, if you could give me the name and number of your vet, I'll pass it on to him. He's a good guy. And right now, the entire Anchorage Police Department will come to your aid if you need them to. So, like I said, have faith and let me handle things, okay?"

"Yes sir, and thank you. The idiot wanting Jekyll is someone I'd love to pay back with a little of the hell he gave to my dog. Jek was really abused with broken ribs and cowered for a long time whenever I put my hand down to pet him." I stroked Jek and gave him a hug. He reciprocated by licking my cheek.

"Von Bickerstaff had a tough life before meeting you, that's for sure. But, he has the perfect partner now. Do you want me to call you after meeting with Cameron today?"

"No. If the news isn't good, I'll toss and turn all night. I need to get a good night's sleep, so why don't you fill me in tomorrow."

"As you wish, my boy."

"Pat, this little dog means everything to me. The thought of losing him sends shudders through me."

"I know. We love the fur ball too. Like I said, I'll hire a lawyer to get this resolved. But, let's take one step at a time."

"I'll try. Well, the urge to climb Flattop has passed. I might go to the store since we're running low on carrots."

He laughed. "A dog loving carrots is so peculiar."

"I know. But, thank God they're cheap. Having a rather basic dog suits me fine."

I finished my beer and Pat walked me to the car. Jekyll jumped into the passenger seat and wagged his tail. He had a dandelion flower stuck between his teeth, looking even more ridiculous than his normal self. I laughed and petted him as I drove. *Please God, don't let them take my dog away from me.*

17

I DRILLED THE Family Brennan mercilessly the next week, and Jekyll was there every day providing encouragement. He even tried to do some fancy foot maneuvers, and we all howled with laughter when he tripped over his feet. He didn't mind everyone laughing at him. I think he did it on purpose to keep us cheerful.

Katie had made tremendous progress, which was inspiring to see. She slept through the night now, and even the counselor was amazed at how well she was doing. He said if she kept up the pace, she wouldn't need to be seeing him as much in the future. He wanted to talk to me about Krav Maga as a potential tool for helping other victims of trauma.

On Saturday, we were ready to go car shopping. Pat told the ladies we needed a "man day" and were going to the base gym to work out. Katie asked if I'd bring Jekyll over so they could hang while we were gone. I checked my mail before leaving, and was delighted to see my new Alaska license plate had arrived. It looked pretty cool. "Alaska" was printed in purple letters at the top of the plate, and the words "Purple Heart" were on the bottom.

Pat and I put the new plate on the Trike. We left Jekyll with the ladies, and dropped off the Trike at the dealer. We planned on looking at the Honda, Toyota and Hyundai dealers. Annie's only demand was to buy something with a pretty red exterior color.

We looked at Toyota first, and then went to the other two dealers. I liked the Honda Fit, which had plenty of cargo room for camping or hauling stuff around. Pat was leaning toward a sedan. We went to the Subaru dealership on a whim, and found a sparkling new red hatchback. It got great gas mileage and, with full-time four wheel drive, was perfect for Alaskan winters. On the test drive, Pat gave me a nod, indicating this was the car to buy. We reached a good deal after haggling a bit, and they said we could pick it up at noon the next day. We high-fived each other after doing the deal, then headed to the Harley dealer to pick up the Trike.

When we got back home, Annie had a heavenly smelling prime rib resting on a carving board. She asked Pat to slice it while she finished the mashed potatoes. He excitedly told her about the new car as he went to work on the big chunk of meat. I offered to pick it up from the dealer and surprise Katie like they did me by having the car sit in the driveway when she walked out. They thought it was a great idea. Katie came bounding in with Jekyll in her arms, his tongue hanging out in full pant. He must've been playing hard from the way he looked.

"Hey, boy, it looks like you've been having a good time."

"Woof!"

Katie put him down and he ran over to a bowl on the floor filled with water for him. He lapped it up like he hadn't had a drink in a long while. She sat next to me on the couch. "Guess what, Colt? I had a dream last night and that guy appeared." She jumped up. "I grabbed his pistol away and had him on the ground in less than two seconds. Then I told him to get up and get his candy-ass out of my life."

I rolled my eyes. "Katie, there's one important thing that I haven't taught you, and this is really important. Sit down. It'll only take a minute or two." She looked at me quizzically and complied.

"Sweetheart, there's a wonderful little book written many centuries ago called the Tao Te Ching, and it has many truths that are relevant to this day. I recommend you read it. Here's one of the passages I love.

There are three jewels that I cherish: compassion, moderation, and humility.

With compassion, you will be able to be brave,

With moderation, you will be able to give to others,

With humility, you will be able to become a great leader.

To abandon compassion while seeking to be brave, or abandoning moderation while being benevolent, or abandoning humility while seeking to lead will only lead to greater trouble.

The compassionate warrior will be the winner, and if compassion is your defense you will be secure.

Compassion is the protector of Heaven's salvation."

I paused for a moment before continuing. I could see she was earnestly listening to me. "Now that you know Krav Maga, you need to have the utmost respect for it. Don't run around bragging or showing off about how good you are at it. Just because you can do something, doesn't mean you should. Always remember the three jewels: compassion, moderation, and humility. Plus, let me add one more jewel. Good manners. Having good manners will always serve you well."

"Those are fine words," said Pat. "Mighty fine words. Katie, I have a copy of the Tao in our bookcase if you ever want to read it."

She nodded an okay to her father. "I didn't mean to be bragging about meeting that guy in my dreams, Colt."

"I know you didn't, sweetheart, and understand what you were saying. When we first talked about self-defense, I said you needed to confront the guy in your dreams and that's what you did. I'm so proud of you for the courage you've shown. Now you have a responsibility to use what you've learned wisely, and just remember that it's always better to flee if you can, rather than fight."

"I know. You taught me well. I'm not afraid anymore. Thank you for showing me how not to be afraid."

"You're welcome, pretty girl. But you need to keep up with your lessons. I found a great place that teaches martial arts over on Northern Lights Boulevard. Give some thought to training for a black belt. You're really good at it."

"Do you think I am?"

"I sure do. You might end up teaching or helping me one day."

"I'll defend you any day, just like you helped me."

"Let's hope that never happens. By the way, your counselor says you've been doing really well and I'm proud of you for participating fully."

"He says I only need to see him once a month, if I want."

"What do you want?"

"I don't know, maybe I'll see him once a week for a couple of more weeks and then start seeing him each month."

"That sounds like a plan."

"Hey, can I take Jekyll back over to see Jen again? She wants to show him to some more people."

"Sure, but don't you want to stay and have dinner with us?"

"Well, Jen's mom is having lasagna and it's my favorite food. Do you mind if I go?"

"No, go ahead if it's okay with your parents. Just don't feed Jekyll too much. He'll eat his weight in lasagna if you let him."

"Momma, Daddy, can I go?"

"Yes, Katie, but be home at seven."

"Okay, Momma. C'mon, Jekyll, we're going to have lasagna!"

Jekyll shot out of the house without so much as a goodbye.

The phone rang. Annie answered it. "Pat, it's Mark Cameron."

Pat got up and took the phone. "Hello Mark, what's up?" I thought it was interesting that Pat was now calling Detective Cameron by his first name. "Yes, yes. Good. He did? Are you sure? Excellent! Thank you, Mark. What time? Yes, we can do that. I appreciate all you've done. You'll have to come over some day with your wife for dinner. Good. Okay, I'll call you back to firm up the time. Later." He hung up the phone and swung his fist triumphantly through the air. "Yes!"

"What's up, Pat?"

"Good news, Colt. It seems the guy had a few issues with the law. Mark told him to forget about Jekyll, and they'd forget about running him in. They appear to have struck a deal. The Jekyll matter is now over."

I leaped up and let out a whoop, and we all did a jig. "Thank you, Pat, thank you!" I looked up and said another thank you to the heavens.

"Wow, this has been quite a week," said Annie.

"It has. Man, do I feel good."

Annie and Pat laughed. They could see the tension in me had lifted.

"I have another piece of good news, Colt. The mayor and the Anchorage Police Department want to present you with their hero award the Tuesday after next at one p.m. Forgive me, but I told him we'd be there. Do you mind?"

"I guess not. What should I wear?" The thought of having to put on the "death suit" hit me.

"Casual is fine, jeans and a polo shirt."

"Can Jekyll come?"

"He sure can. They expect him to be there since you two are co-heroes."

"Colt," said Annie, "I want to say this while Katie isn't here. I was against your approach for getting her well, but I was wrong. I've had all these psychology classes and work with kids, but here you come and upset my whole applecart. The proof is in the pudding. I'm amazed at how well she's doing since you've been back from the Kenai. When she just told you she met the bad guy in her dreams and defeated him, I thought, wow, she really is getting through this and it's because of you. I'll never forget how she reached out to you in the middle of the night and you came without hesitation. I love you, Colt, and apologize for being so mean to you."

"It's okay. Katie is an incredible young lady, and I know she'll put all this behind her soon."

"She will because of all you've done. As her father, I can only say thank you from the bottom of my heart."

"Thanks, Pat. Really, I'd do anything for you guys and you have my word on it. And thank you, too, for taking care of the Jekyll situation. You handled it beautifully and I'm indebted to you."

"No problem. I met a new friend in the process. Mark Cameron is an interesting character. He was in the Coast Guard in his misspent youth, but we can't hold that against him."

"No sir, I suppose not. Um, can we eat?"

Annie laughed. "Excellent suggestion. Let me uncork a special Napa Valley merlot for this occasion." In no time, we were feasting on a meal worthy of a five-star restaurant. Conversation came easy; it felt like I'd know these fine people for years.

I ate so much it hurt. After placing my utensils on the plate, I looked at the chef. "Annie, you're a terrific gourmet. If you ever opened your own restaurant, it'd be an instant hit."

"Colt's right, dear wife. This meal is sublime."

"Thanks, you two. I enjoy cooking for both of you."

"Be sure to save some room for dessert," said Pat.

"I don't know if I can eat another bite."

"Trust me. You'll want a piece of what's coming."

"I can't believe Katie passed up a meal like this for lasagna."

"Oh, she has her reasons," Annie said with a smile.

"Speaking of Katie, how do you want to handle things tomorrow?"

"Well, can you pick up the car and have it here by noon? I figure, if you wouldn't mind, I'll pack a picnic basket and we can all drive in her new car to Hatcher Pass."

"Sure, I'm up for that. But, seriously, aren't you two getting rather tired of me by now? I've been practically living over here."

"No, we aren't tired of you. Our home is always open to you."

"By the way, you better be prepared for Katie making a big run for freedom once she gets those wheels. I'd recommend easing up a bit on the reins and giving her more responsibility. I'm not saying give her total freedom, but you need to let her explore."

"I think you're ready to have a brood of your own. You certainly are thinking like a parent."

"Thanks, sir, but Jek is all the responsibility I can handle right now."

"I hear what you are saying, and I'll do my best," said Annie. "But, she'll always be my baby girl."

"Speaking of exploring, I've given notice to my landlord to be out by the end of May."

"Oh, that's so soon."

"I know, Annie, but I need to hit the road shortly or I'll be driving through Maine in mid-November. That's not a good idea."

Just then we heard Katie and Jekyll bellowing at the front door. "Open up, Momma!"

"Woof! Woof!"

"I'm coming!" Annie yelled. She got up and playfully messed up my hair as she walked by.

Jekyll was inside as soon as the door cracked open. He ran over and leaped on my lap. "Hey, boy, what's up? Did you get enough lasagna?"

"Woof!"

Katie came in, proudly holding a big cake. "I made this for you, Colt. It's carrot cake. Jekyll sure wants to taste it."

"Wow! Very nice, Katie. Carrot cake is my favorite, and I'm sure anything made with carrots will be Jekyll's new love too. Thank you for making it for me."

"Jen and I made it. Her mom helped us."

"That's so nice of you guys. Thank you." She put the cake on the breakfast nook table, then came over and gave me a hug.

Annie brought out plates and a box of tissues, placing them on the table next to the cake. Maybe she was out of napkins, I thought. "Alright, everyone, have a seat."

Katie was beaming as we took seats around the cake. "Okay, Daddy, let's start."

"Okay, Sweetie." He looked at me as Annie plucked a tissue out of the box. "Colt, there's another reason we asked you to come over tonight. We—"

His voice broke. Suddenly Annie had tears in her eyes, and then Katie. *What the hell...?* "What's going on, you guys? Does that guy want Jekyll back again?"

"No, Colt, this is all good," said Annie through her tears. She grabbed a couple more tissues and dabbed her eyes. "Do you remember when we gave you the MLC, and I said if we had a son we'd want one exactly like you?"

I nodded.

"Well, we've been talking about this for the last few days, and we decided that we want to adopt you."

"Adopt me? Annie, I'm a little old to be adopted."

"Colt," Pat said, "we don't mean it like that. What we mean is we want you to be part of our family. You lost your parents and don't have a place you can call home with people who love you. We're offering that to you today. We're offering you a place in our family. It's the highest honor we can give for all you've done. I'd be so proud to think of you as my son."

"Say yes, Colt," said Katie. "I promise I'll love you forever and want you to be part of our family."

Annie had the waterworks fully on. "I'm offering you the same love as Pat's mom gave to me. I want you to become a part of our family, Colt, just like his family did with me. You and Jekyll will always be welcome in our home, just as if you were our real son and Katie's brother.

"We also talked to Rachel and she wants the same thing. She wanted to be here today, but she's at the Keck Observatory at Mauna Kea and can't get away. Anyway, she thanks you from the bottom of her heart for saving her sister."

Now I was in tears. "I-I really don't know what to say. I'm not sure you guys would want me after all I've been through. I—"

"We want you, Colt. We love you," said Katie firmly.

"Would you like some time to think about it?"

"No, sir. There's nothing I need to think about. I'd be honored to be part of this family, and I'll do anything for any of you."

"You already have, Colt," said Annie. "You already have."

"Alright," said Pat, "here's to Colt Mercer, the newest member of the Brennan family."

"Yeah!" said Katie. She was clapping enthusiastically.

"Woof! Woof! Woof!" Even Jekyll was getting into the spirit of things. He tried to grab a piece of the cake.

"Whoa there, Jekyll, let Katie cut you a piece."

"Woof!"

Katie had done a good job with the cake—it was delicious. After eating a piece, I could hardly move from being so full. It felt so good to be around these people and I couldn't help but think of times like this with my parents. To be given another chance to be part of a family was amazingly uplifting. Katie retreated to the couch with Jekyll and I helped Annie with the dishes. Pat sat in his easy chair and was watching Katie playing with Jekyll. I walked in with Annie and sat next to Katie. Jekyll gave me a few welcome licks. I cleared my throat. There was something I needed to say.

"Could I talk to you guys about something that's pretty important to me, and, if we're a family, it's a family matter that we need to address."

"Sure," said Pat looking a bit surprised. "What's up?"

"Well, I don't mean to be a party pooper, but there's one more thing we need to do before we get on with our lives."

"What's that?" said Annie.

"We, as a family, need to forgive the man who abducted Katie." I could see Annie recoil at the thought. Her smile along with the joy of the day suddenly vanished. "Please hear me out on this, okay?"

"Go ahead," Annie said tentatively.

I could see I had destroyed the mood of the evening, but I had to do it. "I've been thinking a lot about the guy. You know, you just don't start out life as a criminal. He must've had a really tough life. All of us in this room have or had loving parents who cared about us and mentored us on how to be good human beings. When I think of this guy, I'd be willing to bet he had little love and guidance, and he turned rogue because of it. I'm not condoning his actions; I'm just saying we need to forgive him."

"I'm not sure I can do that," said Pat.

"I don't know if I can either," said Annie. "He was trying to hurt my little girl."

I turned to Katie. "Sweetheart, unless you forgive him, you'll keep your spirit forever trapped in an invisible cage. I'm not asking anyone to condone his actions; I'm just saying let's turn him over to God without our condemnation."

I looked at Pat and Annie. "As hard as it was, I've forgiven the man who took the lives of my parents. Also, in my prayers, I've asked the people I've killed, and their families, to forgive me."

That brought tears to Annie. She understood what I was trying to say.

"Let's do it," said Katie. "I'm willing if you guys are."

"I guess I'm in, but as a father, this is hard for me to do."

"Annie?" She looked at me and nodded her head hesitantly, but affirmatively.

"Okay then, let's gather around in a circle and hold hands."

They did as I asked. "We each need to say something. I'll start, then you, Katie, then Annie, and Pat, as the head of the family you can finish. Okay?"

They all said okay. I bowed my head. "Heavenly Father, we are gathered here as a family to say we forgive the man who tried to harm Katie. I believe he had an awful life on this planet, so I hope you'll surround him in your loving care."

I looked at Katie and nodded at her to offer her thoughts. "Um, dear God, I too, forgive the man. I hope he finds peace with you and that he can find the kind of love my family gives to me."

I squeezed her hand and smiled. It was Annie's turn. After some hesitation, she began. "Dear God, as a mother I cannot excuse what this man has done. But, I remember how lost I was after you took my mother to heaven, and without her love, how close I came to going down the wrong path too. So, I forgive this man and ask that you have mercy on his soul."

It was Pat's turn. I heard him take a deep breath. "God, I echo what my wife has said. Forgiving this man is incredibly hard. But I forgive him and pray that you wash his soul clean with your divine grace. We ask you this as a family."

"Amen," I said. Amen, they repeated. I smiled at each of them. "Thank you all for having the courage to do this. This chapter in the book of our lives is now finished. It's time to move forward to all the good that's out there."

"Amen again," said Katie. "Speaking of good, do you think I could spend the night with Jen? We want to watch *Titanic* again."

"How many times have you seen that movie?"

"Not that many, Daddy, maybe twenty or thirty is all."

"Let me call Jen's mom and see if she really doesn't mind," said Annie.

"I'll start packing a few things while you do that. Goodbye, Colt, and welcome to our family again."

"You're welcome Katie. Jek and I should head home too. I can hardly walk after that wonderful meal. And thanks, sweetheart, for that delicious cake. It was super."

Pat and Annie walked me out to my car. As we were saying good-bye, Katie whizzed by with her arms loaded with stuff she needed for her safari at Jen's house.

"Bye, Colt," she yelled without breaking stride.

I drove home and enjoyed the rest of the evening with Jek. That night, in bed, I thought about how lucky I was. I had a family.

18

I WOKE UP feeling better than I had in a long time, and with you-know-who stuck in my face. "Hey, boy, do you need to do your business?"

"Woof!"

I got up and opened the door. Jekyll did his thing and then trotted over to see if Lilly was home. He let out one of his custom yodels. "Yo-e-o-eo-eee-eo!"

A second later the front door flew open and out came Lilly in her stocking feet. "Jekyll von Bickerstaff!" And just like that, they became a blurry whirlwind of hugs, licks and kisses. "Can he play for a while, Mr. Colt?"

"If it's okay with your parents." In a snap the two of them bolted into her house and the door slammed shut. I suppose that meant Jekyll could play.

I took a shower, had a bowl of frosted flakes and did a little surfing on the internet to prepare for the Grand Adventure. It was nearly ten-thirty, so I needed to get moving to be at the Brennan's by noon. Jekyll and Lilly were playing hide-and-seek in her apartment. Every time he found her, he got a carrot so he was motivated to have the game go on all day. Reluctantly, he said goodbye to his best little friend. We started walking to the car dealer, which would take about twenty minutes. To get ready for the Grand Adventure, I put Jek on a leash to get him used to it. At first it bothered him, but he soon forgot about it after turning his attention to all the new smells along the way.

The car was gleaming and ready to go when we got there. I asked them to put some plastic on the passenger seat so Jekyll wouldn't get the car dirty. I pulled into the Brennan's driveway and honked the horn. They all came out to see what was up.

"Wow, Colt," said Katie, "did you get a new car?"

"This car isn't mine, it's yours. Your parents bought it for you." She turned to her parents with a look of disbelief.

Pat was beaming. "It's yours, Sweetie. Take care of it because you'll be driving it through college."

Katie's surprised expression quickly morphed to pure exhilaration. She hugged and kissed her mom and dad. I held the door open and motioned for her to get in. She jumped into the spiffy-looking red ride. "Oh Momma, can Jen come over and see it?"

"Yes, but the first drive in your new car will be going to Hatcher Pass for a family picnic. Colt and Jekyll are coming."

"Cool!" She was holding the steering wheel looking radiant. Pat sat in the passenger seat. He started going over all the buttons and dials, but Katie was too excited to hear much. Jen came over in a flash and ogled with her friend.

Pat drove the car to Eagle River, wanting to get out of heavier traffic before letting Katie drive. She did well driving up to Hatcher Pass. We parked at Independence Mine and hiked across the valley to an amphitheater with incredible views. Annie had made prime rib sandwiches with horseradish sauce. Boy, were they good. After eating, we watched Jekyll and Katie chase butterflies.

Annie took my hand. "Colt, I slept soundly last night for the first time since this whole ordeal with Katie began. I woke up this morning wondering why I slept so well. And then it hit me. To forgive that man was the right way to put this all behind us."

It was a special day.

19

I SPENT THE week focusing on my Grand Adventure. The huge limiting factor for my trip was my meager savings account. I tried not to be negative, but the numbers weren't adding up.

I gave notice for my apartment, and was down to one week left. Brian and Jamie offered to help me clean so I'd get the $700 security deposit back. Since it was furnished, I didn't have to get rid of any furniture. Much to my delight, the Gilgrens agreed to buy my Honda for four hundred bucks. Brian and I went to a junkyard and found a good deal on a fender, which Pat graciously paid for. We bolted it in no time and the car looked good again. I decided to give Brian my computer as a gift for all he and Jamie had done for me.

All my remaining possessions had to fit in the tight space on the Trike, so I pared things down to the barest of essentials. My Army training helped with how to live on practically nothing. One of the exceptions to this minimalism was packing Jekyll's Zen book, which I'd promised Pat I'd read.

I thought about what I'd be leaving behind. In the last year, I'd met some wonderful people and would miss them terribly. I teared up when picturing Lilly saying goodbye to Jekyll. We'd been working on preparing her, but I knew her little heart would break the day we pulled out. Scotty was only days away from deploying, and that meant his family would have no one to look after them. Maggie is a very capable woman, but everyone needs a break. Then there's Eddie. What a guy. Jekyll would sorely miss his fries, and I'd miss my friend. And the Brennans, how I would miss them. I was pretty close to calling the whole thing off.

The phone rang. "Hey Colt, it's Scotty. We just got orders to fly out next Thursday at 1000. Maggie and I'd like to have you over for a barbeque before I go. It'll be a farewell bash for both of us."

"Sounds good. I, uh, I need to talk to you. Can you come over? There's some beer in it for you."

"Hold on…" In the background I heard him yelling for Maggie. "Yeah, Colt, the boss says I can come over for a while. Give me a half-hour."

"Great. See you then." I hung up and went to see how Jek and Lilly were doing.

She opened the door and frowned. "Does Jekyll von Bickerstaff have to go now?"

"Well, sweetheart, let's see what your mom and dad have to say."

"Come in," Jamie yelled from the bedroom. "Brian went to the store and will be back in a minute. Get a beer if you want."

"No, thanks. My friend's coming over, so I can take Jek home now if he's driving you nuts."

"Oh, he's no bother. He and Lilly are having a ball." She came over and gave me a hug. "So, is this a female friend?" she said with a sly smile.

"No, nothing like that. Scotty, my Army buddy, is coming over to talk. I'm starting to think this Grand Adventure might be a huge mistake."

"Oh. My. Well, this family wants you to stay, so you better not ask for our opinions."

She burst out laughing, which startled me. "What?"

"Oh, I was thinking. This reminds me of a bachelor getting cold feet as he gets closer to the big event at the altar. Brian was a nervous wreck right up to the time he said 'I do.' He knew I'd kill him if he bolted, so he took the lesser of the two evils and showed up."

"You think that's it?"

"I do. No pun intended."

I smiled. "If you get tired of the fur ball, send him home. And thanks, Jamie. I needed to hear what you said." I headed out the door and Lilly and Jekyll followed. We played ball in the yard until Scotty arrived. Jekyll ran over and gave him a yodel hello. Brian returned and I introduced him to Scotty. After a bit of small talk, Brian left with my beast and Lilly.

I handed Scott a beer and we went to the living room. "So, what's up?"

I took a long drink before answering. "I'm having second thoughts, Scotty."

"Second thoughts on what?"

"The Grand Adventure. Maybe it should be called the Grand Folly."

"Why the change?"

"Well, things are going well here. I've met some good people, and then you're deploying. I should stay and look after your family."

Scotty took a drink and then shook his head. "You know, you're as fickle as an old woman. First of all, Maggie has gone through multiple tours of me being gone. She's tougher than both of us. Secondly, you've spent your entire Army career saying goodbye to legions of friends, so that's nothing new to you. Let's cut to the chase, here. What the hell's wrong?"

"Well, thanks for your pathetic attempt at empathy, buddy. All I'm saying is that staying here might be the best choice. Did I tell you the Brennans adopted me?"

"*Adopted* you? What the hell, do you think you're going to move in with them and go back to high school?"

"Not that kind of adoption, knucklehead. They said I'd always have a place to come home to. They now consider me part of their family."

"Colt, here's a newsflash. You've been part of our family for years."

"Thanks, Scotty, I know that but it's not the same as with the Brennans. You and I are peers. They are nearly the same age as my parents and…and they're so much like them, it's eerie. I feel like I'm connecting again with my mom and dad when I'm around them. It's hard for me to describe."

"Well, from all you told me about your parents, I guess you're lucky to find people like the Brennans. They seem like nice people."

"They are, Scotty.

"Okay, let's look at this from a different direction. Indulge me." I nodded yes. "It's nice that you've found a new family, and no offense, but so what? You've barely got a pot to piss in, and you're not going to work in your new family's business. So, what the hell are you going to do if you stay, flip burgers or sweep floors?"

"I don't know. Maybe I'll go to college."

"And do what, become a rocket scientist? You haven't a clue what you want to do with your life, and don't try to blow daisies up my ass about it. College would be a colossal waste of your time, as if you could even afford it."

I frowned and let out a big sigh. "You're right. I haven't got a clue about what I should do."

"You keep telling me your 'heart' says you should go on your so-called Grand Adventure, right?"

"Right."

"Well, I've never believed in that 'heart' bull crap; but, has your heart dictated any new terms to you lately?"

"No."

"Well damn, it sounds like the only reason you're wavering is because you've lost your nerve. You used to be someone with balls."

"There's a guy I took out the other day who'd verify me having balls. But, he's dead right now, so take my damn word for it."

"Colt, I don't mean it that way and you know it. You're one of the bravest men I've ever known. What I mean is, you've lost your way in terms of trusting yourself. You're afraid to try bold things. The Grand Adventure is a bold move. Trust yourself. Trust what your heart is telling you."

"Scotty, I seem to be drifting aimlessly, and don't know how to get on a solid course. I've run the numbers and they're just not adding up. I'm going to have to find work while on my trip and I don't have that many skills. And then there's Jekyll. What the hell do I do with him while I'm working?"

"Colt, who the hell knows. Just have faith and make it happen. You were a master at improvising when you were in the Army. Do you think those skills vanished the day you got out? Have some faith, buddy. Have some faith."

I emptied my beer. "You want another one?"

"No, I can't stay. Maggie is cooking dinner and you're welcome to come."

Thanks, but I'll pass. As you can tell, I'm not good company."

"Colt, you're single. You're unencumbered with the exception of that ugly dog, and you're trying to find your way. So go find yourself. Go on your Grand Adventure. If it doesn't work out, sell the damn Trike and come back. I'm heading into harm's way, yet again. Sitting on that magnificent ride tooling down the road sounds a whole lot better than where I'm going. There'll be no one taking potshots at you for sport or laying IEDs along your path. So, from my perspective, what you're doing sounds damn rosy. Enjoy it. Not many people ever get to do something as incredible as this. If I was as footloose as you, I'd be joining you on your adventure."

"I'd love to do this with you, Scott, we'd have a blast."

"We sure would."

"Thanks, Scotty. Really, I mean it. You're right about everything."

"No problem. I still consider you to be my brother, and you can tell your new family that I have grandfather rights."

"You do and I'll never forget that. You're a damn good friend."

"You are too. The best of the best." He got up and gave me a hug. "I have to go. Stop feeling wishy-washy. Go do this and enjoy every minute of it."

"Okay. I guess I needed a swift kick in the ass."

"I have no problem putting my size 11 up your rear. Just give me a call whenever you need it done." We walked to the door. "Oh, regarding the farewell barbeque, next Wednesday is the only day that's going to work. I'm up to my ears getting those idiot privates ready to deploy."

"Yeah, Wednesday is good, and if it's okay, I'd like to include the Brennans and Gilgrens and maybe a few more. You met Brian Gilgren today."

"I don't mind. Give Maggie a call when you firm things up."

"Sounds like a plan."

"You'll be fine."

"I know." I decided right then and there to drop the confidence draining self-doubting, and focus on the good that was out there waiting to be discovered by me and my dog. The Grand Adventure was going to happen come hell or high water. I was going to have faith.

My stomach growled and I realized I hadn't eaten since breakfast. The urge for a steak at Eddie's hit me. I went to the Gilgrens and whispered into Jekyll's ear. He lit up and, in full yodel, set a new land speed record to the car.

"What did you say to him?" asked a bewildered Jamie.

"I said one word. 'Eddie.' That means only one thing to Jekyll. French fries." I left to the sounds of them laughing.

It wasn't crowded at Eddie's, so he had time to chat. He put Jekyll on his lap and started feeding him fries with catsup. I told him about

Scotty deploying, me leaving, and that we were having a farewell barbeque and he was invited. To my surprise, and delight, he insisted on catering the whole thing on his dime. He said he had a grill that he could tow anywhere. All I needed to do was tell him where, when, and how many would be attending.

Jekyll and I waddled out. After we got home, I called Annie and she suggested having the bash at their place. I then called my vet, Rosanna, the Gilgrens, Maggie, and Eddie to nail down the event. Geez, there's no way I'd want to be an event planner. After the phone marathon, my eyelids were heavy. Jekyll was snoring. We were soon snoring in unison.

20

I SPENT MOST of Tuesday morning fretting about the award ceremony at Dimond High School. Pat called saying to meet him at his house for lunch, and then we'd drive over.

I was short on things to wear since donating my death suit and a bunch of other clothes to the Salvation Army. Jeans and a powder-blue polo shirt would have to do. To pass time, I sat on the couch and thumbed through the road atlas. I had traced my primary route with a yellow highlighter and some alternate routes in blue and orange. The plan was to be in Maine by early October to see a New England autumn. After that, I'd head south to avoid the winter snows. I talked to Jekyll about the trip and the reasoning behind certain decisions. He was a good listener.

We headed to the Brennans around noon. Pat made club sandwiches for lunch. He saw my nervousness and tried to calm me down, saying the presentation would be a "low-key" affair. Annie was already at Dimond because she wanted to see a personal safety presentation being given by the Anchorage police.

We pulled into the parking lot five minutes early. Annie was there, waiting for us. I picked Jekyll up and we followed her into the school. Jek was wagging his tail at breakneck speed, happy to be seeing some unfamiliar kids. Annie directed us down an aisle, and then motioned for me to go through some closed double doors. When I walked in, the whole place erupted in applause. God, it looked like most of the students were there, and they were clapping and shouting, Colt! Colt! Colt!

Jeykll was frightened at first, but quickly recovered. He started yodeling and was soon hitting some of his best high-notes, causing the kids to howl. I laughed too. Annie was beaming. She took my arm in hers and led me to the stage where Katie and a bunch of other people had gathered. I recognized Mark Cameron and the police officer who initially cuffed me. Both were clapping. I smiled sheepishly and waved to them. Then I saw the mayor. He came up, shook my hand, and patted Jekyll on his head. You should've seen him grimace when he got a good view of my pooch. Katie gave Jek and me a big hug. She took Jekyll from me so I could more easily shake hands. I waved to the kids and then glanced at Pat thinking, "low-key," huh? He smiled slyly and clapped.

To my surprise, Scotty was there looking sharp in his ACU. He jumped on the stage and gave me a hug. I thanked him for coming, which must've been hard since he was so busy. After greeting me, he went back to Maggie and their girls, who were waving from the front row. I blew them a kiss.

The mayor tapped on the microphone. "Ladies and gentlemen, let's get on with the show!" Everyone clapped and stomped their feet. The mayor clapped with as much enthusiasm as everyone else before raising his hands to hush the crowd. "There are heroes among us today. Let me introduce Colt Mercer and his dog, Jekyll von Bickerstaff!"

More wild applause. Katie came up with Jekyll. He loved the limelight and let out a huge high-octane power yodel right into the microphone. "Yo-eee-oo-ee-ooh-ar-woooo-eee-oo-ee-ooh-ar-woooo!!!!" His warble brought the place down. I forgot about being nervous. It's difficult to be nervous when you're laughing so hard.

Our normally stoic mayor was bent over in laughter. The kids were applauding and stomping their feet, shouting in unison Jekyll! Jekyll! Jekyll! I held him up and, to the delight of the crowd, he let out an encore yodel. I'd be willing to bet our riot of glee could register on the Richter scale. The mayor composed himself and patted Jekyll on the head. He leaned to the microphone. "That dog could have a future at the Grand Ole Opry!" All the kids laughed and began another round of Jekyll! Jekyll! Jekyll!

The mayor raised his hands. He was clearly enjoying himself. "Let me tell you a little about Colt...." He waited for the crowd to quiet down a bit. When he was satisfied he could be heard, he went on. "Let me tell you a little about Colt. He was an Army Ranger who served two tours in Iraq and another in Afghanistan before getting out and moving to our wonderful city. This man won a Silver Star and a Purple Heart in Afghanistan for gallantry in the field. We thank you, Colt, for your service to our country." More applause.

"Now let me tell you why he's getting the Anchorage Community Hero Award. For those who haven't heard why, it's an amazing story." He motioned for Katie to come stand by him and me. "Katie Brennan, a junior here at Dimond, was walking home from school one day last month when a man in a truck kidnapped her at gunpoint. According to the police, this guy was a hardened criminal. Colt is friends with Katie's family and was on his way to see them when he recognized Katie in the truck and knew something was wrong. He pursued them, and crashed his car into the guy's truck to stop him. And here's the amazing part. He jumped out and went after the guy even after seeing a gun pointing right at him. His dog, Jekyll, leaped up on the guy just as he fired, causing the bullet to deflect, barely missing Colt. The two men battled and the bad guy succumbed as a result. Katie, thank God, was returned safely to her parents."

He turned to me, clapped with everyone else for a while, and then went back to the microphone. "How many of you would run straight to a man pointing a gun at you, knowing you were going to be shot, in order to save someone else?" He paused for a moment to let his words sink in. "This is why Colt is a hero!" Everyone stood up and clapped. Katie gave me another hug as did Annie and Pat.

"Colt, it's my privilege to present you the Anchorage Community Hero Award." I shook his hand and took the award. He smiled on cue when pictures were taken and then went back to the microphone. "Colt, there's a couple more people who have something to say to you. The first is Detective Mark Cameron of the Anchorage Police Department."

Mark stepped up to the microphone and waved. They already knew him. He had talked to them about personal safety before we got there. "Hello again. Let me just say I echo everything the mayor has said, especially about Jekyll having a potential career in country music." Everyone laughed and clapped. "What Colt did was one of the bravest things I've ever witnessed in twenty years of being a policeman. But, that's not why I'm up here today. I have something else to share with you about Colt." He looked at me and smiled. I was puzzled about what else he could say. "I learned a lot about him from Pat and Annie Brennan, the parents of Katie. Colt's had a tough time adjusting to civilian life since getting out of the Army. Pat said he and Jekyll plan to tour the Lower 48 on a motorcycle to try to work out some issues he's facing from his combat days. Colt, I know money has been a challenge for you, so the Anchorage Police Department passed the hat around. We want to present you this check for nine thousand dollars to help you on your journey. Good luck, my friend."

I was stunned. He came over and gave me the check and then a hug. "We all love you," he whispered in my ear. I lost it. A flood of tears streamed down my face. Annie came to my aid. She pulled out a wad of tissues and dabbed my eyes. Katie gave me a hug. Jekyll, who was now in Pat's arms, began struggling to come over and comfort me. Pat brought him over so he could give me a few licks. I patted him and told him I was okay. It took me a couple of minutes to regain my composure.

The mayor went back to the microphone. "One more thing, Colt. I'll kick in another thousand." The whole place erupted in applause. Several kids took off their ball caps and started going through the crowd for more donations. The mayor had to shout to continue to be heard. "I have one more person who'd like to say a few words. Ladies and gentlemen, may I present the Governor of the State of Alaska!"

Out from backstage came the governor, who was clapping as he came forward. He shook my hand, gave me a hug, and walked to the podium. "I'll match your thousand, mayor." I was beside myself now.

"Colt, you're a true hero. There's nothing more to say other than 'thank you' for all you've done. If you ever get down to Juneau, stop by my place and we'll have a beer, er, I mean, a soda." The teenagers laughed at his minor-corrected remark. The governor motioned for me to come to the microphone and say something. I shook everyone's hand again while making my way over. At the podium, I looked at all the clapping kids and cautiously leaned toward the microphone, acting like it might bite me if I got too close.

"Hello, everyone."

"*We love you, Colt!*" shouted someone from the crowd.

"Um, I love all of you too." There was more applause. The kids who went through the crowd collecting came up and put the money on the stage. "Wow." Everyone laughed. "I'm not one for speeches, so please forgive my anemic eloquence. I just want to say 'thank you' for the kindness you've shown me today." I looked at Mark Cameron, the mayor and the governor and mouthed a 'thank you' to them. I turned back to the microphone and pointed to Scotty as I started to speak again. "If you want to talk about heroes, please let me introduce you to my friend, Sergeant First Class Scott Morey. Come up here, Scotty." Scotty looked like he just got noticed at a Taliban tea party. He slumped in his chair trying as best he could to go invisible. Reluctantly, with Maggie's prodding, he stood up and came to the stage. Like me, he had no penchant for being the center of attention. I gave him a big hug and then went back to the microphone.

"If you walk by Scotty, you'd probably not give him a second thought other than perhaps noting that he was wearing a uniform. You'd have no idea that you passed one of the finest, bravest, and most decent of people ever to have lived. You'd never know that here is a man who completed three combat tours since 9/11 in some of the world's most dangerous and hostile places. You'd never know that here is a person who has bravely led men in treacherous battles, and has held terrified dying men in his arms and tenderly comforted them as they took their last breath. You'd never know that here is a person who exemplifies, in every way, the words duty, honor, country. You'd never know the man you walked by is a devoted husband and a superb father of three little girls, who will soon be saying goodbye to their daddy when he deploys next week on his fourth combat tour to Afghanistan. I'm so honored that this exceptional man calls me his friend."

I paused for a moment and looked at him. Tears were in his eyes. Tears were in the eyes of a lot of people in the crowd too. He smiled at me and nodded. I knew he was silently saying that he loved me too. "And here's one more thing you don't know about my friend, Scotty. He lives with someone who is a hero in every essence of the word. She's his wife and her name is Maggie." Everyone stood up and started clapping for my friends. Maggie stood sporting a beet-red face and embarrassingly waved to the crowd. The governor and mayor shook Scotty's hand. Even Jekyll gave Scotty a few choice licks.

After the applause subsided, I went back to the microphone. "Scotty and I have many friends who didn't make it back alive. On my trip I plan on meeting the parents of my friends who were killed in action. I plan on telling them how incredible their children were and how honored I am to have known them. I pray every day for peace and hope you all will join me in that prayer. I'll end by saying something to any of you who may be lost or struggling with life. Do not despair. Once I confided to Katie's mom that the light inside of me had gone out and I feared I'd never see anything but darkness. 'Don't worry,' she said, 'you'll find a new light within you. It won't be the same as the old light, but it will shine just as brightly as the one before.'" I looked at Annie and then back to the crowd. "I have to be honest and say that I've yet to find that new light, but I know I'm on the right path to finding it when

I see kindnesses like what I'm experiencing here today. Thank you all."
I stepped back and waved to everyone, and then went over to get Jekyll
from Pat. He eagerly came to me and started licking my face.

Mark Cameron leaned to my ear. "That was beautiful, Colt. When
you get back, think about a career as an Anchorage police officer. Say
the word and I'll make it happen."

"Thanks, Mark. Will you please tell everyone how grateful I am for
their donations. Lack of money was a huge concern and you lifted that
burden off me."

"It's no problem. Give some thought to joining our team." I nodded okay. The mayor and governor came over and handed me their
checks. I sincerely thanked them. The governor emphasized his invite
for a beer was legit. I told him thanks. Katie took Jekyll from me and
melted into the crowd. Within a minute Jekyll began a new round of
yodels which meant he was having a ball. Kids were yelling and screaming to get near him like he was a rock star. I wouldn't be surprised if he
became the new school mascot.

Scotty drifted over and said Pat tipped him off to the event and he
wouldn't have missed it. Maggie was so happy that I acknowledged her
husband. She kissed me on the cheek and gave me a look that said "you
did well and I'll forgive you for anything wrong you may do for the rest
of your life." I hugged her girls. The governor shook Scotty's hand and
thanked him for his service. He then quietly exited the same way he
came in with the mayor in tow. Scotty thanked me again and said he
had to get back to the grind. The school's uniformed junior ROTC students swarmed around him as he walked out and he shook their hands
and talked to their commander.

Katie yelled for me to meet all her friends and she appeared to have
a ton of them. Jekyll was working the crowd as well as any politician.
I was thinking since he liked school so much that maybe I'd sign him
up for a few obedience classes. I decided to be brave and join Katie for
a while in the horde.

After a while, Pat saw me tiring and mercifully told everyone we
had to go. Katie reluctantly surrendered Joe Cool and we headed out
with Pat and Annie to their car. "That was an incredibly decent thing
you did for Scotty," he said.

"It was," said Annie. "Everyone could see how much you love and
respect him."

"They come no better than Scotty. I've begged him to get out but he'll have none of it. Like I told you before, I'm worried about him going on this tour. You can't beat the hornet's nest over and over again without getting stung. I once arrogantly proclaimed that we'd all die of old age before a bullet found us, but after losing most of those friends, I learned how perilous life is when you're in a war zone."

"It reminds me of an old flying adage. There are old pilots, and there are bold pilots. But there are no old, bold pilots."

"Yes, sir. By the way, I appreciate you asking him and his family to come. I never thought to ask since I figured he'd be super busy getting ready for deploying this Thursday."

"No problem. After what you did, I'm really glad they were here."

We pulled into the garage and went inside. Annie was holding a plastic bag used to gather the money left on stage. She counted the offerings, which, to my amazement, totaled $252. That brought the grand total to $11,252. I could last a good year on that. Pat passed out beers and we retreated to the couch, laughing about Jekyll bringing the house down with his yodeling. Annie said it was cool to meet the mayor and governor. I agreed.

Katie and Jen came in about an hour later and plopped on the couch with one on each side of me. "How'd you like it today, Colt?" said Katie. "Did we surprise you?"

"Oh man, did you guys ever."

"Guess what, Colt?" said Jen giggling.

"What, Jen?"

"Katie said she's going to marry you when she gets out of high school."

"Jen!" Katie turned beet red and reached over me trying to put her hand over Jen's mouth.

"Ha!" I laughed. "By the time Katie's old enough to marry me, I'll be an old man with no teeth using a walker to get around." To emphasize the point, I brought my lips over my teeth and acted like I was toothless. Jen laughed.

"I wouldn't care, Colt."

I could see she was serious. "Sweetheart, I'm practically an old man. Just you wait. Some young buck will sweep you off your feet. You too, Jen."

"I hope he has a car as nice as Katie's."

"Hey, Colt," yelled Annie, "come on over. We have a few things to give you."

She and Pat came out of their bedroom with some fancy-wrapped gifts. "Guys, this is all too much. You really need to quit."

"Yeah, yeah," said Annie. "Come on, open them up." I shook my head and went to the table.

Katie handed me a small box. "Open this one first!"

I shook it next to my head for a hint as to what it was. Finding no clues, I went to town on the gift wrap. The box had an Apple logo on it. "What's this?"

"It's an iPhone," said Jen enthusiastically.

"Go ahead and open it," said Pat. "It's got some pretty neat features, including GPS. Plus, you're on our unlimited family plan so you can talk as much as Katie does with Jen."

"Yeah," Annie beamed, "and it has email too, so there'll be no excuses for not keeping us informed about where you are and how you're doing."

"Well, I could use the excuse of my battery being dead." Annie smirked and handed me the next gift. I opened it and laughed. It was a solar-powered battery charger.

Pat handed me the biggest box. "Here, son, open this." I opened it and found a cool motorcycle jacket with pants and boots. The jacket was made with outrageously loud phosphorescent lime-green cloth that was practically guaranteed to burn retinas. Some high-reflective tape strips would allow me to be seen at night.

I tried on the jacket and really liked it. On cue, they all pulled out sunglasses and put them on to shield their eyes from the intense color. Pat added to the moment by moaning and groaning and dramatically putting his hands up to further protect his eyes. It cracked me up. After a few adjustments I had it fitting perfectly.

"The guy said to tell you the coat is rainproof and made with armor-something fabric and has ballistic polyester in the impact areas. That big reflective triangle on the rear will light you up at night, and there's a bunch of vents you can open for good air flow in hot summers. Oh, it comes with a zippered chest map pocket and a mobile media pocket too. Katie picked out the boots, and they're breathable too."

"All I can say is wow. You guys are way beyond generous. It's too much."

Annie gave me a hug. "No, it's not. I'd never let my son go on such a long trip without these things. We have one more thing. It's a two-year membership with an outfit called Motorcycle Roadside Assistance. They offer free towing and 24/7 response anywhere in the US or Canada. We'll feel better knowing you'll have roadside assistance just a call away."

I shook my head. "Thanks so much, you guys. After today at Dimond and this, I'm truly speechless."

"I know I already said it, but that was a fine speech you gave today, Colt." Pat said. "I laughed when you began with 'forgive my anemic eloquence.' You, sir, are a silver-tongued orator."

I smiled sheepishly.

"Oh," said Annie with a devilish smile, "We forgot one more thing. Come out to the garage." Katie ran ahead and opened the garage door. There was the MLC, I mean Trike, with a cool-looking luggage rack attached. It seemed to be floating in mid-air behind the Trike.

"Isn't this something," said Pat. "It hooks into the trailer hitch so you don't need any wheels for it or a license plate. It has fourteen cubic feet of space and will hold around 300 pounds."

It sure was ultra-sweet, with integrated brake lights and color matching the Trike. I opened the lid and was amazed at the storage space. It was the equivalent of moving from a studio apartment to a mansion. Well, that might be a bit of an exaggeration, but it sure was nice. I put Jekyll in and he fit well. I gave some thought to having him ride back there, but having more storage space trumped those thoughts. "Guys, this is nothing but fantastic. You could put every Christmas gift I've had in the last ten years together and it wouldn't come close to what I've received today. Thank you all so very, very much." I hugged each of them, feeling like I'd won the lotto.

The phone rang and Annie ran into the house to answer it. She came back smiling. "Eddie is on his way to drop off the grill. When I asked him what we could bring for tomorrow's barbeque, he said all we needed to bring was a smile."

"Trust me, Eddie will have you singing his praises after tomorrow."

Eddie rolled in a few minutes later and I introduced him to everyone. He asked if we had any barbeque favorites and the consensus was ribs. I knew Scotty would love it because we practically lived in rib joints at Fort Benning.

Annie insisted Eddie stay for dinner and when he tasted her Chicken Picatta with blue-cheese mashed potatoes followed by a dessert of Key Lime cheesecake with mango ribbons, well, let's just say he met his match in the culinary arena. They spent half the evening going over their favorite gourmet meals, and to their delight, found they liked many similar things. While the gourmets chatted, Pat and I sneaked out to look at the new carrier. Man oh man, was it nice. It would double the stuff I could take. Pat was delighted at seeing how much it meant to me. I felt like a little kid getting his first bicycle.

21

THE NEXT DAY, I didn't wake until late and kicked myself for sleeping in. I got dressed, brushed my teeth, and took Jek out to do his business. Lilly spotted us, and she and Jekyll snapped together like powerful magnets. Jamie came out and said hello. While rolling in the grass with Jek, Lilly pleaded for the fur ball to stay with her for the rest of the morning. Jamie agreed, which was fine with me, since I planned to clean the kitchen today, and then if I had time, the living room.

I made good progress cleaning my place, but had to stop at one to get ready for the barbeque at Pat and Annie's. After showering, I went to the Gilgrens. They wanted to take their own car to leave early if Lilly got cranky.

Lilly looked cute wearing denim overalls and a pink shirt. She begged to let Jekyll ride with them, and he was delighted to be her escort. The day was warm and we all had our car windows down. I heard Jekyll start power yodeling when we turned on 100th Avenue. He knew we were getting close to the Brennans. I was laughing so hard I could barely drive. In my rearview mirror, I saw Jamie and Brian cracking up too. My dog was a mess.

I introduced the Gilgrens to Pat and Annie, and Katie and Jen commandeered Lilly and Jekyll. They took off for Jen's house saying they had to get something for the barbeque. When I went to the back yard, Eddie was on station looking dapper in a white apron. He had a bottle of ale in his hand and looked happier than Jekyll with a French fry. The heavenly smell of ribs and smoking mesquite wood chips permeated the air. Oh my, this meal was going to be good.

Pat was in the kitchen stirring some sauce concoction Eddie had made earlier. He was chatting with Jamie and Brian who had just completed a self-guided tour of their impressive home. Since the girls had Lilly, he suggested they walk to the inlet for a view of the Alaska Range.

They knew a good offer when it came their way and headed out. He seemed pleased that I dropped in to be with him. "Pull up a seat and tell me how you're doing."

I grabbed a barstool and sat down. "You want me to get you a beer?"

"No, I'm fine. I'll start hitting the brewskies once Eddie rings the dinner bell. Man, he knows how to cook. I've never smelled anything so good coming from a grill."

"He's a pro. Did you hear him and Annie trading notes? It makes me laugh."

"It's like watching two epicurean giants squaring off and sizing each other up. I call it culinary Sumo. So, is everything shaping up for you leaving?"

"Yes, sir. Departure day is Saturday morning. Do you have any advice regarding Lilly? Jekyll is her best friend, and it'll break her heart when we go."

"That's a tough one. Talk to Annie. She's very intuitive when it comes to that stuff." He cut the heat down on the saucepan. "What else can we do for you? I want to make sure you're in good shape for the trip."

"May I use your address for my mail? Also, can you and Annie be on my bank account should anything happen?"

"Both are fine. We can go to the bank tomorrow morning if you want."

"The morning won't work. I'm going to the airport to send Scotty off."

"What time is he leaving?"

"1000 hours."

"Would you mind if Annie and I come to wish him farewell? The colonel in me wants to do it."

"I'm sure he'd appreciate the gesture, sir."

"Good. We'll be there."

"Pat, no kidding, I'm really going to miss you and the ladies."

"We'll be missing you too. If you get cold feet, I'll try my best to find work for you at the Corps. You're way up there in terms of hiring preference points being a vet with a Purple Heart. You'd fit fine in our environmental department. We're cleaning up tons of former utilized defense sites all over the state."

"You better not dangle those worms in front of me right now because they're sure tempting to bite."

"My advice is to go on the Grand Adventure. Give it a chance. I'm sure the first few weeks will be hell until you and von Bickerstaff find your rhythm. Just don't give up too early, or on the flip side, push on for fear of wounding your pride. If you decide to come home, we'll discuss job options then. Remember, the Harley is yours free and clear, with no strings attached. If you want to sell it, sell it. I will in no way be disappointed regarding what you choose to do with it." He stirred the pot some more and then looked me in the eye. "If you're ever in trouble or you need anything, call me day or night. I'll be on the first plane out of here. I'm not kidding when I consider you as my son. I was always grateful for my mom taking Annie under her wing, and marveled at how genuinely she embraced her as a daughter. I couldn't fully fathom how strong her love was for Annie since there wasn't common blood. But, with you, I see with crystal clarity how my mom felt. I feel it with you. In the spirit of my mother, I'm calling you my son. I hope you understand what I'm trying to say."

In that moment I truly saw him as my new father. "Pat..." I bit my lip. I was too overwhelmed to speak. I got up and hugged my father. He didn't say anything either and just hugged me back. Sometimes you can say a lot without saying a word.

He patted me on the back and whispered. "Annie feels the same as I do. You're our son."

The front door burst open and in came Jen, Jekyll, Katie and Lilly. The girls had water pistols, and were howling with delight at who shot whom the most. When the riot of canine and kids surged into the kitchen, they all stopped cold at the sight of me in tears. "What's wrong Mr. Colt," said Lilly. "Did you burn yourself?"

"No, Lillybean, I'm just happy."

"Oh. Do you want to see how I can feed Jekyll von Bickerstaff water with this pistol?"

"Sure, Sweetie. Let's go outside and you can show me."

"Okay, Mr. Colt. C'mon, Jekyll von Bickerstaff!" He let out a frenzied woof and out they went.

"Colt, are you okay?"

"I'm fine, Katie. Your dad said something incredibly nice to me, and it made me feel like I was talking to my own father."

She came over and gave me a hug. Jen lightened things up by shooting me with the water pistol. "All right, this is war!" I grabbed Katie's pistol and chased Jen out the back door. We had a great time playing with the squirt guns. I was drenched by the time Pat brought Scotty and his family to the back yard. I nailed Scotty in the face with a jet of water. Lilly squealed with delight. I gave the pistol back to Katie and introduced the Moreys to everyone. Julianna, Sophie and Amy timidly gravitated to the other kids. After a few minutes, they were frolicking like they'd known each other forever. Lilly and her new best friend, Sophie, were running with Jekyll in their grasp, trying to escape the monsoon the other girls were shooting at them. Lilly had the front half of Jekyll and Sophie the back half. His wagging tail was hitting Sophie in the face like a windshield wiper. He was yodeling with joy. It was hilarious.

Rosanna walked up. "I heard all the noise and a familiar yodel, so I knew I must be getting close to the party."

I gave her a hug and introduced her to everyone. When she saw Jekyll in the haphazard grasp of the two little girls, she burst out laughing. Annie came over and shook Rosanna's hand. "Thank you for all you've done with Jekyll. He must've been one of your toughest challenges."

"He was. I lobbied hard to put him down, but Colt would have none of it. I'm proud to say I was wrong."

"Hey, you two, some advice please. Lilly loves Jekyll more than anything. She's going to be devastated when we go. I just don't know what to do, and am open to your thoughts."

Annie replied quickly. "The answer is easy; get her a dog of her own."

"I agree," said Rosanna. "You know, I have a wonderful little mixed-breed male pup who'll be about Jekyll's size when he grows up. He needs a good home and Lilly looks like she'd give him all the love he'd ever need."

"That's a great idea. Would you mind if we discuss it with her parents when they get back?"

"Not at all."

The three of us talked a bit more. When Jamie and Brian emerged from the woods, I brought them over to Annie and Rosanna. Annie presented the dog-for-Lilly idea and Rosanna turned it up a notch by describing the sweetest, most adorable puppy a family could ever hope to have. Brian and Jamie excused themselves to talk it over. They came back smiling. "Can we come see the pup tomorrow?"

"You sure can, Jamie. Come by anytime between noon and five. Oh, and Colt, bring Jekyll over and I'll trim his nails and get him ready for the Grand Adventure. It'll be my farewell treat."

"Thanks, Rosanna. Can you trim my nails too?"

"Sure, but I might take off your little toes with the clippers I use."

I laughed. "Hey Jamie and Brian, how about this; if you guys want, I'll take Lilly for an ice cream cone at McDonalds while you go see the puppy. If he's not what you want, then Lilly will be none the wiser."

"That sounds perfect," said Jamie, "and we can take Jekyll with us for his pedicure."

"Excellent. We have a deal." I had a thought about how to help Lilly bond with the new puppy. "Hey if you decide to adopt the pup, we need to have a good cover story so Lilly will transfer her love from Jekyll to him. I propose a kinship angle. How's this. Let's call the puppy Finley von Bickerstaff and say he's Jekyll's cousin from Shaktoolik, Alaska. Jekyll is concerned that it's far too cold for Finley in Shaktoolik, and wants Finley to move to Anchorage where it's warmer. Jekyll wants Lilly to adopt Finley because she's a special girl who can see beauty even when it's not apparent. Jekyll says only Lilly's sweet and tender heart can love Finley the way he needs to be loved, the way she loves him."

"Colt, you make me want to cry," said Jamie. "Finley von Bickerstaff? Seriously, you might want to give some real thought to writing a book about this for children."

"I second that." said Annie.

Rosanna joined the fun. "I'll buy a dozen copies if you write it." I laughed at the notion of me being a kid book author.

Eddie announced hot dogs would be ready in five minutes. Annie cupped her hands to her face. "Hey kids, I have hand wipes on the table. You need to clean your hands!"

Katie and Jen herded the kids to the table, and soon every kid was being wiped down. I told Pat that Eddie was ready for the sauce. When he brought it out, Eddie generously applied the concoction to the ribs, which released another pleasing aroma.

Annie borrowed a couple of portable picnic tables from the neighbors and those, combined with the one they had, provided plenty of space for everyone to sit. She had one of the tables reserved for the kids, and put extra napkins on it for the inevitable spills. Eddie asked for anyone wanting hot dogs and beans to come first. He also had a generous assortment of chips and dips.

After the kids were squared away and happily munching, Eddie announced that the real food was ready. "I hope you enjoy my famous 'baby backs,' which are cooked Kansas City-style. Help yourself to all the sides. Beers and sodas are in the ice chest. Let the fun begin!"

The view inside the grill made me drool. Eddie had enough slabs of ribs to feed an army and he was generous in doling them out. My rack of bliss stretched four inches past each side of the oversized paper plate. When I tasted the first rib, the tangy, smoky-sweet caramelized sauce lit up my taste buds, and the meat melted in my mouth. I ran over to Eddie and gave him a saucy kiss on his cheek. He didn't mind; he knew a genuine compliment when he saw, or should I say, experienced it.

I made no effort to hide my gluttony. Soon, everyone was powering through the ribs and swooning like me. Pat and Annie stood up and started clapping after tasting the meal prepared by our master chef. Following their cue, we all stood up and applauded, even the kids. Eddie loved the gesture and bowed an exaggerated bow to his new legions of followers. He grabbed a plate and piled on the food. Pat motioned for him to sit with him and Annie.

We ate and ate. Scotty and I visited the grill twice more. After everyone had their fill, there were several racks of ribs remaining. Eddie wrapped them in foil and gave them to Annie.

Pat stood up. "Will everyone form a circle and join hands while I say a prayer for Scotty and Colt." After we circled up, he bowed his head and began to speak. "Heavenly Father, we ask that you bless Colt and Scotty and watch over them as they begin their new journeys. For Colt, we ask that you guide him to discover the noble purpose he is seeking; for Scotty we ask that you wrap him in your divine protection so he can return safely to his wife and family. May your light and love shine upon their paths. In your name, we pray. Amen." Everyone said amen.

"God bless you, Scotty."

"God bless all of us, Colt."

We all pitched in to clean everything up. Eddie then said he needed to get back to the Grille to close things down, so I helped him hook the grill to his truck. I thanked him for making this a special day, and for all he'd done for me as a friend and mentor. He wished me good luck on my quest and hoped I'd find what I was seeking. I hugged him long and hard, and waved as he drove off.

Rosanna came over. "You have a lot of good friends and I'm glad one of them is me."

I gave her a heartfelt hug. "I'll never forget your generosity and friendship. The start of me getting better was the day I met you and Jekyll. You'll never know how much you mean to me."

"Colt, you always get back when you give. With you and Jekyll, I've gotten far more back than I gave. You have a friend for life, kind sir. I'll never forget you and Mr. von Bickerstaff."

I smiled. "Well I suppose a lot of people will never forget the sight of my furry friend but not in the way you mean."

She laughed. "He does have a face you'll remember, probably in your nightmares. I have to go. Thank you for inviting me. Tonight was special."

"Thanks for coming, and thanks, in advance, for giving Jek a tune-up." I gave her another hug at her car and headed into the house where everyone remaining had gathered.

Before I could join the others, Scotty came over with a beer in his hand. He motioned for me to move into the empty living room. "That, my friend was a meal I won't soon forget. It was over the top."

"I won't forget it either. Eddie is an animal behind a grill."

"I need to go soon, so I wanted to say bye to you in private while I have the chance."

"Thanks for taking the time. You know I wish you the best."

"Colt, let's cut to the chase here, and say what needs to be said. If something happens to me, will you make sure Maggie and the kids will be okay?"

"I will, and you know you don't have to ask that question."

"I need to hear it even though I know you'll do it. I have to tell you when Manny got nailed, well, it shook me right down to the core. The odds aren't in my favor. You can only go to the show so many times before your luck runs out. But, like we say, embrace the suck. It's all you can do."

I nodded. Only a soldier who experienced combat could fathom what he was saying. "Do you know where you're going yet?"

Scotty frowned and sipped his beer. He looked at me despondently. "Yeah, they called me yesterday. They're separating me from my men and sending me to liaison with the Brits at a remote outpost called Checkpoint Toki. From what I hear, it's a God-awful death trap so poorly equipped and undermanned that it's become a magnet for insurgent bullets and mortars. It's somewhere in the bad-ass Helmand region. Colt, it's a real serious shithole teeming with well-armed bad guys and IEDs as plentiful as you can imagine in your worst dreams. Some Brit journalist called it the most perilous place on earth. I'm not trying to be fatalistic, but I call them as I see them. My head's in the noose with this tasking."

"Jesus, oh Jesus..." I gasped and suddenly felt weak, like I was going to pass out.

"Damn it, Colt, get ahold of yourself. If Maggie sees you freaking out she'll know something bad is up."

I felt my stomach roll and dashed outside. Thank God I made it to the woods before losing my meal in several convulsive bursts.

Scotty came out holding his bottle of beer. "Swirl the beer around in your mouth and spit it out. Pull yourself together and do it now."

Pat saw me run out the front door and then Scotty coming after me. He left the house and began looking for us. "Colt! Scotty!"

"We're over here," Scotty quietly said.

Pat saw me propped against a tree, looking ghastly. "What's going on?"

"Sir, you tell my friend to straighten his ass up right now."

"Colt, what happened?"

I bent over and hurled again. "Colt, are you sick?"

"He's not sick, sir. I just told him where in Afghanistan I'm going to be deployed. Drink some more beer, Colt."

I stood up and leaned against the tree. "Damn, Scotty. Damn, damn, damn."

"Sergeant Mercer, you get yourself squared away and I mean now. Maggie will NOT see you this way."

"Scotty, where are you going?"

"Sir, I don't want you freaking out on me too. Let's just say that my other three tours will seem like a vacation compared to this place."

"How long, Scotty?" I asked between gulps of air. "How long will you be there?"

"Maybe six months. Maybe more."

"Dear God..." I couldn't say more.

"Scotty, you have my word that Annie and I will look after your wife and kids while you're away."

"Thank you, sir. Maggie has a real good support system with the wives of others who are deploying, but I appreciate your offer."

"Damn it, Scotty, I told you to get out after Manny bought it." I felt the anger welling up in me.

Scotty grabbed my shoulders and pinned me hard against the tree. "Don't you go there, not now. We've been down that road. I'm asking you, as my friend and brother, to collect yourself so my wife won't have to endure any more anguish than she already has to bear. I'm on the edge myself, trying to keep it together, so I'm begging you."

He cut through with that remark. He was right. Maggie and the kids didn't need any more to worry about. I looked him in the eye and nodded okay. "Scotty, you know if I could, I'd put on the uniform and head out with you tomorrow."

"I know you would. I promise I'll do my best to keep my head down. There's no way I'm going to offer to go outside the wire. I'll do my liaising from behind a fortified wall."

I stood up and tried my best to regain my shaky balance. "Pat, if you don't mind, could I have a few minutes alone with my friend?"

"Sure. I'll tell Maggie you're talking to Scotty about the Grand Adventure."

I waited until he walked away. I drank more beer. My stomach was iffy regarding further eruptions. I looked at my friend. "Scotty, there's some things that need to be said between us. I'll never forgive myself if you don't come back and I haven't said these things to you."

"What do you have to say? We don't have much time before Maggie and the kids come looking for me."

"Scotty, I could go on all night about how good a friend you are, but you already know that. I just want to say that I love you, my brother, and I thank you for everything you've done for me. After my parents died you saved my soul. You saved my soul." I wanted to shout to the heavens how important this man was to me. I kicked myself for not being able to find the words that would convey what I needed to say. But, those kinds of words didn't exist.

"Colt, you're everything I could ever want in a friend. I'm honored to call you my brother. If I don't come back, just know that I'll be watching over you and my family. Now, I want you to stand tall and go back into that house with me like we haven't got a care in the world. My family is the most important thing I have on this earth, and I want them to remember me with a smile on my face and not panic in my eyes." He was fighting to hold back his tears. "Tomorrow, I want you to do me a favor. Don't come to the deployment ceremony because you're on a hair-trigger emotionally, and I don't want you falling apart in front of my family. Instead, be with Maggie and the kids afterward. The first day I leave is always hardest on her, and she could use your support. I want you to be calm around her tomorrow. Don't cry in your beer with her, okay?"

"Okay, Scotty. I promise I'll rise to the occasion. Only you'll know how I'm feeling. Let's go back and act like we've been having a ball talking about old times."

"That's the spirit." He gave me a playful slap on the back. I smiled meekly and nodded my head.

We walked into the house laughing and pushing each other around. Everyone laughed when I fell on my butt after Scotty gave me a good push. Pat caught on to what we were doing and laughed at the two fools.

Scotty said he needed to head home for some last minute packing. Jamie and Brian followed his lead, and I asked if they'd take Jekyll home with them. Jamie caught on to that request and gave me a look asking if everything was alright. I slightly shook my head negatively as I was smiling. Only she could see my gesture. She nodded her understanding and, not missing a beat, smiled and laughed like she hadn't a care in the world. She got her family out quickly with Jekyll in tow.

I didn't walk with the Moreys to their car. Instead, I smiled and waved from the front porch. After Scotty helped Maggie get in the car, he closed her door and looked at me. He mouthed the words *thank you* and I nodded in reply acting happier than a pig in mud. They drove off and I walked back into the house. Katie and Jen were laughing on the couch and I forced a smile when they saw me.

Pat looked at the two girls. "Katie, you and Jen need to go over to her house so we can clean up. You can spend the night."

"Oh, cool, Daddy!"

Annie looked at Pat with an odd expression. He never once told Katie to go over to Jen's house. Katie and Jen made a mad dash to her room and came running out, each holding safari essentials. They were gone in a flash.

"Pat, did you clear this with Jen's parents?"

He shook his head no. When Annie saw me sitting ashen on the couch she caught on that something was wrong. "Let me call Jen's mom and I'll be right back."

Pat came over and sat next to me. He put an arm around me. I knew if I started crying now, I'd never stop. Annie joined us on the couch. "The news isn't good," Pat said to her. "Scotty was told he's being deployed to a hellhole in Afghanistan."

"I'm so sorry, Colt. I thought things were getting better over there."

I looked at her. "No Annie, they aren't. They're sending Scotty to a place where odds are staggeringly high that he'll be coming back in an aluminum box. Not even God would feel safe where they're sending him."

"I can't imagine how he must feel. I couldn't tell a thing by looking at him."

"I know. He kept it from me too, until just a few minutes ago."

"What can we do?" said Pat. "I don't think you should be alone."

"Would you mind me staying here tonight? I think if I go home I'm going to lose it."

"Sure," said Annie, "you can stay in the guest room."

"The couch is fine, Annie. I won't be sleeping."

"Why don't you let me pour you a good stiff drink."

"No, dear," Pat said shaking his head. "He has an empty stomach."

"But we just ate."

"He lost his meal outside."

"Oh. Okay then, how about me getting you an antacid and a glass of water?"

I nodded and she went to the kitchen to get them. I chewed a couple and knocked down some water to kill the chalky taste. "You know, it's getting late and I'd really appreciate just being able to sit here and reflect for a while."

"Okay. I know what you're going through," said Pat.

"No, you don't." My anger leaped into my vocal chords. "You have no idea what I'm going through. No offense sir, but things look a whole lot different when you're at forty-thousand feet over a war zone compared to being on the ground, experiencing savagery and carnage firsthand. Scotty and I have seen things that I once thought could only happen in hell. You have no idea, none."

"Colt, I wasn't in the air over there. I was on the ground, and I do know, certainly not as much as you or Scotty, but I know. I lost three airmen and had to call their parents to tell them the news."

"I'm sorry, sir. That was disrespectful and unwarranted. Please forgive my anger for surfacing." He nodded, silently accepting my apology.

"We'll give you some space," said Annie. "There's plenty of stuff in the fridge if you get hungry or need something to drink. If you need us, knock on our door. We'll pray for Scotty and his family."

"Thanks Annie. I'll be praying for them too."

They turned off the lights except for the one next to the couch. Annie kissed me on my forehead and, without saying a word, retreated to the bedroom.

I sat there and started thinking about when I first met Scotty and all the things we'd done. We grew from kids to men together. I was there when he married and I was there to see him proudly introduce me to his firstborn. I remember holding Julianna in my arms when she was one day old, and being so scared I might drop her that I was shaking. But not Scotty. He was always fearless. Kids, combat, you name it, Scotty was the man. I guess that's why it rattled me so much when he told me tonight he was on the edge. Rocks don't crumble, or so I thought. Manny not making it shattered his invincibility notion. With Scotty, it was always the stupid, careless guy next to him that would buy the farm. Well, Manny wasn't stupid and Manny wasn't careless. Manny was the best of the best. I hoped Scotty would stay true to his word and keep his ass down, but I knew he was never one to cower in a corner.

I felt a surge of guilt for getting out while Manny and Scotty soldiered on. What both of them needed was me by their side watching their six. How many others may be dead right now because I wasn't there to protect them? God, I could go crazy thinking about these things. I shut my eyes, and wearily massaged my temples with the heels of my hands. It was going to be a long night. I reached over and turned off the light. Even though it was late, there was still enough sunlight for me to see.

I heard voices at the front door and then the sound of a key quietly being inserted into the lock. The doorknob twisted and Katie poked her head in. She saw me sitting there and ducked out again. I heard her say goodbye to someone. She tiptoed over, sat down, and leaned in close to whisper in my ear. "It took me a while to figure out something wasn't right. Daddy never says I can go with Jen. He always says that's for Momma to decide."

"You're very perceptive. Does Jen's mom know you left?"

"She walked me to the door. What's wrong, Colt?"

I looked at her and tried to decide what to say. The truth seemed the only proper thing to say. "Just before he left, Scotty told me that they're sending him to a dangerous place in Afghanistan. The kind of place you won't come back from."

She could see my lips quivering. I was trying with all my might to control my tears. She got up, went to her bedroom, and came out with a pillow and blanket. She sat at the end of the couch and put the pillow on her lap. She knew I knew what this meant—I did the same thing with her not that long ago. I slid over and put my head on the pillow. She tossed her blanket on me. "It'll be okay, Colt," she whispered. "Trust me, it will be okay."

I suddenly felt very tired...

I awoke the next morning with my head still on Katie's lap. Annie and Pat were now there, quietly sitting in chairs across from the couch. "Good morning, Colt," said Annie with a tender smile.

I sheepishly sat up. Katie looked me over to see how I was doing. When I smiled at her, she returned the smile and then got up and hugged her mom and dad. She went to take a shower without saying a word.

"She had Jen's mom walk her home last night after figuring out something wasn't right. She stayed up all night with me. That's one very special young lady."

"You're her brother," said Annie. "She'd walk through fire for you."

I could see the pride on Pat's face. It's not often when a teenager does something noble and his little girl just showed what she's made of. We sat for a while without saying a word.

Katie came bounding out of the bathroom looking all peaches and cream and no worse for wear. "Can we have pancakes for breakfast, Momma, with blueberries?"

"Sure, Sweetie. Do you like blueberry pancakes, Colt?"

"Yes ma'am. That'd be great."

Annie headed into the kitchen with her arm around Katie. I saw her giving Katie a thumbs-up. It made me smile.

Pat looked at me. "Colt, Annie and I still want to come with you to say goodbye to Scotty."

"Sir, he doesn't want me to come because he's afraid I'll lose it. Instead, he asked me to look in on Maggie after she gets back from seeing him off."

"Scotty impresses me on many fronts. He's a good guy."

"I know, sir. They come no better."

We sat down for breakfast. Katie wolfed down her stack of pancakes, excused herself, kissed us goodbye, and left to pick up Jen for school. "Goodbye, brother!" she yelled as she ran out the door.

"Did I already say how special that girl is?"

"You did," said Pat. "We're seeing some incredible growth in her. The difference in our little girl between the abduction and now is stunning. And the remarkable thing is it's all for the good."

"She'll be a fine young woman soon. I don't envy you guys when she goes to college. Every male for miles around will be trying to win her heart."

"Well, that's no problem. Annie and I know Krav Maga."

I laughed. "Can you imagine the guy who tries to come on to her after she says no? He'll be on the ground so fast it'll make his head spin." We all laughed.

"Well, you guys, I need to run home to get cleaned up. Please tell Katie how grateful I am for her being there last night. I'd be a mess this morning if it wasn't for her."

I got home and checked in with the Gilgrens, telling them what happened and how Scotty asked me to look in on Maggie after she got home from seeing him off. I then told them it might be nice to take the Moreys and Lilly to McDonalds for a Happy Meal and ice cream to help take their minds off saying goodbye to their dad. While I did that, they could go see Rosanna with Jekyll. They said it sounded like a plan. I took Jek home and gave him some attention.

At 10:30, I gave Maggie a call. She was on her way home with the kids. I could tell she had been crying. I asked her to meet me and Lilly at the McDonalds on Tudor and she agreed. I then took Jekyll over to the Gilgrens. They put Lilly's car seat in my ride. I asked them to call me if they decided to adopt the pup and I'd tell Lilly the story of Finley von Bickerstaff to prepare her for him. We headed off, leaving Jekyll looking puzzled for not taking him.

We met in the McD parking lot and walked in. The kids dashed to the play land and Maggie and I took a seat nearby to monitor them. She didn't feel like talking. I held her hand while we watched the kids happily playing in the pen filled with balls. Sophie and Lilly were becoming as tight as Katie and Jen. I ordered a bunch of Happy Meals and the kids pounced on them like Jekyll going after his Blue Buffalo.

After the meal, Maggie ordered ice cream cones and we became a mob of cone-licking fools.

Jamie called, saying how cute the puppy was and that Jekyll was having the time of his life playing with his cousin from Shaktoolik. I was given the okay to spring the story on Lilly. Maggie decided this was a good time to say goodbye. I told her I'd drop by later and to call me if she needed anything.

I took Lilly into the non-play area and told her the amazing story of Finley von Bickerstaff, and how Jekyll thought that only she could love this puppy because she was such a special girl. Lilly excitedly said yes to adopting Finley, and promised to love him just like she loved Jekyll. I asked if she wanted to meet Finley and her eyes widened. She started clapping and squealing, "Yes! Yes! Yes!"

On the way home she drilled me regarding Finley. Where is Shaktoolik, what does Finley von Bickerstaff eat, does Finley von Bickerstaff like carrots, does Finley von Bickerstaff have funny ears like Jekyll, does…? I marveled at how many questions a child could ask.

We pulled in and I heard the familiar "yoo-ee-ooo-ee-ooowoo" followed by a series of squeaky yips. When Lilly saw both her old and new loves, she erupted. "Finley von Bickerstaff! Jekyll von Bickerstaff!" The von Bickerstaff dynamic duo showered her with pure love. Jamie and Brian watched with tears in their eyes. I needed to get Jekyll out of there for Lilly to be with FvB, so I braved an encounter with the rolling mass of boundless bliss. "Lilly! Oh Lilly! Do you like your new puppy?"

"Look, Mr. Colt! Here's Finley von Bickerstaff. He looks just like Jekyll von Bickerstaff!" She scooped up the little dog and brought him to my face. "Don't you just love him?"

I picked him up and looked him over. "I do. He sure is a cute pup." Jekyll was yodeling and jumping up on me with sheer delight. He adored his little cousin from Shaktoolik. The pup looked like he was handling all the attention quite well.

Jamie and Brian came up. "Momma, Finley von Bickerstaff is from Shacaooleelicklick and Jekyll wants me to adopt him because only I know how to love little dogs, huh Jekyll?"

"Yee-ar-ooo!"

"See, Mommy. I just have to have him."

"Well, Lilly, you'll have to love Finley a lot and help clean up after him. Do you think you can do that?"

"I can, Mommy. Only I can love him the right way. Ask Jekyll von Bickerstaff."

"We already did, baby. Jekyll says you have a special love for dogs."

"I do! I really know how to love them, Mommy."

Lilly was so engrossed with the puppy that she scarcely noticed us leaving. It looked like the bonding between her and the pup was immediate. I still had Lilly's car seat, so I pulled it out and brought it back.

"Colt, look at them," said Jamie. "The answer to Jekyll leaving was so obvious. I can't believe we didn't think of getting a puppy. Your cover story is just so precious and funny. Thank you for making this happen. Oh, Rosanna said to tell you everything's fine with Jekyll and you can come in any time for your pedicure."

I smiled. "I'm going to miss her."

"She's great, and bless her, she's giving us a discount for taking Finley on."

"That sounds like Rosanna."

"Hey, Colt, how are you doing?" said Brian.

"I'm pushing myself to keep going and have a ton of things to do. I don't see how I'll get everything done by Saturday."

"We plan on coming over tonight to clean your place. In fact, if you give me your key now, I'll run our Dyson through the place."

I handed the key to him. "Thanks Brian. I really appreciate this."

"Cleaning your apartment is more than a fair trade for all the things you've given us. We'll have it gleaming by tomorrow night."

"Brian, I'm not sure when I'll be back. I feel like I'm taking advantage of you guys by not being here to clean the apartment."

"Colt," said Jamie, "this has been a draining week for you. Truly, your place is nothing to clean. Stay away as long as you want and don't worry about it."

"Thanks so much, you two. I'm so, so glad Lilly found a new friend."

"We are too. Be sure to tell Annie what happened."

"I will. God, I've got so many things to do."

"Get out of here, Colt."

"Yes, ma'am." Jekyll and I headed to Pat and Annie's. Katie and Jen happily agreed to watch Jek while Annie, Pat and I went to the bank to add them to my account. On the way we ignored any talk of Scotty's send-off. I filled them in on Finley von B. and Lilly. Annie earlier told

Pat about the cover story and he thought it was hilarious. My disposition didn't favor levity. I could only muster a half-hearted smile.

At the bank, we had to wait in line, which wasn't good since my patience level was low. A lady ahead of us apparently couldn't make up her mind on what she wanted. I felt like screaming *hurry the hell up!*

"Patience, Grasshopper," Pat said after seeing my face turning red.

"What did one vulture say to the vulture next to him?" I asked.

Pat shook his head indicating he hadn't a clue.

"Patience, my ass."

A half-hour later we were back at their house after taking care of business. Annie made a simple meal of grilled cheese sandwiches with a salad. While eating, we talked about the things I had left to do before leaving on Saturday. Pat suggested letting Jekyll stay with them so I could clean my place and do all the last-minute things without having any interruptions. I agreed. I stopped by the Moreys to make sure they were okay, and then went home to find Jamie and Brian hard at work in my place. Lilly was having a grand time playing with her new furry friend. With the help of my friends, we had the apartment sparkling by eight. After they left, I sat on the couch and used the quiet time to program my friends' phone numbers and email addresses into my new iPhone. I sent Scotty an email letting him know Maggie was okay. After downloading a few apps and playing around with them, my eyelids got heavy so I went to bed.

I woke up gasping with the familiar nightmare of me holding Johnny in my arms with a bullet hole between his eyes. Only this time it wasn't Johnny. It was Scotty. A tsunami of fear coursed through me. I prayed that God would spare my friend from harm.

22

THE ALARM CLOCK jarred me awake. I felt groggy and drained. A shower helped. I headed to Pat and Annie's to complete packing the Trike for the journey. Annie wanted to make breakfast for me so I called saying I was on my way. While driving, I mentally ran through everything needing to be done in terms of leaving. Earlier, I had given notice to the utility companies and asked the post office to forward my mail to the Brennans. I couldn't think of anything else to do.

Jekyll bounded out and greeted me with some power licks. He was glad to see me and the feeling was mutual. Annie had crème brûlée French toast and fruit on the table. It practically melted in my mouth. Katie offered Jek a nice chunk of it, which he wolfed down. He gave her some inspired farewell yodels when she left for school.

Pat and Annie had taken time off from work to help me get on my way. Between this and the leave they took for Katie, I'm sure they wouldn't be having much of a vacation this year. It made me feel special.

After cleaning up and putting away the dishes, we went to the garage, which we were using as the Grand Adventure storage depot. Over the last few weeks, I'd visited motorcycle touring sites on the net and had seen what they recommended to take on extended trips. From that, I put together a checklist and we had all the stuff laid out on the garage floor. Key items included my driver's license, passport, birth certificate, Jekyll's vet papers, motorcycle registration, proof of insurance, Canadian nonresident vehicle liability insurance, and photocopies of everything. Plus, there was camping gear, clothes, and food.

We went through the checklist item by item and packed the stuff into the Trike. After four hours, we were nearly done. Annie made lunch while Pat and I finished up.

"Geez," said Pat. "This has required as much planning as a military operation."

"I know, sir. My Army field training sure is coming in handy for the Grand Adventure."

"Let's go in and have some chow. I'm hungry."

"Me, too. Why you don't weigh 400 pounds with her cooking escapes me."

"Moderation, my boy. Everything in moderation."

I laughed. "That's a concept Jekyll never mastered."

Annie wasn't finished with the meal when we walked in so I sat down with Pat and showed him a few of my downloaded apps.

"Did you know that you can use Siri to write and send your emails?" asked Pat.

"No, sir. Can you show me how to do that?"

"Sure. You start here..."

To my amazement, Siri, the iPhone genie, listened to what I said, wrote it down, and sent the email to Pat's iPhone. I felt like a caveman who had just woken up in this century.

"Colt, did you know you have some email?"

"No, sir. How do you open them?"

"Easy. You do it like this. Hey, you have an email from Scotty."

He handed me the phone and I started reading it. "Oh, no."

"What is it?" said Annie with a look of concern.

"A truck bomb injured eighty soldiers in eastern Afghanistan." I kept reading. "It was in the Wardak province just outside Outpost Sayed Abad. Lots of destroyed shops. Oh, my God!"

"What?" demanded Annie.

"Because of the casualties, Scotty's unit has been reassigned as replacements for the ones being evacuated. Scotty's liaison tasking with the Brits is cancelled. He's going to Outpost Sayed Abad with the others! It's a *good* outpost. The protective barriers around it absorbed most of the truck bomb's explosive force and the damage is reparable. He's jazzed about going there! Oh, yeah! Oh, yeah! Thank you, God!"

I leaped up and hugged Annie and then Pat. I grabbed Jekyll and danced around the room. God had answered my prayer.

"Colt, I don't mean to be a party-pooper here, but this news seems a bit like *'other than that, Mrs. Lincoln, did you like the play?'* Eighty soldiers got injured. Why is Scotty going there good news?"

"Sir, I've been to Outpost Sayed Abad and it's built like a fortress. It absorbed a big-ass truck bomb with no one getting killed. Compared to where Scotty was going, this place is immensely safer. I'm so, so happy!" I hugged Annie again. I'm calling Maggie to tell her the good news."

"You might want to leave off the part about eighty soldiers being wounded."

"Right. Good idea." I called Maggie. From the animation in my voice, she knew I was stoked about it being a good place for him to be. I didn't mention the hellhole he nearly got sent to.

After lunch, I went to the Moreys. While Jekyll played with the kids, I told Maggie more about Scotty's new outpost, focusing on how safe it was. The relief on her face was palpable.

Pat and Annie wanted to treat me to one last dinner with the family, so I said goodbye to the Moreys around six-thirty and headed back over. The Last Supper would be an encore performance of Eddie's grilled ribs. We talked well into the evening about my planned route. Jen came over and Annie made popcorn with real butter. Now there's a treat if ever there was one. At eleven, I reluctantly said goodbye and Jek and I headed home.

I went to bed happy and said "thank you" out loud to God for answering my prayer for Scotty. Tomorrow we were starting the Grand Adventure. I said one last prayer, and that was to find my noble purpose.

23

MY SLEEP WAS far from restful. I tossed and turned all night, mentally running through my packing checklist and where each item was stowed. Not satisfied, I repeated the process again and again in an obsessive-compulsive meltdown. Jekyll, in contrast, slept peacefully. His checklist consisted of Blue Buffalo and carrots, so he had nothing to fret over.

I got up and took a shower. Afterward, I used my towel to wipe down the bathroom surfaces to ensure everything looked good for the landlord inspection. Jekyll crawled out of bed and greeted me with a yawn and stretch. "Hey boy, welcome back to the living. Today is the big day. Are you ready?"

"Woof!" He ran to the front door. After doing his business, he raced over to Lilly's apartment and unleashed a power yodel.

"No, Jek! It's too early to play with Lilly and Finley." A second later the door flew open, and out came Fin and Lilly, in her pajamas and barefoot. Jekyll bellowed joyously.

"Hi, Mr. Colt! Finley von Bickerstaff sleeps with me, did you know that?"

"I didn't. Does he sleep through the night?"

"He does, and I make sure to hug him before he goes to sleep."

"I bet he likes that, sweetheart. You know, today is the day Jekyll and I leave on our big adventure. We're sure going to miss you."

"I'll miss you too. Will you be back next week?"

"No, Sweetie. We're going to be gone for a long time, but I promise I'll write and tell you how we're doing."

"But I can't read, Mr. Colt."

"We can ask your mom to read the words for you. Will that work?"

"Yes. Mommy is a good reader."

"Good, I'll try to send you some pictures too."

Jamie came out looking groggy. "I thought I heard the front door open."

"Sorry, Jamie, Jekyll broadcast a hello yodel and Lilly came right out."

"Do you have everything ready at your place?"

"Almost. I'll make the bed and that should do it. Hopefully, there'll be no issues."

"Don't worry. Your place looks immaculate."

"Do you want me to watch Lilly and the fur balls so you can get some more sleep?"

"No, I'm awake now. Why don't you let Jekyll come over to spend a little more time with Lilly and Finley."

"Sounds good. Jek, do you want to play with Lilly and Finley?"

"Woof!"

"Come on, Jekyll von Bickerstaff! Let me show you where Finley sleeps with me."

Just like that, the von Bs were running with Lilly into her place.

"Are you okay regarding breakfast?"

"I am. Annie and Pat want me to have breakfast with them. I appreciate you guys offering to take me over."

"No problem. I'll wake Brian so we can get ready to take you."

"Thanks, Jamie. You know, I'm going to miss you all immensely."

"We'll miss you too. You have our email, so drop us a few lines to let us know how you're doing."

"I will. I promised Lillybean I'd write to her."

"She'd love that. Do you think you'll come back after your adventure?"

"Good question. Right now, nothing is set in stone. One of these days, I'll have to entertain the notion of working for a living. Or, maybe I'll stop in Vegas and seek my fortune there. I'll have to play the penny slots because that'll be all I can afford."

She laughed. "Hey, remember us when you're rich and famous."

"I will. You guys are friends forever. Send Jek over if he starts driving you nuts."

"He'll be fine. See you after the landlord."

I went back and did a final spit-shine of the place. The landlord came and was happy. Per my request, he gave me the $700 security deposit in cash. I planned to use it as fuel money for the first leg of the trip. I handed him the keys and shook his hand. With that, the Grand Adventure had begun.

At the Gilgrens, I gave Brian the keys and title to my Honda. They were ready to go, and we walked to their car.

"Mr. Colt, will you sit with me and the doggies?"

"I'd love to, Lilly."

On the way, Lilly didn't grasp that this was the final goodbye, but I did. My throat started to tighten. I held her hand the whole way. By the time we pulled into Pat and Annie's driveway, my eyes were brimming with tears. I got out and gave Brian and Jamie goodbye hugs. Then it was time to say goodbye to Lilly. Pat and Annie came out and stood on the porch.

"I love you very much, Lillybean. You're my best friend, you know."

"I love you too, Mr. Colt. Can I say goodbye to Jekyll von Bickerstaff?"

"You can. He'd like that a lot."

I gave her a long hug and then turned to Jekyll. "Okay, boy, it's time to say goodbye."

Lilly scooped him up and hugged him. She started crying. "I love you so much, Jekyll von Bickerstaff. You're my friend." He tenderly licked her cheek.

"Lilly, we have to go now. Give Jekyll one last hug."

"Oh Momma, no, no." This was killing me. I was breaking this little girl's heart. Lilly reluctantly brought Jekyll to me, giving him a kiss on his muzzle. I put him down and gave her a final hug. Jekyll then did something extraordinary. He went over to Finley and gently picked him up by the scruff of his neck and dropped him in front of the crying little girl.

"Woof!"

"Jekyll says he wants you to love and take care of Finley for him," I said, doing my best to ad-lib the tender scene.

"I will, Jekyll von Bickerstaff," she said, trying to hold in her sobs. "I'll love Finley von Bickerstaff just like I love you."

"Woof!" With that final bark, Jek ran over to Pat and Annie. Annie scooped him up and waved to the Gilgrens. Jamie helped Lilly and Finley into the back seat and then blew me a kiss. Jekyll began yodeling softly and poignantly. It touched my heart. I stood in the driveway and waved to Lilly. She was holding Finley and wiping tears from her eyes. As their car went around the corner, she waved to me. I waved back and then they were gone. I looked at Pat and Annie. They could see the pain in my face. Annie gave Jekyll to Pat and came to me. She hugged me without saying a word. Pat took Jek inside.

"I truly love that little girl."

"I know you do. I know you do." She hugged me a little longer. "You need to go on this trip, Colt. I know it's hard, but you're doing the right thing. I feel it deep inside. Come on, let's go in."

Katie and Jen were in the living room, both in tears. They had watched the goodbye from the window. They gave me a hug.

"All right, everyone, enough of the sad faces," said Pat. "This is the start of Colt's Grand Adventure and we need to celebrate it."

"You're right, sir. This should be a special day."

"Okay then," said Annie. "Let's start breakfast. Colt, I'm making a stick-to-your-ribs meal that'll have you feeling full for five hundred miles. The menu includes breakfast burritos, hash browns, and pecan waffles."

"Wow. After this meal I should get to Canada before being hungry again."

We all dug in. I made no effort to disguise my appetite, and didn't start losing steam until after the second burrito and fifth waffle. I knew this would be the last good meal I'd have for a long time. Katie and Jen were impressive with what they consumed, and Pat did his part to make sure there were no leftovers. Jekyll sampled the entire fare and appeared to favor the hash browns. Of course, I had to put catsup on them to satisfy his discriminating palate. Annie packed a lunch for me, which seemed like complete overkill given the way my waistline had expanded. But, I was grateful to have an easy meal on my first day.

Katie and Jen took roost on either side of me in the living room.

"So, Colt, how will you go to the bathroom?" said Jen, playfully.

"I won't. I'll just hold it for a month or two."

"Yuk. No really, what'll you do?"

"Well Jen, number one is easy, especially on a lonely road. Number two, well, I guess I'll need to find a place with trees or bushes."

"Gross. And what about a shower?"

"Hmmm. I was planning on stopping once a week at a campground that has showers. Or even jump in a creek or lake when I get to warmer parts of the country. Maybe once a week is too ambitious. I might try once a month. What do you think?"

"OMG! No one will be able to get near you. People in cars will have to hold their noses when you pass them."

"I once went thirty-eight days without a shower in Iraq. That's my record, and it got over 120 degrees in the desert."

"I'll never join the Army, that's for sure."

"Will you email us, Colt?" Katie asked. The seriousness of her tone evaporated the levity.

"I will, Katie. I promise. But, I'll likely be spare with sending emails. The whole idea of my trip is to have time to think about things. I'll probably email something to your mom and she can forward it to you guys. You can email me whenever you want, but please be patient for replies."

"I don't get it," said Jen. "Why do you have to go on a big trip?"

"Jen," said Annie, "Colt has known nothing but the Army since he got out of high school. He's going on this trip for a lot of reasons, and one of them is to think about what he wants to do for the rest of his life."

"You should be a teacher," Jen replied. "Everyone at school thinks you're cool."

"My dad was a teacher, but I don't have the patience he did. I might eat unruly kids for lunch." I grabbed her and pretended to bite her arm. She giggled.

"Jen," said Annie, "if you don't mind, could we have some time with Colt?" We want to say goodbye to him as a family. Katie can come over after he leaves."

"Uh, okay. Are we still going to see a movie today?"

"Yes," said Katie. "We can see two if we go to the matinee."

"Sounds good. Maybe I can talk my mom into a Taco Bell contribution." She gave me a hug. "I hope you have a good time and get to shower at least once a week."

"Thanks, Jen. I'm glad you're concerned about my smell factor." She laughed and said goodbye to Jekyll before leaving.

None of us said anything for a while. Annie took Jen's spot on the couch. "I promised myself not to make a scene, but I can see the futility of that notion."

"I'm going to miss you all so much."

"Colt, will you really miss me?" Katie asked hesitantly.

I stood up. "Come on, sweetheart. Let's go outside." I led her out the back door. "Let's walk to the inlet." I took her hand and we started walking on the dirt trail in the woods. I stopped about halfway there and looked at her. "Katie, I'm so proud of you, and I love you so much. You truly are a special person. Instead of being sad about me going, will you please be excited for me, and say a prayer that I find what I'm looking for?"

"I'll try, Colt, but I'm going to miss you so much." A tear rolled down her cheek.

"Me too, but I need to do this. I've had a hard life and feel so lost right now. I hope to find some kind of clue, out there, about what I should do."

"You can stay here and I'll help you."

"I know you would, sweetheart. But the help I need requires something spiritual. That's why your mom and dad are supporting my trip. Do you understand?"

"I suppose."

"Anyway, thank you for all you've done for me. You really came through after I got the news about Scotty. I'll never forget that."

"I'll never forget what you did for me, either."

"See, we're joined by special things."

"I love you, Colt."

"I feel it. And I love you too." I gave her a long hug. "C'mon, let's take a last look at the inlet. I bet you can see Denali today." We were rewarded with a magnificent view of the Alaska Range. "Katie, I'm so optimistic about you and your future. I know you'll love college, and trust me, the guys will be swooning over you."

"Do you really think I'm pretty?"

I looked at her, surprised. "Are you serious?"

"Yes." She squirmed a bit.

I could see she wasn't quite sure of herself. "Katie, you know I don't blow daisies, and I'll tell you like it is, right?" She nodded. "Well, I'm telling you straight up, you're one of the most beautiful young ladies I've ever laid eyes on. Your freckles and red hair would have me weak-kneed if I was ten years younger. Trust me, you're beautiful, and you'll grow up to be a stunningly attractive woman. I hope you'll never get caught up in your beauty and think you're better than others because of it. Just remember that physical beauty is fleeting, but true beauty will last forever. Katie, you're beautiful inside and out. You're the real deal."

"Thanks, Colt. I won't forget all the things you taught me."

"Sweetheart, if you ever need to talk, call or email me. I'll always be there for you."

"You can call me too. Even at night. I'll always be there for you too."

"Sounds like a plan. Now, we better go back before your mom and dad send out a search party. Wanna race?" I didn't wait for an answer and began running back to the house.

"Hey, no fair!" she laughed as she sprinted after me. By the time we got back to the house, we were both out of breath and laughing. We walked in finding Pat and Annie in tears.

"Uh, oh. You guys aren't going to make this difficult, are you?" Annie didn't say a thing. She dabbed her eyes with a tissue.

"So, do I get a turn to be with you?" Pat asked.

"Sure. Do you want to go to the garage and get the MLC ready?"

He nodded. "I'll be back in a little while, okay, my lovely wife?"

She smiled meekly and nodded her head. "Colt, wait a second. I have one more thing for you to take." She picked up a book from the coffee table. "Pat's mom gave me this journal when I was twelve years old. She told me to write down anything that touched my heart." She stroked the book with reverence, as if it had magical powers. "The quotes and sayings in here resonate within me. I want you to have it on your journey. I think the words will help you as well."

"Annie, are you sure? I know this means a lot to you."

She smiled and handed me the book, whose ragged edges affirmed years of wear. Katie came over and took her hand. "Momma treasures her little book, you know."

"I'll treasure it too." I looked Annie in the eye as I spoke, to let her know that I understood the enormity of her gift.

"Go on out, you two," she said to Pat and me as she brought a tissue again to her eyes.

I followed Pat and he raised the garage door. Sunlight flooded the space as the door rose. The Harley looked great and was ready to go.

"I went over it last night, Colt. The tire pressures are fine and you're good to go on fuel and oil."

"Thanks for doing that, sir." I looked at him. His eyes were moist and red. "Pat, I can't thank you enough for all you've done. It still feels like a dream, the way you and your family took me in. I'll never forget you. If something happens to me, just know how much I love you all."

He gave me a long hug. "Look what you did for our family. For that, I'll be eternally grateful. I pray you'll find what you're seeking."

"I hope I find it too, but right now, I haven't a clue where to even look."

"That's where faith comes in, Colt. Never lose faith. Now, you need to be with Annie. She's taking your leaving hard. She has bonded powerfully to you, my boy."

"You're a lucky man to have her, sir. I wish one day I'll find someone like her."

"I knew Annie was the one for me before I even started to shave. Sometimes, you just know."

"Well, I guess I'm slightly retarded at picking women."

"Here's some advice on that if you permit me."

"Sure."

"Three words. *Time and deeds.* That's all you need to know if she's the one. Time and deeds."

"I'll remember that. You boiled it down to its essence."

"How about you go inside and be with Annie. Katie and I will go out back and play with von Bickerstaff."

I nodded. We went in and Pat picked up Jekyll. He motioned for Katie to come with him. She knew what he was saying. I sat next to Annie. She leaned into me.

"I hope you know how much I love you and will miss you."

"I do, Annie. I do. You know I feel the same for you."

She reached for another tissue. "Promise me you'll email us and maybe call once in a while."

"I will. But we know I need some time to just 'be.' Could I ask you a favor? Read the emails I send, and decide if you want Katie to see them or not. There may be some times when I'm despondent or mad at the world and I don't want her to be exposed to that."

"That's a good idea. I hope you don't mind if Pat and I send you a hello or two. You don't have to respond. I just want you to know we're thinking of you."

"Sure. I'd love that."

"I hope you find your noble purpose, Colt. You deserve a happy life."

"Thanks, Annie. I wish I could say I have confidence in this endeavor, but it could just as easily be a huge boondoggle."

"I'm sure Pat already told you to have faith, so I'll repeat what he said. Have faith, Colt."

I laughed weakly. "You sure know your husband. He said that very thing. I will, but during the trip, I'd appreciate you reminding me to keep the faith."

"I will. Over and over, if necessary. You better get ready to go. I'll be praying for you every night. You know all you have to do is call if you need help, or just someone to talk to."

"I know, Annie. Thank you for everything."

She stood up and gave me a tender hug. "You need to get dressed for your trip. Is there anything I can do for you?"

"No, ma'am. I'll change in the bathroom if you don't mind."

"That's fine. I'll say my goodbyes to Jekyll von Bickerstaff."

It took about five minutes to put on my gear. My riding jacket practically lit up the room with its bright color. Pat had the Weather Channel on when I came into the family room. The forecast predicted a fair day, but a front would be moving in by the evening. I might be sleeping in the rain. I looked at Jekyll, who was in Katie's embrace. "Are you ready, boy?"

"Woof!"

He leaped off Katie and ran to me. I picked him up. "Well, all that's left to do is outfitting Jek with his helmet and goggles and then we're ready to go."

"I'll give you a hand with that," said Pat.

It didn't take long to get Jekyll ready and in his harness. I hugged my family one last time, and then hit the button to start the engine. It roared to life. They all had a hand on me as I slowly pulled out of the driveway. We all were tearful. I pulled the sun visor down on my helmet to hide my tears. I was on the street now. Jekyll suddenly let loose. "Yo-eeee-oo-ee-ooh-ar-woooo-eee-oo-ee-ooh-ar-woooo!"

"Goodbye, Jekyll!" Pat yelled. I twisted the throttle and headed out, fighting the overwhelming urge to end the Grand Adventure right there. I now knew how Scotty felt when he had left his family. The feeling could be succinctly described as an immediate, gut-wrenching void.

24

THIRTY MINUTES AFTER leaving the Brennans, I was on the Glenn Highway. This stretch of road runs through Fort Richardson and offers beautiful views of the Chugach Mountains to the east. I looked at the mountains, knowing I wouldn't be seeing them for quite a while. I saw the Fort Rich/Arctic Valley exit sign ahead, and suddenly knew I had something to do. I needed to say hello to Manny. I took the exit for the big Army base, stopped at the visitor center, and got a pass to visit the National Cemetery. The guard at the front gate smiled when seeing Jekyll in his goggles and helmet and motioned me through after inspecting my pass.

At the cemetery, I parked and carried Jekyll to Manny's grave. Grass had grown on his plot, but the headstone had yet to be laid. I read where 700 WWII vets are dying each day from old age, so between them and the current war dead, the government has been busy supplying headstones to all who have served.

I kneeled and looked at Jekyll. "Jek, my brother is buried here. His name is Manny. Manny, this is my friend, Jekyll." I touched my hand to the grass. "Manny, I…" I couldn't say anything more. The morning's goodbyes and the thought of Manny being on the wrong side of the dirt hit me. I started bawling and cried nearly a half-hour. Jekyll sat quietly and let me get it out.

A lady placing flowers on a grave a few rows over saw me in tears and came over. "Would you like a flower to put on the grave?"

"That would be nice." She handed me a white rose and I placed it where the headstone should be.

"Thank you." I stood up, wiped my eyes, and tried to compose myself.

"I lost my husband last year in Iraq. He's over there."

"I lost far too many of my friends there and in Afghanistan. Far too many."

She took my hand in hers. We stood for a long while, neither of us attempting to fill the silence. A cool breeze drifted by. She looked at me with empathy in her eyes. "I'll leave you to be with your friend. God bless you."

"God bless you too. Thanks again for the flower." She smiled and walked away. I turned my attention back to my friend. "Manny, I'm going to see your parents. I'm going to see the parents of our friends too. I'm on a trip to find my soul. Maybe you could ask the 'Hombre' up there to give me a clue or two along the way. I love you, brother, and I miss you. Please look out for Scotty. I'm worried about him." I saluted my friend. "God bless you, Manny. God bless us." I pulled a coin from my pocket and placed it on his grave as a way of saying to his family that someone had visited to pay their respects. Several coins were already there. I looked at Jek. "C'mon boy, we've got a long ride ahead of us."

"Woof!"

Forty-five minutes later, we were at the George Parks Highway Junction. To the left was the town of Wasilla, and to the right, was the city of Palmer. I turned right and decided to top off the gas tank since the next town, Glennallen, was nearly 150 miles away.

I noticed a McDonalds and decided to give Jek a treat. This would be his last fries for quite a while. I must've looked foolish in my phosphorescent lime-green jacket feeding fries with catsup to a dog wearing a helmet and goggles.

I got back on the Glenn Highway and headed east. This was a mountainous region and the scenery was beautiful. The temperature was an agreeable sixty-three, and I felt comfortable with the circulation zippers closed on my jacket. After the Kenai trip, I had put a stick-on convex mirror on the inside of the windshield to see Jek. He looked like he was enjoying himself. We were making good time. After a half-hour, we drove past the spectacular King Mountain. After that came Chickaloon, a 200-person town located at the confluence of the Chickaloon and Matanuska rivers. Chickaloon was established in 1916 as the terminus of the Matanuska Valley branch of the Alaska Railroad.

I planned to stop and stretch every hour. We were getting close to that time as we got to the Matanuska Glacier, which is the source of the Matanuska River. I decided to take a side road down to the Glacier

Park resort. I'd done this before. You can drive close to the termination of the glacier and, after a short hike, be on the ice.

We had a blast playing on the glacier. Jekyll repeatedly fell when his paws lost traction, but he didn't mind. I'll never tire of the broad valley view that was carved by the glacier and the surrounding Chugach Mountains. I did a slow "360" to see the panorama. If ever there was a million dollar view, this was it. After an hour, I headed back to the Trike. Jekyll was holding a piece of ice in his mouth. I mused how the ice had been part of the glacier for over ten-thousand years. Now it was in a dog's mouth. You'd think it deserved something more than that inglorious end.

We were back on the road, and after a while reached Eureka Summit, the highest point on the Glenn Highway. The summit is the divide for three major river systems, including the 300-mile Copper River, which is world-renowned for its high quality, sumptuous salmon. Once you've tasted a Copper River red, nothing else compares.

The scenery began shifting from steep, jagged mountains to broader vistas. We rode past the Lake Louise Road Junction, where a nineteen-mile gravel road leads to this huge lake, a popular vacation spot for Alaskans. We reached Glennallen at six-thirty and I gassed up. After that, I turned north on the Richardson Highway and drove five miles up the road to the Dry Creek State Recreation Site Campground. It was time to call it a day. I checked in and got a spot to pitch my tent. The campground was nice, having toilets, fire pits, and picnic tables. My Marmot tent went up fast; it was freestanding, weighed less than three pounds, and even had a vestibule to store my motorcycle riding gear. I put my sleeping bag and pad into the tent and then changed from my road gear to Carharts and a sweatshirt.

While I did my business, Jekyll decided to greet the other twenty-odd people who were camping in everything from RVs to tents. I spotted him working the crowd and smiled at how people winced upon seeing him, but then succumbed to his charms. From a campsite with a huge RV, a high-strung, yapping Yorkie came bounding out. After a few mutual sniffs, Jekyll had a new best friend. His owners said hello. They were Robert and Karen Anderson, a nice retired couple from Calgary, Alberta. We chatted about our touring plans while the dogs played. After a while, we headed back to our humble campsite and I pulled out our food. "Ready for chow, Jek?"

"Woof!"

"Okay, here's some Blue Buffalo." I poured a cup of food into his collapsible dog dish. He gobbled it up, licked his chops, and looked at me.

"Woof!"

"Oh, come on. You're not going to start this on our first night out, are you? You got a full ration."

"Woof!"

"Would you mind letting me see what Annie packed for us? You might want a taste of that."

"Woof!" He started wagging his tail fiercely. I rolled my eyes, opened Annie's bag, and smiled. She had made a couple of PBJs, tossing in a few bags of potato chips, some boxed fruit drinks, and three packs of peanut M&Ms. Oh, yeah! I wolfed the sandwich down as quickly as Jekyll devoured his Blue Buffalo. He ate a bag of chips while I slurped down a fruit drink. Dessert consisted of M&Ms. The remaining stuff in Annie's care package would be for lunch tomorrow.

After dinner, I put all our food in a bag, and hoisted it high off the ground between two trees to keep it away from bears. That reminded me to get the pepper spray for protection in the tent at night. Clouds were rolling in from the west and it looked like rain was on the way. I got my portable shovel and did some trenching around the tent to channel away any water. To keep the Trike dry, I covered it with a tarp and used bungee cords to prevent the tarp from blowing away. It was now after ten, so we retired to the tent and I decided to send an email to the Brennans and Gilgrens.

Dear friends, had a busy day. It's after ten now and I'm camping at the Dry Creek campground just north of Glennallen. The MLC performed flawlessly today and Jek and I enjoyed the meal you packed for us, Annie. I hope the weather cooperates tomorrow, but I see clouds coming. Jekyll is having a great time and met a little dog here named Jingles. Jek says hi, Lilly, and he has a joke for you. "What happens when it rains cats and dogs? You have to be careful not to step in poodles." Yuk, yuk. I love you all and miss you enormously. God bless us. Much love, Colt.

I took off my jeans, but left my sweatshirt on because the temp had dropped to the low forties. Jekyll followed me into the sleeping bag. "Hey, boy, we made it through the first day. Let's hope the rest of our trip goes as well as today."

"Woof!" I stroked his head and he gave me a few licks on my cheek. We were tired and it didn't take long for us to be snoring. Day one of the Grand Adventure was history.

25

THE FIRST DROPS of rain fell shortly after midnight. We soon were being buffeted by forty-mile-per-hour winds and a horizontal monsoon. I opened my eyes to see Jekyll staring at me with concern. "Wow, looks like we might be testing the limits of this tent." The driving rain, coupled with the winds flapping the tent's walls, was almost as loud as an airplane. The only thing we could do was hunker down and ride it out. I decided to put on my Carharts since it'd be embarrassing to be running around in my skivvies if my tent took flight. I hoped the tarp stayed put on the Trike, but anything could happen in this mess. The sun wouldn't come up until four. Even in the land of the midnight sun, the sun still dives under the horizon. I unzipped the flap and pulled in my riding gear from the vestibule. It was wet. Argh. I'd have to dry it out before hitting the road. I lay back down and brought Jekyll in close. He was cold and appreciated my warmth. "Well, boy, let's hope we don't fly or float away." I had to shout to be heard above the din. It was hard to sleep with all the noise. After a while, the wind died down, but the rain was still heavy. I kicked myself for not bringing in my rain jacket and pants last night. My bladder began transmitting reports of being full. Note to self: have a pee bottle for times like this. After another hour I could wait no longer. "Jek, I have to drain the dragon. What about you?"

"Woof."

"Well, try not to stay out too long, okay? No puddle diving because I don't have a towel to dry you off."

"Woof!"

I put on my motorcycle jacket, opened the flap, and was greeted with cold, drenching rain. "Come on, let's get this over with." He dashed out, squatted, and waiting impatiently for me to do my thing. We were back in the tent in a couple of minutes, both looking like drowned rats. I took off my T-shirt and used it as a makeshift towel, first drying off my hair and then his fur. Being wet and cold doesn't make for happy campers. We got back to the sleeping bag and tried our best to stay warm.

Morning mercifully came and I woke up to Jekyll licking my face. He was telling me that the rain had let up and we should take care of things before it returned. "Hey, boy, let's get my rain gear and have something to eat."

"Woof."

While getting my raingear, I saw the Andersons milling about. They were breaking camp. I waved to them and Jek gave them a hello yodel. Their dog Jingles ran over and started playing with Jek. I put on my raingear, tossed the baggy with the books into the tent, and got out a few granola bars for breakfast. Robert started the engine and the big diesel began growling like an angry bear. While he was warming the engine, Karen came over with a big bag. "Hey Colt, I know you can't cook in all this rain, so I made a few things for you."

"Wow, thank you Karen. This is really nice of you to do."

"It's no problem. We have more than we need and we'll resupply in Anchorage." She scooped up Jingles, said goodbye, and went back to their RV. Robert waved, put the rig in gear, and pulled out. I waved goodbye and Jekyll broadcast a farewell yodel to Jingles, who was barking from behind the front windshield.

We watched them get on the road and disappear. I suddenly felt lonely and hoped the feeling would soon pass. "Well, boy, we'd better stretch our legs before the next rain comes." I went to the dumpster and looked in. There was a pint-sized plastic juice bottle with a locking cap. I pulled it out and now had a spiffy new pee cup. "If it keeps raining like this, I might have to teach you to use the pee cup too." He cocked his head at my remark. No sooner than I said that, the heavens opened up. We ran back to the tent and got in. I pushed the sleeping bag over and unfolded my portable chair. Jek crawled on my lap. We listened to the wind and rain. An hour later, I was bored out of my mind. "You want to see what Karen packed for us?"

"Woof!"

Oh, yeah! There were a couple of sandwiches and a big piece of cake wrapped in plastic. The cake had some orange bits in it. Carrot cake. I guess I'd be fighting the fur ball for that. Next came a big bag of corn chips and a couple of Kokanee Glacier beers. Lastly, there was a box of

Mr. Maple cookies. I was breaking a cardinal rule of Alaska camping by having food in my tent, because a bear's incredible sense of smell can detect even a crumb of food. Reluctantly, I put everything back in the bag and placed it in the vestibule. When the rain subsided, we'd have a feast, but the feast would be a good distance away from the tent.

I got out my iPhone and decided to check on the weather. There was no signal. I sighed and turned off the phone. "What now, Jek?" He went to the wadded up sleeping bag, lay down, and sighed. The rain showed no sign of easing. After another half-hour, enough was enough. I put on my rain coat and pants, and then my sandals. "Come on, Jek, let's go for a walk. I'll pack a sandwich and the carrot cake. We can eat in the toilet if we have to." He was all for getting out and wagged his tail excitedly. I pulled out the sandwich and cake, stuffed them in my pocket, and then put Jek inside my raincoat. I put the hood on my head, opened the tent flap, and stepped outside. Geez. Cold rain blew into my face and I turned my head away. Jek tried to burrow deeper in. This weather sucked. We ate lunch in the malodorous toilet. Karen had made a nice sandwich and cake. I used the facilities after we ate, so I guess there were some efficiencies to our dining arrangement. There was an overhang on the toilet building, so we stood under it for a while. Jek knew it was this or going out in the rainstorm, so he squatted on the concrete and took care of business. I used the sandwich wrapper to pick up his deposit. This wasn't the best of days.

I put Jekyll in the tent and decided to hang Karen's food in the tree with the rest of the food. I lowered my cache. It was full of water. I poured the water out and cursed. I added Karen's stuff, closed the bag again, and hoisted it up. Back in the tent, Jekyll had curled up on the sleeping bag and looked at me pitifully. "What can I say? Today sucks. Suck it up, buttercup."

I sat on my humble little chair, pissed at losing a full day of traveling. I looked around and noticed the books. "Hey, Jek, let's check out your Zen book."

"Woof!" He sat up and looked excitedly at me. I found it curious why he seemed to like this book. Maybe it had an agreeable smell.

"Okay, I'll close my eyes and open the book to a random page. Whatever we see will be what we're supposed to learn today. Fair enough?"

"Woof!"

I acted like a drama queen, closing my eyes, and dramatically turning the pages and stopping at one. I opened my eyes. "Okay, Jek, here's the perfect page for us." I looked at the page number—forty-two. "Jek, my dad was forty-two when he died." That rattled me. I hesitatingly began reading.

"A desperately sad man traveled many miles to see a wise old sage. The sage was sitting outside, relishing the sun on his face when the sad man came to his side. 'Sir, I have journeyed far to hear your learned words.' The sage nodded for the man to go on. 'Kind sir, I have endured many sufferings and fear I will never be happy. Please help me.' The sage looked with empathy at the troubled man. He pointed to the sky, filled with puffy white clouds. 'Must all these clouds be gone for me to enjoy the sun now on my face?'"

I looked at Jekyll. "That's interesting. I guess the sage was saying that your sorrows don't have to be completely gone before you allow yourself to be happy. What do you think?"

"Woof!"

"Good point. Let me read on…"

"Two monks were returning to the monastery in the evening. It had rained and there were puddles of water on the roadsides. At one place a beautiful young woman was standing, unable to walk across because of a puddle of water. The elder of the two monks went up to her and lifted her in his arms and left her on the other side of the road. Afterwards, he continued on his way to the monastery. In the evening the younger monk came to the elder monk and said, 'Sir, as monks, isn't it true that we cannot touch women?' The elder monk answered, 'Yes, brother.' The younger monk then responded, 'But then, sir, how is it that you lifted that women on the roadside?' The elder monk smiled at him and said, 'I left her on the other side of the road, but you are still carrying her.'"

I thought about the story for a while…

"Woof!"

"Sorry, Jek, I was thinking. Okay, here are a couple of insights from Buddha. *'Thousands of candles can be lighted from a single candle, and the life of the candle will not be shortened. Happiness never decreases by being shared.'* Here's the next one: *'If you light a lamp for somebody, it will also brighten your own path.'"*

I thought about Annie saying I would find a new light within me. Maybe Pat's mom lit a new light within her and she may have lit a new light in me…

I turned my attention back to the book.

"*An old farmer had worked his crops for many years. One day his horse ran away. Upon hearing the news, his neighbors came to visit. 'Such bad luck,' they said sympathetically. 'Maybe,' the farmer replied. The next morning the horse returned, bringing with it three other wild horses. 'How wonderful,' the neighbors exclaimed. 'Maybe,' replied the old man. The following day, his son tried to ride one of the untamed horses, was thrown, and broke his leg. The neighbors again came to offer their sympathy on his misfortune. 'Maybe,' answered the farmer. The day after, military officials came to the village to draft young men into the army. Seeing that the son's leg was broken, they passed him by. The neighbors congratulated the farmer on how well things had turned out. 'Maybe,' said the farmer.*"

I looked at Jekyll. He was keenly focused on me. "Do you want me to keep reading?"

"Woof."

"Okay then. Why you like Zen escapes me." I looked for where I'd left off.

"*A man was walking across a field when he heard a rustling in the tall grass beside him, and turned to see the hungry eyes of a large tiger staring at him. The man began to run, fear giving him greater speed and stamina than he knew he possessed. But always, just behind him, he could hear the easy breathing of the hungry tiger. Finally, the man stopped, not because his strength had failed but because he had come to the edge of a high cliff and could go no farther. 'I can let the tiger eat me, or take my life in my own hands and jump.' The man turned and saw the tiger slowly walking toward him, licking its mouth in anticipation. Resolved to take his own life, the man stepped to the edge of the cliff and bent his legs to jump, when he suddenly noticed a thick vine growing out of the side of the cliff, several feet from the top. Carefully, he let himself drop down the cliff face, catching hold of the vine as he slid past, and thanked God when it was strong enough to support his weight. Hanging now, the man looked up and saw the tiger's eyes peering over the edge of the cliff. It roared down at him, and then began to pace back and forth along the top of the cliff. For the first time, the man looked at the vine that had saved his life. It was thick enough for him to wrap his legs around, resting his arms, and long enough that he might be able to let himself far enough down to jump safely to the ground below. And the moment he had this thought was the same moment that he saw the second tiger, pacing back and forth at the foot of the cliff, licking its mouth, and looking hungrily up at him. Well, thought the man, if my strength and the strength of the vine are great enough, perhaps I can outwait the tigers. Surely, they'll go someplace else to eat when they're hungry enough. And the*" *man prepared to settle in for a long wait. His preparations halted quickly, however, when he heard a scurrying, scratching sound close to his own face. Glancing upwards, he saw two mice, one white and one black, emerge from a small hole in the cliff. They made their way swiftly to the base of the vine, and began to gnaw through it with their small sharp teeth. There was nothing else he could do, a tiger above, a tiger below, and the vine that kept him from their jaws about to break. The man was closing his eyes to begin his prayers, when he noticed, a little to his right, a tiny patch of red color on the face of the cliff. He reached toward it precariously, pulled, and brought his hand back beneath his eyes. There, in his palm, was a luscious, red strawberry. The man swiftly pressed the strawberry between his lips, to his tongue, and hanging between those still visible tigers, he enjoyed the finest, juiciest, sweetest meal of his life."*

I looked at Jek. "I bet if it was a carrot, you'd have gone after it too." He climbed on my lap and licked my cheek. "I'm enjoying your book, Jek. One more story and then we need to take a break."

"Two monks were washing their bowls in the river when they noticed a scorpion that was drowning. One monk immediately scooped it up and set it upon the bank. In the process he was stung. He went back to washing his bowl and again the scorpion fell in. The monk saved the scorpion and was again stung. The other monk asked him, 'Friend, why do you continue to save the scorpion when you know its nature is to sting?' 'Because,' the monk replied, 'to save it is my nature.'"

"I can relate to the monk who got stung. How about you?"

"Woof." I closed the book. "Woof!"

"What? Do you want me to keep reading?"

"Woof! Woof!"

"Jek, you're one weird dog, do you know that? Okay, I'll read one more from a random page and then I need a break. Deal?"

"Woof." I closed my eyes, thumbed through the book, and opened the page.

"A student went to his teacher and said earnestly, 'I am devoted to studying with you. How long will it take before I become enlightened?' The teacher's reply was casual. 'Ten years.' Impatiently, the student answered, 'But I want to master it faster than that. I will work very hard. I will practice every day, ten or more hours a day if I have to. How long will it take then?' The teacher thought for a moment and replied, 'Twenty years.'"

I laughed. "Sounds like me and our trip, huh? I want to find enlightenment in a hurry. Maybe I should give some thought to practicing patience." Jekyll looked in my eyes. I think he was agreeing with me.

I was tired after so little sleep last night. I folded up the chair, moved it to the side, and crawled into the sleeping bag with Jek. After we snuggled in, I stared at the top of the tent for a while, thinking about my parents and Annie and Pat. Then Lilly flashed before me and I smiled at how she always called me 'Mr. Colt.' An overwhelming sense of loneliness swept through me. I pulled Jekyll closer and fell asleep listening to the gentle sound of the rain on the tent. I mentally wrote a poem before drifting off.

So deep, this loneliness.
I pretend to ignore
this sweet, talking rain.

26

IN THE MORNING we awoke with sunlight bathing our humble abode. What a great way to start the day. The first priority was getting things dried out. I lowered our food cache and looked in. Since everything was packed in plastic bags, our food remained dry. After putting my riding jacket and rain gear out in the sun, I placed the sleeping bag on the picnic table to air out. Breakfast consisted of beef jerky and Karen's maple cookies.

While our things dried out, I tossed a stick for Jek to fetch. By nine-thirty, we were ready to go. I outfitted Jekyll with his riding gear and then put on mine. After putting him in the harness, we pulled out of the camp and headed north. As I shifted to third gear, Jekyll let out an excited power yodel. He was glad to be back on the road. So was I.

A bouncy ten miles of frost-heaved road later, we got to Gakona Junction and took the Tok Cutoff. The 125-mile long Tok Cutoff was built during the 1940's and 50's to connect the town of Tok more directly to the Richardson Highway. For those traveling on the Alaska Highway to Anchorage or Valdez, the cut-off shaved 120 miles from the total distance of the trip. We passed the trans-Alaska pipeline, which carries oil 800 miles from Prudhoe Bay on the Arctic Ocean to the pipeline terminus at Port Valdez. A few miles down the road, I pulled over to see a sweeping view of the valley and the junction of Gakona and Copper rivers. Mounts Drum and Sanford towered in the distance. It was inspiring. As we motored on, I was amazed at all the frost heaves, pavement breaks, potholes, and road tilting along the way.

We rolled into Tok nearly five hours after leaving Dry Creek. I gassed up at Fast Eddy's Restaurant, and ordered a couple of burgers, fries, and water to go. My crazy dog made me go back for catsup for his fries. My hope was to get to the Deadman Lake campground in the Tetlin National Wildlife Refuge, which was around sixty-five miles away.

The road was in much better shape than the roller coaster morning ride, but there were some seven percent grades. The weather was pleasant with a strong, cool breeze. After getting our camp set up at Deadman Lake, Jek and I took a self-guided tour on the Taiga Trail, a nice boardwalk that started at the campground and ending at an observation deck overlooking the lake. We saw a few ducks in the water and Jek greeted them with energetic yodels. The breeze died down and, suddenly, a million ravenous mosquitoes were cleared for flight. They came at us from every direction. I scooped Jekyll up and made a mad dash to the campground. Even there, the so-called 'state birds' of Alaska were swarming. I jumped into the tent and hoped the wind would kick up again.

"Geez, Jek, I've got over twenty bites on me. How about you?" He looked none too pleased. I swatted ten of the buggers that got in with us. If the wind didn't pick up again, it'd be interesting trying to get our food out to eat. I had bug juice, but it was stowed away in the Trike. Digging it out would mean a multitude of bites. I also wasn't thrilled about exposing my tush to the horde if I had to use the restroom. I sighed. "Well, boy, we're stranded for a while. How about I read something from Annie's book tonight? I'll flip through and pick a page like last night, okay?"

"Woof!"

"Okay, here we go." I closed my eyes and turned the pages. I stopped and opened my eyes. There were no page numbers, only dates. The date was April 4, 1981. All of the entries were handwritten by her, so when reading them, I would imagine her voice.

"Be patient toward all that is unsolved in your heart and try to love the questions themselves, like locked rooms and like books that are now written in a very foreign tongue. Do not now seek the answers, which cannot be given you because you would not be able to live them. And the point is, to live everything. Live the questions now. Perhaps you will then gradually, without noticing it, live along some distant day into the answer. Ranier Maria Rilke."

I looked at Jekyll. "Wow, this guy is deep. *Live the questions now.* Let's read another." I turned a few pages and came to a quote that Annie had put a smiley face next to. She must've really liked this passage.

"The first step to the knowledge of the wonder and mystery of life is the recognition of the monstrous nature of the earthly human realm as well as its glory, the realization that this is just how it is and that it cannot and

will not be changed. Those who think they know how the universe could have been had they created it, without pain, without sorrow, without time, without death, are unfit for illumination. Joseph Campbell."

Jekyll sat on my lap. I petted him and read the next entry.

"Peace originates with the flow of things—its heart is like the movement of the wind and waves. The Way is like the veins that circulate blood through our bodies, following the natural flow of the life force. If you are separated in the slightest from that divine essence, you are far off the path. Morihei Ueshiba."

"Woof!"

"I know, Jek, I liked it too." I turned the page.

"Most of us are not raised to actively encounter our destiny. We may not know that we have one. As children, we are seldom told we have a place in life that is uniquely ours alone. Instead, we are encouraged to believe that our life should somehow fulfill the expectations of others, that we will (or should) find our satisfactions as they have found theirs. Rather than being taught to ask ourselves who we are, we are schooled to ask others. We are, in effect, trained to listen to others' versions of ourselves. We are brought up in our life as told to us by someone else! When we survey our lives, seeking to fulfill our creativity, we often see we had a dream that went glimmering because we believed, and those around us believed, that the dream was beyond our reach. Many of us would have been, or at least might have been, done, tried something, if we had known who we really were. Julia Cameron."

I thought about this for a while. How was I raised? I'd have to ponder this some more. I became curious regarding what Annie's last entry was, so I flipped to the back and started reading.

"I couldn't sleep tonight because my heart is breaking. Colt is leaving in the morning. If feel like an emotional cyclone is swirling inside of me. How could I come to love someone so much in so little time? I may not have birthed him, but he is now my son and I love him with all my heart. I've cried many tears for his hurts and his pain. He has suffered far too much in his tender years. I see in him a reflection of me. I see a frightened boy in search of meaning, just as I was a frightened girl in my youth. I so wish I could surround him and protect him always with my love. When I think of Colt, I remember the words of Elisabeth Kübler-Ross. 'The most beautiful people we have known are those who have known defeat, known suffering, known struggle, known loss, and have found their way out of the depths. These persons have an appreciation, a sensitivity, and an understanding of life that fills them with compassion, gentleness, and a deep loving concern.

Beautiful people do not just happen.' Colt is a beautiful person; he just doesn't know how beautiful he is yet. I pray, God, that my son finds his way in Your loving arms."

Tears flowed as I read her words. *She called me a "beautiful person." Me.* I put the book down and hugged Jekyll.

27

A BREEZE RETURNED in the morning, keeping the mosquitoes at bay. Last night, when getting gear from the Trike, the blasted things nearly picked me up and carried me away. I decided not to have instant oatmeal because the wind might die down in the time it took to boil water, leaving us exposed once more to the hordes. Instead, I packed while eating a granola bar and the rest of the maple cookies. This wasn't the best of meals, but it was better than yesterday's dinner of beef jerky and beer.

After gearing up, we were on the road again. I loved the deep engine rumble of my Harley and how it eagerly responded to a flick of my wrist on the throttle. Jekyll was liking life again. His head was swiveling to and fro, and he barked hello to every car we passed. I glanced at him in the mirror and it made me happy to see him enjoying himself. We came to the Tetlin National Wildlife Visitor Center. I pulled in and took off Jek's goggles and helmet, but kept him in his harness. No one said anything when I walked in.

The visitor center was built in 1988 and looked like a trapper's log cabin with a sod roof. I viewed wildlife displays and liked the exhibit that lets you "travel" through the ecosystems of the refuge and interact with the history of the area.

We got back on the road and I topped off the tank at the Border City Lodge. As we neared Port Alcan, I saw a sign saying this stretch of highway was named the "Purple Heart Trail" to honor veterans wounded in battle. It made me feel good to have this beautiful area dedicated to my friends who sacrificed so much for freedom.

I passed the U.S. customs station and saw another sign saying *Welcome to Yukon*. "We're in Canada, Jek!" He gave me a bark in reply. The Beaver Creek Canada customs station was up ahead. There were about ten cars ahead of us, so I was able to stop and get out my papers. I noticed a Canadian customs officer looking at me. I suppose he didn't often witness a dog wearing a helmet and goggles yodeling a Yankee hello.

I rolled up. "Good morning, sir."

"Please turn off your engine and take off your helmet." I complied with his request. He looked me over before continuing. "Passport, driver's license, proof of Canadian nonresident vehicle liability insurance, and proof that your dog is vaccinated."

I handed him the documents. He inspected them and handed them back.

"Is the purpose of your trip business or pleasure?"

"Pleasure. I'm traveling from Anchorage to the Lower 48 on vacation."

"Where will you be going in Canada during your stay?"

"I'll be on the highway, bound for Wenatchee, Washington."

"Do you have a criminal record?"

"No, sir."

He walked around the Trike and looked at my license plate. "Purple Heart, eh?"

"Yep. Army Ranger."

"How long do you plan on being in Canada?"

"Just a few days."

"Are you bringing any firearms or explosives?"

"No."

"Are you bringing any alcohol, tobacco or gifts?"

"No."

"Any narcotic drugs or prescription drugs?"

"No."

"Woof!" Jek was looking at the guy like they were long-lost friends.

"Interesting dog you have there. Drive safely and have a nice time in our country."

"Thanks. I've always wanted to see Canada." I nodded goodbye, put the Trike in gear, and motored away.

It didn't take long to go through the nondescript border town of Beaver Creek and I was glad to be on the open road again. There wasn't a lot of traffic, which suited me fine. I hit another stretch of frost-heaved road and had to slow way down. It felt like a carnival ride in a few places. Jekyll wasn't thrilled being flung around in his harness, but he didn't voice his displeasure.

After two hours, we crossed the Donjek River Bridge. Jekyll howled the whole way across it. I think the distinct change in road noise caused by our tires being on a different surface got him fired up. Five miles later, I saw a turnout and decided we needed to stretch our legs. The view was fantastic, with mountains and a wide, silt-filled river. I saw an interpretive sign and read it to Jek. *"The Icefield Ranges include the highest and youngest mountains in Canada. They form the main group of peaks in the St. Elias Mountains and include Canada's highest mountain, Mount Logan, at 19,545 feet plus six other peaks over 16,000 feet."* I got out the map and looked for a place to camp. "Look, Jek, Burwash Landing is thirty miles away and there's a campground."

"Woof!"

"Alright, let's mount up and get going. We'll get there in thirty minutes if the road is good."

I pulled into the Dalan Campground and checked in. It had treed campsites, wood, fire pits, and water. The campground was on the north end of Kluane Lake, the largest lake in the Yukon. The guy said we didn't have to worry about bears. It was breezy, so mosquitoes weren't a problem. I started a fire and put water in a pot to boil. Dinner tonight would be two packs of freeze-dried lasagna. I set up the tent while Jekyll enjoyed all the new smells in the area. He lapped up water from the lake and playfully chased dragonflies.

I poured boiling water into my meal pouches, and then dumped a cup of Blue Buffalo into Jekyll's bowl. When he heard the magical sound of the nuggets hitting his bowl, he hustled over with a power yodel. "Okay, Jek, dig in." As he devoured his meal, I checked on mine. It was ready. I plowed through the first pouch and went to the second. Jekyll barked to remind me not to be miserly. He wolfed down his share and licked the containers.

While I cleaned up, Jek visited our neighbors. I found him sitting in the lap of a little boy named Julien from Dauphin, Manitoba, who was feeding him roasted marshmallows. My silly dog looked like he'd entered Nirvana. I rolled my eyes. Jekyll never met a stranger. I chatted with Julien and his family and had a few marshmallows myself. I was as bad as my mooching dog.

After the marshmallow-fest, we went for a walk. Julien joined us and we had fun walking and playing. It felt good doing normal things again. I handed him my iPhone and asked him to take a picture of Jek and me standing in front of the lake.

I reset my watch to Yukon time and turned on my iPhone to see if there was any coverage. To my delight, I got three bars and saw messages from Scotty, Annie, the Gilgrens, and Katie in my inbox! I opened Scotty's first. His troop was getting settled in at Outpost Sayed Abad and all was well. Maggie and the kids were adjusting to life without him. I replied, telling him where we were and sent him the picture Julien took of me and Jek. Next, I opened the Gilgren's message where Jamie wrote Lilly's dictates. *Dear Mr. Colt and Jekyll von Bickerstaff. I miss you. I am teaching Finley von Bickerstaff to fetch the ball, but he likes to do other things. I have a joke for you. What's a wolf's favorite holiday? Howl-oween. Love, Lilly.*

I replied. *Hello, Lillybean! That was a great joke! Jekyll was laughing so hard that he fell off the chair. We're now in Canada, camping at Kluane Lake near the town of Burwash Landing. The lake is really big. Jekyll says hi and has another joke for you: "Why did the Eskimo call his dog Frost? Because Frost bites!" We're having fun, but we miss you. Bye, sweetheart. Colt and Jekyll.*

I opened Katie's email. *Dear Colt, I miss you and Jekyll so much. Momma didn't take your leaving well. Daddy and I took her for an ice cream cone the day you left, but she cried when she saw a little dog in the car next to us. I hope you know how much she loves you. Daddy has been quiet lately. I think that's his way of missing you. As much as they miss you, I miss you even more. I love you, Colt. I hope you're okay and I think about you constantly. Momma says we shouldn't bother you because you need to be alone to find out who you are. That seems funny to me because I already know who you are. You're the most wonderful person I've ever known. I never used to pray much, but I pray every night for you and Jekyll. I hope you won't ever forget me. I worry that you'll never come back. Jen says hello and hopes you're finding enough bushes and trees for, well, you know. I've decided to learn Jujutsu. Ju relates to flexibility, suppleness, and gentleness and jutsu means technique or art. So Jujutsu is the art of suppleness or gentleness, which seems like a good match for me. Now I'm a Jujutsuka, or student of Jujutsu. My sensei was impressed with all the moves you taught me and how well I execute them. He'd like to meet you one day. I promise I won't bother you after this. I hope you find what you're looking for. Love, Katie.*

I took a deep breath and sighed after reading her email. Katie was a special young lady and I missed her just as much as she missed me. I thought for a moment about my reply.

Dear Katie, it's so good to hear from you, especially after a long day on the road. Jekyll and I are camping at Kluane Lake in the Yukon and we just got back from a walk. Attached is a picture taken today by a young boy named Julien from Dauphin, Manitoba. He and his family are driving to Dawson City in the Klondike to see relatives. Julien roasted marshmallows for Jekyll. He has a new best friend. If he'd had roasted carrots, I think my dog would've exchanged owners. Tell Jen I haven't had to use the outdoors yet because we've been staying at campgrounds. Jujutsu is an excellent choice—good for you! Thanks for the wonderful words in your email. Leaving you and your family was incredibly difficult. I got as far as Fort Richardson and had to pull over and cry. I never used to cry and now I can't seem to keep my tears in check. Love brings out emotions in many different ways. I can't explain why I need to go on this trip, other than my heart requires it. I know that's not a very good explanation, but it's the best I can do. Katie, I was a good soldier, but just because you're good at something doesn't mean it's right for your soul. My hope is to find what God wants me to do with my life because I haven't a clue. I'm drifting through life now, and it's eating away at me. I read a quote from your mom's journal last night, and I've been thinking about it all day. "Be patient toward all that is unsolved in your heart and try to love the questions themselves, like locked rooms and like books that are now written in a foreign tongue. Do not now seek the answers, which cannot be given you because you would not be able to live them. And the point is, to live everything. Live the questions now. Perhaps you will then gradually, without noticing it, live along some distant day into the answer." 'Live the questions now' is resonating within me. I know when I find my purpose, my soul will be at peace. That is why I'm leaving you. I'll end with another quote in your mom's journal by Joseph Campbell: "If you do follow your bliss you put yourself on a kind of track that has been there all the while, waiting for you, and the life that you ought to be living is the one you are living. Follow your bliss and don't be afraid, and doors will open where you didn't know they were going to be." So, my dog and I are in search of our bliss. You have my love. ps. I will never, ever forget you.

The low-battery warning flashed. I wrote one last sentence. *Would you please tell your mom and dad that I'm fine, and I'll write them soon. Love you! Colt.* I sent the message and opened Annie's email, but then the phone shut off. Rats. I got out the solar charger and tried to find a way to charge the phone while driving. After fumbling around, I found a clever way to do it by tying the charger to my jacket's front pocket zipper and then running the wire from the charger to my iPhone. It didn't look pretty, but it would work.

I decided to call it a day and brought both books into the tent. Not surprisingly, Jek chose the Zen book to read first. "Okay, let's begin. I'll do a random page as is our new tradition. Ready?"

"Woof!"

I closed my eyes, flipped the pages, and stopped. "Page eighty-three. What do we have here?"

"Enlightenment is like the moon reflected on the water. The moon does not get wet, nor is the water broken. Although its light is wide and great, the moon is reflected even in a puddle an inch wide. The whole moon and the entire sky are reflected in dewdrops on the grass, or even in one drop of water. Enlightenment does not divide you, just as the moon does not break the water. You cannot hinder enlightenment, just as a drop of water does not hinder the moon in the sky. The depth of the drop is the height of the moon. Each reflection, however long or short its duration, manifests the vastness of the dewdrop, and realizes the limitlessness of the moonlight in the sky. Dōgen Zenji"

"Woof!"

"That wasn't bad. Here's another."

"Where beauty is, then there is ugliness; where right is, also there is wrong. Knowledge and ignorance are interdependent; delusion and enlightenment condition each other. Since olden times, it has been so. How could it be otherwise now? Wanting to get rid of one and grab the other is merely realizing a scene of stupidity. Even if you speak of the wonder of it all, how do you deal with each thing changing? Daigu Ryokan."

I thought about this and it hit me. I've been seeking a mono-dimensional world, where there is only right and no wrong, and beauty with no ugliness, and peace with no war. I could drive for a million miles and never find that place. It doesn't exist, not in this world. It was like that Zen story I read last night where the sage didn't wait for all the clouds to be gone before enjoying the sun. He enjoyed the sun between each passing cloud...

"Woof!"

"Okay, sorry. I need to think after reading these, Jek."

I turned the page.

"After winning several archery contests, the young and rather boastful champion challenged a Zen master who was renowned for his skill as an archer. The young man demonstrated remarkable technical proficiency when he hit a distant bull's eye on his first try, and then split that arrow with his second shot. 'There,' he said to the old man, 'see if you can match that!'

Undisturbed, the master did not draw his bow, but rather motioned for the young archer to follow him up the mountain. Curious about the old fellow's intentions, the champion followed him high into the mountain until they reached a deep chasm spanned by a rather flimsy and shaky log. Calmly stepping out onto the middle of the unsteady and certainly perilous bridge, the old master picked a faraway tree as a target, drew his bow, and fired a clean, direct hit. 'Now it is your turn,' he said as he gracefully stepped back onto the safe ground. Staring with terror into the seemingly bottomless and beckoning abyss, the young man could not force himself to step out onto the log, no less shoot at a target. 'You have much skill with your bow,' the master said, sensing his challenger's predicament, 'but you have little skill with the mind that lets loose the shot.'"

I smiled. I learned that truth in the Army. There were a lot of good shooters, but very few good snipers. I turned back to the book.

"*The meaning of your life depends on which ideas you permit to use you. Who you think you are determines where you put your attention. Where you direct your attention creates your life experiences, and brings a new course of events into being. Where you habitually put your attention is what you worship. What do you worship in this mindstream called your life?* Gangaji"

That one hit me hard. '*Where you habitually put your attention is what you worship.*' It was like a light bulb went on in my head. I thought about all the negative things I'd been 'worshiping' and the list was long. I suddenly knew there was major work to do on myself.

"Hey, boy, let's take a break from your Zen. I need time to digest what we read. Why don't we shift to Annie's journal for a while." He picked up the journal and carried it to me with his tail wagging. "Thanks, boy. I'm tired, so I won't read many, okay?"

"Woof."

I was glad he didn't argue. I turned to a random page.

"*Hold on to what is good, even if it is a handful of earth. Hold on to what you believe, even if it is a tree which stands by itself. Hold on to what you must do, even if it is a long way from here. Hold on to life, even when it is easier letting go. Hold on to my hand, even when I have gone away from you.* Pueblo saying."

I thought about my dad and how I forced myself not to think of him or Mom because it was just too painful. Maybe it was time to hold his hand once more. Mom's too. The thought of that brought tears to my eyes. I closed Annie's book. "Sorry, Jek. I can't do this anymore. Let's go to bed."

We crawled into the sleeping bag and I stroked his head. "You know, the passages we've read sure echo within me." He licked my face in empathy. I looked up. "Sorry, Mom and Dad, for keeping you from my thoughts. I'm inviting you back and want to hold your hands again."

A flood of childhood memories came to me. For the first time in my adult life, I welcomed my parents back to my thoughts. Snug in my sleeping bag, I pretended to hold their hands. That night, I floated down the Colorado again with my father. I told him all my troubles and he smiled and held my hand. I was safe again.

28

I FELT LICKS on my face and turned over, wanting to sleep some more.

"Woof!"

"Go back to sleep, Jekyll. It's the middle of the night."

"Woof!"

"Twenty more minutes, that's all I ask. Twenty more..."

"Woof!"

I opened my eyes groggily.

"Woof! Woof!"

"What? Do you have to go out?"

"Yeee-ooooo-ooo!"

Reluctantly, I sat up. "What time is it?" I looked at my watch. It was half past ten. "Oh, my God, I've slept the morning away. You need to go out, huh?"

"Woof!"

"Okay, give me a second to get dressed." I put on some clothes, opened the tent flap, and was greeted with a brilliant blue sky. "Come on, Jek, let's get on with our day."

"Woof!" He bounded out and took care of business. Then he romped around and leaped at a butterfly. Julien and his family had already left. I pointed the solar charger into the sun so it could start pumping electrons back into my cell phone. What to eat? Hmmm. I didn't feel like making breakfast, so a granola bar would have to do. Jek eagerly ate a chunk of it. I got out the map. The next town, Haines Junction, was about seventy-five miles away. "Hey, Jek, if we get going soon, we can get a burger and fries in Haines Junction. What do you think?"

"Woof! Woof!"

"Okay, let's break camp and hit the road." I ate another granola bar to tide me over and added water to Jekyll's bowl. He lapped it up while I packed. After putting on my riding gear and outfitting Jek with his helmet and goggles, we headed out. We got on the road and soon came upon an enormous gold pan at the Kluane Museum of Natural History. We passed Burwash Landing and went through a few more dips and frost heaves. I was careful not to go too fast and looked at the mirror to see how Jek was doing. His tongue was hanging out and he was enjoying himself. I thought about last night's readings and the next forty miles melted away.

Even though the thought of a burger drove me on, I couldn't help but stop when I noticed a nice turnout to view Kluane Lake and the background Kluane Ranges. They were grand. We sat on the Trike and marveled at the panorama. Back on the road, we came to Haines Junction at twelve-thirty and stopped at Madley's General Store. I walked in with Jek in the harness. They had a vegetable section, so I picked up a bunch of carrots. Jek let out an excited woof. He was no doubt suffering from carrot withdrawal. They were featuring barbeque chicken that day and its aroma trumped my urge for a burger. I ordered a half-chicken to go with a big soda.

We feasted on our meal in the parking lot. I even ate a carrot. There's nothing like a good meal to make life feel grand. I gassed up at the FasGas station. It was one-thirty and I wanted to put some more miles on before calling it a day. Whitehorse was about seventy miles away and the Marsh Lake Yukon Government campground was fifty miles beyond that. At a modest rate of forty miles per hour, we'd be there by five-thirty. That sounded good.

About ten miles out of town, Jekyll let out a monster yodel. All of the sudden, a black bear and her two cubs ran across the road a hundred yards ahead of us. Before I could even hit the brakes, they were back in the woods. "It's okay, boy. Just a momma bear skedaddling across the road. Good spot, though."

"Woof!"

I reminded myself to pay more attention. The rumbling of the engine was soothing and I had to fight the urge to let my mind wander. Further down the road, we got some more great views of the snow-capped Kluane Icefield Range. Traffic had stopped ahead, so I downshifted to slow down. Jekyll gave another yodel. This time there was a herd of elk crossing the highway. I didn't expect elk, thinking only caribou or moose inhabited this region. We waited fifteen minutes. The lunch soda had worked its way through me, so I took the opportunity to water the forest. Jekyll cavorted around and enjoyed stretching his legs.

A half-hour later, we were in the outskirts of Whitehorse. I saw another FasGas station and topped off the tank. Although we had eaten only three hours ago, I was hungry. Maybe the chicken we had for lunch had been skinny. The thought of a burger hit me again. The FasGas guy said there was a McDonalds just up the road on Fourth Avenue. Jek lit up when we rolled into the arches. I ordered two Big Macs, extra-large fries, and plenty of catsup. We sat in the parking lot and chowed down. I think Jekyll loved the Grand Adventure simply for the gourmet meals we were having. Last night, marshmallows; today chicken, burgers, and fries. I'm sure a nutritionist would gasp at our fare, but, hey, calories don't count when you're on vacation.

We cruised through Whitehorse, which is a nice, compact town. I know it gets bone-ass cold here in the winter, but it was sure pleasant in the summer. I glanced at my watch. We were running behind, but we'd still get to the campground by six.

At Marsh Lake, I got a nice camp site and quickly pitched the tent. The manager said bears weren't a problem, so it would be okay to leave our food in the Trike. I pulled out my phone and got zero signal strength. Rats. I should've read my emails in Whitehorse and needed to better anticipate where coverage would be.

Exercise helps to alleviate disappointment, so we took a walk around the campground's half-mile loop. I gathered firewood, started a fire, and gave Jekyll a half-ration of Blue Buffalo. He didn't call me on it after the chicken lunch and McD dinner. After eating, he sat on my lap and we watched the fire. There's something primal about seeing flames dancing. By eight-thirty, the mosquitoes were getting feisty, so we headed to the tent. On a whim, I got a pencil and writing journal from our stowed gear. Jek was tired and curled up on the sleeping bag. Soon his eyes closed.

Although I brought in the journal to jot down my thoughts, I looked at Jek and started sketching him. Soon, I was absorbed with this endeavor, drawing his facial features, the crisscrossing scars on his muzzle, and what was left of his ears. After that came his compact body and the color splotches on his fur. I did my best to capture how contented he looked. I finished the sketch and held it next to him. Not bad. I flipped the page and began to write...

Dear Annie, after many hours on the road, the day is growing long. I'm in the peaceful confines of my humble tent, with a riot of thoughts racing in my head. Jekyll is curled up and sleeping contentedly. He loves traveling and has a peculiar penchant for me to read Zen to him every night. I don't think I'll ever understand all his quirks and idiosyncrasies, but those are the things that endear him to me. We've also read your journal, and the words in both books have rocked my world. Annie, how can I begin to say thank you for sharing your journal with me. Yours is a daring journey of epic highs and unbearable lows. I feel you've handed me a portal to another world, a world with an infinity of possibilities. I see in your entries your struggle for meaning and purpose, and your search for answers to your many 'whys.' Ultimately, I think you and I know the answers to which we seek will never come in succinct, easy-to-understand snippets; rather, we will have to 'live the questions' as one of your entries stated. I see over and over how you've staked your existence and bet your happiness on faith and hope. To place all bets on faith and hope is courageous, but I see clearly that you've won big with that bet. How I envy you for what you have. Now, I have the opportunity to make the same bet as you. I don't know if I can be as courageous.

Last night I read the Pueblo saying in your journal, which ended with 'Hold on to life, even when it is easier letting go. Hold on to my hand, even when I have gone away from you.' Annie, I've always beat down the memories of my parents because it was always too painful to think of them. I understand now how destructive this was to my psyche. My parents still live in my heart. Pure joy floods through me as I say those words. My parents still live in my heart!

I dreamed last night that I floated down the Colorado again with my dad. We had such a grand time, Annie. We had years of catching up to do. We built a big fire on the shore, and he told me the campfire tales I loved to hear as a kid. He told me that Mom and he were very happy, but he couldn't share any details. All he said was I would, one day, come to know the wonder of it all. I told him about what happened to me since they left, but he said Mom and he already knew. I apologized for being a failure, and for disappointing them so. He looked puzzled when I said that, and took my hand in his. 'Son,' he said, 'Mom and I love you so. We have never left you. Your mom whispered for you to ski the day you met Jekyll. I told you to turn around in the vet's office and go back to him. Your mom said to turn left on the road after picnicking with Scotty's family. We wanted you to meet the Brennans. I suggested you tour the land when Pat asked what you'd do with the motorcycle. We are the cool wind that caresses your cheek on a warm day, and we will never abandon you. We dance with joy that you've opened your heart to hear us.'

I wanted to sleep forever and be with him, but Jekyll roused me from my slumber. I spent hours talking to them today while we were on the road. It feels so good to be with Mom and Dad again. They love you and Pat and thank you for loving me. I hope you can feel their love.

I read the last entry of your journal. How utterly humble I felt upon reading it. I love you and Pat just as much, and I, too, cried rivers of tears the day I left. I never thought of myself as 'beautiful' before. I was a warrior, and warriors are not beautiful. My heart, though, has always told me that I wasn't a warrior, despite how I excelled at it. My heart has been whispering that I am beautiful and I must do beautiful things.

Tonight, I read this from your journal, by Siddhārtha Gautama: 'You can search throughout the entire universe for someone who is more deserving of your love and affection than you are yourself, and that person is not to be found anywhere. You, yourself, as much as anybody in the entire universe, deserve your love and affection.' How true this is.

I'll close with a story from Jekyll's Zen book. Chuang Tzu, ancient Chinese Taoist, once experienced a dream in which he was a butterfly fluttering here and there. In the dream, he had no awareness of his individuality as a person; he was simply a butterfly. Suddenly, he awoke and found that once again, he was a human lying in bed. But then, he thought to himself, 'Was I before a man who dreamt about being a butterfly, or am I now a butterfly who dreams about being a man?'

I feel like I've been sleeping for years. What will I be when I awake?

I love you, my dear Annie. I thank you and Pat for helping me awake, for helping me feel alive once more.

29

WE HAD A lazy morning. I dictated last night's letter to Annie into my iPhone, but there still wasn't any signal to send it. I opened my map on the picnic table, placing some rocks on the edges to keep it from blowing away. Jek barked for me to pick him up so he could see the map too. "Look, Jek, we're here and the town of Teslin is eighty-five miles away. It doesn't look very big, but I think we can get gas there. Don't be thinking about fries at the arches on this leg of the trip."

"Woof!"

"We have a decision to make. Right here is the junction of the Alaska and Cassiar Highways. If we stay on the Alaska Highway, it goes on this side of the Rockies. The scenery will be great, but we'll have to go nearly to Alberta before starting south to Wenatchee. If we go on the Cassiar, we'll be between the Coast Mountains and the Rockies, and we might make better time. I'm leaning toward the Cassiar. What do you think?"

"Woof!"

"That's a good point. We could get more rain going on the Cassiar since it's closer to the ocean. Hmmm. Tell you what, let's flip a coin. Heads for Cassiar and tails for the Alaska Highway." I pulled out a quarter, tossed it high in the air, and watched it land.

"Heads! Cassiar it is."

"Woof!" Jekyll was excited about the choice.

"Okay, the Cassiar junction is about 200 miles from here. We can get there in about five hours, eat and gas up. Are you ready?"

"Woof!"

"Good. Let's hit the road." I put on our riding gear and started the engine. Jekyll let out an excited yodel. He loved riding on the Harley. I patted him and he licked my hand. I put the big machine in gear and gave it some gas.

We were making good time. About fifty miles down the road, Je-kyll bellowed when he saw several caribou crossing the highway. We watched them for a while. My iPhone delighted me by having a signal. I sent the email to Annie and finally got to read the one she'd sent to me.

Dear Colt, we miss you so much already. Pat is outnumbered by us ladies and is moping about. That's what he says, but he can't fool me. His heart is breaking, just like mine. You're no longer here and there's a huge void in our lives. As with Rachel leaving for college, I'm once more immersed in the turbulent times of letting go. I love you, my dear son, and every tear I shed proclaims my love of you. Please read the last page of my journal. I love you, my beautiful boy. Annie

I read the email aloud to Jekyll and then looked upward. "Thank you, Mom and Dad, for bringing me to these people." Jekyll seemed to understand the significance of the moment and seemed as happy as I. "Come on, boy, let's find our purpose." I started the engine, put it in first gear, and pulled away.

A short while later, we crossed the Teslin River Bridge. Jekyll howled the whole way across. We came to the picturesque community of Teslin, on the shores of the ninety-two mile long Teslin Lake. Back in the Klondike gold rush era, steamers plied its waters to bring supplies to the miners. The region was heavily forested and beautiful.

We came to the Nisutlin Bay Bridge, the longest bridge on the Alaska Highway. Jek once more howled as we crossed. We pulled off at a rest area and got a great view of the bridge. I asked an elderly couple to take a picture of Jek and me. When I looked at it, I had to smile. The picture was from my waist down. I waited until they left and asked a young lady to take another.

Seventy-five miles of hills and a few steep grades later, I pulled into a large gravel turnout and read a sign saying *Welcome to the Continental Divide*. Here, the divide separates two of the largest drainage systems in North America, the Mackenzie and Yukon River watersheds. The Mackenzie flows northward and empties into the Beaufort Sea. The mighty Yukon traverses Alaska before joining the Bering Sea. It occurred to me that right here were three divergent entities, each going on separate, but epic journeys. The Mackenzie, the Yukon, and me.

We descended into the beautiful Rancheria River valley. An hour later, we arrived at the intersection of the Cassiar Highway at four in the afternoon. I pulled into Junction 37 Services, a place having gas and an RV park and filled my tank. The cashier said they had showers for campers, so I checked in, got a camping space, and fed Jekyll dinner. I left him in the tent, where he promptly fell asleep, and took a long, hot shower. Afterward, I ordered a BLT at the café and ate it on the way to our camp.

"Woof! Woof!"

"I'm here, Jek. Hang on a second." He bounded out wagging his tail and looking refreshed. "My, don't you look chipper. I'm going to look at the map in case you're interested."

"Woof."

I put the map on the grass and sat down. Jek crawled into my lap. "I bet you're thinking, why is Colt clean-shaven and why does he smell so good, huh, boy?"

"Woof!"

I stroked his head. "Okay, the Cassiar's 450 miles long. I'd like to do at least 250 miles tomorrow, which would put us here, at the town of Iskut. We could push on to the Stewart junction, but it'd be a nine-hour drive. I'm not feeling that. How about you?"

"Woof!"

"Yeah, you're right. There's no sense killing ourselves when we don't have a deadline to be anywhere. Okay, let's go for the leisurely drive to Iskut." I put the map away and tossed a ball for Jek. He wasn't interested in retrieving; his nose was the air, sniffing for marshmallows. He left to make the rounds at the campground, leaving the ball to be fetched by me. There were plenty of people for him to say hello to. I started looking for him after finding the ball, and would've walked right by a campsite had it not been for him giving me an "I'm here!" yodel. Like a gold miner, he had struck pay dirt in the form of a little girl who was feeding him a perfectly toasted, foamy-white piece of heaven. I walked up to the family of four. "Pardon my dog's shameless mooching. He's developed a powerful fondness for marshmallows since we've been on the road."

The man stood up and shook my hand. "My name's Don Oldham. We thought your dog might be feral when he walked into our camp. I was ready to shoo him away, but then he looked so darn friendly."

I smiled. "He's a charmer, no doubt about it."

"What's his name?" said the little girl feeding old chubberpus.

"Jekyll von Bickerstaff." They all laughed. I had to repeat Jek's name three times before they could properly say it. They invited me to join them and wanted to know about my wunderhund. I guess a missing ear and a bunch of ugly is a natural conversation starter. As I was telling them his story, Jek brought me the little girl's stick with a marshmallow on the end of it. He was sharing the bounty.

The Oldham's were heading home to Whitehorse after spending a week in Vancouver. Don was a printer and his wife, Wanda, did the editing for the family business. He got excited when I told him we were touring on a Harley Trike. He had a love for motorcycles going back to his teen years. After chatting, or should I say, after Jek had his fill of marshmallows, we said goodnight. Don followed us back to camp, asking a ton of questions about my ride and where we were headed. It made me smile. I'd acted the same way with Pat after seeing the Trike in his garage. Boys and toys. No matter what country you're in, there are constants in life. I showed him the riding harness for Jek. He was impressed with it and my floating storage compartment. He reluctantly said goodbye when Wanda sent their son, Ryan, to get him. I think Wanda runs a tight ship.

I brushed my teeth to get rid of the sugar taste from the marshmallows and gave Jek some water. We began our goodnight routine. I lay on the sleeping bag and Jek handed me his Zen book. "Okay, boy, let's see what we'll read tonight." I picked a random page near the beginning of the book.

"One day the Master announced that a young monk had reached an advanced state of enlightenment. The news caused some stir. Some of the monks went to see him. 'We heard you are enlightened. Is that true?' they asked. 'It is,' he replied. 'And how do you feel?' 'As miserable as ever,' said the monk." I laughed at the irony of his remark and read on. "Here's a Zen proverb: 'Happiness is a simple thing: you are happy when you are not trying to be happy.'"

I turned a few pages.

"Just live that life. It doesn't matter whether it is life or hell, life of the hungry ghost, life of the animal, it's okay; just live that life, see. And as a matter of fact, no other way. Where you stand, where you are, that's what your life is right there, regardless of how painful it is or how enjoyable it is. That's what it is. Taizan Maezumi Roshi"

I gave this some thought. "You know, Jek, I spend a lot of time dwelling on the past or worrying about the future. When I do either, I sacrifice the current moment and that's the only place where life exists."

"Woof!"

"Ready for another one?"

"Woof!"

"Here's a Zen saying: *'Make 'being' your priority, not 'becoming.'*"

I looked at Jek. "That's a good saying. One more, then we'll switch to Annie's journal, okay?"

He wagged his tail agreeably.

"When the spiritual teacher and his disciples began their evening meditation, a cat that lived in the monastery made such noise that it distracted them. One day the teacher ordered that the cat be tied up during the evening practice. Years later, when the teacher died, the cat continued to be tied up during the meditation session. And when the cat eventually died, another cat was brought to the monastery and tied up. Centuries later, learned descendants of the spiritual teacher wrote scholarly treatises about the religious significance of tying up a cat for meditation practice."

I smiled. "That sounds a lot like the Army. Let's switch to Annie's journal." Jekyll dutifully retrieved her journal and dropped it on my chest. I flipped to a random page again.

"The same stream of life that runs through my veins night and day runs through the world and dances in rhythmic measures. It is the same life that shoots in joy through the dust of the earth in numberless blades of grass and breaks into tumultuous waves of leaves and flowers. It is the same life that is rocked in the ocean-cradle of birth and of death, in ebb and in flow. I feel my limbs are made glorious by the touch of this world of life. And my pride is from the life-throb of ages dancing in my blood this moment. Rabindranath Tagore*"*

What a nice passage. I turned the page. "One more and that's it, okay?"

"Woof."

"Alright. Let's see.

"People are often unreasonable and self-centered. Forgive them anyway. If you are kind, people may accuse you of ulterior motives. Be kind anyway. If you are honest, people may cheat you. Be honest anyway. If you find happiness, people may be jealous. Be happy anyway. The good you do today may be forgotten tomorrow. Do good anyway. Give the world the best you have and it may never be enough. Give your best anyway. For you see, in the end, it is between you and God. It was never between you and them anyway. Mother Teresa*"*

I looked at Jekyll with tears in my eyes. "This passage is the summation of my mom's life and Annie's life too. I wonder what Annie was thinking when she wrote this. It was over twenty-eight years ago. She was just a teenager, right around Katie's age. She sure has lived this passage." I closed the book. It would be too hard to continue. I got up, fluffed the sleeping bag, and crawled in. Jekyll followed my lead, and I stroked his head. "We read some powerful words tonight, huh, Jek?" He licked my cheek. *"Make 'being' your priority, not 'becoming.'"* You know, I thought by making this trip I'd become someone my parents would be proud of. All my focus has been on becoming. Maybe life is simply about being. I know I'm a good person deep inside. Maybe I should *be* who I am for a change."

"Woof!"

"Thanks, boy. You're a smart dog. Odd, but smart. My mom and dad brought us together, you know. They told me that in my dream."

I fell asleep saying those words to my dear friend.

30

BREAKFAST CONSISTED OF three packets of instant oatmeal. After finishing, I put some Blue Buffalo into the leftover oatmeal and gave Jek a treat. We were on the road by eight. Five miles down the road, we passed a sign saying *Welcome to British Columbia.* We were in a huge, hilly conifer forest, the perfect drive for a motorcycle. "Perfect" ended a mile later with the first drops of rain, which soon turned into a cold, steady downpour. Jekyll wasn't a happy camper, and could easily become hypothermic if I wasn't careful. As if things couldn't get worse, the road became narrow and winding, with an abundance of potholes and blind curves. Rain from cars in the other lane pelted us as we passed.

We pulled into a place called the Cassiar Mountain Jade Store and walked in looking like a couple of drowned rats. It was a nice place and, not surprisingly, had all sorts of jade products. Jekyll was shivering, so I went to the restroom and used paper towels to dry him off. He looked mournfully at me. "I'm sorry, boy. That's some bad weather out there. We'll stay here until you're dry and warm." I turned on the bathroom faucet and fed Jek warm water from my cupped hand. After that, we went into the store and I took my time walking around. They offered free coffee, so I helped myself to a cup. I asked one of the friendly staff about the weather and the news wasn't good. Rain for the next three days, she said. Rats. They had an interesting interactive mining museum and we watched one of their artisans conducting a jade-cutting demonstration. I learned more than I wanted about jade and how it was mined in the area.

After an hour, Jekyll was warm and dry again. He perked up when we ate some granola bars. Since there were no accommodations in the area, we had to keep pushing on. I ran out and grabbed a couple of large plastic lawn bags and a towel from the Trike. We'd use the lawn bags as makeshift raincoats. I punched holes in one of them for my head and arms and put it on. It looked like hell, but fit pretty well over my riding jacket. Next, I wrapped the towel around Jekyll, and put him in the lawn bag. I punched a couple holes in it for air, and then put him in the harness. He couldn't see a thing, unless he peeked out an air hole, but he knew this was better than being exposed to the elements. I put on my helmet and reluctantly went back outside. The plastic bag was a good idea for Jekyll, but a bad idea for me. The wind from driving tore it to shreds. I pulled over, ripped it off, and shoved it in my pocket. Cold rain ran off my helmet and down the inside of my jacket. Enough was enough. I saw a sign for the Water's Edge campground and pulled in. They were full. I offered to pitch my tent in the woods, but the guy said no. He said all the campgrounds in the area were full except for those in Iskut, about sixty miles away. What the hell, I was going for it. I told Jek the news and he quietly accepted it.

We got back on the road and plodded on. I began to shiver. The road had several steep grades, which would've been fun to drive on a clear day, but right now it was miserable. Jekyll hardly moved in his cocoon. He was toughing it out. After many more miles of Godforsaken road, I saw a dilapidated pickup with its hood up on the side of the highway. I downshifted to slow down. It was pouring now and I was tempted to just keep driving, but it didn't seem right to leave someone stranded. I pulled over. A native man, looking to be in his early twenties, was bent under the hood staring forlornly at the engine.

"Y-you need any h-help?" My teeth were chattering, and it was hard to say the words.

"You look like the one who needs help," he said tersely.

"H-hey, d-don't throw a-a-attitude at m-me. I'm o-o-ffering you a-s-sistance."

"The belt's broken. You got a spare belt in your motorcycle?"

"N-no, b-but I-I'll h-haul your skinny a-ass t-t-to town if y-you w-want." He leered at me. I saw his hands tighten into fists. This could get ugly fast.

Jekyll poked his muzzle out the hole.

"Yeee-ooooo-ooo!"

"What the hell is that?" he said, startled.

"I-it's m-my dog."

"Is he possessed?"

"N-no. H-he's just r-r-rather odd."

The guy laughed.

Jekyll's yodel seemed to ease the tension. He held out his hand. "My name is Joseph Quash. Where're you heading?"

I shook his hand. "I-I'm C-Colt. I-Iskut. I h-h-ope to f-find a c-campground t-there."

"Man, that's an hour down the road. Lots of hills and steep grades."

"I k-know. Y-you w-want a r-ride?"

"I'll make you a deal. If you give me a ride to my home, you can stay with my family. We live in Telegraph Creek, which is that way." He pointed in a direction different than we were heading.

"G-give m-me a s-second t-to t-talk it o-over w-with m-my d-dog."

"Are you serious?"

I nodded and walked away so he couldn't hear. "S-Should w-we d-do it, J-Jek?"

"Woof!"

"A-are y-you s-sure?"

"Woof!"

"O-k-kay." I went back to the man. "M-my d-d-dog s-says w-we c-can trust y-you. C-climb aboard." The Trike was sluggish going down the road with the extra weight. I went fifteen miles back the way we came. He tapped me on the shoulder and motioned for me to turn left on Telegraph Creek Road. The rain was pelting me as we went. Joe had it bad too, even though he had on a fisherman's slicker. It didn't keep the rain from hitting him in the face.

After three miles, the pavement ended and we were now on gravel. I was beginning to think the day couldn't get any worse, but that thought was premature. We got to a nasty grade that dropped into a canyon. It was steep, narrow and full of switchbacks. The rain caused the road to be slick. Joe tapped on my shoulder and motioned with his hand that we were going to descend again. Mother of God. A twenty percent grade appeared. I downshifted to second gear and we dropped down, really down. I downshifted to first gear, something I'd never done when going down a hill. "We call this the Grand Canyon of Canada," Joe shouted above the rain. I mentally called it the big suck.

A few miles later, we got to a 180-degree right turn followed by another jaw-dropping descent. I saw a sign saying the Tahltan River Bridge. Halfway across the bridge, I jammed on the brakes, and, with much effort, got off my ride. I was pissed. "W-where a-are y-y-you t-t-aking m-me?" When I'd offered him a ride, I didn't think I'd be hauling his sorry ass halfway across the Canadian wilderness in a driving rainstorm.

"T-t-twelve m-more m-miles. W-w-e're almost t-there." He was cold too. He had a big grin on his face. I knew this grin. When I was in Ranger school and they ran us into the ground, we all grinned at each other when they said we had another five miles to run. When you're at the end of your rope, all you can do is grin.

I struggled to get back on my ride and put it in first gear. I popped the clutch and stalled the engine. I started it again and this time managed to get going without looking like an idiot. A merciful short while later, we got to the town of Telegraph Creek, where we passed a quaint church with a large steeple. Joe tapped my shoulder and pointed to a house on a hill. "T-that's our h-house. G-go up this d-driveway."

I turned on the narrow driveway and went up yet another steep grade. He pointed to a carport and I pulled in. He got off first. I took off my helmet, totally spent. An older man came out of the house, surprised to see a Harley in his carport.

"C-c-olt, t-this is m-my f-f-father, G-George Q-Quash."

I weakly nodded.

"Where is your truck?" the man said.

"F-fan b-belt b-broke. C-Colt g-gave m-me a r-ride."

"Yee-oo-eee-oo-eee-oo."

"What do you have in there?"

"M-m-my d-d-og."

"Come inside, you two."

I tried to get off, but couldn't. George had to help me get off and then walk to their log house. Joe wasn't in much better shape. George opened the door and yelled, "Mary!" His wife came and looked shocked to see her hypothermic son and a stranger in a phosphorescent lime-green jacket in even worse shape. When they took the plastic bag off Jekyll and saw him in all his glory, I thought they'd run for the hills. Instead, Mary took charge.

"George, I'm going to make coffee and you need to get them out of their wet clothes."

"C'mon, young man," George said. "Let's get you to Joseph's room. We're the same build, so I'll get you some of my clothes." He sat me on Joe's bed. I was having trouble grasping my zipper, so he unzipped it for me and helped take the jacket off. Then came my shirt and T-shirt, which were dripping wet. He went to his room and came back with a T-shirt and sweats. He helped me put them on. Joe was in better shape than I, and changed into some dry clothes without assistance. Mary walked in with two mugs of steaming hot coffee. "Drink this, you two."

I awkwardly extended my shaking hand to reach the cup. George helped bring it to my lips. I took a sip and it felt as hot as lava. I swallowed and felt the hot fluid go all the way to my stomach. Between the dry clothes, the warmth of the house, and the hot coffee, my body started coming out of its catatonic state.

"Th-thank you, sir and ma'am. I g-guess I was on the road too long."

"Drink more coffee." Mary looked at my still shivering body and wasn't satisfied with my progress. "Draw him a bath, George. He's not warming up fast enough." He left and soon I heard water running. She helped me empty the cup. "You take a warm bath, young man. I'm making dinner and you're welcome to join us."

"Thank y-you, ma'am."

Jekyll looked at me with concern.

George and Joe helped me to the bathroom. I took off the clothes and sat in the tub. The water seemed scalding hot, but I knew it was just my cold body reacting to warmth. Jekyll started yodeling. There was a knock at the door. "Colt, your dog wants to be with you."

"Thanks Joe. Let him in." Jekyll stood with his front paws on the tub assessing me. "I'm better now, boy. What a day."

"Woof!"

He sat on the floor while I let the water infuse me with its warmth. It was stupid of me to stay on the road so long. Stupidity is excusable if you're an idiot greenhorn out in the bush with no knowledge. But I knew better. I was an Army Ranger. Stupidity with knowledge is true stupidity. Geez, I was starting to think in Zen. Thank God for the kindness of these people.

When I felt normal again, I got out of the tub and redressed. I could smell dinner and knew what it was. Every Alaskan knows the distinctive aroma of salmon.

The family had gathered at the table and was patiently waiting for me. There was Joe, his parents, and two sets of elderly people. I think they were the grandparents.

"Come in," said George. He introduced me to his father and mother, Robert and Greta. Then he introduced me to Mary's parents, Anna and Frederick. I shook their hands. They were old, probably in their eighties or nineties.

George motioned to a chair. "Please sit here."

The elders smiled agreeably at me. "My grandparents are happy you helped me today," said Joseph. I nodded to them.

Frederick pointed to Jekyll and began talking in an animated way, making hand gestures and pointing his fingers in the air next to his head. As he spoke, tears poured from his eyes. The other elders were crying too. I was puzzled since I hadn't a clue what he was saying. George turned to me. "We are part of the Tahltan native people. When Frederick was a little boy, he had a dog. It was an aboriginal breed called the Tahltan Bear Dog. He was a little taller than your dog, about the size of a fox. He was black in color, with white patches on his chest and feet. He had erect, pointed ears and a short, bushy tail. Just like your dog, Bear Dogs had a peculiar yodel." Frederick spoke some more and blotted his eyes with a tissue. Robert said something and began crying too.

George spoke for them. "Our ancestors used the warrior dogs to hunt grizzlies and black bears, and they also assisted in hunting everything from elk to beaver. They carried the dogs in sacks and released them when fresh tracks were sighted. While the heavier animals sank in the snow, the light bear dogs easily ran on the surface. They would harass their quarry with high-pitched barking and mercilessly nip at them until the hunters arrived to dispatch them. The bear dog had the courage to face a bear, but the gentleness to be with humans. Frederick's dog slept with him and was his best friend for many years. There were good spirits in his dog."

I told George about Jekyll saving me from the bear at Eklutna, and how fearlessly he had attacked the bear to defend me. I scooped Jek up and put him on my lap. He licked my face, and I gave him a hug. George told them my story.

Frederick asked if he could hold my "bear dog." I brought Jekyll to him and he accepted my dog's licks to his cheek. As he smiled, I could see wrinkles upon wrinkles. Tears were pouring down his weathered cheeks. It brought tears to me.

"Did he ever get another bear dog?" I asked George.

"No," he said quietly. "Bear Dogs went extinct in the 1930s." How sad, I thought.

Mary brought a big tray from the kitchen. It was loaded with a huge salmon. She put it on the table and returned with a large pot of boiled potatoes. "I hope you like our dinner. It's freshly caught Chinook salmon."

"Thank you ma'am. I've fished for them in Alaska and love how they taste."

She served the elders first and passed the platter to me. I was starved after being so cold and put an ample chunk of the fish on my plate. When the potatoes came my way, I wasn't shy in loading the carbs on my dish. The elders took the first bites and proclaimed it to be a worthy meal. When the others began eating, I took it as my cue to dig in. My, oh my, was it delicious! I wished Annie were here to taste it.

"Mary, this is wonderful."

"You're our guest. Do us the honor of having seconds."

"Yes, ma'am, I will." I ate away. It was just so good. After my second full plate, I excused myself to go out to the Trike to get some Blue Buffalo for Jekyll. He was hungry, so I gave him another ration after he devoured the first bowl.

Mary invited me to sit on the couch next to her mother. The old woman put her wrinkled hand on mine. The small gesture touched my heart and made me feel welcome. I looked at the wrinkles on her hand that took years to form and wondered how many people were graced by her loving hands over those years. Jekyll came to me and I picked him up. George and Joseph were sitting on a love seat. The old men came in carrying native flutes. Mary moved a couple of dining chairs to the center of the room for them. "Our parents want to play for you and your bear dog," said George.

Frederick began playing a hauntingly beautiful song. His old hands moved effortlessly over the holes in the flute. Robert joined in exquisite harmony. The music of their flutes was pure and simple. I had never heard anything so beautiful in my life. I don't know why, but tears started pouring from my eyes. Anna patted my hand with hers. Jekyll started yodeling softly, melding with the music, as if he was summoning the spirits of the Bear Dogs with his deeply longing tones. Frederick was moved to tears, but his skillful old hands navigated the flute as if he was young again. I knew he was playing for his beloved bear dog. I closed my eyes and listened. I don't know how to explain this exactly, but my soul felt untethered to the earth and was floating through the air. I'd never in my life experienced a mystical moment, but I was experiencing one now. I kept my eyes closed after the music stopped. A deeply moving sense of peace permeated my body. I wanted them to play forever. I reluctantly opened my eyes to see all in the room in tears. "That was the most beautiful thing I've ever heard," I said to George.

Robert spoke to George. "He sees the spirit dancing in you. He thinks you may have some blood of our people in you."

I smiled and nodded at him. The way I felt now, he might be right. "Would you ask them to play another song for me?" George spoke and the old men graciously accommodated my request. They conferred with each other and then spoke to George. "They say this song is for those who are seeking. They think you are a seeker."

I listened once more to the mesmerizing music. Jekyll joined in and I put my hand on him while he sang. The calming, beautiful melody seemed to cleanse my soul. After they finished, I hugged them both. I didn't know if it was culturally acceptable to do, but I couldn't help myself. I gestured to Frederick, silently asking to hold his flute, and he handed it to me with a smile. I was convinced there had to be magic in it and ran my hands over its length. I gave him another hug after handing it back, and he touched me on the cheek with his hand. Sometimes, there's no need for words when expressing genuine love. Jekyll offered his thanks to the elders after I had my turn.

I thanked Joseph for inviting me to be with his family. The agonizing drive to his house now seemed trivial. I would've driven a million miles to be with these wonderful people. I sat back on the couch and suddenly felt drained. It had been a long day. Mary saw my weariness and said to follow her to the guest room. I bowed to the elders and thanked George for his hospitality.

I was asleep almost as soon as my head hit the pillow. It felt wonderful to be in a bed again. Jekyll was just as tired. He snuggled in next to me and we made music of our own that night. It was a symphony of snoring.

We didn't awake until noon the next day. When I sheepishly came out and said hello to Mary, she said George and Joseph had left to repair and retrieve his truck. She had some biscuits and honey for me in the kitchen. When I was done with breakfast, she said to go out to the garage to be with Frederick and Robert.

I quickly ate the meal and made sure Jek got a share. We ambled out to the garage and saw the two men hunched over a work bench. When I said hello, Robert motioned for me to stop. He came over and turned me around so I was facing away from them. He reached up and closed my eyes with his hand. I heard him move away and join Frederick at the workbench. This was kind of odd, I thought. How long should I stand there with my eyes closed? After a couple minutes of hearing them talking, and what I thought was filing something, I heard them move toward me.

"C-Colt," one of them said. I felt his hands on me, so I took that to mean open my eyes. It was Frederick. He was sporting a broad grin. Robert was next to him, holding a flute in his hands. He handed it to me. It had a carving on it that looked like Jekyll. They had scratched the muzzle to reflect his scars and filed off one of the ears. It was beautiful. I started crying. They were crying too. Both of them put their hands on me. Robert and Frederick began softly singing a beautiful chant in their native tongue. This was a sublime moment in my life. I had no doubt these kind men were calling God to be with me.

31

FREDERICK AND ROBERT did their best to show me how to play my flute. They showed me how to hold it and how to breathe. They laughed when I blew into it like it was a trumpet. Robert patiently taught me to blow gently and adjust "Jekyll" to get the best tone. By the time George and Joseph got back, I could play a decent-sounding monosyllable note. Joseph came in and smiled when he heard my pathetic attempt to play.

"My grandpas got up early this morning to work on the fetish for your flute. Grandpa Frederick has had this flute since he was a boy. It's made from an old cedar tree his grandpa found on a riverbank. He says our spirits are in the wood. I hope you can understand the true meaning of this gift."

"I do, Joseph, and I'll treasure it always. Will you please thank them for me."

"I don't need to thank them for you. They see the gratitude in your eyes."

I nodded. "What is a fetish?"

"Your little dog carving is called a fetish. You move it to adjust the tonal quality of the flute. We use the word fetish to describe an object that has great power. My grandpas think your dog has great spirits in him. Grandpa Robert is a shaman, and he blessed the carving this morning. After a shaman blesses the fetish, it has magical power. He asked the spirits to show you the way. He says yours is a troubled heart, but it is getting better."

I looked at Robert and touched the Jekyll fetish. I smiled and he smiled back knowingly.

"Joseph, would you ask your grandpa to bless me?"

Joseph spoke to his grandpa and his grandpa smiled after replying.

"He says Grandpa Frederick and he have already blessed you. They sang the song of our Innuit brothers. I know this song. In your language, it goes like this: *I think over again my small adventures, my fears, those small ones that seemed so big, all those vital things I had to get and to reach, and yet there is only one great thing: to live and see the great day that dawns, and the light that fills the world."*

"It's beautiful. Would you tell them how touched I was to hear their music last night."

"I will, but they already know. That's why they gave you the flute." He told his grandparents and they nodded.

"Will you ask them what the hardest thing is to play on their flute?" He asked and nodded his head knowingly when they replied.

"My grandpas say silence. Silence is very hard to play."

Jekyll, my Zen master, would understand that answer. I'd have to think about their response for a while.

Mary yelled for everyone to come for lunch. I didn't want to put the flute down. I could feel the mystical power in it. Frederick brought an exquisitely crafted leather bag for the flute and put it in. He placed it on the workbench. I gave him a hug when he turned around. He was short and I felt his bones. He said something to me which I didn't understand, but I saw a smile on his weathered, high cheek-boned face, and I knew he was happy.

It was raining hard when we walked back to the house. George and Joseph used umbrellas to shield the elders.

"Hey Joe, can I ask you something?"

"Sure."

"Why were you so nasty back when I pulled over to help you?"

"I'm sorry about that, Colt. We've been having trouble with white people. A big oil company wants to develop a coal bed methane field near our Sacred Headwaters. The Sacred Headwaters is the origin of the Stikine, Skeena, and Nass rivers. Our people believe earth was first created in these headwaters and this is where our culture began. If you want to be practical, these rivers provide a home for our salmon, and it's critical to keep the waters pristine. They say there may be eight-trillion cubic feet of gas here, and half of it is in Tahltan territory. We don't want them on our sacred land. The oil company opened an office in Iskut, but our elders turned their employees away. It was a non-violent blockade. Now the oil company is suing our elders for loss of revenue. I thought you might be one of their employees on your fancy motorcycle. But then I heard your dog. No employee of an oil company would have a dog like that. I knew then that you were okay."

"Thanks for telling me. If you're having another blockade anytime soon, I'll join you."

"That's a kind offer, my friend. But, it's now in the courts. My grandpas ask that you stay a few days. They want to teach you how to play your new flute. I could use a hand at our fish camp too. You can eat as much salmon as you want."

"I'd like that a lot. Thank you so much for bringing me here. I needed this more than you'll ever know."

"No problem. My grandpas need it too. You and your little dog have recharged them."

I spent the next four days with this wonderful family, and practiced for hours every night with Frederick and Robert. They didn't teach me about notes or scales or tempo. Rather, they taught me how to make beautiful sounds and how to use my heart to weave those sounds together to form a song. I don't know how to explain it, but when I closed my eyes and stopped thinking, I could play beautiful songs. An incredible feeling of peace permeated through me when I played. Robert said I was summoning the spirits and they were guiding my fingers.

I loved the physical work of fishing. Joseph and his extended family had a fish camp on the Stikine River, and he introduced me to his cousins. We had a grand time. They had a cabin made of spruce logs with many moose racks on the roof. Next to the cabin was a salmon drying shed, where they had nailed small logs to the frame and put salmon on them. The gaps between the logs allowed air to flow through and dry the salmon. I ate enormous quantities of smoked salmon and never grew tired of it.

Word spread of the yodeling "bear dog," and people were soon traveling from miles away to see him. They touched him with reverence and many of the elders had tears in their eyes. Jekyll was enjoying his high status and dispensed many fond licks to his admirers.

On our last day, George told me the village was going to hold a potlatch that night in my honor. He said it would be at their fish camp because they expected a lot of people. I spent some time repacking the Trike and getting it ready for the road. Around three, Mary called me to come back to the house. I was surprised to see all of them wearing beautiful costumes. George gave me a handsome beaded elk-skin jacket to wear.

Jekyll and I rode with Joseph to the fish camp and the others drove in their sedan. For some reason, I took my flute with me, but when we got there, I decided to leave it in the truck. It looked like the whole town was there. All the people wore beautiful costumes with carved masks. Joseph said the masks represented mythological spirit beings. Drums were beating an upbeat tempo and everyone was singing and dancing. There was a fire blazing in the center of the action and several kids were dancing around it in their costumes. They were waving their arms as they danced and looked like flying birds. Several folding tables were set up and loaded with food. Jekyll looked a little intimidated with all the action, so I picked him up. As I was taking it all in, Frederick and Robert came to me. Each put a hand on me and guided me and Jek toward the fire. Robert signaled the drummers to cease playing. Everyone turned to him. The only thing to be heard was the crackling logs in the fire. Robert spoke to the crowd in their tongue. He gently took Jekyll from me and raised him high for all to see. The villagers erupted in shouts and whoops, and the drummers started playing again. Joseph leaned in. "Grandpa said your little bear dog has brought good spirits to the potlatch."

Soon it was time to eat. Frederick brought me to the head of the line. Since I was the guest of honor, I was to eat first. Following me were the elders. There was so much food that I couldn't decide what to try. So, what the hell, I tried a little of everything. George looked at my plate and said I had elk, porcupine, moose, bear, and oolichan, which was dried candlefish. They all tasted good, with the exception of the oolichan. That was definitely an acquired taste. Jekyll feasted too, and to my surprise, appeared to have a fondness for oolichan.

The evening passed agreeably. Several villagers gave me modest gifts of jade trinkets or feathers. I was touched. After all the kindnesses, I had to give something back, so I excused myself and went to Joseph's truck for my flute. I asked George if it would be okay for me to play. He nodded, raised his hands to quiet the crowd, and pointed to me. I felt nervous being the center of attention. I closed my eyes and began to play, reminding myself to stop thinking. Jekyll joined me. His soft yodeling let me know the spirits were there....

When I finished, I opened my eyes. Everyone was looking at me and my yodeling bear dog with tears in their eyes. Frederick hugged me. He was crying. I knew then that what I played was a worthy gift. The potlatch lasted well into the night. I drove home with Joseph feeling elated. It was one of the best times of my life.

After a breakfast of wild berry oatmeal, I said goodbye to my wonderful friends. George told me their house was always open for me and my dog. He handed me a note and said to read it later. I hugged each one of them and then got on my ride. I reluctantly started the engine and backed out. I waved one more time and then I was gone.

32

I TOOK MY time on the gravel road. It wasn't only for safety; rather, this region was incomparably beautiful. It was a sunny day and I made the most of it. I upshifted and downshifted countless times, enjoying every steep gradient and sharply-angled switchback. I hoped I wouldn't have a Wile E. Coyote moment, the part where he ends up off the edge of the cliff, staring down, waiting for the fall to start happening. Jekyll was keeping a sharp lookout to keep me from peril. He let loose with several "Danger, danger!" yodels. I was amazed I did this ride at night in a driving rain, being cold to the bone.

The beauty before me was breathtaking. Carved through layers of sedimentary and volcanic rock by the Stikine River, the spectacular canyon was nearly a thousand feet deep. Joseph said this area was called "Yosemite of the North" by naturalist John Muir. I stopped several times to gawk at the scenery. I could live here and be happy.

It took three hours to travel the seventy miles back to the Cassiar Highway. If it took three days, I wouldn't have cared. The asphalt surface was amazingly quiet compared to traveling on gravel. The Trike was filthy with all the mud being thrown up on it from the gravel road, but it performed flawlessly. Jekyll was enjoying the day and I smiled at seeing his head swiveling back and forth. He was truly my co-pilot, looking for any signs of peril, be it animal or poor road conditions. I patted him on his chest for his diligence and he woofed for that kindness.

We rolled into Iskut and refueled. I bought a big slice of pizza and a soda, and we sat in the parking lot enjoying it. It was noon, and I had to come up with a plan for the rest of the day. The high from seeing the beautiful scenery had subsided, and I was missing my Tahltan friends. I got out my map and stared at the road ahead. "Look, Jek, if we go another hundred miles to the Stewart BC junction, I bet we can find a place to camp. That's only two or three hours from here. What do you say?"

"Woof!"

"I agree. We can do it easy." I got back on the road and passed the mountain-surrounded Eddontenajon Lake. Then we crossed a couple of narrow, wood-decked bridges, which brought howls from you-know-who. We went through another series of steep grades, but compared to the Telegraph Creek Road, these were easy. We climbed to Ningunsaw Summit and, several miles later, I saw a place called the Bell 2 Lodge. I pulled in and was delighted to hear there were camping spaces available. We found our site and I set up camp. I remembered the note George gave me and opened the small piece of paper, which was folded in half. Tears were in my eyes after reading the short story, which George said was from an unknown author. A renewed wave of loneliness swept through me. Almost in desperation, I turned on my phone, hoping to hear from someone. There was an email from Annie.

My dear Colt. As I began reading your email, my heart soared with your gifted words. Halfway though, I was so joyously crying that Pat had to take over. We practically danced around the room afterward. How wonderful that you are with your mother and father again. Your words have echoed in me for days. In my journal is this from the Indian mystic, Osho: "Once you have started seeing the beauty of life, ugliness starts disappearing. If you start looking at life with joy, sadness starts disappearing. You cannot have heaven and hell together, you can have only one. It is your choice." You're on the right path, my dear beautiful butterfly. Keep living your dream. You have our love. Annie

I read her email over and over, imagining her voice as I said her words. I started writing a reply.

Oh, Annie, how I needed your words. I'm near Stewart, BC, and was deep in loneliness, until you brightened my day.

I've just spent four days with an incredible Tahltan First Nations family in the town of Telegraph Creek, BC, and I am missing them so. When I left, my new friend George gave me this note: A wise woman, who was traveling in the mountains, found a precious stone in a stream. The next day she met another traveler who was hungry, and the wise woman opened her bag to share her food. The hungry traveler saw the precious stone and asked the woman to give it to him. She did so without hesitation. The traveler left, rejoicing in his good fortune. He knew the stone was worth enough to give him security for a lifetime. But, a few days later, he came back to return the stone to the wise woman. "I've been thinking," he said. "I know how valuable the stone is, but I give it back in the hope that you can give me something even more precious. Please give me what you have within you that enabled you to give me the stone."

Annie, *in my days with this family, I've had many moments of soulful blossoming. The elders gave me the gift of a flute with a carving of Jekyll on it. It's a long story, but they believe Jekyll is the incarnation of their sacred, extinct Tahltan Bear Dog. They taught me to play it, and I played for the whole village. I cannot, in my poverty of words, ever hope to explain the way my heart guided my fingers to play the song, but it was magical. While I was there, the sadness in my soul was consumed by their unfathomable kindness. How I love them. I read in Jekyll's Zen book a passage from Buddha that captures the heartbeat of my new friends:* "Thousands of candles can be lighted from a single candle, and the life of the candle will not be shortened. Happiness never decreases by being shared." *The elders blessed me with this Innuit song:* "I think over again my small adventures, my fears, those small ones that seemed so big, all those vital things I had to get and to reach, and yet there is only one great thing: to live and see the great day that dawns, and the light that fills the world." *I am happy, Annie. I am blessed. I am beautiful.*

I sent the message and turned off my phone. Writing elevated my spirits.

"Let's go for a walk, Jek."

"Woof!"

I put on my sweatshirt and sandals and picked up my flute. We started walking along the banks of the Bell Irving River. The forested area was beautiful with the Skeena Mountain Range in the background. We walked along the river for a while and sat on a large boulder. I took my flute from the bag and began to play. Jekyll's soft yodel soon accompanied me. As I played, I had an epiphany: *Throughout my adult life, my heart has been in conflict with my warrior veneer.* But no more. I was becoming my authentic self. The evening melted away, graced by the kinetic expression of human and canine souls.

When we got back to the tent, Jekyll burrowed into the sleeping bag and was soon snoring. I realized I hadn't looked at our books for several days, so I picked up Annie's journal and found a passage from Robert Frost. *Suddenly, quietly, you realize that—from this moment forth—you will no longer walk through this life alone. Like a new sun this awareness arises within you, freeing you from fear, opening your life. It is the beginning of love, and the end of all that came before.*

I gently put the book down and crawled into the sleeping bag with Jekyll. He didn't notice my presence. I thanked the Creator, said good-night to my parents, and drifted off to sleep feeling at peace.

33

I AWOKE BEFORE Jekyll and quietly got out of the sleeping bag. After putting on my clothes. I went outside, closed my eyes, and faced the morning sun, letting its warm rays envelop me. As I sat there, it occurred to me that I awoke happy, which was a rare event throughout my adult life. Normally, I'd wake with my mind abuzz on how to cope with the day.

Some campers passed and we said hello. Jekyll heard their voices and bounded out with a "hello" yodel. As he wagged his crooked tail, he put his nose in the air, and began sniffing for any hints of breakfast on the wind. Deep down, I hoped he'd land a scent and we'd follow it to its source. I was becoming as bad as my dog in the art of mooching, and that rang the guilt bell.

"Forget it, Jek. Let's make our own breakfast today."

I looked in our food cache. "Okay, we've got instant oatmeal, granola bars, or beef jerky. What'll it be?"

There was no response.

"Pancakes it is. Let's go to the coffee shop."

"Woof!"

I put him on a leash and tied him up at the front of the store. "Listen, you need to wait here while I order the food, okay?"

"Woof!"

"I'll be back in a few minutes." While waiting for my order, I heard a series of full-throttle power yodels and rolled my eyes. People in the shop began looking in the direction of the racket. It sounded like something had gotten run over. I told the staff to bring my order out and excused myself. I went outside and looked at the maestro of yodel.

"We're gonna have to work on this *Let me go in and order* thing. Your job is to sit quietly while I take care of business."

"Woof!"

His complete and utter joy at seeing me was trumped by me having nothing to eat in my possession. "Hey, I had to come out and tend to yodeling you."

The door opened and a pretty server handed me a sack of goodies. Her smile waned when she saw my train wreck on paws. "Um, here's your order, sir." She backed away, as if Jek's ugliness was partnered with meanness.

"Thanks for bringing it out. I have a mighty hungry dog. Would you like to pet him?"

"Uh, no…" She reversed direction and beat feet to the safety of the building. I smiled and turned my attention back to the revered "bear dog."

"Okay, let's eat back at our campsite."

"Woof! Woof!"

I kept him on the leash as we walked back, not that he'd take off with me holding a bag of food. We ate breakfast and got on the road early.

The town of Kitwanga was about a three-hour drive. I thought we'd go there and see how we were feeling. We passed several wood-plank bridges and Jekyll howled like a banshee as we crossed. He sure had a thing for bridges. Maybe they provided an opportunity for him to croon.

Shortly after the Meziadin Junction, Jekyll let loose a "Danger!" yodel. A grizzly was standing on our side of the road, in no hurry to get anywhere. I jammed on the breaks and downshifted to a halt. We were about a hundred yards from it. The wind was in our face, so it had no idea we were there. We sat and watched as it pawed at the side of the road. In Alaska, moose were drawn to roads for salt, so maybe this bear was doing the same thing. A big RV approached from the opposite direction, and the guy tried to brake as hard as I did. His big rig reminded him that it wasn't a sports car, and lurched around like a drunken sailor. After the bear stopped laughing, it hightailed into the woods.

I shifted to first and gave it some gas. Jekyll scanned the woods where the bear ran, concerned about an encore performance. He gave an "all clear" yodel about a mile away and I patted him on the chest to thank him for his diligence. I glanced in the mirror and swore my silly dog was smiling. He loved touring and took his job as co-driver seriously.

We crossed another bridge, and this time I beat Jekyll to the punch. I began howling which, at first, confused him. He quickly recovered, and we howled in unison. It was so funny (and oddly uplifting) that I decided all future bridge crossings would feature a howling duet.

We arrived in Kitwanga a short time later, and pulled in to the Dollops gas station. My ride was thirsty after the long drive. I checked the oil and was happy to see all was well. Pat would shudder if he saw how dirty his once pristine rig was. There wasn't so much as a square inch of surface that was clean. The devil in me emerged. I put Jekyll on the driver's seat and asked a non-senior to take our picture. I wanted Pat to see the MLC in all its glory. I was feeling good, so I looked at the map to chart our next leg. "Well, Jek, the Cassiar ends in a couple of miles. We need to get on Highway 16 and head east until we get to the town of Prince George. There's no way we can go that far today, so let's just motor on until we get tired. What do you think?"

"Woof!"

Just before the junction signaling the end of the Cassiar, we crossed the Skeena River. I had to inhale twice to howl the length of the bridge. We hung a left on Highway 16, which is called the Yellowhead Highway. Following that came the relatively big town of Smithers. I wasn't used to so much traffic and was a bit edgy. Suddenly, Jekyll started howling. I hit my breaks thinking an animal was running across the road that I didn't see. I pulled over and looked around, startled. Then I shook my head at seeing what caused Jekyll to go crazy. There were yellow arches a block up the road. He'd seen a McDonalds. My dog is a mess. I think there would've been a mutiny if I didn't pull in and order some extra-large fries. Oh, yes, let's not forget the catsup. I devoured a couple cheeseburgers and had a few of Jekyll's fries. I felt like an idiot sitting in the parking lot dribbling catsup on fries before feeding them to my dog. After the fries, Jek helped me finish my vanilla shake. I was still hungry, so I made another pass through the drive-through window, this time ordering a fish sandwich because it's important to have a balanced meal. While munching away, I gave some thought to Jekyll needing to eat better.

I was about ready to start my horse when it hit me to check for emails. My iPhone delighted me with mail in the inbox. It was from Pat.

Hello Colt. I asked Annie if I could assume the role of converser this time, and she grudgingly gave me reign of the keyboard. Though I've been a silent participant in your journey, I want you to know how much I've treasured hearing from you. Annie reads your emails aloud with Katie and me in rapt attention. We've yet to get through one of your emails without tears. Perhaps that is a measure of our love for you.

I miss you, Colt, in ways I never imagined. I can't explain why, but you've moved in and made my thinking crowded. There's not an hour that goes by that I'm not wondering where you are, how you're doing, what you're learning and discovering. I even think about von Bickerstaff. We howled with laughter about him being revered as the incarnation of a Tahltan Bear Dog. He's one amazing little dog, but no more amazing than his owner.

We love how you've been sharing your insights and discoveries with us. You're on the path that includes God, and it fills my heart with joy. The father in me reminds you to be safe and not push it. As your friend, I say enjoy every minute of your adventure. Sometimes I imagine myself on the road with you, having the time of our lives. But, I know this is a journey you need to complete on your own. Someday, before I'm old and decrepit, let's go on a mini-Grand Adventure together. We'll sit by a campfire, tell tall tales, and eat so much junk food that we puke. Real man stuff. I love you, son, with all my heart.

I smiled while reading it and closed my eyes afterward, absorbing his words, the words of my father. I read it aloud to Jekyll, trying to sound like Pat. He was wagging his tail and let out a woof when I said "von Bickerstaff." I thought about what to say, and then dictated a message into the iPhone.

Dear Pat, it was so good to hear from you. I'm sitting in a McD parking lot in Smithers, BC. You-know-who demanded we stop for fries. Imagine a guy in an outrageously loud phosphorescent lime-green motorcycle jacket feeding fries with catsup to an equally outrageous-looking dog in a helmet with orange-tinted goggles. If I stay here any longer, we'll become a local tourist attraction. I'm enclosing a pic of us and the MLC. If you look hard, you might see that it's black in color.

I, too, think about you, Annie, and Katie all the time. I want to share with you the beauty around every turn, and the vastness of this land. If I quit the Grand Adventure today, I'd still have enough wonderful memories for a lifetime. I'll never forget all of this has been possible because of you. I love you, Pat. I love you and your family and the countless kindnesses that you all have given me. My father, your love is my oasis. Your love is my salvation.

I sent the email and began composing another.

Scotty, I'm here in Smithers, a small town in British Columbia. My Grand Adventure is truly grand. I love you, my brother, and hope you're well.

"Let's find a place to stay, Jek."

"Woof!"

We pulled out and motored away.

34

IT DIDN'T TAKE long to find a place once we left town. I pulled into Tyhee Lake Provincial Park and got a campsite. The campground has a developed beach with swimming in the lake. After setting up the camp, I put on my swim trunks, grabbed some soap and shampoo, and looked at Jek. "You, my friend, are getting a bath. C'mon, let's go romp in the water."

I waded into the cool water with Jekyll in my arms. He was excited, right up to the point of getting wet. Then he frantically tried to crawl to the top of my head. I had to hold him out and away from me, before immersing him in the water. I was careful not to get his head wet. As we headed back to shore, he barked with delight, thinking the ordeal was over. Little did he know, we were just beginning. I put shampoo on him and started washing away. While he shook all over, I soaped down and shampooed. I had to chase him down because he knew another dunking was forthcoming. We must have looked pretty ridiculous, being all soaped up and running around. Ah, those Americans, the locals must be thinking.

I dunked my "wet rat," scrubbed the shampoo from him, and brought him back to the shore. After washing the soap off me, I was feeling good, that is, until seeing Jekyll rolling in the dirt to dry off.

I had to repeat the process all over, this time carrying him back to the camp. I toweled him off and we stayed outside until his fur was thoroughly dry. Since I was feeling a bit domestic, I aired the sleeping blanket for good measure.

I gave Jek a half-ration of Blue Buffalo since we already had eaten in town. It didn't take long for him to call me on it. I rolled my eyes and poured him a little more. By now, it was late enough to head to the tent. Jek started rooting through our stuff until he found what he was looking for—his Zen book. He dropped it next to me.

"Woof!"

"Did I ever tell you that you're one odd animal?"

"Woof!" He put a paw on the book.

"Okay. But, let's first get comfortable." I got into the sleeping bag, but left the top off since it was warm inside. After the customary show of closing my eyes and flipping to a random page, I looked at my Zen enthusiast. "Are you ready?"

"Woof!"

"Okay, let's see what we have tonight."

"A renowned Zen master said that his greatest teaching was this: Buddha is your own mind. So impressed by how profound this idea was, one monk decided to leave the monastery and retreat to the wilderness to meditate on this insight. There he spent twenty years as a hermit probing the great teaching. One day he met another monk who was traveling through the forest. Quickly the hermit monk learned that the traveler also had studied under the same Zen master. 'Please, tell me what you know of the master's greatest teaching.' The traveler's eyes lit up, 'Ah, the master has been very clear about this. He says that his greatest teaching is this: Buddha is NOT your own mind.'"

Jekyll looked like he was smiling. "I'm not surprised you thought that was humorous. Okay, here's another."

"A hermit was meditating by a river when a young man interrupted him. 'Master, I wish to become your disciple,' said the man. 'Why?' replied the hermit. The young man thought for a moment. 'Because I want to find God.' The master jumped up, grabbed him by the scruff of his neck, dragged him into the river, and plunged his head under water. After holding him there for a minute, with him kicking and struggling to free himself, the master finally pulled him up out of the river. The young man coughed up water and gasped to get his breath. When he eventually quieted down, the master spoke. 'Tell me, what did you want most of all when you were under water.' 'Air!' answered the young man. 'Very well,' said the master. 'Go home and come back to me when you want God as much as you just wanted air.'"

I laughed. "That hermit sounds like he was once an Army drill instructor."

"Woof!"

"One more, then let's switch to Annie's."

"One of Master Gasan's monks visited the university in Tokyo. When he returned he asked the master if he had ever read the Christian Bible. 'No,'

Gasan replied, 'please read some of it to me.' The monk opened the Bible to the Sermon on the Mount in the Gospel of St. Matthew. After reading Christ's words about the lilies in the field, he paused. Master Gasan was silent for a long time. 'Yes,' he finally said, 'whoever uttered these words is an enlightened being. What you have read to me is the essence of everything I have been trying to teach you here!'"

"I guess there's some universal truths in the world, huh, boy?"

"Woof!"

Jek retrieved Annie's book and I chose a page from her youth.

"Spring has its hundred flowers; autumn has its many moons. Summer has cool winds; winter its snow. If useless thoughts do not cloud your mind, each day is the best of your life. Wumen Huikai"

As I turned the pages, it felt like I was flipping through the years of her life.

"The Way is perfect like vast space where nothing is lacking and nothing is in excess. Indeed, it is due to our choosing to accept or reject that we do not see the true nature of things. Live neither in the entanglements of outer things, nor in inner feelings of emptiness. Be serene in the oneness of things and such erroneous views will disappear by themselves. When you try to stop activity to achieve passivity, your very effort fills you with activity. As long as you remain in one extreme or the other you will never know Oneness. Seng-ts'an"

"This passage is very true, Jek. I guess I've been an extremist in a lot of things. A couple more and that's it, okay?"

"Woof!"

I closed my eyes, chose a page near the beginning of the book, and began reading.

"Ask, and it will be given you. Seek, and you will find. Knock, and it will be opened for you. For everyone who asks receives. He who seeks finds. To him who knocks it will be opened. Jesus, Matthew 7:7"

Annie had drawn a line from this passage to another one further down the page. She circled it twice. "If you will confess with your mouth that Jesus is Lord, and believe in your heart that God raised him from the dead, you will be saved. Romans 10:9"

"Wow, Jek, this is powerful stuff. 'Ask, and it will be given to you. Seek, and you will find.' Well, we sure are seeking, but I guess we haven't asked."

"Woof!"

"Okay, then, I'll ask." I bowed my head. "Jesus is Lord, and I believe in my heart that God raised him from the dead. Please come to me, show me the way, and lead me to my noble purpose." I opened my eyes to see if anything happened. There were no mystical signs. I sighed. More hopes dashed. "C'mon, Jek, let's go water the forest and then go to bed."

We went out and did our thing. A shooting star flashed across the sky. "Hey, boy, maybe that's a sign."

"Woof!"

The night passed and we were on the road again. We traversed several steep grades and howled across a few bridges before rolling into the town of Vanderhoof. As we passed through the town, Jekyll's head began swiveling. When I looked at him in the mirror, I could tell he was sniffing the air. It didn't take a genius to know why. The fry-dog was on the hunt.

I saw a KFC, and, for a change of pace, pulled in. We chomped down a Variety Big Box Meal in the parking lot. Jek favored the popcorn chicken.

I gassed up and we pushed on. When we reached Prince George, it felt like a megalopolis. There are over eighty-thousand souls in this city and it was a shock to be in the hubbub again. We turned right on Highway 97, the Cariboo Highway. Since the next bigger town of Cache Creek was a good distance away, I topped off the tank and used the opportunity to check the tire pressure. I added a couple psi into the front tire.

Three hours later, we passed through the town of Williams Lake, and I decided to look for a campground. That ended up adding another thirty miles to our day. When we finally rolled into the Lac La Hache Provincial Park, I was a weary traveler and my rear, well, let's just say it was feeling every bump. This was a nice place, set in a stately Douglas-fir forest, with flush toilets, tap water, and—Jekyll would love this—a lake and developed beach for swimming. It even had a self-guided nature trail. Man, we were living the high life.

After setting up camp, I headed to the beach for a solo swim. The cold water felt wonderful. I swam out a ways, and then turned around when Jekyll barked warnings that I'd gone too far. I got out feeling exhilarated. Back at camp, I felt a little chilled, and put on my sweats.

Jek looked like he had some pent-up energy, so I got out my flute and decided to go for a walk on the camp's self-guided trail. There weren't many people on the trail, so I pulled out my flute and sat on a tree that long ago had succumbed to gravity. Jek climbed up and joined me. I started playing a tune, imagining I was once more on the Telegraph Creek Road with its many curves and grades. Jekyll joined in and capably hit some high notes with his yodeling. After that song, I played an upbeat melody picturing my friends dancing around the fire at the potlatch, and Jek matched me by lively crooning. When I opened my eyes, several people were standing in front of us. One of them started clapping, and the rest followed suit. I turned about thirty shades of red, but Jekyll eagerly accepted their adulation. A few came up and touched me and Jek, like we were holy. A couple named Paulette and Richard Monteau introduced themselves and said they were from Red Deer, Alberta. They invited Jek and me to dinner. It was an offer I couldn't refuse and we followed them back to their camp.

Richard got some coals going on the barbeque while Paulette ducked into their RV to prep the meal. He was a straight-talking man with an ample paunch who looked to be in his mid-forties. He reminded me of an older Marlboro man who'd traded ruggedness for his wife's good cooking. Paulette had an easy laugh and bubbly personality that perfectly matched her chubby frame. They were wheat farmers, owning a 480-acre spread. This was their first true vacation in ten years, and they were on their way back from a cruise through southeast Alaska.

An hour later, my belly had noticeably expanded from the consumption of two big burgers, a bunch of chips, two sodas and a large piece of cherry pie. Richard matched my eating stride for stride. I now understood how the former Marlboro man lost his mojo.

While I was chatting with Richard about my Trike, Paulette excused herself and went into their RV. She came out with a laptop computer. "Colt, I have something to show you. I recorded you and Jekyll while you played today on the nature trail and uploaded it to the net. Would you like to see it now?"

"Sure."

She hit a button and the video appeared featuring me and my crooning dog. It was beautiful. Paulette stopped it after a couple of minutes. "I think you should listen to the rest by yourself. Here's the link to access it online." She handed me a piece of paper with the link written down. "I promise no one will see this without your permission."

"Thanks, Paulette. I don't care who sees it. That was really nice of you." She asked for my email so we could stay in touch. We talked for a while longer and by then Jek and I were tuckered out. As I said goodbye, Richard invited Jek and me to visit them in Red Deer, promising the best-tasting steak in Canada. I thanked Paulette again for the video and we made our way back to camp. A short time later, we were sound asleep.

35

I WOKE EARLY, determined to get to the Canadian border today. By eight, we were on the road making good time. We passed the town of 100 Mile House—an odd name for a town. A while later, we passed 70 Mile House. I'm sure there's a story behind the names, but I wouldn't give the people naming the towns high marks for originality.

We rolled into Cache Creek a little after noon and gassed up. It was a small town, so when I saw Hungry Herbie's Drive In, I pulled in. Jekyll was happy with the fries, and quickly spotted the bacon on my burger. After he got his cut, my meal was downgraded to a cheeseburger. I'd been charging my iPhone all morning and turned it on to check for emails. Oh yeah! Two emails, one from Scotty and the other from Annie. I opened Scotty's first. Bad chow, bad working hours, and endless complaining by the young troops. The news was all good. Anything not involving blood was good news. I gave him a quick update regarding me and moved on to Annie's email.

Dearest Colt, you made our day with your last email. You should've seen Pat gasp when he saw the MLC! I think his idea of a Grand Adventure is traveling across town to get an ice cream. We're glad you're using it for its intended purpose. I won't ramble on and on, though it's so tempting to do so. Just know you're in our thoughts and prayers. I hope you feel our love.

I smiled while reading her email and sent a brief reply.

I'm in Cache Creek, BC, bound and determined to cross the border today. Yesterday, I met a lovely couple from Red Deer, Alberta. They heard me playing my flute, and unbeknownst to me, recorded my "performance" on camera. I'm enclosing the link and hope you all like it. Annie, it's weird, but I don't listen to the music while I play. I just close my eyes and let my spirit play. On the video I'm sending you, I imagined playing for my native friends. Jekyll always lends his voice anytime I play. We make a good team. Well, off we go. God bless us!

I turned off the phone and we hit the road. We encountered more steep grades, and passed a town called Spence's Bridge. I hung a left at Highway 8, and we motored to Merritt. A sign read *Country Music Capital of Canada*. I looked at my gas gauge and kept on going. We were now on Highway 97C, which they called the Coquihalla Connector. The scenery, as always, was beautiful with Douglas-fir forests and mountainous terrain.

After an hour, we arrived at the junction of Highway 97 and turned right. We were in the home stretch to the border. We passed through an area that looked like they were growing fruit trees. My suspicion was confirmed when we passed through a town called Peachland.

The next town was Summerland. Jekyll unleashed a huge yodel. Sure enough, he'd zeroed in on a McDonalds. Seeking some variety in my diet, I ordered two chicken wraps, a side salad, fries, and a large drink. They forgot to add catsup, which necessitated me running in for a handful of packets. Jekyll didn't touch the fries while I was gone. For him, no catsup was like Halloween without candy. After I dribbled on the red ambrosia, he was in hog heaven. We rolled on with sated stomachs and high spirits, getting ever closer to the good old red, white and blue.

The area was becoming arid as we drove south. A short while later, we came to the "huge" town of Penticton. The sign said the population was 39,993. It might as well have been New York City after where we'd been. I gassed up and looked at the map. We'd be back in the U.S. in an hour if all went well. The road got curvy and narrow for a while. We rolled through Oliver and later Osoyoos. Up ahead was the border.

We crossed into America without a hassle. The customs agent laughed when she saw Jek in his riding gear, and asked the standard border-crossing questions. She saw my Purple Heart license plate, thanked me for my service, and cleared me to move on. Jek yodeled goodbye as I drove away.

We'd been on the road nearly five hours since leaving this morning and both of us were tired. We passed Oroville, Washington, then Tonasket and Riverside. We howled going over the Okanogan River Bridge. I gassed up at a Chevron station in Omak and smiled at pumping gallons once more rather than liters. The cashier gave me directions to a place called Sunset Lakes RV Park. I was delighted to see how nice it was. They offered canoeing, walking trails, and even fly fishing.

I set up camp and washed up. My shoulders were aching from supporting Jekyll in his harness all day. We could use a few days of R&R, and I really needed to find a laundry and a car wash. The MLC was looking shabby, and I was getting low on clean underwear. Our sleeping bag smelled like sweat and dog, so I needed to wash that too. When we got to Wenatchee, I hoped to find a Harley dealer to change the oil and give the bike a tune up. We'd put a lot of hard miles on it, so I wanted to make sure it was in good repair.

Wenatchee was the first hometown on my list of KIA friends and I needed time to think about what to say to his parents. My happy mood faded with the thought of having to revisit painful parts of my past. I fed Jek, but didn't feel like eating. I turned on my phone and was glad to see a message from Annie.

Dear Colt, we listened to your video and felt we were in the presence of holiness. Your music is unspeakably beautiful. We listened to it over and over, and I must've gone through a box of tissues. Jekyll's soft yodeling is eerily breathtaking. We've never heard anything like it. As I've said before, he's a God-dog, and now I'm convinced of it. It's like your two souls join when you're playing. I watched, with fascination, your hands dancing on the flute, as if you've been playing forever. Divine energy has manifested in you, my wonderful son. Those who gathered around you, at the campground, came to hear Spirit. I feel so privileged to have you in my life and in the lives of my family. I have unbounded love for you, my dear Colt.

I turned off the phone because my poor disposition wasn't conducive to replying. I looked at Jek. "Hey boy, they liked our music. I guess we'll have to watch it all the way through, but I don't feel much like doing it now. How about you?"

"Woof."

"Exactly. It's been a long day. Why don't we go for a short walk to stretch our muscles, and then turn in."

"Woof."

We walked around the campground, which was nice, but I didn't pay much attention to the surroundings. I was deep in thought about my friend, John "Hector" Richardson, Jr. I don't know how Hector got his nickname. It was an odd nickname for a guy with pale skin and red hair. I'd have to ask Scotty about it. Anyway, he was "Hector" when I met him at Fort Benning, so I never questioned it.

Hector wasn't a Ranger, so Scotty, Manny and I dogged him until he volunteered for Ranger School. He was so proud to return with a Ranger Tab on his shoulder. He was one of us, the elite. Shortly after, he deployed to Afghanistan.

Hector was part of a 12-man special operations team sent to search for Taliban fighters in the mountains near Nuristan, Afghanistan. This was a nasty hellhole tucked up against the lawless border with Pakistan. After the helicopters departed, Hector and his team traversed a peak and descended down a valley leading to Nuristan. That's when all hell broke loose. The insurgents chose terrain perfect for an ambush. Their kill zone was steep and rocky with a million places to hide. Hector was on point when his team was pinned down by heavy arms fire. He came under fire from several directions, so there was no place to hide. He didn't go out in a blaze of glory. He died an agonizing death. They used him as fodder, shooting him over and over to bait the rest of the team to come help him. It took a series of Apache runs to clear the area. When they finally got to Hector, there were only pieces of him. He was fourteen days shy of his twenty-first birthday.

I didn't sleep well that night. I was back in Afghanistan. Several times I woke up shaking with a concerned Jekyll licking my face to calm me. The sun came up and, after eating a couple granola bars, we got on the road early. I halfheartedly howled as we crossed the bridge over the Columbia River, and scarcely noticed the scenery all the way to Wenatchee. We got there at nine-thirty and gassed up at a Texaco station. The guy there told me how to get to a carwash on Easy Street. The street name made me smile. He also gave me the name and number of the Harley dealer. I called and they said they could work me in at noon. That gave us enough time to wash the Trike and get a bite to eat before dropping it off.

It took a lot of spraying and scrubbing to get the Trike gleaming again. Jekyll sat in a dry corner of the wash bay and directed me a few times to re-spray some dirty areas. We pulled out looking a thousand percent better.

We rolled into the Legend Harley-Davidson dealership at eleven-thirty. They were courteous and promised to have my ride ready by two. Before going in, I put my cash, important papers, Jek's leash, and the flute in a kitchen trash bag. My riding gear and Jek's gear went into the Trike's storage compartment and I left the helmet on the seat. I needed a haircut and they said there was a place about three miles away. One of the staff was going to lunch and offered me a ride.

The barber didn't mind me bringing Jekyll into his shop. I got a short haircut because it's more practical to have short hair on the road.

He recommended the Motel 6 on North Wenatchee Avenue since they allowed dogs. We talked about Wenatchee and he bragged about it being the "Apple Capital of the World." I asked if he knew the Richardson family, but he didn't.

I took my time walking back to the Harley dealer and got there after one. The service manager said there was a small nail in the front tire and they fixed it. The bill caused me to gasp, but, considering everything they did, it was a fair price. I repacked the things in my bag and we headed over to the motel.

The motel room looked like a mansion compared to my tent. I gathered the dirty clothes and went to the laundry room. While doing my wash, I gave more thought on what to say to Hector's, I mean, John's, parents. In the end, I decided there was nothing to say but *"Hello, I'm Colt, and I knew your son. I'm here to pay my respects."* From that point on, they could steer the conversation.

I brought my clean clothes to the room, folded them, and took what I didn't need out to the Trike. As odd as it sounds, I didn't want to eat out, so I poured Jek his ration of food, and brought in some beef jerky and trail mix from the Trike. I absently munched on it while looking at the TV. After that, a nice, quiet soak in the tub sounded good.

I eased into the hot water and it felt wonderful. A tub may be one of civilization's greatest inventions, right up there with the wheel and cheeseburgers. I closed my eyes and took it in. My reverie soon ended. Jekyll walked in, his nails clicking on the tile. He stopped next to the tub and then I heard a soft thud. Even with my eyes closed, I knew what it was. "Let me guess. You want me to read your Zen book."

"Woof!"

"Sshh! Jek, you need to use your indoor voice."

"Woof!"

I looked at him. "You're one weird dog, you know that, don't you? Okay, hand me the book."

"Woof!" He hoisted it up in his mouth. I opened it, careful not to get it wet. Since Jek couldn't see me, I skipped the "eye's closed" ritual, and started reading.

"Once upon a time there was a little boy with a bad temper. His father gave him a bag of nails and told him that every time he lost his temper, he should hammer a nail in the fence. The first day the boy had driven thirty-seven nails into the fence. But gradually, the number of daily nails dwindled down. He discovered it was easier to hold his temper than to drive

those nails into the fence. Finally the first day came when the boy didn't lose his temper at all. He proudly told his father about it and the father suggested that the boy now pull out one nail for each day that he was able to hold his temper. The days passed and the young boy was finally able to tell his father that all the nails were gone. The father took his son by the hand and led him to the fence. You've done well, my son, but look at the holes in the fence. The fence will never be the same. When you say things in anger, they leave a scar just like this one. You can put a knife in a man and draw it out, it won't matter how many times you say I'm sorry. The wound is still there.'"

I thought about the rage in me. It hadn't surfaced since Manny passed, but I knew it was still there. I drifted back to the day we buried him...

"Woof!"

"Sorry, Jek. Where was I?" I turned a page.

"A student went to his meditation teacher and said, 'My meditation is horrible! I feel so distracted, or my legs ache, or I'm constantly falling asleep. It's just horrible!' 'It will pass,' the teacher said matter-of-factly. A week later, the student came back to his teacher. 'My meditation is wonderful! I feel so aware, so peaceful, and so alive! It's just wonderful!' 'It will pass,' the teacher replied matter-of-factly."

I smiled. It was the first time I had smiled all day. "One more, Jek. Then let's go to bed." From habit, I closed my eyes and flipped a few pages.

"No one saves us but ourselves. No one can and no one may. We ourselves must walk the path. Buddha"

I closed the book and handed it to Jek. "I bet Buddha would've loved 'walking the path' on a big Harley." He left with the book in his mouth. I toweled off and brushed my teeth. When I came into the room, Jekyll was on the bed with his Zen book sitting next to Annie's.

The bed felt too soft after being on the road. I gave some thought to sleeping on the floor, but, after a while, I got used to it and it felt good. A bad dream visited me during the night, and I was glad Jek was there to let me know everything was alright.

36

I AWOKE TO knocking on the front door. Jekyll's sudden barking ensured the shock was complete. I got up and walked to the door. "Yes?"

"Room service, sir. You're past checkout time. Will you be ready soon?"

Geez, I slept in late. "Um, can you give me another fifteen minutes?"

"Sure, sir. But you need to hurry. We have this room being occupied again at noon."

"Okay. Thank you." I looked at Jek. "Can you wait for me to shower before doing your business?"

"Woof."

"Okay, I'll hurry." I showered, shaved, and combed my hair, wanting to look presentable to Hector's parents. After dressing, I gathered our things and thanked the attendant for her patience. Jek ran to the grass and promptly did his thing. I was hungry, so that was our first mission of the day.

Jekyll had his McD radar going, and quickly detected an arches on North Mission Street about two miles from the motel. Breakfast consisted of coffee, a McMuffin, and fries with catsup for McJek. We ate quietly in the parking lot. I took off my riding gear except for my helmet so his parents wouldn't think I was a bad-ass biker. It felt odd riding without my gear.

We pulled into their driveway around noon. It was a typical suburban house, like the one of my youth in Prescott. I took off my helmet, put Jek on a leash, and tied him to the Trike. I re-tucked in my shirt, and left my helmet on the seat of my bike. I was nervous and took in a deep breath before walking to the front door. An elderly lady was looking at me through the screen door. She had on a bathrobe and didn't look friendly. "Good afternoon ma'am. My name is Colt Mercer, and I served in the Army with John Richardson. I wanted to pay respects to his parents. Do they live here?"

She didn't answer. Instead, she yelled, "Margaret!"

A woman came to the door looking to be in her forties. "Yes?"

"Good afternoon ma'am. I served in the Army with your son. May I come in for a few minutes?"

She looked me over, and hesitantly opened the door. "Come in."

I offered my hand and she shook it. She motioned for me to sit on their couch. With gaunt eyes and a stoic expression, she didn't look like a happy person. The older lady went to the sliding glass door leading to the backyard and opened it. "John, you need to come in. Someone's here to see us." A minute later, a tall man with glasses appeared. He had salt-and-pepper hair and looked like an older version of Hector. The old lady spoke again. "He says he served with Johnny. What's your name again?"

"Colt Mercer, ma'am. Pleased to meet you, sir." I went over and shook his hand. I think he was surprised someone from his son's Army days would just show up.

"Have a seat, Colt."

"Thank you, sir." I returned to the couch and cleared my throat. "I was in the same battalion as John, and we were good friends. I'm out of the Army now, touring the country on a motorcycle. So, I thought I'd drop by to tell you what a privilege it was to know him." His mother left the room, leaving me with the father and grandmother.

"I miss my son more than I can say," he said, with tears in his eyes. "They wouldn't let us see his body, did you know that?"

"Yes, sir. I'm very sorry for your loss. I wasn't there, but I heard he died bravely."

He nodded. "Did you know he was almost twenty-one when he died?"

"Yes, sir. He emailed me saying he was looking forward to his birthday."

Hector's mother returned with a shoebox. She sat next to me and opened the box which was full of letters. She ran through them and found the one she wanted. "I know every one of these letters by heart. Your name is Colt, right?"

"Yes ma'am."

She opened a letter and began reading. "My good friends Colt,

Manny and Scotty are dogging me to go to Ranger School. Colt says you're not a soldier until you have a Ranger Tab on your shoulder. He's right, Mom, so I'm sending my name in for consideration." She looked coldly at me. "You're the one who goaded my boy into becoming a Ranger. If he didn't do that, he never would've been on that special operations team in Afghanistan. How does it feel to have my only son's blood on your hands, Mr. Colt Mercer?" Her voice was laced with disdain.

I reeled back. "Ma'am, I—"

"Get out of my house and never come back. Get out!" She stood up, pointed to the door, and screamed. "Get out!" I was stunned. I stood up and looked at Mr. Richardson. He stared at the floor and didn't say a thing. Tears were pouring from his eyes. I bolted out the door, ran to my motorcycle, and got the hell out of there. I could barely see from crying so hard. After a few miles, I saw a dirt road and took it, pulling in between some trees. I threw off my helmet, buried my face in my hands, and cried uncontrollably...

"Hey, mister. You! What are you doing in my orchard?"

I looked up to see an old lady with white hair standing ten feet away with a rifle pointed at me. My day had just gotten even better. I wiped my eyes. "I'm sorry ma'am. I just needed to pull over for a while."

"Are you one of them Hell's Angels? Are you doing drugs?"

"No, ma'am. I'm just going through a hard time right now." Jek jumped off and ran to her, wagging his tail.

"That sure is an ugly dog."

"No, ma'am, he's a beautiful dog. You just have to look deeper to see the beauty. He got that way saving me from a bear."

"Where you from, mister?"

"Alaska, ma'am. I'll be on my way."

"Why are you sitting in my orchard crying like a baby?"

I started bawling again. She lowered her weapon and walked up to me. "You're hurting bad, aren't you?"

"Yes, ma'am. Real bad."

"Follow me up to my house, son." She went to her pickup, put the rifle in a rack behind the seat, and started the engine. She leaned out the open window. "C'mon!"

I put Jekyll in his harness. It was hard to see through my tears, so

I tailed the vague outline of her truck. We got to her house about five minutes later, and she invited me in. She told me her name was Vivian and said to sit at the kitchen table while she made a pot of coffee. I explained what had happened today, along with a rambling account of my life. I must've sounded pathetic, but she listened patiently.

"Colt, I went to school with Margaret's mother, so I know the family. Margaret has never been right since her son died. She's mad at the world, and you're just another poor thing for her rage to pounce on." She got up and came back with her *Bible*. She thumbed through the pages. "Listen to this. It's from Jesus in Acts 1:7: *'It isn't for you to know times or seasons which the Father has set within his own authority.'*" She closed the book. "Unless you've assumed the role of God, you have nothing to be blamed for. He was in a dangerous profession, going into harm's way. His demise could be blamed on the President for sending troops over there, his commander for putting the soldiers into the battle, or the Taliban who pulled the trigger. I bet she even blames her husband for encouraging Johnny to join. That's all for God to sort out, not Margaret or you. Just know the essence of her rage isn't you. She lost her little boy and her heart is broken. Give her your love, and pray that God heals her soul."

Her words made perfect sense. "Vivian, I needed to hear what you said, more than you'll ever know."

She put her hand on mine. "I want to say something else that you're not going to like. You've had a recent winning streak in meeting the Brennans and getting those donations for your trip. I hope you didn't get jaded into thinking your quest will be nothing but a series of fairy godmother episodes. Today was a wake-up call. I'm here to tell you that you need to drop the fairy godmother in favor of some serious soul searching. You're going to have to earn your calling, because it won't be handed to you by your well-off friends. Being damaged takes a long, long time to get over, and it may never happen. Last summer, I lost Bill, my husband of fifty-two years. He was the light of my life. The world doesn't seem right without him in it and I'll never get over losing him."

I winced at her remarks. They cut deep. "I'm sorry for your loss, and hear what you've said. You're right on the fairy godmother thing. Deep down, I suppose I was hoping to see a burning bush or find words chiseled on tablets laying everything out for me." A wave of hopelessness swept over me.

"Colt, all I'm saying is: earn it. Earn the life you're seeking and accept that you'll have to work harder than you ever have to get there. I find my strength now in the Lord. You might want to give thought to that too."

"Yes, ma'am. I've put all options on the table to try to find my way. As for soul searching, back in Alaska, a special lady named Annie gave me her journal. It's full of quotes and passages, and I've gotten a lot of insights from it. I read it every night to Jekyll, along with his Zen book."

"Your dog likes Zen?"

"Yes, ma'am. He won't sleep until I read him a story."

She laughed. "You have an interesting little dog there."

"I'd prefer to read a dog obedience book to him every night, but that wouldn't fly. Actually, I enjoy the Zen book as much as he does."

Vivian went to the fridge and plucked off a paper that was held by a magnet. "This was Bill's favorite passage, written by Mark Jenkins. I think you'll like it. *Adventure is a path. Real adventure—self-determined, self-motivated, often risky—forces you to have firsthand encounters with the world. The world the way it is, not the way you imagine it. Your body will collide with the earth and you will bear witness. In this way you will be compelled to grapple with the limitless kindness and bottomless cruelty of humankind—and perhaps realize that you yourself are capable of both. This will change you. Nothing will ever again be black-and-white.'"

"Wow. That hits home. Today sure has been a day of kindness and cruelty. I think I would've liked your husband."

"He would've liked you too."

I looked at my watch and frowned. "Vivian, would you mind if I said goodbye? I want to visit John's grave and pay my respects, then head down the road."

"Not at all. Why don't we both go to the cemetery. I've had a yearning to visit Bill's grave and can show you the way."

"That would be great. I stood up and gave her a hug. "Thank you so much."

"No problem. Let me get you a bag of apples to take with you. I grow Pink Ladies, which are a cross between Golden Delicious and Lady Williams. The first bite tastes tart and is followed by a delightful sweetness. Just like me."

I smiled. "You are sweet. They'll be great after our steady diet of fast food."

At the cemetery, I got out my flute to play for Hector. Vivian helped me find his grave, which had a white government headstone. I touched it, silently read its inscription, and then whispered, "This is for you, Hector." I closed my eyes and began playing my flute. Jekyll added his voice to the effort. I think he knew we were paying respects to the dead. Vivian hugged me after we finished.

"That was so beautiful. Will you play a song for my husband?"

"I'd be honored to. Would you mind me saying a few more words to my friend, and then I'll join you?"

"Not at all. Take your time. I'll be over with Bill." She left and Jekyll followed her.

I knelt down and said goodbye to my friend, asking God to bless him and be with him always. I touched the grass for a few moments and left a coin on his headstone. I stood tall, saluted, and whispered, "Rangers lead the way."

I wiped tears from my eyes while walking to the grave of my new friend's husband. She was busy pulling weeds and stood to welcome me. Bill had a large granite headstone. Next to his name was Vivian's name with her birth year but no deceased date. "All they have to do when I die is add the death date to the stone and plant me next to Bill," she said. I smiled meekly and started playing my flute, imagining my own father being buried here. When I finished, Vivian was in tears. "That was so beautiful. I thank you so." We hugged for a long time. After putting on my riding gear in her truck, we said goodbye. There was another thing for me to do on the Grand Adventure. I had to play my flute at the grave of my parents in Prescott.

37

I GOT ON Highway 2 and blazed out of town, hoping that distance would somehow mute the words of Hector's mom, which were still echoing in my head. I scarcely noticed the scenery and just drove and drove, debating the foolishness of visiting KIA parents. Spokane came and went on Interstate 90, and then we were approaching Coeur d'Alene, Idaho. Jekyll reached his limit and started barking and struggling to get out of his harness. I took an exit and stopped on the shoulder of the off-ramp. He leaped off the Trike and immediately squatted. After finishing, he looked at me like he was madder than a box of frogs.

"Sorry, Jek. I needed to get away. I'll make it up to you." I stomped my feet to get some feeling in them, and got out some water for him to drink. He was really thirsty. I gave him a full ration of food and drank the rest of the water while he chowed down. Both of us didn't feel like going another mile. "Jek, let's find a motel and spend the night." He moaned when I put him back in the harness. "Not much longer, boy. Keep an eye out for a McDonalds and we'll pull in."

"Woof!"

Finally, my dog began acting normal. I was glad he didn't stay mad for long.

I saw a Motel 6 sign, took the off-ramp, and got a room. I asked for directions to the nearest McDonalds. There was one on West Appleway Avenue, about two miles away, so we headed over.

After dining, I stopped at a gas station, filled the tank, and cleaned the windshield. When we got back to the motel, I took a shower and felt better after washing off the road grime. Maybe I washed off the bad karma too. Jekyll was on the bed looking happy. "Thanks for forgiving me, Jek. I just needed to get away from there."

"Woof!"

I scratched behind his remaining ear and thought about the day.

Other than meeting Vivian, today was an absolute disaster. Maybe the smart move was heading to Prescott and ending the trip there. I could take I-90 to I-15 and ride it all the way south. As I toyed with the thought, I noticed Annie's journal. Maybe I'd find an answer there. Jekyll eased in close when I started reading.

"Out of suffering have emerged the strongest souls; the most massive characters are seared with scars. Kahlil Gibran*"*

How true it was. I read the next entry.

"What seems to us as bitter trials are often blessings in disguise. Oscar Wilde*"*

Well, Mr. Wilde, today sure didn't feel like a blessing in disguise. I looked at the journal again.

"It's never too late to be what you might have been. George Eliot*"* I read the words several times to Jekyll. "The question is, what should I be?"

"Woof!"

"I know. Sometimes I wish I could say 'to hell with it' and just rent a crystal ball. This quest thing can get damn tedious."

"Woof!"

"Okay, I'll read on. You're kind of impatient tonight, do you know that?"

"Woof!"

"Here's one from Maya Angelou. *I've learned that no matter what happens, or how bad it seems today, life does go on, and it will be better tomorrow. I've learned that you can tell a lot about a person by the way he/she handles these three things: a rainy day, lost luggage, and tangled Christmas tree lights. I've learned that regardless of your relationship with your parents, you'll miss them when they're gone from your life. I've learned that making a 'living' is not the same thing as making a life. I've learned that life sometimes gives you a second chance. I've learned that you shouldn't go through life with a catcher's mitt on both hands; you need to be able to throw something back. I've learned that whenever I decide something with an open heart, I usually make the right decision. I've learned that even when I have pains, I don't have to be one. I've learned that every day you should reach out and touch someone. People love a warm hug, or just a friendly pat on the back. I've learned that I still have a lot to learn. I've learned that people will forget what you said, people will forget what you did, but people will never forget how you made them feel.'*"

I stroked Jek's head. "That was beautiful. I know how much I miss my parents. Do you remember playing that day when Paulette and Richard saw us, and how those people around them came up and touched us? I think they'll remember us for a long time. Annie said they liked it too, and so did our friends at Telegraph Creek."

"Woof."

"Maybe that's what we should do. Play our music and maybe make a record. What do you think?"

"Woof."

"Yeah, that doesn't sound like our noble purpose. Maybe doing it on the side, but doing it for a living doesn't get me excited. It's like we're trying to make money off something divine."

"Woof."

"Hey, we're both tired. One more and that's it, okay?"

"Woof."

"*Even as fire finds peace in its resting place without fuel, when thoughts become silence, the soul finds peace in its own source. When the mind is silent, then it can enter into a world which is far beyond the mind: the highest End. The mind should be kept in the heart as long as it has not reached the highest End. This is wisdom, and this is liberation. The Upanishads*"

I turned off the light, and then turned off my mind.

38

I WOKE UP feeling refreshed. Our next stop would be Tioga, North Dakota. Come hell or high water, we were going to see all the families on the list. I turned on my iPhone and dictated an email...

Dear Pat and Annie, forgive me for being incommunicado the last several days. The last few days have been tumultuous, and last night I thought of packing it in. Let me tell you what happened.

I visited the first parents on my KIA list, and it was an unmitigated disaster. His mother told me I had his blood on my hands because I urged him to become a Ranger. Had he not become a Ranger, she said, he wouldn't have been on the special ops mission resulting in him being killed. She threw me out of her house and said never come back. I was so beside myself, I had to pull over. Annie, I sat there and cried my eyes out. I didn't think the day could get worse, until the owner of the property pointed a rifle in my face wanting to know why I was trespassing on her land.

After seeing how distraught I was, she invited me to her home, and we talked a long time. She knew my friend's family, and said I mustn't let his mother's rage bring me to despair. Annie, she was a blessing. Her name is Vivian and I'm convinced God directed me to her. She lost her husband of fifty-plus years the summer before, so we visited the cemetery and she showed me where my friend Hector was buried. I played my flute for him and then for her husband. We said goodbye and I drove nonstop to Coeur d'Alene, Idaho, debating the whole way if visiting the KIA parents was folly. I was on the brink of scrapping the Grand Adventure, but something happened in my dreams last night...

I dreamed about Hector's mom and her swirling vortex of rage. In this dream I talked to her, and told her about my wonderful parents and my years-long rage at the man who ended their lives. I told her I learned how this rage kept me from my parents, the very thing I loved most. It was only after I forgave him that my parents returned to me. At first, she said I was foolish, but I confirmed my words by having her talk to Mom and Dad. She cried as she listened, and bravely made the choice to forgive, and let her rage go. I left her smiling and holding her son's hand as she waved goodbye. After sending you this email, I'm going to write my dream in a letter and send it to Hector's mom. I hope she'll find comfort from it. In my dream I also talked to Mom and Dad about visiting the other parents of my fallen friends. They had a simple response: "Your dreams traverse the universe and touch others with the highest good. Consider the smiling face of Hector's mother as you weigh your decision." I woke up knowing I had to continue. I'm heading to Tioga, North Dakota. By the way, I'm adding another stop to my journey. I'll be going to Prescott to play my flute at my parents' grave.

Annie and Pat, I've learned so much in the last year. In your journal, Maya Angelou says, 'I've learned that people will forget what you said, people will forget what you did, but people will never forget how you made them feel.' I want to do something to make people feel. What that is, I don't know. But it's what I want to do. Is this progress?

I sent the email, wrote a letter to Hector's mom, and then shared a couple of Vivian's apples with Jekyll. After that, I looked at my map. We could make Bozeman easily today. As I looked at the I-90/I-94 junction, something caught my eye. The Little Bighorn Battlefield National Monument. Custer's Last Stand. It'd be a 132-mile round trip detour, but I had to see it.

I ate another apple and packed our things. We left the hotel at ten. Before we left, I got directions to a grocery store and motored over. I filled a cart with Blue Buffalo, bulk trail mix, cashews, granola bars and a bag of baby carrots. Craving something salty, I grabbed a bag of salt-and-vinegar chips. At the checkout, on impulse, I added a cold soda and a York peppermint patty. The lady looked at me funny, acting like she never saw someone in a lime-green riding jacket with an odd-looking dog in a harness.

I ate the peppermint bar while walking to my ride, chugged down the soda, and, after a gargantuan burp, started the engine. We were bound for Missoula.

I admired Lake Coeur d'Alene as we left the beautiful, forested city. The drive to Missoula was gorgeous. As the distance from Coeur d'Alene increased, the density of the forest decreased. I fed Jekyll carrots from my pocket as we drove, and even ate a few myself. By the time we arrived in Missoula, the land was much more arid. Just past the airport, you-know-who's radar detected a familiar site, and he sounded a McD yodel alert. I pulled in, tied him to the Trike, and went in to use the restroom. I ordered our meal and came out to find an excited dog. Jek ate the fries, of course with catsup, while I enjoyed a chicken salad. I slurped down a large vanilla shake and he helped me finish the last of it.

Three hours later, we wearily rolled into Bozeman, an attractive college town with impressive bordering mountains. I gassed up and checked the tire pressures, which were all good. While paying for the gas, I asked about a place to camp, and the guy gave me directions to a place called Sunrise Campground. It proved to be a good tip. I set up camp and fed Jekyll. I bought a soda and slurped it down while eating the bag of salt-and-vinegar chips purchased in Coeur d'Alene. Jek tried a chip and his face contorted from the vinegar taste. I finally had found something he didn't like. I gave him a few carrots to get the taste out of his mouth and he lapped up a lot of water. I finished my meal with a handful of cashews. After tasting that chip, Jek wanted no more of my food.

I looked at the map. Billings was 140 miles away, or about two hours. Little Bighorn was an hour after that. I decided to get up early to have plenty of time to visit the battlefield.

While I was fixated on the map, Jekyll contented himself with chasing grasshoppers. After catching one, he didn't eat it, but rather it go, like it was a game of tag. It was so funny that I got out my journal and sketched him playing. He looked so happy. A train went by and he howled. It was a long train, so it took several breaths to keep up the howling. Afterward, he looked at me with bravado, like he himself had chased the iron horse off.

"You know, it's a privilege to watch your mind at work. Did I ever tell you that you're a very odd dog?"

"Woof!"

The sun was going down, so I got out my battery-powered lantern and we went into the tent. Jekyll sat on the sleeping bag. "We were living the good life in motels, huh, boy? Now it's back to pedestrian living."

"Woof!!" He picked up his Zen book and dropped it in my lap.

"I know, you want your Zen, but give me some time to go over our finances. Our burn rate is higher than I was anticipating. Let me total things up, and then I'll read your book, okay?"

"Woof!"

"Thanks, Jek. You're a good dog. I'm proud to call you my friend."

"Woof!"

"Okay, let me focus."

I got out my receipts and used the iPhone's calculator to do the adding. The total made me frown, but I told myself not to worry, we'd be okay. When I turned to tell Jekyll I was ready to read his book, he was sound asleep. I switched off the lantern and joined him.

39

JEKYLL WOKE ME at sunrise. I'm glad he did, though it was hard to open my eyes. I ate some more apples and gave him the last of the carrots. We were on our way before eight and the traffic was light all the way to Billings. This was cowboy country. Billings was a big town—the biggest town we'd been through since leaving Anchorage. It had some impressive cliffs, which looked to be about 500 feet tall. Jekyll howled when he saw a McD. I barely had time to take the off-ramp. We ate quickly and, after gassing up at a nearby station, headed down the road.

We came to the I-90/I-94 junction, and I veered right, staying on I-90. An hour later, I took Exit 510, and pulled into the monument. The ranger said pets weren't allowed out of vehicles, so I took their cell phone audio tour where you experience a narrative story of the Battle of the Little Bighorn. I listened to a narration of soldier movements and warrior accounts, and tried to imagine being in this cauldron of battle, and how I'd use the terrain for defense. In this exposed area, there wasn't much the troops could do, being so outnumbered by Indians hell-bent on protecting their way of life. I closed my eyes and heard the rifle fire, the desperate screams of the wounded, the smell of gunpowder, and the Indians' war cries. Suddenly, I was back in Afghanistan, hearing the noises, seeing the blood, smelling the cordite from ammunition. I covered my ears to shield them from the imaginary noise...

Someone touched me and I nearly jumped out of my skin.

"A-are you okay?" An elderly woman was looking at me with concern.

It took me a moment to get my bearings. I was sweating, even though it was a cool, windy day. "Yes ma'am, I was living the battle in my head."

She stayed a moment, looking me over to see if I was truly okay. When she noticed the Purple Heart license plate, I think she put two-

and-two together. She walked back to her car and said something to her husband. He saluted me as they drove to the next stop on the tour.

I got off the Trike and pulled out some water. I drained the bottle and got another one for Jek. "Jek, I need you to wait here while I visit some of the gravestones, okay?"

"Woof!"

"I'll be back in a few minutes." I tied Jek to the Trike and walked from Custer Hill to a deep ravine about 400 yards away. It was here that at least twenty-eight bodies had been found. One of the gravestones said "U.S. Soldier Fell Here, June 25, 1876."

The 7th Cavalry lost 16 officers and 242 troopers. I closed my eyes and said a prayer for them and for the Indians killed in battle. Both had gotten a raw deal. I thought about the arrogant Custer and his battle-savvy foe. It's ironic how winning this battle hastened their demise. In the distance, I heard yodeling, so I needed to hurry back before the park rangers scolded me for having an unruly pet. Before leaving, I stood tall and saluted the dead.

Jekyll was relieved to see me return. I patted him a few times and got out the map. I was tired of cruising the interstate, and wanted something less civilized. After studying the map, the roads simply weren't going to cooperate. The interstate was basically the only game in town, at least to Glendive, which was near the Montana/North Dakota border, about 215 miles away. That was a good three-and-a-half hour drive. "Jek, you're not going to like this, but we've got a long stretch of road ahead of us. Are you up for it?"

"Woof."

"I know, but you can see there's nothing between here and there except for Miles City, but that's still two and a half hours from here."

"Woof."

"Okay, we'll see how we're doing at Miles City before going on." I let him run into the prairie grass and take care of business.

We rolled into Miles City and gassed up. I took a few moments to look around. Surrounded by vast stretches of plains and badlands, Miles City in every way exemplified the West. I sure saw why they call Montana "Big Sky Country." There was a KFC, so I ordered the Big Box Meal with a 32-ounce drink. Jek ate his fill of potatoes and gravy, along with the popcorn chicken and a biscuit.

Back on the road, I saw clouds to the west. Uh-oh. I'd been lucky since the Cassiar, and hoped my luck would continue. An hour later, it ran out. We were in the middle of nowhere when rain started coming down, and there wasn't an overpass within a hundred miles. I saw a gravel side road, pulled onto it, and quickly got out my portable chair and the tarp. I bungeed the tarp to my Trike to make a makeshift lean-to. I crawled under it, and sat on the chair with Jek. Then things got interesting. It started to rain and hail. I put on my helmet and bent over to shield Jek. Pea-sized hail turned into nickel-sized, which turned into quarter-sized. Lightning was flashing near, followed by booming thunder. Strong winds started lashing at the tarp and I grabbed the ends to hold it down. God almighty! Jekyll was howling, and all I could do was hold on.

It took over an hour for the storm to pass. When we emerged, the sky was almost clear. I watched the thunderhead move to the east. The roads were drenched, so I decided to camp right where we were. After the adrenaline surge of the storm, I was tired and so was Jek. After setting up the tent, we went in and quickly fell asleep. Fortunately, the night brought no more rain.

Jekyll woke me the next morning, barking. I thought he had to go out, but then I heard movement outside the tent. When I poked my head out, there was a Montana Highway Patrol car parked next to us with its lights flashing. The officer motioned for me to come out. I quickly put on my jeans and sandals and exited the tent with Jekyll in my arms. He looked us over, said something into his microphone, and then stepped out of his car. "Are you armed?"

"No, sir."

A message sounded on his speaker saying no warrants or violations. "Do you know it's illegal to camp along an interstate?"

"No, sir. I got caught in the thunderstorm yesterday, and the roads were wet afterward. It was too dangerous to travel."

"I see you're from Alaska. Where're you headed?"

"I'm touring the country, but right now, I'm headed to Tioga, North Dakota."

"Why?"

"I'm going to visit the parents of a friend of mine who was KIA in Iraq. In fact, I'm going to visit all the parents of my KIA friends throughout the country."

"How's that going?"

"Not good. I got thrown out at my first stop in Wenatchee, Washington."

"I saw your license plate. Purple Heart, huh?"

"Yes, sir."

"What did you do?"

"Army Ranger and a Sniper. Nine years, three combat tours."

"Impressive. Who's your dog?"

"This here is Jekyll von Bickerstaff."

"Woof!"

He came over and patted Jek. "That's a hell of a name. Looks like your dog has seen some action too."

"I found him in the bush last winter and then he saved me from a bear."

He offered me his hand. "My name is Dave Rayfield."

"Pleased to meet you, Dave. Been a cop long?"

"Ten years. Before that, I did a stint in the Air Force."

"Have you heard the latest on the weather? Yesterday wasn't pleasant."

"Yeah. The front has moved through. Temps today should be in the seventies."

"Excellent. Thanks for the dirt."

"How long do you plan on being gone?"

"It depends on how my money holds up.

"Well, if you get short, give some thought to joining us. We could use someone with your talents."

"Thanks, Dave, but I've seen enough killing to last a lifetime. Right now, I'm just trying to figure out what I should do. And regarding that, I haven't a clue."

"I know what you mean. I felt lost after getting out of the Air Force. I stumbled into this job, and came to love the freedom it offers. My beat covers thousands of square miles."

"I'm sure I would've loved being a patrolman if I did it right out of high school. But now, I wish they'd ban all weapons and wars. Hell of a thing for a soldier to say."

"If you change your mind, give me a call. Here's my card."

"Thanks. Can I use it to get out of a speeding ticket?"

"Hand it back." He turned the card over, took out his pen, and began writing, saying aloud the words he was writing. "Fellow officers. Please let my friend, Colt, off with a warning. He's a genuine hero." He handed the card back to me. "I could get my ass chewed if you ever try to use this, but what the hell, give it a try if you need to. Good luck on your trip, and take your time getting ready."

"Thanks, Dave. It was a pleasure meeting you."

"You too. Good luck trying to find your way." He shook my hand, got in his car, and motored away.

"Well Jek, let's get out of here before someone less friendly shakes us down."

"Woof!"

We were on the road in fifteen minutes.

We rolled into Glendive before noon and I spotted a Subway. I got a foot-long turkey sandwich with plenty of veggies and chips for Jekyll. He was starting to get downright pudgy with all the high-calorie fast food we'd been eating. I could feel my waistline expanding too.

I got out the map. I knew I could use my iPhone to display maps, but I was a dinosaur, preferring paper. Tioga looked to be about three hours away. I had to get on Highway 16 until it intersected Highway 2. Tioga was about forty miles east of the intersection. "We've got another three-hour drive ahead of us, Jek. I'll give you a half ration of food now and a half ration when we get there. Fair enough?"

"Woof!"

We rolled on. To say this region is isolated is an understatement. There was nothing but miles and miles of miles and miles. Argh. I used the time to think about my friend, Marc Norgaard. His family traced their roots to Norway, and they were North Dakota homesteaders. Marc had an easy smile and a certain stoicism that I could see came from living in this harsh land. He always took things in stride and often talked about joining his dad's business when he got out. His dad owned a company supporting the oil industry.

Marc got it in Iraq. He was in a convoy that got attacked with enemy fire ranging from small arms to rocket propelled grenades. When the Humvee ahead of him broke down, Marc ran to assist them. He took over firing its turret machine gun after its gunner got hit. Before a bullet found him, he'd fired over 300 rounds, killing or wounding fifteen insurgents. Marc was a brave man.

An hour passed as I thought of him. Then another. We got to the intersection of Highway 2 and then rolled into Williston, North Dakota. It was a compact town teeming with activity. They sure had a lot of trucks for such a small town. Most had oil industry decals on their doors.

I pulled off the road, got out my iPhone, and found several Norgaard families in the area. I looked up Marc's obituary and struck pay dirt. His father's name was James Norgaard. I found his address and used my iPhone's map to see how to get there.

I planned to get cleaned up in a motel in Tioga before seeing his parents, just like I'd done in Wenatchee. I almost laughed when I entered the town. There were a few grain silos and not much else. The only place to stay was out on the austere prairie in my tent. To hell with it. The Norgaards were going to see me just as I was. On the last mile to their place, I thought about what to say. Once more, nothing came to mind. I said a silent prayer that it wouldn't be a repeat of Wenatchee.

40

Four months later...

I WAS LYING in a meadow of grass in Randolph, Vermont. I'd found a slice of heaven. Jekyll was snoozing peacefully, enjoying the crisp autumn day. I sent an email to Pat and Annie.

Oh, Annie, how I wish I could adequately describe the beauty of Vermont in October. Before me in every direction, a riot of colors—sugar maples ablaze in scarlet and gold, brilliant yellows of birch leaves, and rich, dark oranges of the oaks. Unspoiled mountainous terrain ignited in color contrasting beautifully with country roads bordered with sumacs' bright reds and oranges, and everywhere fat orange pumpkins and pastures abundantly green. Never has beauty so splashed in my eyes, painting my memory with splendor.

For the last week, we'd been staying at the Lake Champagne Campground, and we were having the time of our lives. Using this 123-acre wooded oasis as our basecamp, we'd been traversing Vermont, taking in the incredible fall colors. I loved it here. I loved the quaint towns with tall church steeples and plainspoken people with easy smiles. I loved picking and eating fresh vegetables and fruits grown a mile away at the Lincoln Farm stand. I loved the peace filling my soul.

So much had happened in the last four months. Going to Tioga had been a Godsend for me, a time I'll never forget. James and Kathleen Norgaard turned out to be remarkable people. From the moment I said hello to the day I left, I was treated like one of their own. Jim actually offered me a job in his company as his right-hand man. I worked next to him twelve to fourteen hours a day, six or seven days a week. I ended up with twenty-thousand more dollars in the bank and a heart brimming with happiness.

North Dakota is experiencing a modern-day version of the California Gold Rush, but this time, the commodity is oil. A 360 million years old stratigraphic layer, known as the Bakken Shale, is the source of the good times. The Bakken is spread over 25,000 square miles of prairie in North Dakota, Montana, and Saskatchewan. Refineries love the Bakken's oil for its "light and sweet" properties, and some estimate the reservoir could hold over 200 billion barrels of recoverable oil. Getting oil out of the Bakken is a challenge because the non-porous rock is unwilling to give up its riches. Advanced technology has come to the rescue, in the form of horizontal drilling and a process known as hydraulic fracturing, where millions of gallons of water, chemicals, and sand are pumped into the formation under high pressure to fracture the rock and release the oil.

Jim's company provides slickline services to help extract the oil. I learned a lot about this technology and the jargon, and became a competent worker. Slicklines are used to place and recover wellbore equipment and tons of other things, like adjusting valves downhole or installing repair tubing down the well. We used slicklines to do well workovers to sustain, enhance, or restore producing wells. We also did well pipe perforations by lowering a gun with explosive charges to create holes in the casing through which oil can flow. Jim called it "Rockin' the Bakken." He is a wizard at his craft; there's no other word to describe his genius.

I learned to appreciate the hard, isolated land and the men who worked there. But, there was a price to pay for good wages and employment. Admittance to the oil patch requires brutal working hours, extreme winters, and most importantly, separation from families. This oil boom has caused a severe shortage of places to let, forcing the necessity for "man camps," facilities that feed and house hundreds of workers. Working conditions, coupled with living in these camps, is as austere as anything I faced in the service. But working here has nothing to do with patriotism. In today's times, people need work and are willing to endure a lot for a paycheck.

Jim and I had plenty of time to talk as we drove all over the region servicing wells. We talked about Marc, and a lot about me. Jekyll rode everywhere with us, and Jim ended up loving him almost as much as I did. I stayed at their home, and Kathleen was simply a peach. She worked as hard as Jim in her sphere, which included doing the books for the business, to having home-cooked meals for us, to running tons of errands for equipment needed at the well sites. She was a force.

I took every idle moment to read Jekyll's Zen and Annie's journal.

We'd gone through them four times by the time I left. I knew them well. I filled my journal with drawings of Jekyll, drawing him from various angles, and in various moods. Some of them looked nice, I thought. We both lost weight and looked fit from working long hours and eating good food. The nearest McD was a 96-mile round trip from Tioga. Going there once a month became our special treat to each other.

I spent a lot of time thinking, especially after talking with Jim and Kathleen at dinner. They had taken the news of their son's death in stride. Not that they were cavalier about it, rather, they held tight to the belief they would see him once again in another life. Their North Dakota toughness helped them through the ordeal. I admired them for their convictions.

When I got my first month's pay, my eyes nearly popped. It was $4,835! Little did I know, but slickline workers command top pay in the oil patch, and this was like a gift from the gods. I put the paychecks in my wallet since there wasn't anywhere to spend money. Annie said she almost fainted when I finally got around to mailing them to her to put in my bank account. My one major spending extravagance was replacing all my socks, T-shirts and underwear with first-rate products from Fruit of the Loom.

I reluctantly said goodbye to the Norgaards when fall came because we needed to make it to New England before the snow flew. I'd stumbled on this campground after taking a fortuitous wrong turn. This place was heaven, with laundry, showers, picnic areas, big camp sites, all the firewood you could burn—you name it, they had it. I truly love Vermont. As I lay in the grass among brilliantly blazing sugar maples, looking at puffy clouds passing by, I took inventory of what I'd learned so far on my journey.

I learned that:

- People are inherently kind and I am an inherently kind person too
- I feel good when I'm kind to others
- I have to listen to my heart, instead of the chatter in my head
- Forgiveness is a vital nutrient for happiness
- I want to do something to make people feel good
- I should let go of the past, not worry about the future, and simply live in the moment
- Pain is an effective teacher and rage is nothing more than my soul crying out for love
- Self-love is a choice, an essential ingredient to a happy life

- I am deserving and worthy of love
- Life, or God, expects something from me
- Self-pity is a terrible use of time
- Beauty is everywhere. I just have to see it
- It's never too late to be who I really am
- I am not a jinx; the fate of my friends is in the hands of God
- I am not God
- Only God knows the reasons for all things
- The main thing is the main thing (thanks, Jek!)

I smiled. It was a long list.

41

THE NIGHT PASSED with the glorious sound of soft rain hitting the tent. Jekyll started the new day with several licks on my face. When that failed to rouse me, he let out a thunderous woof in my ear. That worked well. It was hard to be mad when I saw his happy face. The visible vapor from my breath proved it was getting cold. We needed to leave soon or we'd be stranded in New England. If I had a regular vehicle, spending the winter here would be fun. But I had an urge to see Maine, go up Cadillac Mountain, and play my flute to welcome the first rays of the rising sun hitting the United States. I wanted to see the rugged beauty of the state, from ocean shorelines to coastal forests. I also wanted to sample Maine food, and know the delights of fresh buttery lobster, blueberry pie, and real maple syrup-drenched pancakes. "C'mon, boy, let's get on with the day."

Emerging from the tent, we saw ice in the puddles. Uh-oh. While eating breakfast, I looked at the map and did some rough calculations. If I drove on interstate highways, we could be at Cadillac Mountain by evening. It would be a hard drive. I got out my iPhone and looked for a place to stay. There was a Hampton Inn at Ellsworth, Maine, and they allowed pets. We could stay there, and easily do the twenty-five miles from there to Cadillac Mountain in the morning. I had a plan. I used the iPhone to make a reservation, and took a minute to email Pat and Annie.

Hey you two, ice in puddles here filled me with incentive to push on. I'm bound for Maine! I made reservations tonight at the Hampton Inn in Ellsworth, Maine. Tomorrow morning, I'll be at the peak of Cadillac Mountain. We'll welcome the first rays of sun to hit the United States with Jek yodeling and me fluting. Big drive ahead of me today. I'm really looking forward to this! Talk to you soon. All my love...

We broke camp and made the first leg of the trip to I-95 with no problem, that is to say, if you didn't mind being jammed together on a freeway of insane drivers. Before having a nervous breakdown, I exited and gassed up in Kittery, Maine. I stopped at a Subway there. Jek would've preferred fries, but he made do with chips. We still had three to four hours to go. We headed north, passing numerous hamlets along the way. At Augusta, we turned onto Highway 3 and took that road all the way to Ellsworth. I gassed up at a Mobil station and asked how to get to the Hampton Inn on Downeast Highway.

Man, we were tired when we got to our room. I fed Jek and ate a granola bar as I filled the tub. After my bath, I set the alarm to 3:30 AM, and then sent Pat and Annie a message saying we arrived okay. Jek was asleep on the bed, so I gently picked him up, lifted the covers, and crawled in with him. We were snoring in less than a minute.

42

THE ALARM SOUNDED and I grudgingly turned it off. I dragged myself to the bathroom, took care of business, then shaved and brushed my teeth. We had apples and beef jerky for breakfast and then went on our way. It was one of the rare times I had driven the Trike in darkness.

It took a while to drive the twenty-five miles to the summit. The road had so many switchbacks that I worried about missing the sunrise. At the summit, the place was packed with others wanting to see the first rays of the sun too. I got out my flute and looked around. We still had some time before dawn, so we walked around and found an outcrop of rocks 300 yards away from anyone else. Perfect. We found a good boulder to sit on, and waited. It was a bit windy, but not unpleasant. Impatient, I stood up and looked eastward. Then I saw the beginnings of light! I closed my eyes and started playing, imagining I was a bird, waiting for the sun to rise. At seeing the first rays, I took to the skies, soaring through the air, wheeling and turning, effortlessly gliding over the beautiful coastal forest. I pictured Mom and Dad standing next to me, and played a song for them. Jekyll was yodeling with me, and hit a lot of nice high notes. I felt the warm rays on me and opened my eyes, imagining the sun thanking me for playing with its warmth. I played another song for the sun and God. I was happy and it was obvious in my music. Then, our reverie was jarred by a voice. A female voice.

"Excuse me…"

I looked around. There was a very pretty lady looking at us with tears in her eyes. She looked to be in her mid-twenties. "Hello," I said with a smile.

She smiled back and wiped a tear from her eye. "That was the most beautiful music I've ever heard."

"Thanks. Would you care to join us?"

"I'd love to."

She came over and hugged me. "It truly was beautiful," she said as she held her hug. I hugged her back.

"Really, I can't carry a tune unless my dog is yodeling to keep me in rhythm."

She laughed, and then impulsively kissed me. It startled me and I drew back, breaking her kiss.

"I'm so sorry. Forgive me. I'm normally a very shy person."

I looked into her pretty blue eyes. Even though she wore no make-up, she was the most beautiful girl I'd ever seen. Now it was my turn to be impulsive. I kissed her back, slowly at first, and then passionately. It'd been a long time since I kissed a woman. "Sorry, I got a little carried away. You'd never know it, but I'm a shy person too. My name is Colt." I extended my hand and she shook it.

"My name is Jillian Brooks. I go by Jill."

I sat down and she joined me. Jek was in full tail wag, excitedly looking at this woman.

"What's your dog's name?"

"This is Jekyll von Bickerstaff, a dog of exceptional courage and dubious lineage."

"Woof!"

"Hey Jekyll von, von… What's his name again?"

"Jekyll von Bickerstaff."

She laughed and patted him on his head. "I bet there's a story behind that name."

"There is. Maybe you'll let me share it with you one day."

"I'd love that." She leaned in and kissed me again. It was heavenly.

I looked in her eyes. She looked familiar, but that couldn't be, not on this coast. "Where're you from, Jill?"

"There's no place I call home. I'm a military brat. My dad was career Air Force."

"I was in the Army for nine years and got out over a year ago. What did your dad do in the Air Force?"

"He was an officer. Exactly what he did, I don't know. He's been out for a while."

"So, do you live on the east coast?"

"For the time being, while I'm in college. Right now, I'm on a break from school, so I took a tour bus to see Acadia, and greet the first morning sun on the States. What about you?"

"I'm touring the country with Jekyll. I wish I could say I'm on a break from college too, but the fact is, I'm just trying to find my way."

"It sounds like a grand adventure. I'm envious."

I looked at her. "That's what I call it, my 'Grand Adventure.'"

She laughed. "Great minds think alike, I suppose."

I smiled in response. I felt like I knew this lady. It was eerie. Jekyll sat on her lap and licked her face. He acted like they were long-lost friends. She hugged him and kissed his muzzle. I looked at her face as she stroked Jek. Her facial bones were delicately carved, and were perfectly matched to a complexion of soft, smooth skin with a freckle here and there. There was Irish in her blood, I'm sure. Her short, auburn hair blew casually around in the breeze. She was peaches and cream, through and through.

She looked at me and smiled. I was embarrassed that she had caught me staring at her.

"You're beautiful, you know. That's not a come-on line. You truly are beautiful."

"Ah, you're too kind," she said, blushing. It only added to her beauty. I couldn't resist kissing her again. She responded in kind. A tingling excitement raced through me. I opened my eyes and saw her looking at me, her bright blue eyes aglow. She drew me back in, giving herself freely to the passion of my kiss.

"You, sir," she said, touching her finger to my lips, "you know how to kiss a woman."

I smiled. "It's been a long time since I've kissed a woman. A long time."

"I haven't been with a boy for a long time either. It was college or a boyfriend, but not both."

"So, what are you doing for the rest of today?"

"My bus leaves at one."

"Would you like to go for a bike ride? It's a great way to see the country if it's not raining."

"I'd love to. Colt, I… I'm normally not like this. I can't believe I kissed you." She looked deeply into my eyes. "I heard you playing and had to come to you. I hope yours isn't a Siren's song."

"I'm no Siren or pied piper. I'm just a guy on a quest to find my noble purpose."

"You sound a bit like Don Quixote. Are you off in search of windmills?"

A shiver ran through me. "Before starting this trip, the thought of being Don Quixote, incarnate, had occurred to me. I've yet to call my dog 'Sancho Panza,' so perhaps my sanity prevails."

She laughed. "Can we wait here a little while? I'd love to just sit and feel the sun's warmth on my face."

"Sure, I planned to do that anyway."

She leaned into me, tilting her face toward mine. It felt like we'd been together for years. Jekyll sat on my lap. The three of us enjoyed the morning sun.

A half hour later, we were ready to get on with the day. I looked at my iPhone and found a trip that we could do, and get her back by one. It was called the Park Loop Road, a twenty-seven mile avenue for navigating through Acadia National Park. We held hands walking back to my ride. She was impressed when she saw it.

I put my flute away and, since I didn't plan on going very fast, switched from my riding boots to sandals. I took Jill's pack and bungeed it to the floating storage compartment. She laughed when I put on Jek's helmet and goggles. I offered her my helmet, but she preferred me to have it since I was driving. She sat in back of me and was thrilled going down the switchbacks. Jekyll yodeled at the sheer fun of the hairpin turns, and we laughed at his antics. She held on to my waist and squeezed me to let me know she was enjoying the ride. We had a blast driving along the rocky shore, and stopped several times to walk about. Jek romped and frolicked while I held hands and kissed my beautiful companion. We drove through forests and mountains and completed the loop in three hours. I don't think there's a prettier twenty-seven miles on the planet. We pulled into a place called Docksider, a quaint café that had an outdoor seating area. This was where I had my first taste of Maine food. The lobster was sublime. Jill had haddock with a bowl of clam chowder. We sampled each other's dish, and I even ordered fries with catsup for Jekyll. It was nearing twelve-thirty. I wished the day would last forever.

I put my hand on hers. "We need to head back so you can catch your bus. Can we stay in touch? I already feel like I've known you forever."

She leaned in and kissed me. "Colt, this has been the most perfect day. I've had a grand time." She looked at me with her brilliantly blue eyes. "I believe God has drawn me to you." She hesitated for a moment. "If you want, I can miss the bus. The decision is yours."

My mood turned buoyant. "I could think of nothing better." I kissed her again.

The next two weeks were a blur. We fell head-over-heels in love. We stayed in a motel, hardly coming up for air. Jekyll loved Jillian too. I bought her a helmet, and when we weren't making love, we were zooming across the Maine countryside. I've never felt so good, or so happy, in my life.

I told Pat and Annie about her, and they asked for a picture of us. Jill was afraid they wouldn't like her, and wanted to meet them in person instead of sending a photo. I was ready to drop everything and fly back, but she wanted to wait until we were sure our relationship was right. Well, as far as I was concerned, it was more than right—it was perfect. Asking her to marry me loomed large, but I'd need to ask her father for her hand first. We talked of life together. She wanted kids, and I couldn't agree more.

Her degree was in teaching and she knew it was her calling. I talked about my noble purpose and maybe going to college one day. I told her about my past, from my parents to soldiering. She comforted me when some of my stories got hard to tell. We discussed where we could live and be happy. I mentioned Coeur d'Alene, Idaho and Vermont, and she thought both sounded interesting.

When we drove into the country, we'd pull over and lie facing upwards, and I'd point out the names of the stars in the sky. I laughed when she didn't know what the Big Dipper was, and showed it to her, explaining how it was part of the Ursa Major constellation. She said she loved me so much it was almost scary. Life couldn't be better. I thanked God for smiling on me. After all these years, my ship had finally come in. She agreed to go with me to Orlando, and would think about joining me on the Grand Adventure, if that went well. Life was so good.

43

WE SPENT OUR last day in Maine going to the LL Bean store in Freeport. Afterward, we had a great meal at Harraseeket Lunch & Lobster Company. For dessert, we ordered cherry cheesecake and a whoopie pie. Jek had me add cheesecake to his list of culinary loves. I carried him in my harness the whole day, and fortunately, no one hassled us.

We stayed at the Hampton Inn in Freeport, making love throughout the night. The alarm clock seemed to beep far too soon. I hit the off button. "Hey, Jill," I said as I kissed her good morning, "do you want to sleep a little longer while I get ready?"

She didn't respond. I patted Jek on the head and got up. I took a cool shower to help me awake. After shaving, I was ready to yield the bathroom to the sleeping beauty.

"C'mon, Sweetie, rise and shine."

She stretched, yawned, and looked at me. "You're a fabulous lover, my dear man. How I love you."

I smiled. It felt good to hear. "I love you too, with all my heart. I'll take Jek out while you get ready."

She smiled and blew me a kiss. I played with Jek outside, feeling great, carefree and happy to be alive. Jill was showering when we came back in. Jekyll was still feeling rambunctious and jumped on the bed. He accidentally crashed into Jill's pack and all her stuff spilled out. I stooped down to pick it up and saw her open checkbook on the floor. The name on it wasn't Jillian Brooks. It was Rachel—Rachel Brennan. I gasped. Oh, my God. She was Pat and Annie's daughter.

She came out of the bathroom, bouncing and bubbly, and then she saw me glaring at her.

"Colt, what's wrong?" she said with alarm.

"Jekyll knocked over your pack and this fell out, Jillian, or should I say, Rachel?"

"Colt, please, let me explain."

"You damn well better explain!"

She swallowed hard. "Sit down and let me talk to you, okay? Please, Colt."

"I'm not sitting." My face was a glowering mask of rage. "Talk and talk now!"

She cringed at my sudden fury. "Yes, it's true. Momma has told me all about you from the day you first met them. She told me everything, Colt, from saving Katie, to you caring so much for Jekyll and your friend Scotty. I cried the day they told me they gave you the Trike, and eagerly agreed to include you in our family. I tried to console my mother after you left on your trip, and I've read every one of your emails, laughing with you and crying with you the whole way. I fell in love with you and your words, and had to meet you. From your email, I knew when you'd be at Cadillac Mountain, so I flew out here to meet you. I knew you'd never be open to loving me if you knew who I was, so I made up my story. The fact is, I've been in love with you long before we met. You're the love of my life."

I was seething with anger, pacing back and forth, and her words just inflamed me. "Do you, in any way, know how much your parents mean to me? Can you fathom how deeply I've betrayed them?" I was shouting the words. "My God. My dear God. What can I ever say to them? And you, you've been like a voyeur, planning all this, learning my weaknesses and vulnerabilities. *'Tell me about the Big Dipper.'* Well, Ms. Master's Degree in Astrophysics, you played me like a fiddle."

"Colt, I didn't—" I cut her off, bristling with indignation.

"Did you ever consider your little sister? She's been through so much. Her friend Jen said she wanted to marry me one day. Now she's been betrayed by her older sister. Her sister! You better be careful because that little girl knows how to kick some serious ass. I don't suggest facing her anytime soon. As for reading my emails, that'll end right now!" I took out my iPhone and slammed it on the floor. It exploded into pieces. Jekyll went running for cover.

"Colt, I love you. I want to spend—"

"Not another word from you! Do you think that's how a relationship begins, on lies and deceit? Don't ever, EVER talk to me again.

You've stolen away the people I love. I can never face your family again." I gathered my gear, grabbed Jekyll, and gave her a withering glare, my face distorted in anger. "Go to hell, Rachel Brennan!" It was the last thing I said before slamming the door.

44

I DROVE SEVEN hours, crying and cursing and crying some more. She had stolen my family from me. I was close to running out of gas, so I filled up in Danbury, Connecticut. I asked for and got directions to a Hampton Inn. I pulled in and got a room. We hadn't eaten all day, so I fed Jek in the parking lot and let him do his business. I didn't feel like eating. Jek slinked into the room, and went to the farthest corner. He sat there with his head hung down, looking pathetic. "Jekyll, come here, boy, I'm not mad at you." He hesitantly came over. I scooped him up and put him on the bed.

"She lied to us, Jek. She isn't who she said she was. She's ruined the one thing that was good in my life. Annie and Pat will never forgive me." I gathered him close. "We've lost them, boy. I've lost parents all over again." I started crying and Jekyll did his best to comfort me. Her scent was still on me. I needed a shower.

I went to bed early that night, and felt like a zombie the next day, so I decided to stay another day. I took Jekyll out for fries and catsup to let him know everything was okay between us. He stayed by my side and loved me like the true friend he was. While he was napping, I closed my eyes and tried to talk to my parents. There was nothing. I wished I could talk to George and the elders again at Telegraph Creek, or Vivian, or Jim and Kathleen. Or Scotty. Mostly, I wished I could talk to Pat, Annie, and Katie to tell them I was so, so sorry. My life was back to being a mess. I closed my eyes and prayed, but all I got in return was the hum of the air conditioner.

Jek and I got on the road the next day, and it was a marathon trip. I drove five hours to Harrisburg, Pennsylvania, and checked into a Motel 6. I ordered pizza, and shared it with Jek. He mostly ate the pizza bones, which is what my parents used to call the crust.

I used the drive finding new ways to despise Rachel, and wondered if she'd have the guts to tell her parents what she had done. I could just imagine the shock and hurt on their faces when they found out I was intimate with their precious daughter. The image of Pat tracking me down with a shotgun loomed large. They had taken in a stray, and the stray ended up biting them. I had tried to warn them when we first met, but they still had wanted to be my friend. God, I felt awful.

I went to bed early to get plenty of rest for tomorrow's five-hour drive to Roanoke, Virginia, the next stop on my KIA list. By leaving early in the morning, I could get there by noon. I drifted off thinking about Giovonni Moretti, whom I had met shortly after my first tour in Iraq. Gino was as Italian as you could get. His parents, Emilio and Contessa, emigrated from Milan, Italy and opened an eatery in Roanoke. Gino grew up in the family kitchen. We used to beg him to make manicotti and panettone dessert bread. He joined the Army the day after 9/11, and didn't last a fortnight after returning from his second Iraq tour. He died by his own hand, a pistol shot to the head. Though not a KIA, I considered him to be a KFA, Killed *From* Action. That he survived his first tour in Iraq was a miracle in itself. He suffered three major concussions from IED blasts. On his second tour, he lobbed a grenade in a house to nail an insurgent sniper. There was a family inside, and two little girls succumbed to the blast. He was never the same after that. After he got home, the trauma to his soul was too much to bear. Gino was a sweet soul. Sadly, the military is losing fine men and women like him at the rate of one a day to suicide. Given how I was currently feeling, I now understood why Gino took his life. Sometimes life doesn't seem worth living.

I fell asleep with those nasty thoughts dancing in my head, and woke up two hours later gasping. Jekyll did his best to calm me. I was drenched in sweat, so I took a shower. As the cool water flowed over me, I thought about how I actually was doing that damn Rachel a favor by dumping her. At least now she wouldn't have to put up with a broken excuse of a man, plagued by flashbacks and nightmares.

Further attempts at sleep were pointless, so I ate a couple of granola bars, packed our stuff, and headed for Roanoke in the darkness. We arrived at the Moretti's restaurant well before noon. The front door was locked, so I went around back and knocked on the service door. A cook let me in and introduced me to the surprised parents. They were polite, but spoke little English. I didn't have the energy to deal with the language barrier, so I simply told them that Gino was my friend. His father shook my hand and his mom hugged me. They invited me to lunch, but I politely declined, saying I was in a hurry to get to Orlando, and wanted to see Gino's grave. They gave me directions and said good-bye. I left thinking they deserved better from me.

Gino was buried in the Fair View cemetery, which had veterans from every war going back to the Civil War. I knelt at my friend's grave, said my words, and started playing my flute. This time, there was no beautiful music. I normally didn't hear what I played, but I sure did this time. It sounded like a screeching alley cat. Jekyll looked at me oddly, wondering what the hell I was doing. I adjusted the fetish and tried again. More alley cat. What the hell? Frustrated, I saluted my friend, left a coin on his headstone, and left.

After gassing up, we motored out of Roanoke admiring the Blue Ridge Mountains. This part of the country was beautiful. My next stop was Orlando, but that was over 700 miles away. If I pushed, we could make it to Charlotte, North Carolina, in three or four hours.

We stopped at a McDonalds in Woodlawn, Virginia, and five minutes after leaving, I couldn't remember what I'd eaten. When we finally reached Charlotte, I checked into a Hampton Inn, fed Jek, and drew a hot bath. He almost fell asleep while eating. I picked him up, put him on the bed, and stroked his head until he drifted off. Then I eased into the hot water and enjoyed its soothing effect. I tried to figure out what happened to my flute. Maybe it had gotten broken bouncing around in the storage compartment. My mind wandered. I thought about how Scotty was doing; I missed communicating with him. I thought about Pat and Annie and how much I loved them. I heard Jekyll having a dream in bed. I thought of the day we'd met and how I'd felt like a sap for adopting his sorry ass. And then I thought how much I loved him, even when others were appalled at his looks. For some reason, I always could see the beauty in him. He might've been just a stray, but he meant the world to me. I thought about the word "stray." That's how I felt when Pat and Annie said they wanted to be my friend. I had been a stray too, just like my dog. I thought more on this. I loved my dog with all my heart, yet he was flawed. Damaged. Abused. Dreadfully ugly. Yet...he was beautiful. Just like...me. I started crying.

45

I WENT TO bed thinking about the ride the next day. It would be an eight-hour drive to cover the 525 miles to Orlando. That wasn't going to happen. I guess we'd just get on the road and see how far we could go. I drifted off, still wondering about my flute.

Scotty crowded my thoughts when I woke the next morning. It was killing me not knowing how he was doing. I called the front desk and asked where I could buy a cell phone. They said there was Best Buy a block away. I ate breakfast, played with Jek, and drove over.

I planned to buy a new iPhone and get it in my name. It didn't seem right to freeload on the Brennan's phone plan now. They would soon be kicking me out of their family anyway. A nice lady at Best Buy asked me how often I used my previous iPhone. I told her about the Grand Adventure and how I used my phone for emails, and only occasionally to make a call. She said it would be far cheaper to buy a no-contract cell phone, and with the savings, I could get a netbook for emails, internet access, and even things like journaling. She said the bigger screen would be much easier to see and many netbooks had an 8-hour battery life. Her idea of using it to write a journal rang a chord in me. Maybe it'd do me good to write down my thoughts. While she activated my new basic cell phone, I looked at some spiffy-looking netbook computers. I walked out 900 bucks lighter, but had two devices and a year's worth of internet connectivity.

On the way out of town, we stopped at a McDonalds. I downed a couple chicken wraps, and, after Jek ate his fries, we went to the drive-through again and ordered a vanilla ice cream cone. I got two licks before Jekyll had to have his cut. He ate the whole thing in less than a minute.

Two hours later, we passed through Columbia, South Carolina, and then Savannah, Georgia three hours after that. I thought about being stationed in Fort Benning, which was about 250 miles away. Savannah was "the" place for Scotty, Manny and me to head for R&R. I loved its dramatic old architecture and especially the microbreweries. We used to jump on I-16 and drive for hours just to visit Moon River Brewing for their Swamp Fox India Pale Ale and grass-fed beef burgers. Or we'd go to nearby Little Tybee Island, and rent kayaks to paddle through the salt marshes. Those were fun times. I'd love to show Rachel this—

God. How could I even think of her? That got me pissed. There were too many memories in Savannah, so I motored on. When Jekyll started squirming, I pulled into a Motel 6 in Richmond Hill, Georgia. I didn't feel like eating out, so I ordered a pizza. While waiting for the pizza, I plugged in both my new toys to charge, and set up my account on the netbook. There were numerous new emails from Pat and Annie, and two from Katie. I deleted all of them. I'd already thrashed myself mentally for what had happened, and didn't need them piling on. I didn't need to hear, *"How could you?"* Their accusing and hurt words would dance in my head for years, and I simply couldn't deal with that. There was nothing from Scotty. I sent him an email saying where we were and that things were fine. He had his hands full trying to stay alive, and didn't need to be sidetracked with my drama.

I ate the pizza while learning about my netbook's features. Jek downed the pizza bones and I fed him his ration of Buffalo afterward. We played a little outside, and then I took another bath. The long days on the road, coupled with lack of sleep and emotional trauma, were getting to me. I came to enjoy how the warm water soothed my aches and pains. I could hear Jekyll snoring on the bed.

I closed my eyes and tried to quiet the chattering monkeys in my head. It was still another 275 miles to Orlando, which would mean a five-hour, ball-busting day. Damn, I was getting tired of the road. I thought about what to say to the parents of David Bennion.

Davey's story was especially tragic. He died on his third tour to Iraq. After two Bronze Stars for heroism, Davey died not on the battle-field but at his barracks in Baghdad while taking a shower. A water pump was improperly grounded, and when he turned on the shower, electricity raced through his body. My friends said it wasn't pretty. He died a long, agonizing death. The last I heard, his parents were suing the contractor who installed the system for negligence. This wasn't an isolated incident. At least 12 other servicemen have been electrocuted in Iraq from faulty electrical systems. It's a damn shame.

I added more hot water. Rachel kept flashing before me, no matter how hard I tried to banish her from my head. She had said she fell in love with me after reading my emails. Could that be possible? I'm sure she was just toying with me…but…why would she go to such lengths to torment me? She was the daughter of Pat and Annie, so it hardly seemed believable that she'd take perverse pleasure in bringing me down. I saved her little sister, for God's sake.

I decided to reread my old emails, from her perspective. What had she seen to "fall in love" with me? My mind swirled around this notion. Although tired, I got out of the tub, opened my netbook, and read every email from Anchorage to Cadillac Mountain. It took hours…

Afterward, I closed my weary eyes. God, I'd covered a lot of territory in those emails, literally and figuratively. They covered a broad arc of emotions, from delving deeply into my soul, to the silliness of my dog, to playing my flute for native villagers and fallen friends. I cried when reliving a few of the entries. Some were gut-wrenchingly poignant. I guess I could see how someone would find them interesting, and maybe they'd even come to like me. But, that interest would be based on pity. Poor little Colt. Let me take you in, just like a stray dog. Well, piss on that. Like I told Pat and Annie long ago, nothing is more pathetic than someone soliciting friendship through pity. I still had my pride.

Jekyll stirred from his sleep and I stroked his fur and gave him a hug. After taking him out, we went to bed. I tried to talk to Mom and Dad, but there was nothing but silence. That pissed me off too. I was mad at a lot of things.

46

THE ROAD TO Orlando was a brutal five-hour grind. With the warmer temperatures and humidity, I began experiencing a new and dreadful condition from being on a motorcycle for hours. To put it mildly, my ass was on fire. I was sore, itching, and in supreme agony. I walked bowlegged into a Walgreens, and described my situation to the pharmacist. He was an older man, and knew exactly what my problem was. Waddling in wearing a motorcycle jacket was a dead giveaway. He said sweat combined with humid heat creates what's infamously known throughout the South as monkey butt, a condition that causes you to walk like a monkey to prevent your skin from rubbing. He went to get something off the shelf. He handed me a bright-yellow container, and told me to use it. I looked at the label. There was a smiling monkey with a red ass and the words Anti Monkey Butt Powder. He told me to keep my nether regions as dry as possible and liberally use the powder. I smiled at the name, but I stopped laughing when I put it on in their restroom. How do you spell relief? Anti Monkey Butt. I bought three more bottles of it and was half-tempted to sit in a tub filled with it instead of water.

I looked up Davey's parents after checking into a Motel 6. Fortunately, there aren't many Bennions in Orlando. I called and they said they were free and didn't mind me bringing Jek over. I put on a generous amount of my new powder and drove to their home. It was a nice place, close to Disney World. Davey must've had a ball growing up in the Land of the Mouse.

We talked for a couple hours, with me telling them how I knew Davey. She served chicken salad sandwiches, chips, and sweet tea. I remembered how much I enjoyed sweet tea from my days at Fort Benning. They told me how they were still in litigation, wanting justice for their son. They expected it to drag out for a long time, but were willing to gut it out if it meant saving the lives of other servicemen. Davey was buried at Arlington, so I wouldn't be able to pay him my respects. While we talked, Jek played with their golden retriever named Daisy. They were nice people.

I drove back to my motel room, relieved that everything had gone well. The next stop on my KIA list was Johnny's parents in Dallas. That one was going to be tough. After that would be Manny's parents in Santa Fe. That would be enormously tough. I sighed. It had been a long day.

I checked my email. There was one from Scotty and two more from Pat and Annie. I deleted the Brennan emails and opened the one from Scotty.

Colt, got your email. All is well here. Maggie says be sure to try some pan-fried alligator, okra, and key lime pie. Glad your trip is going well. I envy you!!! Scotty

I said a silent 'thank you' to God for him being okay, and sent a quick reply, telling him about my visit today. Jek began barking at the door, wanting to go out and play. He needed some levity after the last few days. Despite my monkey butt, I felt like playing too. We had fun chasing each other and cavorting around.

I took a shower and could've sworn my nether regions were flashing the water to steam. Another dose of powder after showering helped. Jek was happy as we went to bed, and my spirits were elevated a little too. Playing had done us both good.

I woke up early the next morning, and looked at my map while Jekyll continued sleeping. The next leg of our trip was going to be a mother—1100 miles, which translated into eighteen hours on the road. Damn. With my flaming ass, this wouldn't be a joy ride. Tallahassee was a four-hour drive, so it would be today's target. I packed and roused Jekyll. We were on the road by eight.

We made good time on I-10. Tallahassee came into view less than four hours later. My rear was singing again, so I pulled into a Hampton Inn. For a change of pace, I ordered Chinese food from a place that delivered. The Mongolian barbeque was delicious and Jek liked it too. Next came a pint of fried rice and I washed it down with a diet soda. Jek devoured the fortune cookie before I could crack it open to read the message. The thought of my fortune going through his system made me smile. Somehow, it seemed fitting.

I drew some water to soak my ailing caboose. Jek felt like playing while I soaked. He put his front paws on the rim of the tub and woofed. I flicked some water at him, and he took off running around the room. He "sneaked" back into the bathroom, popped his head up, and woofed again, delighted at surprising me. I flicked water at him again, and he took off, repeating the process. It was hilarious. How I loved my little dog. Wait a minute… what did I just say? *I loved my dog?* Of course I loved him. But, he was just a stray, flawed…but I didn't love him out of pity…I loved him because of who he was. My dog was just as damaged as I was, and yet I loved him despite all his "flaws." In fact, his flaws made him "him." I toweled off, powdered up, and jumped into bed. As I drifted off, a spark flashed in my hard head. What if things had been different? What if I hadn't been damaged goods and had met Rachel conventionally? Would Pat and Annie be happy when she introduced me? I would think yes. I was a good person, and was raised by wonderful parents. I tried to be kind to people, was a loyal friend, and lived my life with honor and integrity. Okay, now toss in my flaws. I've seen awful things and killed people, but only to save others or defend my country. Even if you threw in the flaws, the good things were still in me, just like they were with Jek.

I began to see the real problem. I loved Jek with all his flaws but couldn't love myself. Others found me easy to love, but I always felt unlovable. Why? I got up, opened my netbook, and read my "what I learned" list I'd written in Vermont. I realized that all I was doing was spitting out philosophies from books. Putting those philosophies into practice was something altogether different. Unless there was a major paradigm shift in my thinking, with square one being to love myself, I'd forever be doomed to this rancid existence.

The morning came with me feeling a bit shaky after the revelations. I needed to get on the road again to clear my head. Pensacola was 200 miles away. We could do that easy.

I did a lot of thinking as we rode. Jek spotted a McDonalds shortly after we howled on the bridge crossing Escambia Bay. I ate a chicken salad and Jek had his usual. After dinner, I went to the restroom and added a liberal amount of powder to my unmentionables. We gassed up and hit the road again. It was easy traveling in terms of finding our way. We'd cruise the I-10 all the way to Lafayette, Louisiana before hooking northwest to Dallas.

We crossed Mobile Bay on a bridge so long that it tested our howling endurance. Gulfport, Mississippi was only an hour away, so I decided to push for it and then call it a day. I found a Hampton Inn just off the freeway. We were both really tired. As I was soaking in the tub, it hit me that a journey isn't about adding miles to a vehicle; it's learning the country and having experiences. We needed to have some fun. I toweled off, went to the lobby, and grabbed a bunch of tourist brochures. Back in the room, Jek and I perused them, and one caught my eye—the Biloxi Beach Company. They had kayaks and jet skis to rent. That sounded cool. I called the front desk and booked another day.

The next day, we drove to the Biloxi Beach Company and rented a jet ski. I put on a life jacket and, over that, Jekyll in his harness. He was apprehensive when we headed out to sea, but after a while, my silly seadog was howling with pure delight. Over and over, he'd bark for me to jump a wave or do 180 spins, and couldn't resist giving an "ahoy" yodel to every boat or jet ski we passed. He loved jet skiing as much as motorcycle riding. We had an outright blast. After the jet skis, we cavorted along the beach, and then our day got even better. We found AnJac's Barbeque and Burger Company. I ordered a full slab of ribs with potato salad, baked beans, and a Barq's root beer in the bottle. My, oh my. Their pecan wood smoking added incredible flavor to the meat. Jek loved the rib bones. Although stuffed, I couldn't leave without having the peach cobbler. Most of it went to you-know-who. We went back to the motel feeling elated. I swore Jek was smiling. We needed more days like this.

There were two emails in my inbox, one from the Brennans, and one from Lilly. I ignored the Brennans and opened Lilly's.

Dear Mr. Colt, I will be six in two weeks! Did you know that? Finley von Bickerstaff can count to two with his paw. He is as smart as Jekyll von Bickerstaff, but not quite. Momma says to tell you I'm going to have a baby brother. I want to name him Mr. Colt. Momma says maybe. I have a joke for you. What dog can tell time? A watchdog. I love you. Lilly

I responded.

Hello Lillybean! That was a great joke! Jekyll laughed so hard he fell off the bed. We're now in Gulfport, Mississippi. We rented a jet ski and went out on the ocean! It was so fun. Happy birthday to you in advance. You're such a big girl, and soon you'll have a little brother. Wow! Jekyll says hi and has another joke for you: Why did the dog say meow? He was learning a foreign language. Ha! We're having fun, but we miss you. Bye, sweetheart, and happy birthday! Colt and Jekyll

I returned to my inbox and frowned at the many unread emails from the Brennans. It was time to end my association with them. With a few keystrokes, their emails were deleted and any future emails would be blocked. Next morning, I planned to call my bank, and have them transfer my money into a new account with just my name. On several levels, they would be out of my life. After my trip, I'd sell the Trike and send the proceeds to them. It was the only honorable thing to do.

My day was too good to be ruined by all this. I turned off the netbook and took Jek's harness to the shower to rinse off the salt water. Jekyll was sleeping soundly on the bed after the long day. He didn't know it, but tomorrow he'd be getting a bath. His coat was salty from playing in the ocean. I took out my journal and flipped through my many Jekyll drawings. Suddenly, I had a flash of inspiration for Lilly's birthday gift. I could write her a book about Jekyll, and include my sketches.

I turned on my netbook and typed the title:

Jekyll von Bickerstaff

Not bad, but it needed a subtitle to dress it up. Hmmm. Got it. An Uncommon Dog. I typed on.

Jekyll von Bickerstaff

An Uncommon Dog

I began typing the story, and before I knew it, it was three in the morning, then four. The sun came up, yet I wasn't tired, even after pulling an all-nighter. In fact, I felt refreshed and recharged.

Jek stirred, so I saved the document and then we went out and played for a while. After that came his bath. To my surprise, he didn't mind being bathed, in fact, he seemed to enjoy it. Maybe he just hadn't liked the cold water in Canada. I dried him off with the hair dryer and then we shared a couple of granola bars.

We got on the road at nine. Destination: Lafayette, Louisiana, about three hours away. While riding, I kept writing Lilly's book in my head, and time seemed to melt away. We passed through Baton Rouge and then rolled into Lafayette. We stopped at a McD and between us consumed two Big Macs, two orders of fries, and a large vanilla shake. It was a little past noon. I got out my netbook and typed the rest of the story. After that, I found a nearby Kinkos and motored over. Jek curled up and fell asleep in the shade of the Trike.

The staff at Kinkos were friendly, and worked with me to get what I desired. They scanned my sketches and added my text. After a couple of hours, it was done. The book had 30 pages, consisting of 972 words, and 24 sketches of Jek. I asked for twenty copies and FedEx'd a couple to Lilly and Maggie. The rest I'd pass out to kids we might meet on the road. I hoped Lillybean would like the gift.

Jek was still napping when I came out. I read the book to him and he seemed impressed. After that, we rolled out, got on I-49, and headed to Shreveport.

The lack of sleep caught up to me two hours later when I started drifting out of my lane. Jek let out a thunderous warning yodel that woke me up real fast. If not for my co-pilot, it would've been nasty. I patted him for his diligence and he barked cheerfully. We found a La Quinta Inn after turning on I-20 and I almost kissed the lady when she said they allowed dogs. Jek woke me up three hours later wanting chow. I fed him and ate the last of the trail mix, which was stale.

After eating, Jek quickly fell asleep, but I couldn't. Maybe a hot bath would relax me. I drew the water and eased into it. Soon, Rachel came into my thoughts…the first day we met…making love. What if…what if she really did love me? She had been right: if I had known she was a Brennan, having a romantic relationship with her would never be considered.

No matter how much I circled around the issue of loving Rachel, there was a bigger issue I now knew I had to face. Why didn't I love myself? I thought about when I had first started not liking myself. When in Iraq or Afghanistan had it happened? Then it hit me—it didn't happen in Iraq or Afghanistan. It happened in…Prescott.

I started crying. I relived the day my parents were killed. I was supposed to go with them to the Gateway Mall, but lied to them saying I was feeling poorly to get out of going and went dirt biking instead. Had I gone with them, they would've had to pick me up, and wouldn't have been anywhere near the drunk driver. I killed my parents because of my lie. And I've tried my whole adult life to suppress that one overriding fact. I killed my wonderful parents, and for that, I deserved a life of hell on earth. I thought some more on this, especially how it related to my Army days. I scored high enough on the Army aptitude tests to get multitudes of cushy non-combat jobs, yet I chose the toughest, grimiest, most dangerous jobs out there. Maybe, deep down, I knew being a sniper would be a just punishment, and that's why I did it. Jesus. None of this was Rachel's fault. I didn't deserve her love. That love would elevate me from this hell.

God, I was a mess.

47

JEK WOKE ME at nine the next morning. After taking him out, a cool shower helped wake me up. La Quinta offered a free breakfast, so I devoured several waffles with black coffee and fruit. Jek waited patiently for me while tied to the Trike, and I rewarded his good manners with a waffle. My weariness from traveling and being on an emotional roller coaster was obvious for anyone to see. Maybe I'd hole up in Dallas for a while to recharge, and take more time to think. Meeting Johnny's parents was going to be hard. I looked them up before leaving and wrote down their address. They lived in north Dallas at a place called Preston Gate. It sounded expensive. We got on the road after gassing up. Dallas was three hours away. I could do that easy.

As the miles clicked away, I thought about my parents. A flash of insight hit me on why I couldn't talk to them. *"We dance with joy that you've opened your heart to hear us..."* My dad said that to me in the dream I'd had in the Yukon. When I stormed out on Rachel, my heart closed like a steel trap. As long as I didn't forgive her, I'd be cut off from my parents.

"Okay, Rachel, if you did what you did because you really loved me, then I forgive you!" Jekyll barked at my outburst and I patted his head. "It's okay, boy. I'm trying to reconnect to my parents."

More miles passed. I turned my thoughts to me. It's pretty amazing when you figure out you've purposely made your life a living hell. But there were no two ways about it. I killed my parents. If only. If only I'd gone with them that day, they'd be alive, and my life would be totally different. *You deserve what you get*, a voice inside me said. As if on cue, a dark line of clouds appeared on the horizon. How fitting.

Before I could say boo, I was in a downpour. It got so bad that I stopped on the shoulder of the freeway, hardly able to see. We were west of Canton, about sixty miles from Dallas. There was nowhere to hide, and nowhere to run. We'd have to sit where we were and tough it out. It was like the heavens turned a fire hose on us. Suddenly, Jekyll unleashed a panic yodel. I got off my bike and looked around. *Crap!* There was a tornado about a half-mile away, heading toward us. I jumped on the Trike and took off with Jekyll howling like a banshee. The rain-slicked road was like ice, but I kept the throttle wide open.

Then a voice boomed in my head. *"Stop! Stop now! Stop!"* It was my mom. I stood on the brakes and fishtailed to a stop. The car behind me nearly plowed into us. I heard a roar like a freight train. The tornado passed just ahead of us, crossing the interstate! Had I not stopped, it would've gotten us. I pulled off the road and dropped to the ground. Five minutes later, the sky was blue. A beautiful rainbow appeared. I looked upward. "Thank you, Mom." I was shaking, and so was my dog. "Let's sit here for a while, okay Jek?"

"Woof!"

I've seen a tornado before on TV, but it's nothing like experiencing one up close. My God. Cars were zipping by now like nothing had happened. But everything had happened. My mom was talking to me again. There was a rainbow. If this was a sign, what the hell did it mean? After Jek relieved himself, I put him back in his harness, and we motored on. We were soaked, but it was warm here, so I wasn't worried about hypothermia.

We rolled into Dallas an hour later. Geez, this city was enormous. The freeways were huge, and jammed with fast-moving traffic. It scared me. I took I-635, the Lyndon B. Johnson Freeway, to bring me north of the town. I saw a La Quinta and took the exit. What a day.

When we got to the room, I peeled off my damp clothes and hung them up to dry. Jek's fur was damp, so I used the hair dryer to dry him off. I poured him some Blue Buffalo and took a quick shower to warm up. It was just past noon, but it seemed much later. I put on my jeans and a sweatshirt, and decided to get something to eat. There was an In-N-Out Burger next door, so I put Jek on a leash and we walked over. I wolfed down a double cheeseburger and Jek feasted on fries and catsup. We walked back to the motel, and I brought in one of my books to read again to Jek.

An hour later, I felt like taking a walk. Since traffic was everywhere, I put Jek on a leash. I opened the door, stepped out, and got the shock of my life.

"Hello, Colt."

It was Annie, standing next to Pat. They were about five feet from the door.

"Yo-eee-eo-ee-ooooo!" Jekyll shot over to them, pulling the leash out of my hand. Annie scooped him up and hugged him. Jekyll was beside himself, yodeling, barking, crying and licking her all at the same time.

I recovered quickly from the shock. "There's nothing you can say to make me feel any worse than I already do." I retreated back to my room, knowing their words would haunt me for the rest of my days. *How in the hell had they found me?*

"Colt, you stop now!" Annie yelled. "Now!"

I turned around and faced her. Then Pat said, "Now WE want the floor for two minutes, just like I gave it to you when Annie demanded you leave that day. Two minutes."

"You don't get it, do you! I can't be hurt any more than I am. Go away!" I started closing the door. Pat hit it with all his force, nearly falling into the room. Jekyll ran in and bit my leg. *My dog bit me!* I lurched back from the shock of it. That gave Annie time to shut the door. They were in my room. I felt like a trapped animal.

Annie latched on to me, crying. I thought she was going to start pummeling me and recoiled backward, tripped on the bed, and fell to the floor. I started to get up, but Jekyll jumped on my chest, and Pat helped hold me down. "Damn it, Colt, settle down. We aren't here to hurt you. Give us two minutes, damn it, two damn minutes."

I saw the anguish in his eyes. "I didn't know, Pat. I didn't know..." I started weeping. "I didn't know," I said over and over.

Annie helped me up to sit on the bed and hugged me. "We know, Colt. Rachel told us what happened. We know. And it's okay. It's okay..." She kissed my cheek and tenderly stroked my hair. We love you so much, my dear sweet boy."

Pat was hugging me too. "We've been so worried about you."

That's all we said for a long while.

When I had no more tears in me, I looked at them. "I am so, so sorry for having betrayed you."

"You didn't betray us," said Pat. "She told you she was someone else. You didn't betray us."

"Colt," said Annie softly, "There's nothing to apologize for. You did nothing wrong." She kissed me on the cheek. "Why would you even think we'd be upset with you falling in love with our daughter?"

"Nothing could make us happier than that," said Pat. "If you asked for her hand, I would've said yes a thousand times over."

"I don't deserve happiness. I killed my parents." I gasped when I said it. It just came out.

"You didn't kill your parents, a drunk driver did," said Pat, looking perplexed.

"If I hadn't lied to them and then gone for a ride on my dirt bike, they would've had to come get me, and the drunk wouldn't have been anywhere near them. They'd be alive now if it weren't for me." I just couldn't control myself, and launched into a rambling tirade about deserving a life of hell, and how I saw now that I subconsciously sabotaged my life to make sure it happened.

"Oh, Colt, my dear boy," Annie said in tears. "You've been carrying this around for so many years. What an unimaginable burden."

"There'll never be another light in me, Annie. I can read as many self-help and Zen books as there are on the planet, but they won't work. I'm already in hell." Tears poured again from my eyes.

Annie pulled me close. Her face was inches from mine. "You listen to me, mister. That's BULLSHIT! Let's settle this right here and now. Mr. and Mrs. Mercer, I know you talk to your boy. If it was, in any way, his fault, you tell him now. NOW!" She looked at me. "Did you hear anything from them? DID YOU HEAR ANYTHING FROM THEM?"

"No, ma'am," I said meekly.

"Well, there you have it. The only one persecuting you is you. You're going to forgive yourself right now. DO IT!"

I looked at her, tears pouring from me. "I forgive myself."

"SAY IT LIKE YOU MEAN IT, MISTER. SAY IT!"

"I forgive myself."

"Say it again!"

"I forgive myself, I forgive myself, I forgive myself…"

"Today is the day the new light in you was lit," she said softly. "Welcome back to life. Welcome back to love." She held me tightly. I closed my eyes and cried and cried. Years of agony seemed to pour from me.

Pat kissed my forehead. "It's time to live again, Colt. It's time to come in from the cold. We're here for you. All the way."

"Colt," said Annie, "lean back and just close your eyes and breathe deeply. We'll be right here." I was exhausted, mentally and physically. I fell asleep with Annie stroking my hair. It felt wonderfully soothing.

I woke up four hours later. Pat and Annie were sitting in the chairs. Pat had Jekyll on his lap, and Annie had my Jek book in her hand. She smiled when I looked at her. "Your book is beautiful, Colt. Just beautiful."

"She's right, Colt. It was touching how you captured Jekyll's story."

"I made it as a birthday gift for Lilly."

"May I have a copy or two? I'd love to give them to Katie and Jen."

"Yes ma'am. I made twenty to give out on my trip. Does Katie hate me?"

"No, Colt," said Annie. "She's not very happy with her big sister. You were her first love."

I nodded. "And what about Rachel?"

"She's devastated. She's head-over-heels in love with you."

"We had to fly to be with her," said Pat. "She was a wreck."

"Colt," said Annie, "Rachel is a special girl. She never dated much because no one ever measured up. What I mean by that is, Rachel is an incredibly gentle and sensitive soul. She needed to find someone with those same indescribable qualities. When she said she fell in love with your words, it was like you were transmitting a signal straight to her soul. She had to be with you, as if the universe was demanding it. I don't know if I can explain it beyond that."

"I understand. I was in love with her as soon as she said hello."

"So, what are you going to do about it, young man?"

"I don't know, Pat. I'm so messed up in my head."

"Don't say that, Colt," said Annie. "Not anymore. That's old news."

"I don't know if it's that easy."

"Yes, Colt, it is. Happiness is a decision, and you make it every day."

"Annie, I reread all my emails to you. It's like I know the theory, but I can't put it into practice."

"Yes, you can," she said firmly. "My life is testimony that you can. Since making the decision to be happy at 14, I look in the mirror every morning and say 'happiness is a choice, and I choose happiness.' Your new life started today. Put away your Icarus wings and start living."

"Amen," said Pat.

"I saw a tornado today. I was driving right toward it, but Mom said, 'Stop!' If I hadn't stopped, it would've gotten me."

"You've had a hell of a day."

"Yes, sir. There was a beautiful rainbow after the storm."

Annie jumped in. "Take the rainbow as your parents' way of saying that you deserve happiness." I nodded.

"So, what will you do now, Colt?"

"I don't know, sir. I really don't know. I still have four more sets of parents to see on my KIA list, and also my parents."

"I think it's lovely that you're going to play your flute for them," said Annie.

"I-I don't think that'll happen. After I broke up with Rachel, the only thing that comes out of my flute is noise."

"It'll come back, just give it time," said Pat.

"I don't know, sir. Maybe it got bounced around in the Trike."

"What can we do for you?"

I looked at him. "Would you two consider coming with me tomorrow and meeting Johnny's parents?"

"We'd love to. What else?"

"Well, sir," I almost whispered, "would you consider coming with me to see my parents' grave?" Tears started with that question.

"We'd be honored to pay our respects."

"Colt, we'll let you rest," said Annie. "We'll be here tomorrow morning to be with you."

They hugged me goodnight. It's hard to describe how peacefully I slept that night. I felt so light; it was like I could float away.

48

JEKYLL WOKE ME by gently licking my cheek. I opened one eye and saw his cheery mug.

"You bit me, you know that, don't you? You didn't break the skin, but it left a mark."

"Woof!"

"Okay, you're right. I deserved it. Next time though, how about just giving me a stern growl. Let me get up. I need to look in the mirror."

I went into the bathroom and stared at myself. *"I choose happiness."*

"Woof!"

"Thank you, Jek. You're right, I do deserve happiness. I'm glad you're my friend, you know."

"Woof!"

"Let's go out, and then I need to call Johnny's parents."

"Woof!"

I called and introduced myself to a surprised Mrs. Matthews. She and her husband agreed to meet with me and the Brennans. Since we wouldn't meet until three, I asked if it would be okay to pay my respects at Johnny's grave. She told me how to get there. I rang Annie and asked them to meet me at my room at two.

Jek and I stopped at the arches on the way to the Dallas-Fort Worth National Cemetery. I skipped breakfast, and still wasn't hungry, but I knew I had to get some energy into my body. Jek didn't suffer the same appetite affliction, and went through his fries and catsup in a flash.

At the cemetery, I hesitantly took out my flute, and walked to my friend's grave. I read the words on his headstone, and put a coin on it before talking to him. "Hello, Johnny, it's me, Colt. I miss you, my dear friend. I hope you've met Manny. He's up there too. I've been through a lot since saying goodbye to you. I'm ready to start living again. I'm going to try to play my flute for you, so please forgive me if only noise comes out. I want to play about us wandering through the Hindu Kush, you know, when we hiked ten miles out of the valley that one day. Do you remember that spot where we stopped for lunch, and you said how beautiful it was?"

I adjusted the Jek fetish, closed my eyes, and began to play. When I heard Jekyll softly yodeling, I knew I must be playing okay. I imagined being a bird soaring in the rarified air of the Kush, and everywhere I looked, there was peace and harmony. I played for a long time to my friend. When I finished, several people were standing around me. The men had their hats off, holding them to their hearts. It was a touching moment.

Before heading back to the motel, I washed the Trike at a car wash. Pat and Annie arrived shortly after we returned, and we headed to the Matthews' home in their car.

"Pat, something's been gnawing at me. How did you two find me?"

"It wasn't a grand feat of clairvoyance on our part. We had Mark Cameron track you down. I reported you as "missing," and, like a bloodhound, he followed your "scent." Every time you used your credit card, he knew where you were. We had your KIA list and Mark confirmed you were still following it. From Orlando, we knew you'd be heading to Dallas. When you stopped in Shreveport, we got on a plane to Dallas. We waited for you to use your card again. When Mark told us the location of the hotel you checked into, we came immediately."

"Wow. I'm amazed you went to such trouble to find me."

"It isn't any trouble if you love someone and know they're hurting," said Annie.

Brad and Vicky Matthews were delightful people. Brad looked like an older version of Johnny, tall and lean, with the same Texas drawl. Vicky was about a foot shorter than her husband, though I suspect she could more than hold her own with him. I told them how close I was to Johnny, and how devastated I had been when he died. They asked me to describe his last battle, which I did, including how he died in my arms. Vicky never knew that part, and tearfully thanked me. Knowing her son died being held and comforted by someone who loved him brought peace to her heart. Brad insisted we stay for dinner, and he and Pat grilled steaks on the barbeque, while Annie and Vicky made the rest of the meal. I was so glad Pat and Annie were there with me.

We got back to my motel at nine, and talked about options regarding Prescott, from flying to driving. In the end, Pat's eyes lit up when I suggested he join me in driving the Trike on the Grand Adventure.

Pat and I traded off driving the Harley to Prescott. While one of us drove, the other stayed in the car with Annie. Although Jekyll could have rode the whole way in the comfort of the car, he insisted on co-piloting the Trike, even when Pat was driving. I'm not sure if he thought the Harley was his, or that it was his job to protect the family. Knowing my silly dog, validity could be claimed for both reasons. We had a delightful time with Manny's family in Santa Fe. Even though there was a language barrier, our mutual love found a way to communicate. We stayed two days with them and took in the sites of lovely Santa Fe. On our last night there, they invited us to be with their family and friends for a farewell dinner. We danced and sang and feasted on empanadas, gorditas, tamales and cookies called *arepas*, and had a remarkable time. They made us feel like family.

We took four days to get to Prescott. I asked them to take a detour to Sedona, and they soon saw why. I took them on a hike I used to do with my parents, through hidden canyons bordered by towering red-orange rock formations. It was jaw-dropping beautiful. I said a prayer for Mom and Dad in the Chapel of the Holy Cross, a beautiful Catholic church with magnificent views in every direction. We stopped at the Javelina Leap Vineyards & Winery, and had dinner at the historic Page Springs Steakhouse. Though cool outside, I felt bad leaving Jekyll in the car. He got over being left alone when I brought him a piece of my steak. We overnighted at the Arroyo Roble Hotel, which had incredible views.

The next day, we bought swimsuits, and spent the morning at Slide Rock State Park. We had a blast going down the famous slippery natural water chute. Jekyll enjoyed it as much as the rest of us and howled all the way down. We waded along the creek and basked in the sun. I recommended Pat ride from Sedona to Prescott, which is the perfect drive for a motorcycle. We stopped in Jerome, which they call *"The largest Ghost Town in America."* It's located on top of the mile-high Cleopatra Hill. Founded in 1876, Jerome was once the fourth largest city in Arizona, and produced an amazing three-million pounds of copper a month in its heyday. The mine shut down in the 1950s, and today, the town is re-inventing itself as a tourist and art community. We visited the Jerome Winery, and Annie delighted in tasting what they called a "sassy" white Zinfandel, along with Pinot Grigio, and a smooth

Muscat. It was fun. We had lunch at The Mile High Inn and Grille. They claimed to have the best hamburger in Arizona, and after having one, I'd argue their case to anyone. Pat called Katie to see how she was doing while I hustled some fries and catsup out to you-know-who.

From Jerome, it was a beautiful, hour-long drive to Prescott. Pat drove the whole way, and said he had the time of his life. I think his dream of riding the MLC through magnificent country had been realized.

Memories of my childhood came flooding back to me as we drove through my hometown. Prescott was still Prescott, even after all the years of me being away. I took Pat and Annie to see the house where I grew up. The people owning it had done a reasonable job keeping it up, but I didn't like the brown color they painted it. Mom had insisted it be turquoise blue because she liked the friendliness of the color. I showed them where I went to high school, and then asked if we could wait until tomorrow to visit my parents. They agreed. We still had some time before dark, so we went to Pronghorn Park, where I had spent many nights stargazing with Mom and Dad. I was on an emotional roller coaster where wonderful memories were followed by waves of sadness.

We checked in to the Motel 6 on East Sheldon Street, and I said goodnight to them at eight that night. I wanted to get a good night's sleep before visiting Mom and Dad. It had been a wonderful day with Pat and Annie. We never once mentioned Rachel.

49

THE ALARM SOUNDED at seven, rousing me from my sleep. I took Jek out, and then went in and showered. I looked in the mirror as I toweled off and said my new mantra. *"I choose happiness."*

Pat knocked on my door saying they were running late. He said they'd meet me at the cemetery. I offered to wait, but he said to go on because Annie was having "female troubles." Plus, he thought I should have a little time alone with Mom and Dad.

My emotions churned while driving the short distance to Mountain View Cemetery. This would be the first time I'd be visiting Mom and Dad since leaving for the Army. I pulled into the cemetery so nervous that my hands were shaking. I got out my flute, and walked to their final resting place. I put the flute on their headstone and picked up Jekyll. "Here's where my parents are, boy." The tears started. I read their names to him. "Daniel Michael Mercer. Christa Rose Mercer." We stood there for a long time. I was crying so hard that I didn't notice Pat and Annie, who were now standing on each side of me. Annie put her hand on mine. I smiled at her, and then looked at my parents' headstone. "Mom and Dad, here are two of the finest people I've ever met, Pat and Annie Brennan."

"We're so pleased to meet you," she said softly. "You've raised a wonderful boy, and we love him dearly."

"I'm honored to meet you," said Pat. "Your son means the world to us."

We stood for a while, not saying a thing. Jekyll was quiet in my arms.

"Colt," said Pat, "if it's okay, there's someone else who wants to meet your parents. Turn around. She's behind you." I looked at him, puzzled, and turned around. Rachel was standing twenty feet behind us. Jek leaped out of my arms and bounded over to her. She picked him up and gazed timidly at me, not knowing if I'd erupt again in anger. I looked at Pat and he smiled. "I called her yesterday in Jerome, when you left to feed von Bickerstaff, and told her to be here today. Go be with the one you love, son."

I hugged him and Annie, and was bawling like a baby as I walked to her. She put Jekyll down and raced to comfort me. "Colt, I love you so much. Don't ever leave me again, don't ever leave me again."

I couldn't say a thing. I just held on to her tightly.

Pat and Annie came to us, and we all hugged each other. "Colt," whispered Pat, "go introduce our daughter to your parents. I'm sure they want to meet her."

I took her hand and lead her to my parents. "Mom and Dad, this is Rachel. You'll be hearing a lot about her in the future." I kissed her tenderly.

"Mr. and Mrs. Mercer, I've come to ask your son to marry me. I hope you'll give me your blessing." She turned to me. "Colt Mercer, will you marry me?"

I looked at Pat. He nodded his head yes.

"I-I have to talk to Katie first. If she says yes, then I'd be honored to be your husband."

"You don't have to ask Katie," she said softly. "I have her permission to ask you."

I smiled and hugged her. This was the happiest day of my life. I turned to the ones I loved. "Before we leave, I'd like to play for my parents."

"We'd be honored to hear you play," said Annie.

I picked up my flute and played like a beautiful, free soulful bird, with my dog singing his best beside me.

EPILOGUE

JEKYLL AND I finished the Grand Adventure with my next grand adventure, Rachel, in tow. We visited the parents of my KIA friends in California, and took our time traversing Highway 1, which hugs the beautiful, rugged Pacific coastline. Jek and I taught Rachel the art of bridge howling, and we gave it our all over every span from California to Alaska. We had the time of our lives.

I asked Pat to marry us, which laypeople can do in Alaska after obtaining a marriage commissioner appointment. He tearfully performed the ceremony at Hatcher Pass in the majestic Talkeetna Mountains, just north of Anchorage.

It was Annie who helped reveal my new career and noble purpose. She shopped my Jek book around to a hundred literary agents, and I got published. To my surprise, it won two national awards, and became a bestseller. I followed it with two more children's books. One is entitled *Finley von Bickerstaff*, featuring a little dog from Shaktoolik and a special young girl named Lilly; and the other is *Seymour C. Sparrow, An Exceptional Little Bird*, about a sparrow desperately wanting to be in the zoo, only to be told he was too common to be admitted.

We live comfortably on the proceeds of my writing endeavors, allowing me to be a stay-at-home dad for a rambunctious boy and a darling baby girl. Daniel Patrick is three years old, and we'll celebrate Christa Anne's first birthday next week. We often take the kids to visit Grandpa and Nana Brennan in Alaska. I savor my time with these extraordinary people.

My wonderful wife got her Ph.D. in astrophysics from Yale, and currently works at the Jet Propulsion Laboratory in Pasadena, California, working on the next generation Mars Exploration Rover project. Our relationship grows stronger each year. Even with the most gifted of words, I could never describe the depth of our love. She is simply the gentle caress who soothes my soul. I thank God for her each day.

Katie's in her second year at the UC Davis School of Medicine and plans on being a psychiatrist, helping children who have experienced emotional and physical abuse. She's still looking for Prince Charming, and I know one day she'll find him. Pat laments on his daughters pursuing higher degrees, and wishes one would've become a mechanic so he could retire before eighty. Don't let him fool you, though, he's a very proud father. And me, well, I'm no slouch when it comes to academia. I received a Master of Fine Arts degree at UCLA, and have been a frequent guest lecturer there. I also keep busy working with organizations aiding and empowering our wounded warriors. Nothing is more rewarding or humbling than helping the heroes who have sacrificed so much. As I well know, the emotional trauma of war is often more potent than physical wounds.

Scotty, thank God, made it back from Afghanistan, and retired several years ago. He began a new career with the Anchorage Police Department, and works as a School Resource Officer at Dimond High School. He and Maggie are happy.

And then there's my beloved companion, Jekyll. He's getting on in years, but still has a zest for life. His life's purpose, after keeping me straight, is raising our children. He and Danny are inseparable companions. Jek's job got bigger with the arrival of Christa, and he's doing his best to teach her to walk. Danny keeps him supplied with a steady stream of carrots, but the vet dictates only occasional treats of fries and catsup. I kept the Trike, and we still go on rides together. We howl crossing bridges, and still find it exhilarating. Jekyll is always there, in so many ways, as my faithful companion.

So, what have I learned in life? Goodness. Where to start....

In retrospect, mine was a slow and circuitous road to redemption. It took years for my life to come into focus, but when it did, I was able to jettison my limitations and distortions. If ever I encounter a Zen master, and he asks what I've learned, I would offer but six words: *"Be. Advice beyond this is excessive."*

As the years go by, I am convinced, more than ever, that love is the universal elixir, the essential element of life. I've learned how love comes in an infinite variety of forms that collectively become an incredibly powerful and transformative force. My transformation began with my dog's love and the love of many kind and caring people, but, in the end, had I not learned to love myself, their efforts would have been futile. To become whole again requires allowing love in, and for me, the key to love was self-forgiveness.

I discovered the only moment that matters is the present moment, and I do all I can to make it one of peace. Annie was so right when she said happiness is a choice. Each day, I read a quote on my bathroom mirror by the Vietnamese Buddhist monk, Thich Nhat Hanh: *"Every morning, when we wake up, we have twenty-four brand-new hours to live. What a precious gift! We have the capacity to live in a way that these twenty-four hours will bring peace, joy, and happiness to ourselves and others."*

During my motivational speaking engagements, I always include two passages, the first by Jesus: *"Ask, and it will be given you. Seek, and you will find. Knock, and it will be opened for you."* I follow this with the words of the thirteenth century poet, Jelaluddin Rumi, which helped guide me to my noble purpose: *"Let yourself be silently drawn by the stronger pull of what you really love."*

A few years ago, I saw this passage that I cherish, by the German poet Rainer Maria Rilke: *"Perhaps the dragons in our lives are princesses who are only waiting to see us act, just once, with beauty and courage. Perhaps everything terrible is, in its deepest essence, something that feels helpless and needs our love."*

And, oh, what I've learned from the greatest of teachers and wisest of sages who happens to be my dog. I owe so much to my kind-hearted yodeler, who brought light to my darkness and joy to my despair. The highest irony was thinking I rescued him, when in fact, it was he, in every conceivable way, who rescued me. With love and patience I could never exhaust, he taught me how to be a human being. He coaxed out who I was, and magnified the goodness in my heart. By making his ugliness slip to irrelevance with charm and cheeriness, he taught me to play the hand you are dealt. He taught me to forgive quickly and love unconditionally. He taught me the power of patience, that passion is the best motivation, and to celebrate the joy that comes with giving. He guided me to happiness with potent doses of optimism and exuberance. He taught me that life isn't about anchoring in port for fear of angry seas. Rather, you journey into the unknown, accept that seas will rage and winds will howl, and rejoice when you return, for you will have lived deeply. His unqualified love reverberates within me, and I try my best to reflect it to the world. He took on the challenge of me, and I am tangible proof that love can transform even the most hardened of hearts. Jekyll von Bickerstaff. I love this little dog.

ACKNOWLEDGMENTS

Writing the acknowledgments is always pleasurable because it means the endeavor is finished and I get to express my gratitude to the people who saw me through this book.

Thank you, John Suler, Ph.D., Professor of Psychology at Rider University, and author of *Zen Stories to Tell Your Neighbors,* for graciously permitting me to use your wonderful Zen stories in my book. Thanks also to J. H. McDonald for your translation of the *Tao Te Ching.* The dog jokes between Lilly and Colt are from the public domain. I am deeply grateful to the sages whose wisdom I quoted throughout this book, and to Ann Lawton, a good friend, for her crackerjack wisdom.

No book would ever see the light of day without an exceptional editor, and I've been doubly blessed. Thank you, Wanda Oldham, for your intuitive wisdom, boundless enthusiasm, and superb editing. You made this a delightful experience for me, and I'm proud to call you my friend. Thanks also to Barbara Munson, who agreed to take me on *"only if the book speaks to me."* How fortunate am I that it did, and your many insights have made this a better book. You are simply a joy to work with.

Merge love, caring, empathy, enthusiasm, patience, humor, strength and support into one word. That would be mother. Thanks, Mary Miller, my wonderful mother.

To my wife, Carmen, who is from Germany, I'll use your language to describe my feelings for you: *Du bist meine große Liebe* (you are my greatest love).

And lastly, special thanks to you, the reader. May the light of God shine always on your path.

ABOUT THE AUTHOR

Born in Germany, Jim Miller has traveled and lived throughout the world. With degrees in physics and geophysics, Mr. Miller has worked as a sailor, seismologist, geophysicist, scientist, and environmental engineer. After thirty years in Alaska, he and his wife now live in Arizona.

You are welcome to contact the author by email at:
jamesmillerbooks@gmail.com
or visit his blog:
jamesmillerbooks.blogspot.com
or browse his web site:
jamesmillerbooks.com

RESOURCES

In this book, Colt said of his invisible wounds that the light within him died, to which Annie replied, "You are right, that light will never shine again. But, in time, you will discover a new light within you, a different kind of light, and this light will shine just as brightly as the one before." I urge you if you are hurting to take the steps necessary to find a new light within you. God bless you.

POSTTRAUMATIC STRESS DISORDER (PTSD). According to the *National Center for PTSD*, anyone, including children, suffering a traumatic event is susceptible to PTSD. Symptoms usually start soon after the traumatic event, but they may not appear until months or years later. They also may come and go over many years. If the symptoms last longer than four weeks, cause you great distress, or interfere with your work or home life, you might have PTSD. There are many types of treatment for PTSD. You and your doctor can discuss the best form of treatment for you.

SYMPTOMS OF PTSD:
- Reliving the event (also called re-experiencing symptoms). You may have bad memories or nightmares. You even may feel like you're going through the event again. This is called a flashback.
- Avoiding situations that remind you of the event. You may try to avoid situations or people that trigger memories of the traumatic event. You may even avoid talking or thinking about the event.
- Feeling numb. You may find it hard to express your feelings. Or, you may not be interested in activities you used to enjoy. This is another way to avoid memories.

- Feeling keyed up (also called hyper-arousal). You may be jittery, or always alert and on the lookout for danger.

IF YOU ARE THINKING ABOUT SUICIDE. No matter what problems you are struggling with, hurting yourself isn't the answer. Call 1-800-273-TALK (8255) to talk to a counselor at the *National Suicide Prevention Lifeline* crisis center near you.

SUICIDE WARNING SIGNS:

- Talking about wanting to die or to kill themselves
- Looking for a way to kill themselves, such as searching online or buying a gun
- Talking about feeling hopeless or having no reason to live
- Talking about feeling trapped or in unbearable pain
- Talking about being a burden to others
- Increasing the use of alcohol or drugs
- Acting anxious or agitated; behaving recklessly
- Sleeping too little or too much
- Withdrawing or isolating themselves
- Showing rage or talking about seeking revenge
- Displaying extreme mood swings

PET ADOPTION. According to the Humane Society of the United States, four million cats and dogs—about one every eight seconds—are put down in U.S. shelters each year. So be a hero—adopt a pet and save a life. Finding a pet to adopt is easy. Go to http://theshelterpetproject. org and enter your zip code for a list of adoptable dogs or cats near you. In the Foreword, Clarissa Black beautifully articulates her Pets for Vets program which is dedicated to supporting veterans and providing a second chance for shelter pets by rescuing, training and pairing them with America's veterans who could benefit from a companion animal. If you already own a dog or cat, do your part to reduce pet overpopulation by spaying or neutering your pet.

FINAL THOUGHTS

Every life is a story;
you write yours every day.
— James Miller

*****

The past has no power over
the present moment.
— Eckhart Tolle

17006753R00185

Made in the USA
Charleston, SC
21 January 2013